THE SABATINI
PROPHECY

"Adventures of Davey Boehm" Series
By Thomas L. Blair

The Sabatini Prophecy (2006)

The Terces Dimension (2007)

THE SABATINI PROPHECY

By
Thomas L. Blair

AXIOM HOUSE
Virginia

PUBLISHED BY AXIOM HOUSE

PO Box 2901, Fairfax, Virginia 22031

http://www.axiomhouse.com

The depiction "*@xiom*" is a logo for Axiom House.

Library of Congress Control Number: 2006920405

ISBN 0-9760237-1-7

Printed in the United States of America
February 2006

20 19 18 17 16 15 14 13 12 11 10 9 8 7 6 5 4 3 2 1

For My Wife Kathy, And My Children,
Steven, Michelle, Jennifer, & David

‸ Contents ‸

THE SABATINI PROPHECY

☙ Prologue ❧

Wherefore springs the source of magick?
Neither the written word nor the talk of
men can interpret this mysterie. The
answer cometh from within thy selfe!

— Translated from Storia Di Incanto; circa 1456

The Watcher In The Shadows

THE LIGHT OF A RISING MOON cast ghostly shadows along the branches of an ancient oak. For centuries, the majestic tree had thrived in a small clearing, a symbol of prosperity and good fortune. The tree had overcome weather, pestilence, and the ravages of time, but now it faced a more sinister challenge. Death lurked below its branches, brought there by an evil force. The tree's leaves shivered in the breeze, whispering of the wickedness that had come to harm it.

Brandishing lit torches, eighteen hooded men moved beneath the tree. Their bodies swayed with a growing fervor as the torchlight flickered across their black hoods. They formed a circle around a securely tied man, a blindfold covering his eyes. In morbid fascination, they taunted him with long sticks and shouts of derision.

Moments earlier, the men had piled branches around the trunk of the tree and poured gasoline over the wood. The fumes lingered in the air, foretelling of their dark plan. "Hang the witch; burn the tree!" they cried, their words slurring with the false bravado that came from drinking whiskey.

A figure emerged from their ranks and raised his torch in rhythm to their chants. Leaning his head back, he emitted a beastly howl. He was their leader, a huge hulk of a man with a heart as black as night. His hooded minions called him the Minotaur, a special name within their secret brotherhood. He relished the image of fear the name invoked, but he was not a mystical creature – just a man with an evil soul.

The Minotaur pointed at two of his followers and motioned them forward. "Take him to the tree," he commanded, indicating the bound man.

The two men dragged their hapless victim towards the massive oak. One carried a long rope with a noose on its end; he threw the rope over a high branch, letting the noose hang freely. The other placed the noose over their victim's head. Then they awaited their leader's signal to pull him up. The rest of the hooded men roared their approval. "Hang the witch," they screamed, their voices rising as one.

A watcher stood among the trees at the edge of the clearing, viewing the scene with tearful eyes. No one could see him in the dark shadows or knew he was there. He held a bow and quiver of arrows, fighting the impulse to shoot at the hooded men. *If only I could help him*, he thought, wanting to do something, anything, to stop them from harming his friend, Tsusga Gineli. Regretting his promise not to interfere, he muttered bitterly to himself. "Tsusga Gineli doesn't deserve this."

The Minotaur raised his hand for silence as he pulled the blindfold from the bound man's head. "Witch, behold those who have judged you," he bellowed, gesturing grandly towards the hooded men.

Tsusga Gineli stood tall and straight, seemingly unaffected by the Minotaur's words or the shouts of his minions. No trace of fear showed in his eyes, despite the rope around his neck. His long black hair waved in the night air as he stared at his tormentors. Then an expression of sadness crossed his face.

The Minotaur glared triumphantly at the bound man. For seven long years, this man, the so-called Tsusga Gineli, had thwarted his efforts to destroy the ancient oak. The Minotaur had waited, cleverly fabricating a string of lies that convinced his followers the man was a witch. They were a slow-moving and cowardly bunch, yet the Minotaur had prevailed, almost believing the deceit himself. Now, on this very night, he would eliminate both the man and the tree. Only one small victory was missing; he wanted to hear the man beg for his life.

The Minotaur circled his enemy, jabbing at him with his torch. "Your hour of judgment has come. You have bewitched this tree and turned it against us; the prosperity we once enjoyed has left our valley. Tonight, the tree will accompany you into the depths of hell. Admit your foul deeds and plead for our mercy!"

Tsusga Gineli managed a step forward, unhindered by the ropes binding him. He glanced briefly at the sky and a sudden shadow fell over the clearing. The hooded men failed to notice the clouds forming overhead or the waning of the moonlight. Their eyes stayed upon their victim, anticipating his supplication.

Tsusga Gineli spoke in melodious and forceful tones, denying the accusations against him. No pleas for mercy came from his mouth. Instead, he delivered a poetic message – a rhyming prophecy full of dire warnings and predictions. When he finished speaking, he studied the men confronting him. He saw confusion and a trace of fear on their faces. *Perhaps they will heed my words and leave while they can,* he thought with a flicker of hope.

A stunned silence fell over the clearing as the hooded men considered Tsusga Gineli's words. All of them were thinking the same thing: *What kind of man said such things while facing death?* As they pondered this question, their concerns grew. They wondered if the bound man spoke truthfully and looked towards their leader for reassurance.

The Minotaur did not disappoint them. He emitted a laugh so

horrible it sent shivers along their spines. Anger bubbled up from the dark pit of his soul, filling his voice with scorn. "So…the witch threatens us instead of showing remorse. Can he not feel the rope around his neck? Will we cower at his lies while he stands helpless before us? No, we will not!"

The Minotaur's fierce determination convinced his minions. Their doubts disappeared as the strength of his malice took control of their minds. "Hang the witch; burn the tree," they chanted in response.

The Minotaur nodded his approval. "We shall wait no longer." Beneath his black hood, a contemptuous smile spread across his face. He signaled to the men holding the rope and threw his torch towards the wood stacked around the tree. The hooded men followed his example, filling the air with their own torches.

Suddenly, the torches halted in mid-air as if frozen in time. One by one, the fires went out and the smoldering stubs dropped to the earth. The men holding the rope gave it a forceful jerk, intending to haul Tsusga Gineli upward. To their surprise, the rope fell away from his neck and wriggled in their hands like a vicious serpent. With cries of alarm, they dropped the rope and fled towards their comrades. Then an amber glow began to spread along the branches of the tree. Awestruck, the hooded men tried to back away, but their feet seemed glued to the ground. They gave each other baffled looks, a sense of dismay forming in their minds.

Thankful the ropes binding his victim's arms and legs were still in place, the Minotaur reached for the revolver in his waistband. *I'll put a stop to this with a bullet,* he thought. At that moment, the ropes around Tsusga Gineli separated from his body and flew towards the Minotaur. The pieces turned into snake-like creatures that knocked the revolver askew and swarmed over his huge bulk. The Minotaur screamed in terror as the ropes bore him to the ground.

Freed at last, Tsusga Gineli stared grimly at the dark clouds overhead. A vision of this night had come to him several months ago. Despite his efforts, he could not change what fate had decreed. With resolve, he focused his mind and summoned his magic power. Then he raised a hand towards the sky and the clouds swooped lower.

The hooded men watched with disbelief as Tsusga Gineli moved freely while their leader screamed under the onslaught of the ropes. Realizing their folly, they began to tremble. When they saw Tsusga Gineli's eyes turn into white-hot coals of fire, they sank to their knees and begged for his forgiveness.

Ignoring their pleas, Tsusga Gineli pointed at the gasoline-soaked wood at the base of the tree. It rose into the air, rotated as a solid mass, and broke apart. The pieces flew at the hooded men, knocking many senseless. Then Tsusga Gineli pointed at the Minotaur. A mysterious force lifted his rope-covered body and tossed it towards his minions. They all cried like lost children when he fell among them.

Once more, Tsusga Gineli reached towards the clouds. As he did, a white globe of energy enveloped his body. The hooded men tried to look away from the brilliant force, but they could not. Their eyes watched as he spoke to them one last time. "Let ye who survive this night, remember well my wrathful might!"

Then the sky erupted with tremendous fury. Lightning streamed from the clouds, striking the hooded men. Claps of thunder, so loud eardrums shattered and minds went numb, followed immediately. The lightning came repeatedly, one merciless bolt after another; the earth trembled with each terrible strike. At last, the dark clouds dissipated and a deadly quiet fell over the clearing. The hooded men lay on the ground, severely injured or dead.

Slowly, the watcher emerged from the shadows, shocked by what he had seen. He had watched as the globe of energy surrounded Tsusga Gineli's body. When the globe finally faded away, his friend vanished with it. In sudden anger, he yelled out at the hapless bodies on the ground. "He warned you – why didn't you listen?" His question went unanswered, a lonely cry in the night.

After a few minutes, the watcher left the clearing. Fresh tears spilled from his eyes as he walked to his village. It was the year 1937; he was barely more than a boy, yet his heart carried a heavy burden. Tsusga Gineli had told him the reason for this terrible night, but asked him not to speak of it until the prophecy came true.

The watcher knew many years might pass before the time would come. He would wait patiently – the moment would eventually arrive. Tsusga Gineli never spoke falsely; his friend might be gone, but his words would hold their truth.

❧ Chapter 1 ☙

---

*Even great things begin small. Behold, a
tree shall flourish from a tiny seed; a
molehill shall become a mountain. Is this
not proof of the existence of magick?*

— Translated from Storia Di Incanto; circa 1460

A Great Oak Welcome

SIXTY-SEVEN YEARS later, birds of all shapes, sizes, and colors
landed upon the large elm outside of Davey Boehm's window. After
settling into place, they burst into song – if one could call it singing.
On this particular morning, their song didn't offer the gentle melody
of normal bird warbling. In fact, it didn't have any musical qualities
at all.

The birds grew louder and louder, as if each were trying to outdo
the other. Of course, they hadn't intended to make such a racket.
Later, they were a bit embarrassed about letting their little party get
out of control. The birds were excited, that's all – excited and more
than a little curious about the person they had come to see.

At first, this rather perplexing cacophony was lost on Davey. He
was fast asleep, having arrived late at night after a long and tedious
trip from New York. Besides, he was having a pleasant dream about
baseball and in no mood to be disturbed.

In reality, Davey was not very good at baseball or any other sport, but in his dream, he was a legendary homerun hitter who had just stepped up to bat with the bases loaded. Fear showed in the pitcher's eyes as the ball leapt from his hand, low and outside. Stepping into the pitch, Davey swung with tremendous force and sent the ball soaring. He dashed towards first base as the fielder ran desperately backwards. The crowd cheered wildly, but then the cheers suddenly changed. Instead of yells and gleeful shouts, they became peeps, chirps, and caw…caw…caw. Davey stopped running and looked towards the stands. No one was there.

"Hey, what's happening?" he yelled, but the sound coming from his mouth was nothing more than a gurgling, frog-like croak. Suddenly, his eyes popped open and he found himself sitting up in bed. The strange noises from his dream still rang in his ears. Only now, they came from the raised window near his bedside. Slowly, his brain stirred into wakefulness and the bliss of baseball faded away.

Initially, Davey didn't know where he was. His eyes grew wide with shock as he surveyed the dimly lit room. Everything seemed blurry and unfamiliar. With fumbling fingers, he pulled his glasses onto his face. The room greeting his eyes was not his snug little bedroom in New York City. The sleek modern furnishings and colorful wallpaper of his forty-second floor condominium were gone. This room was larger and filled with country-style furniture.

In one corner of the room, a stack of suitcases sat idly. Resting on the floor beside them was his computer, Friday, so named after he had read *Robinson Crusoe* two years ago. However, Friday was not showing its smiling screensaver face – the one he had animated from a picture of a giant lizard with a flickering red tongue. Instead, Friday's monitor was blank; its brain disconnected.

Davey flopped down with a groan and pulled a pillow over his head while yesterday's events roared back into his mind. He remembered standing at the airport as his parents boarded a big jet bound for China – he also remembered sitting between his aunt and uncle for what seemed like forever as their pickup made its way to North Carolina. By the time they reached Great Oak, he was a weary bundle of nerves.

He went right to bed as soon as they arrived – well, almost. First, he and his uncle put his belongings in his room. After that, he was so tired he could have slept anywhere despite his anxiety. No question, fate had turned his life upside down.

Four weeks ago, Davey had come home from school and found his parents waiting for him. He immediately knew something was up because of their guilty glances. What followed was a conversation so traumatic, he remembered it word for horrible word. It started when his dad announced they were going to China for an *entire* year. His company wanted him to evaluate some furniture factories that it was thinking of buying.

The news left Davey stunned, but as he grasped the importance of his dad's words, he leapt excitedly into the air. "I'm going to China! I'm going to China!" he shouted repeatedly while jumping around the living room. A picture formed in his mind, one of him dressed as a modern day Marco Polo riding a white horse. *Davey Boehm, Great Adventurer*, read the caption under his picture.

His dad quickly put an end to that fantasy. "I'm sorry son, but you will be staying in the United States."

"Very funny, Dad," Davey replied, positive he was kidding. Yet the grim look on his father's face belied the idea. As the shocking truth sank in, Davey tried everything he could think of to change his dad's mind.

"No, not a chance," his dad invariably responded. "The part of China we'll be going to is rather primitive. It's too dangerous for a thirteen-year-old boy."

"Besides, you have school," his mother added.

"Why can't I go? It can't be all that dangerous or *you* wouldn't risk it. If it's school you're worried about, I'll attend school in China."

Much to Davey's chagrin, his father shook his head. "I've already checked that out. There's not a single accredited school for American children in the whole of Kansu Province. You can't be absent from your studies for a year."

Davey was truly befuddled. "What will I do while you're gone?"

Then his mom chimed in again. "Well, your dad and I have come up with a great idea. You're going to live with your Aunt Sally and Uncle Bill in Great Oak. We've discussed it with them and they're thrilled. You can continue your schooling there and get better acquainted with them at the same time."

A big, incredulous scowl formed on Davey's face. "Mom, I just started seventh grade at my school here. I already know everyone and don't want to begin over somewhere else."

His dad shrugged as if it was no big deal. "The middle school in Great Oak won't be much different from your private school here. You'll quickly make new friends. After all, it's only for a year."

Davey glanced at his mother with pleading eyes. "Mom, why can't you stay here with me?" His question had a childish, whining tone, which he hated. He preferred more adult-like approaches.

His mother, whom he could usually talk into anything, offered no help. "I'm sorry Davey. Your father's career depends upon the success of this trip and he needs me with him. We'll be busy all the time, attending social functions, hobnobbing with the local authorities, and entertaining the plant managers and their wives. Don't worry, you'll like living in Great Oak. We wouldn't send you there if we had any concerns about it."

"I don't want to live anywhere except New York. I'm not going to North Carolina. I'll be miserable there and I'm just not going!" Davey shouted, knowing it was a mistake even as he said the words.

His dad reacted by laying down the law. "Son, you've never been to Great Oak, so don't tell us how miserable you'll be. Spending time in a small town will let you enjoy a simpler life, one focused on the outdoors. It will get you away from your computer and into activities that will put some muscle on you."

Davey's face turned red; it always did whenever he became terribly upset or angry. In this case, he was both. *Whatever you say Dad*, he thought. He had heard his father's toughen up speech before. Feeling indignant and helpless, he shut himself up in his room for the rest of the evening. The picture of the great adventurer had faded from his mind. Replacing it was an image of a boy dressed in overalls, a goofy grin spread across his face. This time, the caption read, *Davey Boehm, Country Bumpkin.* He was sure it was a premonition.

Now, Davey sighed as he looked around his new bedroom. So here he was, stuck in North Carolina for a year with Aunt Sally and Uncle Bill, two people he barely knew. Oh, they were nice enough all right. It wasn't that. However, they weren't his parents. Plus, he was missing out on China. The whole thing made him scream, which is exactly what he had done at his parents until he was blue in the face. Still, it hadn't done any good. Their decision was final – end of story.

Feeling dejected, Davey threw his pillow across the room. The clock on the bedside table stared at him with big red numbers, proclaiming it was 6:00 a.m. "Phooey," he said aloud. Liking the sound, he said it again, only louder this time. With so much noise outside, there was no point in trying to sleep. It sounded like a mob was out there.

Davey climbed out of bed and walked towards the window. A gentle breeze fluttered the curtains like sails on a boat. He pushed them aside and peered cautiously out. The rising sun flashed in his eyes, making it hard to see, but the birds in the tree saw Davey perfectly. As soon as he appeared, they erupted into a chorus of sound so cheerfully loud it was frightening.

The tree where they perched stood near the house, some branches practically touching the siding. As Davey's vision cleared, an incredible sight appeared before his eyes. Birds literally filled the tree, hundreds of them, all lined up on the branches. They weren't merely sitting there, no indeed. Every bird was staring straight at him.

Davey didn't know what to think. While the sight of so many birds startled him, it didn't surprise him entirely. Over the past several years, unusual things like this had happened to him with increasing frequency. Whenever he walked along the street, dogs and cats would approach him. They would wag their tails and circle him as though he was a long lost friend. In Central Park, squirrels and rabbits followed him around, three or four at a time. Sometimes, a whole gang of them would come up and sit quietly beside him while he was reading on a bench or sailing his model boat in the pond. *Odd*, he thought whenever this happened, *how very odd*.

At first, it had only been four-legged creatures, but lately birds had started to pay Davey this special sort of attention. He could hardly sit outside anymore without one or two birds fluttering around overhead or even perching on his shoulder. Last month, right after his thirteenth birthday, a severe cold kept him in bed for a few days. On the very first day, seven ravens crowded onto the sill of his window. They stayed there the entire day, often pecking on the glass as if reminding him of their presence. This seemed particularly strange because he had never seen ravens in New York before.

Although these interactions with birds and animals seemed random and irrational, Davey felt like they weren't. He didn't know why they were happening, but he was certain about one thing. They were occurring for a reason. He tried discussing it with his mother several weeks ago. They were in Central Park, and he noticed her studying him while five squirrels sat nearby as he innocently ate an ice cream cone. She had a strange look on her face, as though worrying about something. Suddenly, he stared into her eyes. "Mom, why do you think birds and animals like me so much?"

She looked pensive, as if thinking it over. Finally, she sighed. "I don't know. Maybe something about you attracts them. There are some strange genes mixed up in your little body – most of them from my side of the family."

Naturally, her answer prompted more questions. "I don't understand. Animals and birds don't act the same way around you, so how could it be genetic? Has anyone else in your family had these experiences?"

She shook her head. "I'm not sure, perhaps my grandmother did. It may sound strange, but there's a lot about my ancestors I don't know. Look at it this way. Genetic or not, you have a special gift, one which may come in handy some day."

Her remark made Davey even more curious. "I've always wondered about your family. We talk about Dad's parents and grandparents all the time, but all you ever say about your relatives is that they're all dead."

His mother frowned, clearly regretting the subject had come up. "When you're a little older, we'll have a long talk about them. For now, all you need to know is that they were people of a different sort."

Davey found this confusing because he didn't understand her meaning of the word different. Did she mean different in a good way or in some other way? He didn't like the latter possibility, so a veritable flood of questions poured from his mouth. However, she wouldn't say anything more, leaving him worried. She was keeping some terrible secret from him. He was sure of it.

Now, looking out the window of his aunt's house, Davey thought about his mother, missing her and wondering what she would say about this weird gathering of birds. They were really raising a racket – almost demanding his attention. *There must be a reason why they are here,* he thought.

As he watched them, his imagination came up with an answer. The birds were some sort of a welcoming committee – just stopping by to say hello. He didn't know why birds would do such a thing, but he liked the idea. His bad humor gradually faded and he smiled. "All right," he said, sticking his head out the window. "Hello and thank you for coming. But if you don't mind, take the volume down a bit...and not so early next time, okay?"

At the sound of his voice, the birds grew silent and just stared at him. *This is too bizarre for words,* he thought. Then he noticed a cluster of ravens at the top of the tree. They seemed somewhat aloof from the rest of the birds, as if they had a more important role in this little drama. For a fleeting moment, he had the ridiculous idea that they were the same ravens who had perched at his window in New York. The ravens stared at him as though awaiting his acknowledgement.

This prompted Davey to embellish his remarks. "Really, I mean it. Hello to the robins, the finches, the mockingbirds, the blue jays, the woodpeckers, and a very special hello to the ravens at the top. You weren't in New York recently by any chance?" Davey watched the ravens closely when he said this. *Did I see a flicker of recognition in those beady eyes?* he wondered.

Then he continued. "I was a little homesick this morning, but I feel better as a result of your gracious welcome. So thanks for being here. I'll look forward to seeing more of you during my visit."

The birds broke into song again as if applauding Davey's words. This time, there was even a little melody in their warbling. Finally, with several nods of his head and a wave towards the ravens up at the top, Davey quietly shut the window. Rolling his eyes, he sighed heavily. "I am totally losing it," he muttered aloud.

All of a sudden, a different sound startled him – a low scratching noise, which came from somewhere nearby. Davey looked back at the window, thinking the birds were pecking on the pane. To his astonishment, not a single bird was in sight – none on the tree and none on the windowsill. He froze in his tracks, listening. *There it is again,* he thought. Now, he was sure the sound came from somewhere inside. He made a running dive for his bed and began looking around.

The scratching became louder, accompanied by a clicking sound. That's when he realized the bedroom door was banging against the door latch. The way the door pushed against the latch made it obvious that something big was trying to get into the room.

Davey grinned from ear-to-ear because he guessed what it was. He started for the door with an excited shout, but one foot caught in the bedding and he tripped. Instead of reaching the door, all he succeeded in doing was falling on his face near the doorway. At that exact moment, the door swung open.

A large golden retriever stared down at him. Davey was sure the dog was laughing, black eyes crinkling at the corners, tail flopping back and forth. "Well hello," Davey said. "Are you part of the welcoming committee?"

"Woof," barked the dog.

"I'll bet you planned on waking me up. Sorry, but the birds got here first." Davey sat up and began rubbing his elbow where it had banged against the floor. "Did you see me fall? I was doing a stunt man's trick in case you didn't know. Just call me Dangerous Dave from now on."

"Woof, woof," the dog replied and then licked him in the face.

Davey grabbed the dog's collar and wrestled him to the floor. The friendly retriever played along, licking him again. A few minutes later, the dog's ears perked up and his head turned towards the door. Davey heard his aunt's steps on the wooden floor downstairs. "Bristol, where are you? Time for breakfast," she called. The dog rose, stared at the open doorway, and then looked longingly at Davey.

"You must be Bristol," Davey said. "Well, you'd better go eat."

The dog licked him one last time, twirled in a circle, and ran out the door, his claws clattering on the floor in the hallway. Davey smiled wistfully as he watched him go. The animal's presence put a slightly different slant on things. He had always wanted a dog, but his condominium in New York didn't allow them. Now, he had Bristol, which made his spirits rise.

He turned and surveyed his new bedroom with less pessimistic eyes. It was kind of nice actually. The peaked roof of the house cut into parts of the ceiling, creating some interesting angles. A small wooden desk sat in an alcove on one side, a good home for Friday. Alongside the desk was an overstuffed chair, an inviting place to read, and behind the desk were two large windows covered by denim curtains.

Pushing the curtains aside, he looked down on an expansive back yard. Large trees, so tall they towered above the house, stood everywhere. Their leaves shimmered in the morning light as they twirled in the soft breeze.

Wow, what a great backyard, he thought. *Some of those trees look climbable too.* He had always wanted to climb a tree, yet never had the chance – mainly because the only trees in New York were in the parks; it was against the rules to climb them. *First thing after school, I'm going to climb a tree,* he promised himself.

"School!" Davey exclaimed, almost shouting. He had just thought about school. The moment had arrived – the day when he would start a new school. Ever since his parents had decided to ship him off to North Carolina, he had been dreading this day.

Davey readily admitted he wasn't a very popular kid at his old school. He pretended it didn't matter to him, although it did. *You can't change the way others feel about you, so don't worry about it,* he often told himself. In Davey's opinion, his problem was that he was short for his age, thin, and worst of all, nearsighted. He wore thick eyeglasses, which gave him tunnel vision. This effected his coordination and made him a terrible athlete. Sports were an important activity at his school, so being a poor athlete was not a distinction he relished.

Since Davey felt physically inferior to most of his classmates, he was a loner. Oh sure, he had a few friends, but they weren't close ones. Mostly, everyone treated him as though he were a nerd. They called him nicknames like "the brain" or "computer head" because he was a top student.

Still, making good grades gives me some status, he thought. Besides, he had a quick wit and sometimes made clever wisecracks in class – ones making the other kids laugh. That had raised his popularity a notch.

Then there was Alice Sterling, a cute dark-haired girl whom he secretly liked. For some reason, she had spoken to him twice in the last week. All she had done was ask about a homework assignment, yet she could have asked anyone. Instead, she had picked him, which meant something. Davey believed it meant she liked him too, but he'd probably never find out now. He groaned with exasperation. He liked his old school and knew where he stood among his classmates. Having a place in the pecking order was a source of comfort, even if it was somewhere near the bottom.

In Davey's mind, a school in a small town would be completely different. He would be a total nobody in an environment where how far he could throw a football, or hit a baseball, or spit tobacco juice for that matter, were the important things. What he was good at wouldn't mean anything. His sense of humor would probably be over everyone's heads, or worse, get him punched in the face.

With his gloom returning, Davey opened his suitcases and began unpacking his clothes. He tried to think about Bristol and climbing the trees in Aunt Sally's back yard, but anxiety over his new school kept creeping into his mind. It was going to be a disaster. He was sure of it, a complete and total disaster.

ୡ Chapter 2 ୰

---

*Let resolve be birthed from the depths of
despaire. Fate shall often reward thy
choice to meet her with open arms.*

— Translated from Storia Di Incanto; circa 1493

Linda Gets A Blue Sheet

AT SEVEN O'CLOCK IN THE MORNING, Linda Peabody checked
her mailbox in the faculty room at Great Oak Middle School. She
had become accustomed to doing this each Monday because it was
critical to a teacher's welfare; Mondays were when important notices
showed up, like which reports were due by the end of the week. The
notices came on orange sheets, so a teacher couldn't miss them.

"If you pay attention to your orange sheets, you'll stay out of
trouble," Eunice Bluestone barked during teacher orientation last
month. In addition to being Linda's boss, Eunice was an intimidating
woman. She looked more like a tackle on a football team than a
school principal and had a personality to match.

At orientation, Linda also learned that a blue sheet might
occasionally appear in a teacher's mailbox. This was a bad thing
because it meant Eunice was giving the teacher extra work. Blue
sheets were the way Eunice punished teachers in her little school, one
she ran like a military dictatorship.

"Receive more than six blue sheets in a year and the axe descends upon you," Eunice bellowed, moving her arm in a chopping motion while she marched in front of the teachers like a drill sergeant. Her eyes glittered brightly, as if she would enjoy hacking a teacher with an axe. Linda resolved never to get a blue sheet right then and there.

So, as Linda removed the thin stack of papers from her mailbox, she stared with horror at the blue sheet lying on top. The words on the sheet made it even worse. "Linda Peabody – see Eunice Bluestone immediately. This means now!"

"Good grief, what could I have done?" Linda muttered. She had been teaching at the school for only a month and the blue sheet made her feel like a failure. Looking around, she hoped none of the other teachers had noticed the blue sheet. Tears formed in her eyes and she bit her lip to keep from crying, something she did a lot of lately.

But Emily Watson, the kind of busybody who stuck her nose into everyone else's business, was watching Linda. She swooped over and snatched the blue sheet right out of Linda's hand. "Doesn't resemble any blue sheet I've ever seen," she announced, passing it around for everyone's inspection.

"Me neither," said Bernice Baumgartner, a hook-nosed woman who had been teaching at the school for six years. "Usually, the old battleaxe lists your mistakes and your punishment for making them. I should know – she gave me five last year."

"You must have done something really stupid," Coach Dobson exclaimed. "See Eunice Bluestone immediately? Wow, I feel sorry for you."

"Maybe she's going to fire you," George Mulroney whined. He taught history and seemed afraid of his shadow most of the time.

The blue sheet had now reached Pamela Dickson. She was a large and bossy woman who thought she was the best teacher in the school. However, Linda had heard all of the comments she could stand. She grabbed her blue sheet from Pamela's hand and marched down the hall towards the principal's office.

"Well, excuse me," Pamela said haughtily, offended Linda hadn't waited for her opinion about the deadly sheet.

Linda was an attractive young woman. Her blond hair was usually tied up in a ponytail and the freckles across her nose made her appear younger than her twenty-three years. In fact, she didn't look much older than many of her students. All of her life, Linda had walked around with a perpetual smile. Unfortunately, she hadn't found much to smile about recently. A cloud of bad luck seemed to follow her around – a cloud she couldn't escape.

Linda's problems had begun about six months ago. Back then, the most important event in her life was her forthcoming marriage to Michael Benson, a young man she started dating several years earlier. Both Linda and Michael were studying to become teachers at Wilson College when they met. Their ideas and interests were almost identical and they quickly became friends. Soon, they wanted to be together all of the time. This led them to develop a plan; they would get teaching jobs at the same school after graduation. That way, they could continue their relationship.

The first challenge to their plan arose at the end of Michael's senior year. He had accepted a teaching position at Huddleston Academy, a prestigious private school two hundred miles away. Linda still had another year of college, which meant they wouldn't see much of each other for a while.

Linda was a popular girl and Michael didn't want her dating anyone else while they were apart. After thinking it over, an idea came to him – they could become engaged. The more he thought about it, the more he liked the idea; they could be married when Linda graduated the following year. All he had to do was persuade her to accept his proposal.

Michael thought about how to ask her for days. Finally, he came up with a clever notion – one so silly and romantic she would have a hard time turning him down. Right before graduation, he dressed up like a clown and hid in the bushes outside her dormitory. When Linda walked out the front door, he leapt from the bushes while singing her favorite song from the opera, Pagliacci. As he did this, he held out a sign reading: *Marry Me and I'll Be Your Clown for Life.*

Everyone who witnessed the event thought it was hilarious, mainly because Michael had an awful singing voice.

The sight filled Linda with so much happiness that she said yes immediately. Then she collapsed in a muddle on the front steps and cried for thirty minutes. Hoping for their support, Michael had secretly told Linda's friends about his plan. They rushed out behind her, cheering while he danced around and played the fool.

Their engagement required Michael and Linda to become serious about their plans. Since Linda was the top student in her class, they believed she had an excellent chance of landing a position at Huddleston Academy too. Therefore, their next objective was to secure her a job there, one that would start the following year.

To their amazement, everything worked out perfectly – at least initially. Just as they had hoped, Huddleston announced several openings at the beginning of Linda's last semester. Linda quickly applied, and three weeks later, Percival Smith, the head of the English department, invited her for an interview. After it was over, she knew Percival had been impressed. Sure enough, she received an offer of employment within a month. Linda graciously accepted and immediately turned her attention to planning her wedding. A few weeks later, Linda learned she would be Valedictorian of her class. Marveling at her good fortune, she wondered if life could get any better.

Of course, Michael and Linda weren't together every day during her last year of college. Still, he visited on weekends, telephoned every night, and sent e-mails whenever he had a spare moment. Everything seemed to be fine, but several months before her graduation, Linda noticed Michael's attitude was changing. The nightly telephone calls began to dwindle and the e-mails slowed to a trickle. Then various excuses for missing his weekend visits came along. After Michael hadn't come to see her for a month and the telephone calls and e-mails had stopped completely, a letter from him arrived.

Linda carried the letter around for several hours before reading it. By then, her hands were shaking so badly she could barely open the envelope. In the end, it really didn't matter. She already knew what was in it. Tears streamed down her face as she read his words. He was so very sorry. He had met someone else, another teacher who was truly his soul mate; their engagement was off. *The big rat, he didn't even tell me in person,* Linda thought.

After Michael's letter, Linda became a wreck. A grim expression replaced her perpetual smile and her eyes clouded with tears at the slightest provocation. Her friends gave her hugs and gently prodded her to move on with her life, but that wasn't easy for Linda. Her heart was broken. Of course, she could no longer consider teaching at Huddleston Academy. She wrote Percival Smith an apologetic letter and rejected his offer of employment, thank you very much.

Linda was clueless about what to do after her graduation. She had only applied for a job at Huddleston Academy. All the other teaching jobs she might have considered were no longer available. Not that it mattered as far as Linda was concerned. She couldn't muster enough energy to interview for a job anyway. Instead, she moved back into her parent's house and moped around.

While her parents were sympathetic to Linda's plight, they were a tough, no nonsense sort, and didn't hold with a lot of self-pity. They firmly believed Linda would snap out of her depressed state if she got busy and found a job. So her father sent out a message to their relatives around the state. "Linda needs a teaching job, preferably as an English teacher. Let us know if there are any openings at your local school."

Much to everyone's surprise, Linda's eighty-two year old Great Aunt Gilda responded right away. She reported that the English teacher at Great Oak Middle School had broken both legs in a motorcycle accident and could no longer work. The school was in a bind because the kids were starting school in a few weeks. No one had showed the slightest interest in the job, let alone anyone who might be qualified.

Without telling Linda, her parents mailed her resume to the school's principal. Almost immediately, a letter offering her the position came from Eunice Bluestone. Her parents opened the letter and were ecstatic. The job was Linda's — no interview was necessary. Of course, such a quick offer might have made some people suspicious. However, Linda's parents felt her circumstances required immediate action, so they investigated no further. Their next challenge was to persuade Linda to take the job.

That evening, her parents explained the whole thing. It was a simple decision really — all the pieces were in place. Great Oak was only a few hours away, so Linda wouldn't be far from home. There was plenty of room for her in Aunt Gilda's old rambling house and the school was close by. Linda would be doing the family a big favor too. Aunt Gilda was getting along in years and needed a little looking after. As an added incentive, Linda's dad offered to put new tires on her old yellow Volkswagen and fix the transmission, which refused to go in reverse no matter how much she begged.

Linda could hardly say no. She needed a change, something new and challenging to help her forget Michael. The job in Great Oak made perfect sense. Nothing else had come along and Aunt Gilda was one of her favorite relatives. It was an easy decision, one requiring little thought. She sighed, blinked out a few tears, and said, "I'll do it."

Her parents breathed a collective sigh of relief. They were sure everything would work out fine, perfectly peachy keen. Linda was getting back to normal, and the rest would take care of itself.

The first sign that life in Great Oak might not turn out exactly as imagined was when Linda caught her initial glimpse of Aunt Gilda's house. Her father had said the house was roomy, which was true, but he had not said the house was so old it resembled a haunted mansion in a horror movie. After living there for a month, Linda still hadn't gotten used to all the creaks and groans of the house during the night.

As for Aunt Gilda, she needed a lot more than a little looking after in Linda's opinion. Oh, she was a sweet and kind old woman and Linda truly enjoyed her company. Nevertheless, she was so full of wacky ideas and quirky behavior, Linda constantly worried about her mental state. Sometimes, Aunt Gilda seemed perfectly normal. Then she would do or say something, which made absolutely no sense. For example, she wore her pajamas backwards whenever she wanted to dream about her deceased husband, or painted her fingernails and toenails green before working in the garden so the plants wouldn't be afraid of her. Every morning when Linda left for school, she wondered what weird things Aunt Gilda would do while she was away.

Her father just laughed when Linda phoned and told him about some of Aunt Gilda's antics. "We always thought she was a bit batty," he said, in between her stories.

Linda didn't find much humor in the situation. "Dad, you don't understand. She believes her husband, Charles, still lives here. She talks to him all the time, and he's been dead for ten years."

This little tidbit only made him laugh harder. "Don't worry, Charles was a good man. If he's still around, he won't hurt anyone."

However, Linda *was* worried...and not only about Aunt Gilda. Her teaching job was a disaster, Eunice Bluestone wasn't the least bit friendly, and the other teachers mostly ignored her. That is, unless Linda asked a question at a teachers' meeting. They all laughed gleefully whenever this happened because Eunice acted as if Linda was an idiot.

The school building itself was a half-century old and resembled a prison more than a school. Tall towers stood at each end of the two-story structure, serving no apparent purpose. Linda sometimes thought guards should be up there, armed with machine guns to keep the kids in line. That would be more in keeping with the high chain-link fence surrounding the grounds and the school's oppressive air.

The student's desks and other furnishings, although still useable, seemed even older than the building. They bore the scars of many years of abuse. All of the overhead projectors, computers, and other equipment were so obsolete; Linda doubted if repairs were even possible should anything break. The school had no budget for repairs anyway, and the other teachers didn't seem to care whether things worked or not.

Still, the students were what really aggravated Linda. They were rude, lazy, undisciplined, and just plain mean. All they wanted to do was waste time or pick on each other. In short, they were a horrible bunch of brats who quickly shattered her fantasies about the rewarding life of a teacher.

So…the appearance of the unexpected blue sheet pushed Linda past the breaking point. She had gotten her fill of Eunice and her demeaning ways. Not only was she ready to tell Eunice what she thought about her school, she was ready to quit and move back home with her parents.

Claire Smithson, the school's secretary, sat hunched over a computer in the outer office of the principal's suite when Linda stormed into the room. Claire was a tall, thin woman with a long neck and a vulture-like nose. Her personality resembled that of a vulture too, or so Linda believed. "Well, well, Linda Peabody, just the person we're waiting for," Claire said wryly.

Linda shook the blue sheet furiously. "I received this," she said.

Claire giggled as if she had done something terribly funny. "Got your attention, didn't I? Sorry, but Eunice wanted you right away. You really didn't earn a blue sheet — at least not yet. Go on in, she's expecting you."

"But—" Linda protested, her anger withering like a dying plant.

"Hurry, no time for chitchat," Claire interrupted, pointing towards Eunice's office. "Get in there!"

Eunice smiled broadly when Linda entered the room. Then she thrust a slim file-folder in Linda's direction. "You are about to have a wonderful experience. We have a new student transferring from New York, and I'm assigning him to you. Sit down and read the boy's records."

Linda's mouth opened and she stared at Eunice. She was speechless.

"Come on girl, hop to it. The boy and his aunt will be here any minute," Eunice barked.

Without a word, Linda sat down and scanned through the file. Besides grade records and aptitude test scores, it contained a psychological profile identifying the boy's strengths and weaknesses. After noticing he had an astonishingly high IQ and perfect grades, Linda focused upon a few of the boy's personality traits. His teachers wrote that he was exceptionally bright, articulate, and a pleasure to teach. He was also shy, insecure, naïve, and overly sensitive about his poor athletic ability.

Linda closed the folder and stared at Eunice, her eyes brimming with excitement. "Why, he's practically a genius," she said.

"Isn't it marvelous? Think how his ability will improve our academic ratings. We'll put him on the Scholar's Team right away."

Linda frowned. "He'll have a tough time fitting in here."

Eunice ignored Linda's comment and continued. "Imagine how surprised Hickory will be when we unveil him – our secret weapon. They have slaughtered us in the regional contest for the last fifteen years. Delia Smoot, the principal, treats me as though I'm running a knucklehead farm up here. This is my chance to show her."

Linda shook her head. "I'd be worried about other things if I were you."

"What do you mean?"

"Well, uh, you know. Our kids are an ill-mannered bunch and fight with each other constantly. You can imagine how they will treat an outsider from New York, especially one as unusual as this boy."

"Nonsense," Eunice roared, slamming a beefy hand down on her desk. "They're a little rambunctious, that's all." She glowered at Linda for a few seconds. "Besides, it's your job to make sure the boy fits in here."

Abruptly, the door opened and Claire Smithson appeared. She made quieting motions with her hands, but only succeeded in looking like an ungainly bird trying to take off. Then a young woman and a boy entered the room. Claire's voice assumed a dignified tone as though announcing the Queen of England. "Mrs. Bluestone, permit me to introduce Sally Winston and her nephew, Hamilton Davis

Boehm."

"Davey," the boy said. "I prefer to be called Davey."

"So wonderful to have you in our little family," Eunice said, sweet as sugar. "Come in and meet Linda Peabody, Hamilton's home room teacher."

"Davey," the boy repeated, much louder this time.

Eunice almost exploded for a second. She didn't tolerate interruptions, but she managed to retain her composure. "Well, all right, excuse me…DAVEY. As I was saying, Miss Peabody will make you feel welcome here – won't you, Linda?"

"I certainly will," Linda said, studying Davey with interest. He was a nice looking boy, but a bit small for his age. A pair of oversized glasses hid most of his face. His brown hair was of average length and neatly combed across his forehead. Hanging over his shoulders was a rather empty looking backpack.

"Look how nicely you are dressed," Eunice continued. "I wish our other students would dress half as well. Maybe your example will inspire them."

Davey shrugged nervously. "It's what I always wear to school."

Linda felt a sudden impulse to strangle Eunice. With her typical lack of discretion, she had embarrassed the boy. Even so, she was right about his outfit. He was dressed like a model from a prep-school catalog. Covering his slender frame was a navy-blue blazer with a crest on the front pocket, a crisp white shirt with a tie at the collar, and a pair of pressed khaki slacks. Brown loafers completed his ensemble. *If the other kids see him this way, they'll laugh themselves silly,* Linda thought.

"Linda, why don't you take Davey for a quick tour and show him where his locker is," Eunice suggested. "I'll go over a few parenting type things with his aunt."

Linda was relieved because Eunice had finally said something sensible. Davey seemed reluctant to leave his aunt's side, so Linda quickly turned him towards the door and gave him a little shove. "Come on, Davey. Let's have a look at your new school," she said cheerfully.

When Davey stepped into the main hallway, he looked longingly at the school's front entrance. On his face was an expression of despair. *Maybe I should make a run for it while I have the chance,* he thought.

For some reason, Linda could sense what he was thinking. Perhaps it was because a similar idea had occurred to her a short time ago. She put her hand on the boy's shoulder and gently pointed him towards the classrooms. "It's this way," she said.

Davey kept his head down and remained silent as they walked along.

Linda did her best to help him relax by chatting merrily. "I know you're probably anxious about starting a new school. Trust me; the feeling is perfectly understandable. I've only been teaching here for a month and I still get nervous. The feeling usually hits me first thing in the morning, so whenever you feel that way, come and see me. I'll think up something fun for us to do – something special. After all, I want you to enjoy it here."

A faint smile fluttered across Davey's face. "Thanks, I'd like that."

Linda felt her heart go out to the boy. Fate, as though sensing her loneliness and frustration, had given her a new purpose. *I'm going to help this unusual boy. Somehow, I'll find a way for him to thrive in this horrible school,* she told herself.

Linda didn't know that her decision marked a milestone in her life. Nor did she realize something very important. Davey Boehm was a lot more unusual than she thought.

⋐ Chapter 3 ⋑

---

*Magick hath many uses. Yet its powere is
greatest when used for acts of good. Thou
magician, be pure of heart and let thy
purpose be noble.*

— Translated from Storia Di Incanto; circa 1535

Hambone

DAVEY'S QUICK TOUR of the school left him aghast. The decrepit
brick building, with its dim hallways, creaky wooden floors, funky
smells, and worn-out furnishings was a far cry from the modern
facility of his school in New York. *This school is ready for the
graveyard,* he thought.

There was one bright spot – he really liked Linda Peabody. As she
showed him around the school, he told her about his parents traveling
to China and his unhappiness over not going with them. He surprised
himself by expressing his feelings freely instead of clamming up as he
usually did around adults. There was something familiar and
comforting about her that made him keep talking.

Davey realized what it was when he almost called her mom.
Luckily, he caught himself in time or he would have been terribly
embarrassed. Similar to his mother, she listened to him as if he was
the most interesting person in the world. She didn't pass judgment
and accepted his feelings without pointing out the flaws in his

reasoning.

Linda revealed a bit of her own distressed emotions in response. "I don't blame you for being upset about China, who wouldn't be? Still, life is full of difficulties; things don't always turn out the way we want. It happens to adults as well as kids — more often than we admit."

They arrived at his locker, which had an old, mud-encrusted shoe lying at the bottom, a relic of its prior user. Linda threw the shoe away, wiped out the inside with some wet paper towels, and convinced Davey to leave his blue blazer and tie there. Then she rolled up the sleeves on his shirt, ruffled his hair a bit, and smiled. "We go for the casual look around here."

Davey looked at her solemnly. "You're afraid the other kids will make fun of me. I've been worried about the same thing for weeks."

Linda did her best to appear optimistic. "The kids here are probably different from those in New York. It may be a while before you get used to them."

Davey didn't find her words encouraging. He wondered what she meant as he stood beside her in homeroom class, waiting for the other students to arrive. But when they began drifting into the room, he understood well enough. They were a tough-looking bunch with shaggy haircuts, unkempt clothes, and sullen, sunburned faces. *I've seen nicer looking kids in street gangs,* he thought gloomily.

The kids wandered about the room, jeering, punching, and yelling at each other. They didn't show the slightest interest in him, even though he was a new face. No one said hello to Linda Peabody either. Watching them, his uneasiness increased. *This is getting worse by the minute,* he told himself.

The bell rang and the room slowly grew quiet. With rather surly glances towards Linda, the students lazily took their seats.

"Class, we have a new student," Linda announced.

Abruptly, Claire Smithson burst into the room. "Yoo-hoo, Hamilton Boehm," she called out, almost stumbling over one of the students who was sitting with his legs outstretched. "Awk," she croaked and swatted at the student.

Linda sighed with exasperation. *What now?* she wondered.

Claire's long skinny neck scrolled around until she noticed Davey. "Oh Hamilton, there you are. Sorry to interrupt, but Eunice wanted him to have a copy of his schedule." She rushed forward, handed him the sheet, and left the room, looking very much like a crane stalking through a marsh.

"As I was saying class, we have a new student. He has just moved here from New York and his name is Davey Boehm," Linda continued.

"Hey...old lady Smithson just said his name was Hamilton!" yelled a chubby-faced kid from the middle of the room.

Linda smiled nervously. "Yes, but his nickname is Davey," she explained.

"Let's call him Hambone," the boy replied. He grinned defiantly at Linda as if he was the one in charge of the class.

Davey frowned because his classmates at his old school had sometimes called him Hambone and he hated the nickname. "I really prefer Davey," he said.

The chubby-faced boy rose and waved his arms, pretending he was leading a pep rally. "Hambone...Hambone," he sang out repeatedly.

"Hambone...Hambone," the class chanted in response.

Davey stared at the boy leading the class. He was a big kid with blunt features, short brown hair combed straight up, and malicious pig-like eyes. His arms and shoulders were meaty lumps of muscle and he wore a t-shirt with a cartoon of a flame-breathing dragon across the chest. Over the dragon was the caption, *Born for Trouble.*

Immediately, Davey realized he was looking at the class bully. He had run into kids like him at his school in New York. They were usually big and got their kicks by intimidating others. His old school expelled them as soon as they started causing trouble. Apparently, the same rules didn't apply at this school. *Definitely not a good omen,* he thought.

Linda walked over to the big kid, put her hands on his shoulders, and pushed him into his chair. "Shut up, Spike," she snapped. "The rest of you can keep quiet too. We will call him Davey like he's asked."

Davey smiled apologetically as if sorry for the commotion. However, the faces staring back at him seemed almost hostile. Then he noticed a blonde-haired girl sitting alone at the far end of the front row. She wore glasses almost identical to his. When their eyes met, she smiled. Davey breathed a sigh of relief – a friendly face at last.

"Since Davey is new here, I'd like for someone to help him learn his way around. Raise your hand if you'll volunteer," Linda said, searching the room expectantly; no hands went up in response.

Davey hoped his face wasn't turning red. He felt like the last kid chosen for a team in gym class, something that had frequently happened to him.

A few seconds passed, and then the blonde-haired girl who had smiled, raised her hand. "I'll do it, Miss Peabody," she said, her voice surprisingly husky.

Linda nodded and turned towards Davey. "Amy Pigeon is going to help you settle in here. Why don't you sit at the desk next to hers while I'll get class started?"

Davey hurriedly took his seat and flashed the girl named Amy a grateful look. He hated being the center of attention.

"Hambone and Birdbrain sitting in a tree, *k-i-s-s-i-n-g*," a voice sang from two rows behind him. A titter of laughter sounded around the room. Davey recognized the voice of the big kid called Spike and wondered if he had already made an enemy.

Linda glared at Spike. "Keep it up and you'll be spending next Saturday in detention," she said crossly.

"Wooooo!" responded the class in unison. The sound rolled around the room like a freight train moving through a tunnel. When it died, an eruption of laughter followed.

"All right class," Linda said wearily. "Since everyone is having so much fun, why don't we really make it a party? Let's practice our diction by reading aloud. Take out your English books and turn to page forty-six. We'll take turns reading *Ralph Waldo Emerson*. Spike, since you're so anxious to be heard, you can read first."

A smattering of groans came from the class. Davey glanced over at Amy, rolled his eyes, and made a pained face. Amy responded with a grin. *At least she has a sense of humor,* he thought.

The remainder of homeroom class was as uneventful as thirty minutes of reading *Emerson's* essay on self-reliance could be. After the bell sounded, a tangible feeling of relief ran through the room. The kids streaked for the door, anxious to escape.

Linda walked towards Davey, looking irritated. Obviously, the unruly behavior of the class had upset her. Davey had found it shocking as well. He had never seen students treat a teacher with such disrespect.

"We didn't have time to gather your school-books," Linda quickly said, trying to hide her frustration. "I'll collect them for you during the day. Your last class will be right here. Come up and get them from me then, okay." She also handed Davey a slip of paper. "This is a note telling your other teachers about you. They probably won't have any paperwork on you until tomorrow, so be sure to show them my note."

"Thank you," Davey said, tucking the note into his pocket.

Linda looked at Amy who was dutifully waiting by Davey's side. "Thank you for volunteering."

Davey tried to look cheerful. "Don't worry; I'll be fine."

Linda managed a smile. "Hurry or you'll be late for your next class."

Davey sensed her unhappiness. He tried to think of something clever that would cheer her up, but Amy was tugging on his sleeve. "Come on," she said, pulling him towards the door, so he just waved as they left the room.

"Why did that kid call you Birdbrain?" Davey asked as they thrust themselves into the throng of kids moving towards their next class. Shouts, laughter, and an occasional shriek reverberated along the corridor, filling the air with a horrendous racket. Underfoot, the worn planks of the floor groaned as though unable to take the weight of so many kids for another second.

"Spike's got a pet name for everyone," Amy shouted. "It's one of the mean things he does. By the way, I'd avoid him if I were you."

"I'm not afraid of him," Davey replied, hoping he sounded braver than he felt.

"Do me a favor. Skip the macho routine and listen. Several mean kids follow Spike around and do his bidding. Once he targets you, they won't leave you alone. Everyone in seventh grade is afraid of them."

"Why doesn't the school discipline them?"

"You can forget about that. Spike's father, Wally Houseman, is on the school board. He owns half the town and bullies everyone the same way his son does. The principal is as scared of him as we are of Spike," Amy replied.

Davey followed her, lost in thought. The more he learned about this school the less he liked it. Amy threaded her way through groups of kids standing in front of several classrooms, detoured around a mass of students clogging the intersection of two corridors, and finally ducked into a doorway. No one said a word when she passed, which seemed odd to him. *She doesn't have any friends,* he thought.

"Well, here we are," she said, breathing hard. "This is math class and Timothy McDonnell is the teacher. Don't let his looks fool you; he's tough as nails. Show him Miss Peabody's note and then sit in the back with me. I'll save you a seat."

Davey glanced at the teacher and his mouth opened in surprise. He looked just like an old dwarf that Davey had seen illustrated in a book. He stood about five feet tall and was nearly as wide. A white handlebar mustache curled up on the sides of his ruddy cheeks, and wire-rimmed eyeglasses perched precariously over his bulbous nose. His head was completely bald except for a patch of white hair flaring around each ear. His trousers, brown sheets of cloth with yellow stripes and bright red suspenders, billowed out from the tops of laced-up army boots. An orange shirt and blue bow tie completed his outlandish outfit.

Davey approached the teacher and timidly offered him Linda's note.

"Harrumph," he said, snatching the note and reading it. Then he frowned suspiciously. "New York, eh lad? Not one of them Yankee troublemakers are you?"

"Uh, no sir," Davey replied.

"Well, why are you in our wee town?" he asked with a trace of Irish accent.

When Davey started to explain, the bell announced the start of class.

"Never mind," Mr. McDonnell said, giving him back the note. "Sit in one of the desks on the front row where I can keep an eye on you."

Davey turned to follow his instructions and noticed that the only empty desks in the entire room were on the front row. Spike sat in the center of the row, his muscular arms resting across the desks beside him. Davey nonchalantly slid into the one nearest the window, two seats away. But when he leaned on the wooden armrest of his desk, the top half almost came apart. He made a quick examination and found that the screws holding the armrest in place were missing. Spike snickered as though Davey had done something really stupid. Ignoring Spike, Davey carefully balanced his arms on the desk to hold it together.

"All right lads and lassies, let's get quiet," boomed Mr. McDonnell. Contrary to the response Linda received from the same group of kids, silence immediately filled the room. He stood at the blackboard and wrote the following equation:

$$6y + 42 = 16y - 8 \qquad y = ?$$

"On Friday, I gave you this simple algebra problem to solve. It's not the least bit difficult, so all of you should have the correct answer. Now, which brilliant student will show the class how they solved it?" he asked cheerfully.

Spike raised his hand and simultaneously turned and scowled at his classmates. No one else raised a hand. *Why is he glaring at everyone?* Davey wondered.

Mr. McDonnell put his hands on his hips and peered suspiciously at the class. "How come Spike is the only one who volunteers in this class?" Shaking his head, he sighed. "All right, Spike, step up and show these scaredy-cats some algebra."

Spike swaggered towards the front of the room and began writing on the blackboard. Davey quickly became bored; he had been solving much harder algebra problems since he was ten years old. As a result, he quickly lost interest in what was happening inside the classroom. Suddenly, a tapping on the window beside his desk distracted him. It was an insistent sound, so he looked over at the window.

Layers of grime covered the outside of the windowpane. The blurry shadow of a small shape was the only thing Davey could see through the glass. To his amazement, the shape began to scrape at the coating of grime on the pane. Soon, the grime was gone from a spot the size of a fingertip.

The scraping stopped, and a tiny eye appeared at the opening. The eye stared at Davey for a minute and then disappeared. Immediately, the scraping started again and the circle slowly enlarged. This mysterious activity intrigued Davey so completely that he forgot about math class, his new school, and everything else.

As the cleared area grew, the claws of two tiny hands emerged into view. Before long, Davey could see the rest of the shape. It turned out to be a squirrel, but one unlike any he had ever seen before. Instead of the normal mix of grey, brown, and white fur, this squirrel had sleek black fur all over – with one exception. On its face, a thin band of white fur encircled each of the squirrel's eyes and then stretched along the side of its head. This made the squirrel look as though it was wearing eyeglasses. Of course, it wasn't, and the squirrel's strange behavior held Davey spellbound.

In the meantime, Spike had finished writing his solution for the algebra problem and come up with the answer: $y = 1.67$. He turned and faced the class proudly.

"Class, how many agree with Spike's answer?" Mr. McDonnell asked.

A few hands went up around the room. Spike glowered at the class, daring anyone to disagree with him.

"Okay, raise your hand if you have a different answer," Mr. McDonnell said.

No hands went up in response.

Mr. McDonnell slapped his bald head dramatically. "How come only a few agree, but no one disagrees? This is math class and you bunch of dumbbells don't add up." He paced in front of the class for a few seconds. "All right," he said, as though having an idea. "How many of you are clueless about the right answer?"

Hands shot up throughout the room.

"Harrumph," bellowed Mr. McDonnell. "You're all deadheads."

Laughter came from the class as Mr. McDonnell glared around the room with mock anger. His eyes landed on Davey, who was staring out the window at the squirrel. Unfortunately, Amy hadn't warned Davey about Mr. McDonnell's habit of picking on anyone not paying attention in class. Afterwards, she felt bad about what happened because she considered it her fault. She watched silently while the teacher zeroed in on Davey like a cat spotting a crippled mouse.

Mr. McDonnell wanted to yell at his new student, but he couldn't remember his name. "You there, why didn't you raise your hand?" he finally bellowed.

Davey had no idea the teacher was talking to him. He ignored the voice because the squirrel's antics at the window still held him enthralled. Upon scraping the grime away from an area about six inches in diameter, the squirrel had done something even more bizarre. It had drawn a perfectly shaped triangle in the grime alongside the cleared area. The squirrel pointed excitedly at the triangle with its tiny hands. *This is just too weird,* Davey thought.

Perplexed, Mr. McDonnell glanced over at Spike. "What is the new lad's name?"

"Try Hambone," Spike whispered with a grin. "It's his nickname. Plus, he's a little hard of hearing, so you may have to shout."

The teacher tiptoed over until he stood near Davey. "Hambone, come in and join us, won't you," he yelled.

Davey didn't see Mr. McDonnell sneaking up on him and he jumped a foot in the air. The movement disrupted his hold on the desk, and it fell apart and crashed to the floor. Losing his balance, Davey spilled out after it, his face landing on Mr. McDonnell's army boots. The class, thinking this was positively hilarious, exploded into laughter.

Davey staggered up and looked into Mr. McDonnell's face, now inches from his. "Uh – I think my desk is broken," he stammered.

Mr. McDonnell ignored the broken desk. "You are Hambone, right?"

"No sir," said Davey meekly. "I'm Davey Boehm."

"Harrumph," responded Mr. McDonnell. "Not Hambone?"

"No sir, just Davey."

"But you are a student in my class," Mr. McDonnell roared.

"Yes sir," Davey said, totally embarrassed. Somehow, he had become the center of attention again.

"Since you are a student in my class and all my students know I insist upon absolute attention, please answer my question," the teacher demanded.

"What question, sir?" Davey asked, wanting to crawl into a hole.

Mr. McDonnell sighed loudly, folded his arms across his chest, and stared silently at Davey. After a few seconds, he turned towards the class as though fed up with such stupidity. His expression caused another round of laughter in the classroom. He glared at Davey again and then spoke slowly as if addressing someone who could not understand plain English. "All right, listen very carefully this time."

"Yes sir," Davey replied.

Mr. McDonnell bounced on his toes and raised his finger in the air. "Is Spike's answer correct? THAT is the question!"

The class giggled uncontrollably at the way Davey was making a total fool of himself. Amy, who was trying unsuccessfully not to join in, wondered if she had made a mistake by volunteering to help him. *This kid is a disaster,* she thought.

Davey squinted at the blackboard, seeing Spike's answer for the first time. "No, it is not," he said quickly.

Suddenly, the classroom became quiet. Spike, still at the blackboard and so consumed with laughter that he had doubled over, jerked upright and looked at Davey with malicious eyes.

Mr. McDonnell feigned surprise. "Not correct? What is the right answer then?"

"It's $y = 5$," Davey replied immediately.

"Do you know where Spike made his mistake?" Mr. McDonnell asked, suddenly very interested in his new student.

"Well, he probably got his pluses and minuses mixed up when he simplified the equation," Davey said earnestly.

The teacher spun in a circle. "Correct, my boy, absolutely correct. Spike, sit down. Davey, take Spike's place at the blackboard."

Spike stomped towards his desk, his face turning purple. Davey stepped to the blackboard without glancing at him.

"The second problem on our homework assignment was a refresher on long division," Mr. McDonnell announced, writing the following problem on the board.

$$8,763.446 \div 56.443$$

"Now, I know you haven't had a chance to do the problem. Still, could you show us how the wee lads in New York would do it?"

"The answer is 155.26," Davey said after a few seconds.

Mr. McDonnell consulted his notes. "Correct, but where are your calculations?"

"Oh, I did it in my head," Davey replied.

Mr. McDonnell was shocked. "It's not an easy problem to do in one's head. Let's make another test," he said, and quickly wrote a second problem on the blackboard.

$$(543.66 \times 2{,}203.54) \div 1{,}332.89$$

Davey took a little longer this time. "The answer is 898.78," he announced.

Mr. McDonnell twirled in a surprisingly fluid motion and two-stepped over to the teacher's desk near the blackboard. Whipping out a small calculator, he furiously punched numbers in the little machine. "He's right," the teacher exclaimed, holding the calculator up for everyone to see.

A gasp of astonishment reverberated through the room. Amy, who was the best math student in the class prior to Davey's arrival, could hardly believe it. *Perhaps he isn't such a disaster,* she thought. Meanwhile, Spike glared at Davey with gritted teeth, his face a mask of anger.

What followed next was an increasingly difficult sequence of math problems, each made up by Mr. McDonnell and solved by Davey in his head. Every time he reported the answer, the teacher became more visibly excited. Finally, he exploded with enthusiasm. "By George, the lad's a bloody genius!"

A few seconds later, the bell rang and math class ended. Mr. McDonnell dramatically eased his bulk into a kneeling position and pretended to give thanks. "Praise the saints and all that's glory, heaven has sent me a math student," he shouted.

❧ Chapter 4 ❧

Forces mystical and wondrous are at work all around thee. Do not forsake events, though they may seem trivial. All is part of the pattern into which we are woven.

— Translated from Storia Di Incanto; circa 1563

Wooga Wooga

"**WELL, BLOODY GENIUS,** you've really done it now," Amy said when they were heading towards their next class.

The pleasant smile on Davey's face faded. "Meaning what?"

"Meaning Spike is going to kill you. His father promised to buy him a motorbike if he wins the class award for best math student. So…Spike rigged it by telling everyone he would hurt them if they sat in front or answered Mr. McDonnell's questions. It's his way of making sure he gets all the points for class participation and wins the award."

"He's terrorized everyone into acting stupid? That's ridiculous."

"Ridiculous or not, it's the way things are around here. If you had sat in the back like I said, this wouldn't have happened. Instead, you sit up front and make Spike look bad by solving the algebra problem. Then you show off by doing equations like a human calculator. That was awesome, by the way. Now, you'll probably get the award – if you live long enough, which I doubt."

Davey shrugged innocently. "I couldn't help it. Mr. McDonnell made me sit up there. After that, everything just sort of happened when my stupid desk fell apart."

Amy started to laugh. "I would die from total embarrassment if anything that dumb ever happened to me. It was…so…pathetic."

"Gee, thanks," Davey said sarcastically.

"I'm sorry – it was just so funny. It serves you right for sleeping in class."

"I wasn't sleeping. I was watching this strange squirrel on the windowsill. It was black with white circles around its eyes and was scraping the grime off the glass."

Amy burst out laughing again. "Not only were you sleeping, you were dreaming. Great Oak doesn't have any squirrels with those kinds of markings. I should know – I've lived here my entire life. Besides, squirrels don't go around cleaning windows."

Davey changed the subject, certain she would really scoff at the idea of the squirrel drawing a triangle on the window. "Well, I don't care if Spike gets mad. I'm not acting stupid in math class to make him happy."

"Look, I'm good at math too. I just don't advertise it."

"It's not something to be ashamed of," Davey said.

Amy sighed. "Even if I wasn't afraid of Spike, which I am, the other kids think you're a nerd if you're good at things like math. Before you know it, everyone calls you a loser and you have no friends."

Her remark startled Davey. For the first time, he noticed her green eyes and the freckles across her nose. He liked the way her blonde hair, held in place by several clips, curled down her back. "No one could think you're a loser," he said seriously. Suddenly, he realized it was an amazingly bold thing to say. He grinned as if he was joking. "Still, you could lighten up a little."

"Sure, just like your head will be lighter after Spike pulverizes it for you," she said. Abruptly, she took off with determined strides.

"Hey, wait up," Davey yelled.

But Amy didn't, not wanting him to see the blush spreading across her face. Hadn't he practically said he liked her? She knew he wasn't joking despite his pretenses. The thought made her feel funny — not funny ha, ha, — funny peculiar. He was certainly different from the other boys. He wasn't tall or handsome, although he wasn't bad looking, yet there was something appealing about him.

Amy deposited Davey at the gym after telling him physical education was next and the boys had separate classes, so she would meet him in the cafeteria for lunch. "Stay away from Spike," she ordered and hurried away without another word.

Staying away from Spike for the next hour turned out to be easy. Coach Dobson, who acted like he had a grudge against everyone, wouldn't let Davey participate because he didn't have the right shoes. "Wear sneakers tomorrow or you'll do push ups," he yelled and made Davey watch while the other kids played basketball, as if watching was some kind of punishment. Coach Dobson didn't know Davey hated basketball. It made him feel more uncoordinated than any other sport, a remarkable feat. Throughout the class, Spike kept giving him nasty looks, reminding him of Amy's warning. He was glad he wasn't out on the court being pulverized.

After class, Davey hid in the boy's bathroom in order to avoid Spike on the way to lunch. When the way was clear, he snuck along the empty corridors until he found the cafeteria. All the while, he felt as if he was living through a horrible nightmare.

Lunch in the school cafeteria had the same circus-like atmosphere as the rest of his classes, only worse. A tidal wave of noise washed over him when he walked through the doors. The room was packed full of kids, all of them screaming, throwing food, and otherwise running amuck. Sunlight streamed in from high windows along the walls, giving the room a cheerful look despite the chaos inside. Giant saucer-like chandeliers hung down on long black cords from the ceiling. Considering the riot-like atmosphere, Davey was surprised nobody was swinging from them.

He noticed a middle-aged woman on a platform at the front of the room. Apparently, she was the teacher in charge. Her curly black hair, which rose up in tendrils around her head, had streaks of blue and red in it. She sat in a chair with her eyes closed as though asleep. *How can anyone sleep in this noise?* he wondered while searching for Amy. He finally found her at a table behind a large column in one corner of the room.

"I hear Coach Dobson yelled at you," she said when he appeared. "You can't stay out of trouble, can you?" Despite her tone, she seemed glad to see him.

"How do you know about Coach Dobson?"

Amy grinned. "You've become a celebrity. The entire school has heard about what you did in math class. Now, as soon as anything happens to you, someone tells me. They seem to think I'm responsible for you. Where have you been, anyway? I was getting worried."

"I had a hard time finding you," Davey said, not wanting to tell her about hiding in the bathroom.

"Sorry, I forgot to mention my special place during lunch. It's the only table in the whole cafeteria where you can get away from all the food throwing and other nonsense. So I always sit behind this big post — mostly by myself."

Davey studied her for a second. *She's a loner like me,* he thought. "Who's the teacher sleeping at the front of the room?"

"She's Mrs. Watson. You'll see her later in history class. For your information, she's not sleeping. She's meditating. She's a bit odd."

"What a surprise."

"By the way, I hope you brought lunch."

Davey pulled a paper bag out of his backpack. "Aunt Sally made me something."

"Good! The food here tastes awful and I'm not sharing my pimento cheese sandwich, even if you are a genius."

"Ugh, pimento cheese, I've got real food. A roast beef sandwich, Fritos, a Snickers bar, and a Cherry Coke." He spread the items out on the table in front of him.

"Uh oh," Amy muttered, looking past Davey. "Here comes Monkey Davis."

"Who?" Davey asked, turning around and staring.

"See the kid in the camouflage pants and green t-shirt? He's one of Spike's little gang. His real name is Albert, but everyone calls him Monkey."

Davey spotted a tall boy coming towards them. "Why Monkey?"

"You'll see," Amy said.

Soon, Monkey Davis reached their table. With almost no neck, round eyes, and gangly arms hanging nearly to his knees, he had the overall appearance of an orangutan wearing clothes. A buzz haircut and flat nose enhanced the impression. "Spike wants to see you out on the playground," he told Davey. Food showed in the gaps of his teeth and flecks of spit sprayed from his mouth as he talked.

Davey stared at him in astonishment. He tried to think of some plausible reason why he couldn't meet Spike, but he was at a loss for words. His only thought was whether Monkey ever brushed his teeth.

Amy shook her head. "He can't," she said firmly.

"Why not," Monkey demanded hotly.

"Because he has to go to the principal's office. Maybe Spike could meet him there," Amy said, straight-faced. Of course, she knew Spike wouldn't.

Monkey stared vacantly at them for a few seconds. Then with a surprisingly quick motion, he scooped up the Snickers bar in front of Davey.

"Hey, that's mine," Davey yelled.

"Wooga, wooga," Monkey hollered, scratching his ribs and imitating an ape. With a spiteful grin, he turned and ambled away, taking the Snickers bar with him.

"Good thing I didn't have a banana or he might have really gone berserk," Davey muttered. He rolled his eyes at Amy, which sent them into fits of laughter.

"I wonder what Spike wants," Davey said, after they stopped

laughing.

"It's one of Spike's favorite tactics. He lures kids out to the playground so his goons can attack them. Hurry up and eat – we need to go."

"What's the rush? Lunch isn't over for another twenty minutes."

"You actually do need to go to the principal's office; Miss Peabody told me in the hallway. You have to sign a form choosing your elective class."

"Choose an elective class?" Davey asked.

"Yeah, elective classes meet on Mondays and Fridays, right after lunch. You can pick one – drama, photography, computers, or speech."

"I wonder what class Spike is in."

"Well, I take computers and he's not in my class," Amy suggested.

Davey grinned. "Perfect, I'm good at computers."

"Is there anything you aren't good at?"

He started to laugh. "Pick a sport...any sport."

As Davey finished his sandwich, he stared out the window at the playground. He saw no sign of Spike and was about to turn away when the squirrel from math class suddenly appeared on the windowsill. The odd-looking squirrel made chattering sounds as though trying to tell him something.

Davey jumped up, grabbed Amy who was carrying her trash away, and pulled her towards the window. "Look, it's the squirrel I told you about."

"I don't see any squirrel," she said when they reached the window.

Davey searched everywhere, but the squirrel had disappeared. Amy pushed him away from the window. "Come on, showing off in math class has affected your brain."

With a frown, Davey followed Amy out of the cafeteria. The squirrel had appeared twice in a matter of hours, acting very mysterious each time. He knew it was not a coincidence. *What does it want?* he wondered. He now had something else to worry about, as if Spike wasn't enough.

☙ Chapter 5 ❧

Magic summons the aide of living things, great and small alike. Even the lowliest of creatures that crawleth below the firmament may partake in the struggle against evil.

— Translated from Storia Di Incanto; circa 1577

Ants

DAVEY'S AFTERNOON TURNED OUT even more eventful than his morning. In computer class, he showed everyone his animated screensaver, which he just happened to have on a floppy disk in his backpack. The teacher, Claudette Jenkins, a thin woman who wore her hair in an elaborate beehive, described Davey's screensaver as fantastic, simply fantastic.

Another confrontation with Spike occurred in history class. The teacher divided the class into three competing teams to answer questions about the Roman Empire. Davey and Amy were on the same team, and his teammates elected him captain after they discovered he knew a lot about the subject. Unfortunately, Spike was the captain of one of the other teams. When Davey successfully challenged Spike's answers four times in a row, Spike grew so angry his face looked like a tomato about to burst.

"You're doing it again," Amy whispered.

"Doing what?" he asked, so happily engaged in the competition that he didn't know what she meant.

"Making Spike mad," she said.

Davey found this truly irritating, but he let his teammates answer the remaining questions without his help. Unfortunately, this didn't appease Spike because Davey's team still won the competition.

Emily Watson, the teacher meditating while everyone ran amuck during lunch, fluttered up to Davey after class. She twirled her hands above his head and then looped them in wide circles around his body. Finally, she stepped back, her face twitching with excitement. The red and blue streaks in her hair wiggled as if they were alive. "I feel a strong aura, a very strong aura. All blue, with touches of green," she exclaimed.

"Is that good?" Davey asked, backing towards the door.

"Oh yes, most certainly," she chortled, slowly raising her arms and turning in a circle. "I see the power as it flows – it makes one glow from tips to toes."

"Well, I must go now," said Davey, thinking she was definitely strange.

"Go young leader and take heart, I saw your glory from the start," she continued, bestowing a blessing upon him while he eased from the room.

"Is it my imagination or are the teachers here too odd for words?" Davey asked when he and Amy headed for their next class.

Amy giggled. "I told you she was odd. We have English with Miss Peabody next. She's my favorite and the only normal teacher in the entire school."

"I like her too, but I think she's really unhappy about something. Deep down inside, she's really sad," Davey said.

Amy stopped for a second. "It's probably because Spike makes everyone be mean to her. He said it was an initiation since she was teaching at the school for the first time, so the kids act uncooperative on purpose. I know it upsets her because I've seen tears in her eyes after class is over."

Davey found this bewildering. "I can understand why he doesn't like me, but why is he picking on Miss Peabody, who is such a nice person?"

"He likes to make other kids do things they wouldn't do otherwise. Choosing her as a target shows his power. That's what I've been saying about him. He's just evil, pure and simple."

Davey still didn't understand. "Why would they be mean to her because he said so?"

A disgusted look came over Amy's face. "See, it's like this. Great Oak has fallen on hard times. Over the years, his family has taken control of the town. They own the furniture and textile factories where almost everyone works. The factories are losing money and his father is eliminating a lot of jobs."

"What does that have to do with Miss Peabody?"

"Their moms and dads are afraid of losing their jobs, so the kids kiss up to Spike. He says his father will keep their parents employed if they do what he asks. Most of them actually believe him."

"I'll bet you don't. You're too bossy to kiss up to anyone."

Amy looked away. While she certainly didn't kiss up to Spike, she didn't openly oppose him either. Despite what Davey thought, she avoided conflicts whenever she could. She often chided herself for being so cowardly, but whenever she tried to change, she lost her nerve.

"We should do something about it. Maybe we can get the class to treat her differently," Davey said.

"That's easy for you to say. You're already on Spike's hit list."

Davey trudged along silently, keeping his thoughts to himself. Amy watched him from of the corner of her eye, feeling a little ashamed. Finally, she groaned. "All right, don't look so disappointed. I'll help."

"That's the spirit!"

"You know, you really are a nice kid. Naïve, but nice," she said softly. Then somewhat embarrassed, she took off running. "Hurry," she yelled. "We can't help her by being late for class."

They arrived at Linda's classroom a few minutes later. Davey noticed Spike, Monkey, and another tough looking kid huddled in a back corner of the room. When Spike saw Davey, he made a remark to the other boys. They turned and looked at him with big grins on their faces.

"Who's the other kid with Spike and Monkey?" Davey asked.

"That's Jeremiah Jones, the third member of Spike's little gang. Spike calls him Torpedo because his head sort of narrows at the top and he butts kids in the stomach with it. I saw him do it to Howie Sherman once and it's very effective. If you admire mindless acts of violence that is," Amy said with distaste.

"I wonder what color his aura is," Davey muttered.

"He wasn't a bad kid before Spike turned him into Torpedo. We were sort of friends back in sixth grade. Now, he's just as worthless as Spike."

The bell rang and Linda began passing out sheets of paper. "All right class, we're going to have a little pop quiz," she announced.

A chorus of moans went up throughout the room.

"These sheets have ten sentences on them," she continued, unabashed. "Each sentence has two different grammar, spelling, or punctuation errors. You have fifteen minutes to find all twenty."

"It's not fair," Spike yelled angrily. "You gave us a pop quiz on Friday."

"Spike, nobody *has* to take the quiz," Linda replied.

Spike threw his sheet on the floor. "Good!"

Monkey, Torpedo, and several others followed suit with whoops of laughter, tossing their sheets in the air.

"However, anyone who doesn't hand in their completed quiz will get a zero," Linda said, looking at her watch. "Okay, time starts now." she added loudly.

Spike and the others students who had thrown their quizzes away stared at each other for a few seconds. Then with a mad scramble, they hastily retrieved them from the floor. "Witch," one of them said in a muffled voice.

Davey glanced at Linda and detected a slight redness on her cheeks. She pretended she didn't hear the remark, although he was sure she had. To him, the quiz was hardly more than a fourth-grade exercise and not the least bit difficult. He finished it quickly and sat quietly at his desk until Linda noticed him.

"Davey, why aren't you working," she asked in a low voice.

He handed her his quiz with a smile. She looked at his sheet for a few seconds and then grinned. "One hundred percent," she said. "Don't forget to see me after class. I have your textbooks for you."

Davey knew Amy had overheard what Linda had said and looked at her with raised eyebrows.

Amy stuck out her tongue. "Spare me."

A short time later, Linda clapped her hands. "Time's up, please pass your quizzes towards the front of the room. Now, we're going to discuss *The Adventures of Huckleberry Finn,* our reading assignment for the semester. By now, you should have finished the first fifty pages. Who will tell the class how they feel about the book?"

She might have been talking at a herd of cows for all the replies she received.

Linda's voice took on an anxious note as she looked around the room. "Oh come on, surely someone has an opinion."

Davey, who had already read the book twice, noticed Amy frowning at him when he started to raise his hand. "Well, you say something. She needs encouragement," he whispered.

Amy looked as though she might be screwing up her courage.

"How about you, Jeremiah," Linda asked, "What do you think?"

"It's boring," he muttered.

"A waste of time," Spike grumbled. "Only an idiot would read this book."

"All the characters talk funny. I can't understand them," Monkey complained.

Suddenly, Amy jumped to her feet. "How can anyone say *Huckleberry Finn* is boring? It's an adventure story about a black slave and a boy floating down the Mississippi at a time when there was practically no law. All kinds of crazy and unexpected things happen to them. It's funny and exciting, and you can learn a lot about the way people acted back then."

"Very good Amy, thank you," Linda said. "Anyone else have a comment?"

"If you sound out the words in the dialogue instead of looking at the way they're spelled, you can understand them," Davey volunteered.

"I sort of tried that and it worked. I really like the book," said Yolanda Smith, a girl who had been on Davey's team during history class.

"I've got an idea," Linda said. "Let's read some of the dialogue as if we're the ones doing the talking. A few of us can play different characters and the rest of you figure out what we are saying."

To Linda's surprise, the class warmed up to the idea. By the end of the period, everyone was laughing at the strange way the characters expressed themselves. That is, everyone except Spike, Torpedo, and Monkey, who sat scowling at each other with their arms folded.

When class was over, Davey and Amy noticed the glow of satisfaction on Linda's face and smiled at each other. "You were great, amazingly audacious," Davey said.

Amy was almost as pleased as Linda was. "Thanks partner," she giggled. Then she hurriedly stood up. "I've got to run because my mom is picking me up. Now remember, I showed you where the school buses wait for the kids. Your bus is number three, so pay attention and don't get on the wrong bus."

Davey saluted smartly. "Aye, aye, sir."

"Stop fooling around and listen," she ordered. "The buses leave in exactly twenty minutes, which means you cannot move at your usual pace. If you're late, they'll leave without you." Then she grinned and ran out of the room.

Davey went over to where Linda was stacking his textbooks on the dilapidated teacher's desk. "You're a good teacher, Miss Peabody," he said, knowing it was what she wanted to hear, yet meaning it just the same.

Linda smiled happily. "Thank you. This is my first year as a teacher and sometimes I think I'll never get the hang of it. After a class like this one though, I feel encouraged." She put her arm around Davey. "Speaking of not doing badly, I hear you had a sensational day. At least, that's what your other teachers told me."

"Yeah, except for Coach Dobson; he got mad because of my shoes."

Linda laughed. "Well, don't let it worry you. He yells at everyone, even the teachers. Did you make friends with some of the kids?"

Davey didn't mention his encounters with Spike and Monkey. "I like Amy Pigeon a lot, but sometimes a person who acts like a friend doesn't hold up in the long run. At least, that's been my experience. Time will tell, I guess."

Linda was astonished at his words. After what happened with her fiancée, she had reached the same conclusion. "Well, I think Amy is the genuine article. Is your aunt picking you up?" she asked, changing the subject.

"No, I'm riding the bus, which is something new. I've never ridden a school bus before."

"We'd better pack up your books and get you going then," Linda said.

In a matter of minutes, they had stuffed his textbooks into his backpack. Linda helped him heft the loaded pack onto his shoulders, which must have weighed at least twenty pounds. "Is it too heavy?" she asked.

"No problem," Davey said, pretending the weight was manageable. *Thank goodness, I don't have to carry this far,* he thought.

Linda looked thoughtfully at him. "Wait, there's another book you might enjoy. I'll bet you like dogs, don't you?"

"Yes, especially since I have one for the first time."

Linda hurried towards a bookcase in the corner and returned with *The Call of the Wild* by Jack London. "My parents gave it to me when I was about your age, so please take care of it," she said, putting the book into his backpack.

"I will," Davey said, and left the room. Much to his surprise, the corridor was completely empty – he had to hurry.

Davey knew exactly where he needed to go. The school had two main corridors and four exits, one at each end. The north-south corridor ran from the front entrance to the playground. The east-west corridor, which is where most of the classrooms were located, intersected the north-south corridor at its center. He had to travel the entire length of the east-west corridor to reach the bus loading area.

Davey went as fast as he could, but the weight of his backpack kept him off balance. Occasionally, he staggered, looking a bit like a sailor after a night on the town. He felt alone and a little spooked as each of his steps echoed off the walls of the old building. Shortly after he passed the intersection of the two corridors, the sound of a locker door slamming shut startled him. The sound reverberated along the corridor, making it hard to locate the source. He thought it came from somewhere behind him.

Unnerved, he spun around and walked backwards for a few steps, but the corridor was still empty. The hairs on his neck began to tingle and he turned towards the exit again, now only ten yards away. He quickened his pace, longing for the safety of the bus.

Abruptly, a furious rattling reached his ears. The sound was identical to the angry warning a rattlesnake might make before it struck. The rattling was coming from the alcove where the exit doors stood, only a few feet ahead. Then the overhead lights went off, cloaking the corridor in darkness.

Davey's imagination ran wild. *There's a rattlesnake up there,* he thought. A few shards of sunlight penetrated through the frosted glass of the doors, providing an eerie illumination. His eyes squinted, but he couldn't see clearly in the dim light, which increased his alarm.

Davey had lived a relatively sheltered life before arriving in Great Oak and he didn't know anything about snakes. He froze in his tracks, unable to think clearly. Suddenly, another frightening sound startled him. A deep cry rose from the corridor behind him. "Who's there?" he asked in a quavering voice, turning towards the sound.

Monkey Davis emerged from the shadows, his arms flapping wildly. "Wooga, wooga, going to get you, Hambone," he shouted.

At that moment, Davey heard the noise of running feet approaching from behind his back. He turned around again, just in time to glimpse a stout figure hurling at him. As he stood there, shocked and confused, the head of Torpedo Jones plowed into his stomach. The impact knocked his glasses off and threw him to the floor. He lay gasping for breath, realizing he should have paid more attention to Amy's warnings. *Don't think about that now. Just get away,* he told himself.

Rolling over in desperation, Davey began a frantic search for his glasses. But Torpedo wasn't finished with him yet. He held him down and shook the severed tail of a rattlesnake in his face while Monkey pulled his backpack from his shoulders.

Davey closed his eyes, shuddering as the rattles spewed out their vicious sounds. After that, the two boys ran down the corridor, carrying his backpack with them. He heard the sound of their laughter fading into the distance. A few minutes later, the overhead lights blinked on.

When Davey was sure they were gone, he shakily rose to his knees and searched again for his glasses. He found them lying on the floor several feet away. *At least they are not broken,* he thought, feebly pushing them onto his face. Then he heard a taunting voice calling from somewhere down the corridor. "Hambone, oh Hambone, look at what I've got." Immediately, Davey knew it was Spike. He staggered to his feet and glanced in the direction of the voice.

Spike stood at the intersection of the two corridors, a meaty hand holding out his backpack. A malicious grin covered his face and his piggy eyes gleamed with triumph. Davey didn't care about the backpack. As far as he was concerned, Spike could keep it, but he had promised to take care of the book Linda had given him. "Give it back," he croaked, his voice hoarse.

"Come and get it," Spike yelled before disappearing into the north corridor.

The thought of what Spike might do to the book made Davey very angry. Otherwise, he would never do what he did, which was run towards the spot where Spike had been standing. Upon reaching the north corridor, he searched ahead for his tormentors. He saw Spike standing about thirty yards away.

"Hambone, oh Hambone, come get your little backpack," Spike teased, pulling open the exit door and running outside.

"Give it back," Davey yelled again and ran after him, not really thinking about where he was going. Upon arriving at the exit, he burst through the doors into bright sunlight. Looking around, he realized he was out on the playground. He halted, remembering what Amy had said about Spike luring kids there so his goons could beat on them. He studied the area cautiously, searching for the three boys. There was no sign of Torpedo or Monkey, but he spotted Spike some distance away. He was busily thrusting a long tree branch into a two-foot high mound of dirt.

What's he doing? Davey wondered, watching him dig into the dirt like a farmer hoeing for weeds. As if answering his question, Spike tossed the branch aside, picked up Davey's backpack, and emptied the contents onto the dirt.

"Stop!" Davey hollered, starting towards him.

Spike glared at Davey and shook his fist. "This is only a warning. If you're smart, you'll go back to New York before you really get hurt." Then he walked smugly towards the end of the playground and vanished around a corner of the school building.

Davey felt a sense of relief. Keeping a wary eye out for Torpedo and Monkey, he turned his attention to the mound of dirt. At first, he thought his eyes were deceiving him. His books, which were scattered across a three-foot area, seemed red and blurry. As he neared, he discovered his eyesight wasn't the problem. The problem was ants – angry red ants. Thousands of them were swarming across his books, searching madly for the culprit who had wrecked their anthill.

Davey slumped down onto the grass, hating Spike, his new school, and everything about it. Then he remembered the school bus and brushed his thoughts aside. If he hurried, maybe he could still catch it.

First, the ants had to calm down so Davey could retrieve his books. He stood up and slowly walked around the big anthill. "Look, it wasn't me who attacked your home," he told the ants. "It was Spike Houseman. If you want to be mad at someone, be mad at him. In fact, I would appreciate your biting him every chance you get."

Davey used the voice he reserved for conversations with dogs, squirrels, and birds. This usually resulted in them acting as though they were his friends for life, but he had no idea if it would work on ants. "If you will just be reasonable," he continued in his most persuasive tone, "I'll get my books out of your anthill and you can take your revenge on Spike. I'm terribly sorry, but I'm an innocent victim just like you."

To his astonishment, the ants stopped their furious swarming and gradually disappeared into the ground. After a few more minutes, they were completely gone. He gingerly gathered up his books and returned them to his backpack. Finally, he heaved the backpack onto his shoulders, thanked the ants for their cooperation, and hurried towards the bus loading area. His worst fears were realized when he arrived. Not a single school bus was in sight. With a solemn expression, he thought about what he should do.

Soon, he began talking to himself as he sometimes did when he was alone. "Aunt Sally's house is not far away – I'm sure I can find my way there. All I have to do is cross the street, go through the park, and walk along Elm Street until I find it. A little hike won't hurt me. In fact, it might be an adventure." Suddenly, he remembered his father saying that he would be doing outdoor things while in Great Oak. Wondering if this was what his dad had in mind, he took a determined breath and headed towards the park.

ℭℌ Chapter 6 ℛ

---

*The pattern of events appeareth like a
great and never-ending tapestrie woven
with mystical threads. At any point in
time, the whole is not readily in thy
sight.*

— Translated from Storia Di Incanto; circa 1604

The Founding Fathers

IF THERE WAS ANYTHING the founding fathers of Great Oak did
well in 1847, it was their design of the town. Back then, the narrow
valley in the Blue Ridge Mountains wasn't even a dot on the map. A
trading post, sawmill, tavern, and small collection of farms were its
only structures. The entire population of the little settlement
numbered less than two-hundred.

Residents of the area called it Walberson's Ferry. The name came
from a mule-drawn ferry, which had carried wagons across the New
River from a dock behind the trading post. The name prevailed,
although Hal Walberson and his ferry had long since departed. Ten
years earlier, the ferry had broken its lines and shattered upon the
rocks downriver. Three people, including Hal, perished in the
disaster.

The residents were an odd mix of folks, each with a reason for
living in one of the most isolated areas of North Carolina. A few were

criminals with checkered pasts, hiding out from lawmen. Some simply desired a rugged lifestyle in a place without many rules. Others drifted there, seeking whatever opportunity they could find.

Although widely scattered, various Cherokee tribes lived in the mountains surrounding the little valley. Their ancestors had lived there for centuries and they had no love for the white men who settled nearby. Despite their promises, these men caused nothing but trouble and constantly tried to steal their land. As a result, the Cherokee kept away from the residents of Walberson's Ferry and stayed out of their affairs.

Unfortunately, their white neighbors did not always do the same. They hunted, cut trees, trapped animals, and mined gold on Cherokee land. Often, the Indians simply escorted them from their property. But repeat-offenders were not so lucky. They disappeared without a trace, their fate unknown.

At the time, demand for lumber was increasing throughout the South. Since trees were plentiful in the nearby forests, signs of growth were appearing at Walberson's Ferry. The sawmill was expanding and men looking for work were moving into the area. Prosperity, like a fair wind blowing through the mountains, was coming.

A few of the more intelligent residents realized that growth without organization would lead to chaos. This was particularly true of a place as lawless as Walberson's Ferry. Thus, they began to plan for the future by seeking a town charter.

Gregory Harrison, the area's most influential citizen, led the effort. Aided by a grant from the State, he formed a committee of six prominent landowners. These six became the founding fathers of Great Oak. Under his leadership, they provided resources for the new town and sought the support of the people living there.

Working together over many long days, the founding fathers laid out a simple but elegant plat for the town. No one remembers why they had such foresight. However, the citizens of Great Oak appreciated the centerpiece of their plat, a ninety-acre park, for years to come. Similar to a town square, only larger and more wooded than most, it set the tone for the town's commitment to nature. Surrounding the park was a wide main street, from which lesser streets spread out like the spokes of a wheel. Along these streets, specific sites were set aside for homes, schools, businesses, and city buildings.

Naturally, there were those who scoffed at the elegant plat. The idea of putting so much effort into a town in the middle of nowhere seemed ridiculous. But Gregory Harrison was a determined man and the founding fathers held their course. When they received a charter from the State, everyone took notice. Soon, the reality of the new town captured the people's fancy.

The final step in the process was the naming of the town. The residents debated the subject for many days. Some wanted the old name retained while others sought to name it after one of the valley's leading families, preferably their own. The founding fathers could have chosen any name they wanted, but they wisely decided everyone should have a say in the matter. They erected a large tent in the park and held an all day meeting on the subject.

The meeting was one of those affairs that everyone told stories about for many years. People came from miles away in order to participate. Many arrived the night before and slept on the ground. In fact, so many came, the tent overflowed. Those arriving late stood outside and learned what was happening from people seated near the entrance.

The discussion inside the tent opened peacefully, but soon grew quite heated. One by one, people wishing to speak came forward. Some spoke cleverly and with finesse, some with bull-headed stupidity. Still, no consensus developed. By midday, there was little agreement upon the name of the new town or on anything else for that matter.

While those inside the tent maintained a vestige of order, those outside did not. Before long, a circus-like atmosphere developed. Men passed around jugs of whisky; tempers began to flare. Curses, name-calling, and flying fists greeted any unpopular opinion; there were plenty of those.

The meeting was deteriorating rapidly when five members of the Houseman clan, stinking like wild animals, pushed their way inside the tent. In those days, they were a loutish family of lumberjacks who lived in the woods. Moreover, they made their living by stealing timber from Cherokee land, which constantly caused problems with the Indians. Everyone held the Housemans in such low regard; their mere appearance brought forth loud jeers and catcalls.

So when they brashly proposed the new town have their name, the crowd nearly laughed themselves silly. Enraged, the Housemans stormed outside where the men who had been drinking whisky all morning were waiting for them. Scorn and insults greeted the smelly tree-cutters, and a fight quickly erupted. The Housemans, too stupid to ignore them and retreat, barely escaped with their lives.

Somehow, this relieved the tensions inside the tent and everyone saw how foolishly they were acting. It also gave Gregory Harrison an opening. He abruptly suggested that an ancient oak standing in the park should serve as the town's namesake. The tree had been a landmark of the area for centuries; the name made perfect sense. To his surprise, everyone liked the idea, and the town of Great Oak was born.

Over the next few years, Great Oak grew steadily. Its first official building, a crude log structure, became the City Hall. Soon, a general store, bank, boarding house, and livery stable joined it. By 1871, twenty brick buildings graced the downtown area and fifty-five houses sat on the wooded hills around the town. The official population stood at seven hundred twenty-two humans, ninety dogs, eighty pigs, two hundred chickens, and sixty milk cows. More of each showed up daily, ready to make Great Oak their new home.

A large furniture factory had started operations as well, benefiting from the nearness of the existing sawmill. None other than the notorious Houseman family owned it. They turned out to be a resilient bunch with a knack for making money. Led by Billy Bob Houseman, they had become wealthy by clearing the foothills of trees.

Their money bought them a place in Great Oak society, despite their lack of couth.

Gregory Harrison became the town's first mayor and remained so for the next forty years. He was a kind and generous man, beloved by all. Most of the credit for the town's progress belonged to him, and rightfully so. Like a patient father teaching a child to read, he guided the town through many difficult decisions. His wisdom set the stage for fifty years of prosperity and growth. Unfortunately, the Housemans eventually undid most of his good work.

One of Gregory's most endearing qualities was his dedication to the welfare of the town. Every morning at six o'clock, he unlocked the doors to the City Hall. He sat in his office most of the day, helping any person with a problem; he never went home without seeing everyone in need. One evening, a clerk found him slumped over his desk, dead from a heart attack at the age of eighty-one.

The town council searched for a suitable way to honor his memory after his funeral. With much fanfare, they finally announced the town park would be renamed Harrison Park. In addition, they erected a bronze statute of him in its middle.

Prominently displayed on the statute were the words, *Gregory Harrison, Father of Great Oak*. After all, he had donated the land for the park and worked tirelessly for its beautification. In fact, he had been its greatest advocate and had delivered frequent speeches extolling the virtues of nature. For once, the citizens of Great Oak agreed – it was a fitting tribute.

The park was a gently rolling tract of land filled with towering hardwoods. The town initially left its slopes and ravines in their natural state. But over the years, weather and disease took their toll on some of the trees. As the woods thinned out, an opportunity for creative landscaping arose.

In 1878, the town council approved a master plan for the park, which provided for a series of manicured clearings between the wooded areas. It also allowed for other enhancements as well. Eventually, a bandstand, pavilion, and hiking trails took their place among the trees.

Nevertheless, the underlying theme of the park remained intact. It was a place dedicated to the serenity of nature. No one could visit it without appreciating Gregory Harrison and the founding fathers. The park stood as a proud symbol of their vision, a quiet enclave where the citizens of Great Oak could gather under the canopy of magnificent trees.

ᴄꙅ Chapter 7 ᴞꙅ

---

*Magick is part of the sacred order of
living things. Hence, be not surprised
should ye encounter mystical beings.
Many spirits inhabit the natural world,
though their purposes may be unknown
to thee.*

— Translated from Storia Di Incanto; circa 1623

The Magic Tree

OF COURSE, DAVEY KNEW nothing about the glorious history of
Harrison Park when he left the school grounds and stepped through
the park's entrance. But he remembered Aunt Sally pointing out the
park in the morning and knew her house was somewhere along Elm
Street, which went up a hill on the other side of the park.

What he didn't know was that a backpack filled with books would
get very heavy, very fast. Less than halfway through the park, he
became hot, thirsty, and tired. His sense of adventure was gone. All he
could think about was the malicious events that had made him miss
the bus.

Looking ahead, Davey saw an ornate bench tucked under the
shade of a lofty maple tree. Alongside the bench, a water fountain
stood like a solitary figure. He hurried towards the bench, pulled off
his backpack, and drank his fill of water. Then he collapsed wearily

on the bench, laid his head against the backrest, and looked up at the spreading limbs of the tree towering above him.

He rested there for what seemed like a long time, although it was only five minutes. As sunlight sprinkled through the leaves of the tree, and a soft breeze blew across his face, he realized the park was a beautiful and special place. *If only I could stay here instead of lugging this backpack home,* he thought.

The bench sat at the edge of a large clearing blanketed with green grass. The bronze statue of a man holding a long staff in one hand and a book in the other stood in the center. Around the base of the statue, groups of yellow, blue, and red flowers accented the tranquility of the scene.

Davey was surprised no one else was around. Finding a secluded spot in the parks of New York was almost impossible, but he seemed to have the entire expanse of Harrison Park to himself. However, he was not as alone as he thought.

Overhead, seven ravens floated high in the sky, watching him diligently, and from a tree less than three feet away, two eyes in the face of a small figure peered at him. The figure crept down the tree and into the nearby bushes, making a slight rustling sound. Davey jerked his feet up, recalling the imaginary rattlesnake in the alcove of the school. Abruptly, the figure leaped out of the underbrush and onto the path in front of him.

Davey laughed with relief. "I'm not surprised to see you," he said. It was the same oddly marked squirrel, which he had seen at school during the day.

The squirrel sat on its hind legs looking at Davey for a few seconds. Suddenly, it jumped onto the bench, ran across Davey's lap, and then hopped back to where it began. Once again, the squirrel sat there, watching him expectantly.

Davey had experienced many odd encounters with animals, so the strange actions of the squirrel were not particularly alarming. Instead, he just spoke calmly. "I know you want something, but what is it?"

Apparently, this was what the squirrel had been waiting to hear. It ran towards the path around the clearing, glanced back at Davey, and beckoned to him. Davey studied the little animal with intrigue. The squirrel's motions seemed almost human-like; it was clearly indicating he should follow it. Despite his weariness, he picked up his backpack. "All right, I'm coming," he said, starting after the squirrel.

The squirrel ran north along the path, stopped every so often to let Davey catch up, and then dashed ahead. Davey was no longer heading east, which was the direction of Aunt Sally's house, but he didn't care. He was too absorbed in finding out where the squirrel was going. When the squirrel reached the end of the clearing, it veered onto another path going further north. The woods closed around them as they left the clearing behind. Unseen, the ravens tracked them from their lofty positions in the sky.

Davey hurried to keep up, his curiosity increasing by the second. The path took on an upward slope and he slowed under the weight of his backpack. Looking ahead, he noticed another clearing, one surrounding a low knoll. The squirrel stopped at the entrance of the clearing and sat perfectly still, twitching its tail furiously. Davey sensed its excitement and understood the reason for it when he arrived. At the top of the knoll, some thirty yards away, stood the most magnificent tree he had ever seen.

"Is this where you were bringing me?" Davey asked, his voice so full of awe it was barely more than a whisper.

The squirrel sat alongside him, nodding its head and chattering softly. Overhead, the seven ravens dove towards the clearing. They aligned their bodies into the shape of a triangle and zoomed down, passing a few feet over Davey's head. With ear-splitting caws, they swooped around the tree in an upward spiral, finally reaching the sky above it. Then they floated in place, slowly rotating their triangular formation over the top of the tree.

Davey watched them with astonishment. He had never seen birds behave in such a manner. The way they maintained their formation while they flew was incredible. Moreover, it was a strange coincidence. The squirrel had also drawn a triangle on the window earlier in the day. *How very odd,* he thought, briefly watching the ravens before turning his attention back to the tree.

The gigantic tree reigned over the park like a stately deity. *Are my eyes deceiving me or is it actually glowing?* Davey wondered. The tree stood at least a hundred feet tall, its massive trunk twelve feet in diameter. Lofty limbs, each the size of a normal tree, branched out gracefully on all sides of the trunk. As a soft wind blew through the clearing, the tree's leaves oscillated with a faint, almost musical sound.

While Davey stared at the tree, a strange tingling coursed through his body. He felt an inexplicable attraction, a magical force emanating towards him. The force drew him forward, as if a powerful magnet was at work. He slowly let his backpack drop to the ground and then walked into the clearing. With each step, the force grew stronger.

Twenty-feet from its trunk, a shoulder-high, metal fence encircled the tree. The shiny-black fence had vertical spikes six inches apart. Pointed brass tips, polished and gleaming in the sunlight, capped the top of each spike.

A wide path bordered by colorful flowers led up the hill towards the tree. The path ended at an ornate gate in the center of the fence. A brass plaque with raised letters hung on the gate. When Davey reached it, his fingers played over the letters as he read the plaque.

The Great Oak

The town of Great Oak takes its name from this ancient oak. Centuries ago, the tree was a landmark for trade between natives who often traveled for weeks to reach it. Cherokee legends speak of a benevolent spirit, which lives in the tree. They claim the spirit grants the wishes of those it favors. Many people believe the spirit is still here and come to seek its blessing. Some say the tree granted their wishes, but these claims are unproven. Visitors should make a wish if they like. Perhaps the tree will favor them.

A brass lock, complete with ornate handle and keyhole, held the gate closed. Davey tried the handle, but the bolt of the lock was securely in place. Then he wandered around the fence, his hand running along the spikes. He found no other opening. When he returned to the gate, the squirrel was waiting.

"I guess visitors aren't allowed inside," he said.

The squirrel looked at him mischievously. If it were a person, Davey would have sworn it was smiling. In fact, the squirrel seemed to be acting a lot more like a person than an animal – a very little person, of course.

Immediately, the squirrel hopped towards the gate, gave a little shove on one of the spikes, and waited while the lock clattered open. With an eerie creak, the gate swung inward. Without hesitation, the squirrel dashed inside the enclosure, motioning again for Davey to follow.

Davey knew something truly strange had happened right before his eyes. He stood pensively at the gate, peering into the enclosure. He wasn't sure if he should go in, but he couldn't resist the force pulling him forward.

He stepped through the gate, hurried to the tree, and gently touched its gnarled and wrinkled bark. A pulsing sensation rushed though his body, which made him jerk his hand back. The sensation was not displeasing, but it startled him. Then he noticed the bark glowing where he had touched it. Behind him, the gate clanged shut and the lock engaged. He ignored the sound, completely enraptured by the tree.

In the meantime, the squirrel had raced up the side of the tree to where one of the branches joined the trunk. The animal looked down at Davey and indicated he should join it in the tree. Davey laughed at the idea. Although the thought of climbing the tree was appealing, the branches nearest the ground were high above his head. "There's no way I can climb up there," he said, looking up at the squirrel.

The little animal ran back down the trunk, stopped at a point about three feet from the ground, and pushed against the bark. When Davey looked at the spot, he saw a flat indentation in the side of the trunk, a ledge big enough for a foot. The ledge had taken on a slight amber glow. He looked at it dubiously, but the squirrel indicated he should put his foot into the indentation.

He followed the squirrel's instructions, grabbed onto the wide expanse of the trunk, and stepped up. As his fingers caressed the rough edges of the bark, he felt the pulsing sensation again. The feeling lasted for only a few seconds. After that, a very pleasant surge of energy flowed through his body.

Having no trouble keeping his balance, but not knowing what to do next, he clung to the tree until the squirrel scurried over to a higher place and pushed again on the trunk. Another indentation appeared, and Davey put his left foot in the new ledge and stepped up once more. The squirrel repeated the process several times and Davey made his way up the trunk, feeling very much like a spider climbing a wall. Soon, he pulled himself onto a branch fifteen feet above the ground.

Davey looked down, shocked by how high he had climbed. Then he noticed the indented footholds in the trunk had disappeared. As an experiment, he touched the bark along the branch where he was sitting. His fingerprints left an amber glow, which faded after a few seconds. Davey had a logical mind, but there was no explanation for this phenomenon. *I have stepped into "The Twilight Zone"*, he told himself.

Davey looked at the squirrel, now perched on a limb just above his head. "This is really weird, yet I'm sure nothing bad will happen to me here. So what do we do now?" he asked the little animal.

The squirrel nodded as if understanding Davey's words. It pointed towards the top of the tree and began to climb again. The way up the tree was easier now. The big branches formed a kind of circular staircase, winding around and sometimes zigzagging up the trunk. Davey followed the squirrel higher and higher, exhilarated by the thrill of climbing the tree. Each time he reached an impasse and couldn't find a nearby branch, the squirrel showed him one he had overlooked.

After this happened several times, Davey chided himself for not seeing a limb practically in front of his eyes. But when he reached a dead-end again, he inspected every branch over his head. He couldn't reach any of them. The squirrel was nowhere in sight and he concluded there was no way to go higher. Suddenly, the squirrel appeared on a branch behind him within his reach. He was sure the branch hadn't been there a few seconds ago. The thought startled him, but not enough to make him stop climbing.

At last, Davey reached a point where he was afraid to go higher. He was at a place where two conjoined branches arched out from the trunk, forming a natural platform. Two smaller branches extended above the platform, providing armrests. He sat down and wrapped his arms around the armrests, feeling as if he had accomplished a great feat. Looking down, he guessed the ground was seventy feet away.

A gentle sigh filled the air. Although Davey knew it was only the leaves fluttering in the breeze, he imagined the tree was expressing its pleasure at his presence. He felt strangely at home on the high platform and fantasized the tree had created it just for him.

An inexplicable feeling came over him as he sat there. He didn't know why, but he felt compelled to tell the tree something about himself. He started from when he had learned his parents were going to China and ended with Spike dumping his books on the anthill.

"I just wish there was a way to make Spike leave me alone. Then maybe I could enjoy being in Great Oak," he concluded.

The tree swayed with a graceful rocking motion, which Davey found remarkably soothing. Gradually, he felt as though the problems confronting him no longer mattered. *Somehow, they will resolve themselves,* he thought.

As he peered out between the leaves surrounding the platform, he could see the countryside for miles. He could even see Aunt Sally's house, which thrilled him because it was not far away. Leaning back against the trunk, he enjoyed the gentle sway of the tree and felt content and serene.

The squirrel, which had vanished while Davey was telling his story, suddenly appeared on the platform in front of him. Davey cautiously reached out his hand and touched the little animal. To his surprise, the squirrel climbed into his lap.

"Thank you for bringing me to this wonderful tree," Davey said softly. Then he had another startling thought. "Are you really a squirrel, or are you somehow part of the tree's magic?"

The squirrel looked at Davey, its eyes twinkling.

"I think there's another reason why you brought me here. Something you and the ravens were trying to tell me – something about a triangle."

The squirrel leaped from his lap, jumping from one branch to the other so quickly he couldn't follow it with his eyes. It disappeared for a few long minutes, only to pop up in front of him again. This time, the squirrel held a small leather pouch in its hands.

"What have you got there?" Davey asked.

Without hesitation, the squirrel climbed into Davey's lap and pushed the pouch into his hand. The leather felt old and brittle and the pouch crumbled as Davey pulled it open. After he dumped the contents into his hand, he gasped. He was holding a gold necklace with a large triangular pendant.

Davey knew very little about jewelry, yet he knew enough to recognize a unique piece when he saw it. Each link in the chain of the necklace was a small gold square with a black symbol etched on its surface. The pendant resembled a pyramid, a large amber jewel in its center. The jewel seemed part of the metal itself, not attached to it.

A few years ago, Davey and his dad had spent a day at the Metropolitan Museum viewing an exhibit of Egyptian artifacts. The symbols on the necklace in his hand had an uncanny resemblance to the hieroglyphics on the artifacts in the museum. He sensed there was a connection, yet he couldn't imagine what it was. Nor could he guess how the necklace wound up in the squirrel's possession.

Davey let the necklace dangle in front of him. A thin ray of sunlight pierced through the leaves of the tree, illuminating the golden brilliance of the pendant. "So this is the triangle you were telling me about," he said, looking at the squirrel.

The squirrel nodded and then motioned for Davey to put the necklace around his neck.

"You want me to wear it?"

The squirrel nodded again, so Davey slipped the necklace over his head. The squirrel nodded once more, apparently pleased.

"Why are you giving it to me?" he asked, examining the pendant again. As his fingers brushed over its surface, they touched the amber jewel. Slowly, an odd transformation occurred. First, the jewel lightened in color until it became transparent. Next, it radiated a warming glow, which Davey found invigorating as it soaked into his fingers. Finally, the interior of the jewel took on a degree of viscosity, as if it were not solid, but filled with a moving liquid. Then the necklace began to vibrate gently.

"How very strange," he exclaimed, looking from the pendant to the squirrel. However, the squirrel had disappeared again. *Where has it gone now?* he wondered. At that moment, he heard a voice calling up to him.

"Hey, you up in the tree; you'd better get out of there!" the voice shouted.

Davey looked down and glimpsed a figure standing outside the fence. He couldn't see the figure clearly, but it appeared to be a boy.

"You'll get in trouble if you get caught up there," the voice shouted.

That's probably why the gate was locked, Davey thought. He tucked the necklace inside his shirt and started climbing down the tree. He kept his eyes on the branches and moved carefully, not wanting to make a fool of himself by falling out of the tree. He didn't look at the boy again until he reached the lowest branch.

"Old man Harrison will have a bloody fit if he sees you," the boy said.

Davey stared at a tall and tanned boy with long jet-back hair. He didn't know what to say at first. "Is he the man who owns the park?" he finally asked.

The boy laughed heartily. "No, that guy has been dead for centuries. The town owns the park and old man Harrison is the park warden. He can arrest you for damaging property or breaking park rules – like climbing the Great Oak."

Davey guessed the boy was older than he was. He liked the friendly sound of his voice and didn't feel particularly threatened, even though the boy was big and tough looking. "Could I really get arrested for being in the tree?"

"For sure, mate. How'd you get up there anyway?"

"The gate was open," Davey replied with a shrug.

"Open? No way – it's never open." The boy jerked on the handle and rattled it against the fencepost. "See, locked tight as can be."

Davey certainly couldn't explain how the gate had opened and closed or tell him about the squirrel. He knew it would sound ridiculous. Instead, he played dumb. "It was unlocked a few minutes ago. Now, I'm not sure how to get out."

"Hey, I've got an idea. See how the branch you're sitting on extends over the fence. Just scoot along it until you get beyond the spikes and swing down. I'll catch you."

Davey didn't know why the boy was helping him, but he seemed trustworthy. Since his idea sounded feasible, he agreed to try it.

At first, he had no difficulty moving along the branch, but when he reached the point where it crossed the fence, the branch began to sway. Holding on for dear life, he wrapped his arms and legs around the branch and inched his way along like a caterpillar. After several more feet, he lost his balance and clung to it upside down.

The boy moved over until he was standing beneath Davey. "You're aces right where you are. Let your feet hang down, but hold on with your hands until I say let go."

The branch started to curve down towards the ground, narrowing the distance between Davey and the boy. Unfortunately, Davey became confused about which part of his body to release and let go with his hands instead of his feet. His legs didn't have a firm grip and they immediately came loose as well, sending him into freefall.

Thankfully, he didn't have far to fall. He landed on top of his benefactor after a drop of three feet and they both collapsed in a tangled heap of arms and legs. The boy pushed Davey aside, who was more or less sprawled on top of him, and struggled to his feet. Then he extended a hand to Davey and pulled him up too.

"Bloody heck, mate! Did you hear me say *let go*?" the boy asked, grinning.

"Sorry, I'm kind of clumsy sometimes."

"Got any broken bones or other deadly injuries?"

Davey looked down and inspected his body. "Not that I can see." He smiled timidly at the boy standing next to him. The boy had an unusual way of speaking, a strange form of slang as though he wasn't from Great Oak.

"Me neither, so no harm done, eh mate? By the way, my name's Jimmy Surefoot," the boy said, returning the smile.

"I'm Davey Boehm. Do you live in Great Oak? You sound like you're from somewhere else."

A wide grin spread across Jimmy's face. "Nah, it's just me *Crocodile Dundee* accent. I talk like this all the time. My mom says it's driving her crazy, but I've been doing it for so long, I can't break the habit. I'm really a Cherokee Indian – half Cherokee anyway. Dad is a full-blooded Cherokee, but Mom is just a regular white woman. Hey, ain't you the bloke from New York that I heard about at school? They say you're a genius."

Davey shook his head. "I'm not really. Are you in seventh grade too?"

"Nah," Jimmy said. "Do I look like a bloody seventh-grader?"

Davey hoped he hadn't offended him. "No, but how did you hear about me?"

"It's all over the bleeding school, mate. Me, I'm an eighth grader – captain of the football team and president of the student council. Nothing happens at school that I don't hear about. Can you really do all that math stuff in your head?"

Davey shrugged, feeling a bit embarrassed. "Yeah, I guess."

Jimmy broke into a laugh. "Then you and my friend Spike must be pals."

Davey's face clouded. "Are you a friend of Spike's?"

"Nah, I'm just sporting with you. I heard your performance in math class freaked him out. Personally, I don't like the bloke. Actually, I can't stand him. My father hates his father and my ancestors hated his ancestors. The Housemans and the Surefoots have been enemies for a long time."

"How come?" Davey asked, thinking no one seemed to like the Housemans.

"Oh, squabbles over land, water rights, and equality, to name a few. A long time ago, the Cherokee caught the Housemans cutting trees on their land. We have been feuding ever since — no smokum peace pipe ever."

Davey breathed a sigh of relief. "Spike is certainly no friend of mine. That's the reason I'm here in the park. He dumped my books on an anthill and made me miss the school bus. He said I should go back to New York before I get hurt."

Jimmy's eyes took on an angry look. "He did, eh? Gives me another reason to hate him, don't it?" Then he grinned. "Where do you live anyway?"

"I live on Elm Street with my aunt and uncle, the Winstons."

"Blimey, my parents are pals of theirs. I even deliver their newspaper. Hey, I have an idea. My bike has a rack where I put the satchels for my newspapers. If you want, you can sit back there with your backpack and I'll give you a lift to your aunt's house."

"That would be great," Davey exclaimed, thinking his day was taking another unexpected turn. *Maybe Amy won't be my only new friend.*

"Listen, you probably shouldn't tell anyone about climbing the Great Oak."

"Do you still think I'll get in trouble?"

Jimmy shook his head. "Nah, I ain't telling anyone, but people around here get all crazy when it comes to the tree. Some think touching it is almost a sacrilege. Others act like it's haunted or something. Best thing to do is keep your mouth shut."

Davey stared at the tree for a moment, silently thinking about the way the branches rearranged themselves and the way the bark glowed when he touched it. *There's definitely something magical about it.*

"I just thought of something. Do you play baseball?" Jimmy asked.

"It's my favorite sport, but I'm a terrible player. It's because of my eyesight."

"All it takes is practice, mate."

Davey shook his head. "I need more than practice – I'm lousy at sports."

"Some of us play every Saturday down at the ball field, which is why I'm asking. My team is missing a player because one of the kids moved away. You could have his spot if you want," Jimmy said.

"You don't know how bad I play. If you did, you wouldn't offer."

"Let's throw the ball around after school tomorrow. Maybe I can give you a few pointers," Jimmy suggested.

Davey was perplexed because no other athletic and popular kid had ever showed the slightest interest in him. "Why would you spend your time helping me?"

"I like you. Anyone who can climb the Great Oak is worth my time. Besides, if I help you with baseball, maybe you'll help me with math. I'm a deadhead when it comes to math."

Davey couldn't help but grin. "You've got yourself a deal."

"I live a couple of blocks from your aunt's house. Why don't we ride our bikes to school together tomorrow?" Jimmy asked.

"I'd like that, but I don't have a bike," Davey replied.

Jimmy laughed. "Well, we're gonna solve that problem real soon. My dad owns the bike shop downtown. He'll fix you up – mate's rate."

"Mate's rate, what's that?"

Jimmy laughed again. "You'll get used to the way I talk after a while. Mate's rate is what Dad gives to my friends. It's his special, ultra low, I ain't making any money on this deal, price."

❧ Chapter 8 ☙

Thy powere should be used to aide those who art less fortunate. This not only strengthens thy soul, but strengthens thy magick as well.

— Translated from Storia Di Incanto; circa 1655

The Orphan In The Woods

WHEN AUNT SALLY noticed how the other school kids were dressed, she rushed home to get Davey some jeans. However, after looking through his clothes, she concluded he hadn't brought any. Of course, this made her laugh. Janie, her sister, had sent her son for a yearlong visit with only dress-up clothes.

Sally was two years younger than her sister was, but she had always been the one with common sense. Janie's head was in the clouds most of the time. Still, Sally and Janie were as close as two sisters could be. They shared a mysterious bond and often knew exactly what the other was thinking.

Fifteen years ago, Janie had married Walter Boehm, a young man from a wealthy New York family. The family was one of the pillars of society, and the young couple had settled into a fancy apartment near where Walter worked in the family business. Three years later, Davey was born – their only child.

Sally had stayed in North Carolina, finishing her college degree.

She planned on moving to New York and living near her sister after graduation. Their parents had died in a horrible automobile accident two years earlier, and the two sisters felt a compelling need to be near each other. They were the only members of their small family left.

Sally's plans changed when she met Bill Winston during her senior year. His roots were in North Carolina and he had no interest in moving to New York. Besides, he had a good job as a furniture designer with a company in Greensboro.

So Sally married Bill, her true love, and they bought a little house in Greensboro. Sally took a position as a staff editor for the local newspaper and they both did just fine – for the most part. A few things were missing from Sally's version of a perfect world. She wanted to have children and she wanted her sister to live near her, but neither one of those things had happened.

Several times over the years, her sister had asked Bill to consider working for Walter's family in New York. "They are in the furniture business just like you and it would make Sally and me so terribly happy," she had explained. Nevertheless, Bill was an independent sort and didn't want favors from relatives, especially where his work was concerned. He simply said thanks, but no thanks, or words to that effect. Sally didn't blame him for his feelings. She just wished it could be different.

Five years later, the job of Bill's dreams came along. Houseman Furniture, a small hundred-year old company, offered him a chance to design his own line of furniture. After a lot of talking it over with Sally, Bill took the job and they moved to Great Oak.

The move made Sally reflect upon the strange coincidences of life. Her grandparents had lived in Great Oak and her mother had been born there. But her mother had hated the town and moved away as soon as she was an adult. She never told her daughters why. Even so, Sally thought she knew after living in Great Oak for a while.

Sally and Janie dealt with the distance separating them by talking on the telephone, visiting each other's homes, and taking vacations together whenever they could. Their husbands had become good friends and even joked about starting their own furniture company some day. Sally prayed at church every Sunday for it to happen. But as time passed, it seemed less and less likely – a source of growing dismay.

Recently, Sally had started having nightmares about something happening to her sister. Janie and Walter were busily engaged in climbing the ladder of New York society, and Sally hadn't seen Janie for a while. In fact, the two sisters had hardly been together since Sally and Bill moved to Great Oak. So when Janie telephoned with the news that she and Walter were spending the next year in China, Sally became upset. It meant another year would pass before they could visit. Then Janie dropped the bomb on her.

"We're hoping Davey can live with you while we're gone," Janie said.

Her sister's words delighted Sally, but she was full of questions. "We'd love to have Davey stay with us, yet what will Walter's parents say?" She knew his parents controlled everything they did.

Janie just laughed. "They won't like it, that's for sure, but Walter and I want Davey with someone who will look after him properly. If we leave him with Walter's parents, they'll just turn him over to their butler. Besides, Walter wants him to spend some time away from New York. He thinks Davey is getting too citified."

"What do you think?"

"I think I'll sleep at night if he's with you and Bill," Janie replied, sounding a little teary-eyed.

"Why don't you just take him with you?"

Janie lowered her voice to a whisper. "We're telling Davey he can't go with us because of school, but that isn't the exact truth. The part of China we'll be in is rather primitive. We've also heard some unpleasant things about the people who are selling the factories. We don't want Davey with us if things don't work out."

Sally found this rather alarming. "What sort of unpleasant things?"

"Apparently, they aren't too reputable, maybe even downright dishonest. That's one of the things Walter will be investigating."

Sally didn't like hearing this. "Maybe you and Walter shouldn't go either."

Janie remained silent and Sally waited, knowing her sister was thinking about how much to tell her. Finally, Janie broke the awkward silence. "Millions of dollars are involved in this purchase. Walter's father has always picked someone else for assignments like this, but he has finally given him an opportunity to prove himself. If we don't go, he may not get another chance."

"Oh Janie, it all sounds so complicated...and dangerous."

Janie laughed, but Sally knew it was just an act. "You worry too much. Just promise you'll raise Davey like your own son if anything happens."

Sally's heart skipped a beat. "Janie, you sound like—"

Janie interrupted. "Promise me Sally, just promise."

"Of course, you know I will. I promise."

Janie started to cry. "Sally, one more thing – Davey is special."

Tears ran down Sally's face as well. "Don't cry Janie, I know he's special. He's your son, isn't he?"

"No Sally, that's not what I mean. He's special in a different way, a way I don't fully understand. He's thirteen years old now and some odd things are happening."

"What kind of odd things?"

"Remember what you heard in Great Oak about our grandparents being witches?"

"Oh Janie, that was just a bunch of malarkey. The old timers around here are always exaggerating stuff that happened long ago. But I do wish mother had told us about our grandparents instead of hiding things."

"Sally, there must be some truth in what they say. Do you remember when we visited Grandmother that time when she was sick? Remember how the neighbor's kids called her a witch and wouldn't play with us? And...remember when we went with her to the park and those ravens and squirrels followed us around? It was so creepy."

"What do you expect? She fed them seeds all the time."

"Well, the same type of thing is happening to Davey and he's not feeding them anything. What if he turns out like our grandparents?"

"Don't be silly. Did you ever see our mother do anything witch-like?"

"No, but perhaps it's the reason why she moved away from Great Oak when she could. Maybe she rejected their ways."

"Janie, I've talked with many of the old folks around here. They don't remember Grandfather, but they do remember Grandmother. When I press them for facts, nobody can honestly recall her doing anything witchy. She was odd and maybe even crazy, but the rest is just conjecture."

"Sally, I'm worried regardless. Just promise me you'll love Davey, no matter what."

Sally promised three or four times before their conversation ended. Afterwards, she decided her sister was just stressed-out and not thinking too clearly. That explained why she hadn't packed the right clothes for her son. With a sigh, Sally made a list of the things Davey needed and went shopping.

ഇ രുഇ രുഇ രു

The next morning, Davey put on the new clothes Aunt Sally had bought. As an afterthought, he slipped the necklace that the squirrel had given him yesterday over his head. It fit neatly under his shirt where it couldn't be seen. Then he hurried down to breakfast.

When he walked into the kitchen, Aunt Sally smiled with satisfaction. The faded blue jeans, white knit shirt, and athletic shoes made him look like he belonged in Great Oak. *He seems perfectly normal to me,* she thought.

"Does everything fit okay?" she asked, busily slicing up bananas for his cereal.

"They're great," he said simply. The big grin on his face filled in the rest.

"You still haven't said much about your day at school."

Davey had purposefully avoided the subject yesterday. He simply told Aunt Sally he had missed the bus, met Jimmy, and rode home on the back of his bike. He didn't mention Spike or climbing the Great Oak. Then he had asked her if Jimmy could stay for dinner, which provided a distraction. As soon as Jimmy left, he went right to bed.

Now, he just shrugged. "It was fine – a little different from New York." He poured a big bowl of Cheerios and heaped a pile of bananas on top. *I'm starving,* he thought, carrying his bowl towards the table where Uncle Bill was sitting.

Uncle Bill passed the milk over as Davey sat down. "Jimmy's a good kid – we know his parents."

Davey grinned. "We're practicing baseball this afternoon."

"Hey, baseball's my game. Maybe I can practice with you sometimes."

Aunt Sally suddenly laughed. "Children shouldn't be exposed to the way you play baseball, Bill."

"Ignore her Davey. She's just jealous because I'm the one who hit a home run in our last game while she struck out twice."

Aunt Sally put her hands on her hips, a big grin on her face. "Go ahead Bill – tell him who was voted our team's most valuable player."

Uncle Bill jerked his thumb in Sally's direction. "You're very own aunt, that's who. Don't ask her about it, though. She doesn't like to brag."

Davey laughed, enjoying the way his aunt and uncle were always joking with each other. His parents had been so uptight lately; they never seemed to have fun.

"See, we play in a local softball league. Kind of silly, bunch of adults running around hurting ourselves. Still, we have a good time," Uncle Bill explained.

Just then, the noise of a commotion reached their ears. It was the sound of a very angry dog barking furiously, intermixed with the screams of several children. The barking had the high-pitched quality of a dog out of control, and the screams were equally as hysterical.

The sounds were coming from the neighbor's backyard.

"What the heck is going on?" Uncle Bill muttered, rising quickly and heading for the rear door. Davey scooped a spoonful of cereal into his mouth and ran after him. In a matter of seconds, they were standing outside on the porch. The barking and screaming had become a continuous jumble of noise, joined by the shouts of a man.

"George...need any help over there?" Uncle Bill shouted.

"Bring your rifle, Bill. One of those wild dogs has come out of the woods!"

Uncle Bill told Davey to wait and ran back into the house. However, Davey didn't wait. For an inexplicable reason, the pendant of his necklace had started vibrating. When it did, a jolt of energy surged through his body. Acting upon a sudden impulse, he ran into the neighbor's backyard.

When he arrived, he saw two young children on a ladder attached to a backyard swing set. The children were wailing in terror, and a middle-aged man, apparently the person named George, stood in front of the swing set waving a long-handled rake. Ten feet away, a rather shabby-looking male German Shepard was snarling ferociously at them.

Shreds of saliva dangled from the dog's mouth. Every few seconds, the dog shifted his position as though purposely keeping the man and the children trapped at the swing set. Twenty feet behind the dog, a dense wall of trees bordered the backyard. Davey ran towards the snarling dog without stopping.

"Hey kid, watch out!" George yelled.

A few seconds later, Uncle Bill arrived with his hunting rifle. What he saw was instantly alarming. Davey was standing close to the dog, staring intently at it.

Uncle Bill didn't know whether to shoot at the dog or not. Davey was blocking his aim, but if he didn't do something, the dog was going to attack him. "For heavens sake Davey, get out of the way."

Davey took a step towards the animal. "He's not going to hurt anyone."

The dog let out a series of high-pitched barks and backed up. Davey noticed one of the dog's back legs had several deep gashes in it. Blood ran from the wound, soaking the dog's hindquarter. In fact, the dog could hardly put any weight on the leg.

"Lay down so I can help you," Davey said gently.

The dog stopped barking and glanced nervously at the trees behind him. Slowly, he collapsed onto his front legs with a whine and rolled over. Davey knelt down and rubbed his ears gently. The dog was painfully thin and completely exhausted. Davey guessed he was less than two years old. *Barely more than a puppy,* Davey thought.

"Will you look at that," George said, lowering his rake.

"Be careful! Some of the wild dogs around here have rabies," Uncle Bill shouted.

Davey shook his head. "This dog isn't wild. See, he's wearing a collar with a tag, which means he's had a vaccination. I think he just wanted the kids away from the woods for some reason. Maybe something dangerous is in there."

"I was getting my ball," volunteered one of the children, a five-year old boy. He pointed a stubby finger at a white soccer ball laying at the edge of the woods. "Something big growled at me. Then there was all this fighting in the woods and the dog came out and chased me."

Uncle Bill carried his rifle over to the woods and cautiously eased into the trees. When he reappeared, he looked strangely at Davey who was busy petting the dog. "You're right; there are fresh bear tracks inside the tree line. They wander down from the mountains sometimes. I've never seen one this close to a house though."

George had tossed his rake aside and was staring at the dog. "Well, I'll be. Most amazing thing I've ever seen. Thank goodness you didn't shoot him."

The dog rolled his eyes and let out a moan of anguish. Davey almost laughed at the way he was hamming it up. However, he didn't, knowing the dog needed food, water, and lots of praise for being so brave. He examined the tag on the dog's collar. "His name is Bupkiss, property of Charlie and Sarah Thompson. Bupkiss, you're a hero, a big hero."

"Hey, I know the Thompsons. Charlie lost his job at the furniture factory and they moved away last month. I guess the dog got left behind somehow," George said.

Davey rubbed the dog's ears. "Poor Bupkiss, no wonder you're so thin. Can we get him some food and water? He really needs doctoring too."

Uncle Bill nodded. "Leave the dog to me, Davey. I'll take care of him. You did good, but now you should finish your breakfast and get to school."

"I'll pay the vet's bill, considering he was protecting my kids," George offered.

Davey looked anxiously at the dog. "Can we keep him Uncle Bill if he has no place to go? Can we at least look after him until he finds a new home?"

Uncle Bill scratched his head. "Well I guess, if Sally says it's okay."

"Did you hear, Bupkiss? You're not an orphan anymore," Davey exclaimed.

᚛ Chapter 9 ᚜

---

*Know that ye art not alone on thy quest.
If thy purpose is good, anon ye shall
obtain allies to aide thee along the chosen
path.*

— Translated from Storia Di Incanto; circa 1657

A Cool Friend

THIRTY MINUTES LATER, Davey took a seat at the back of the
school bus. He recognized a few kids from his classes, yet he sat by
himself. He needed some time to think about the necklace and the
way it had vibrated when the commotion in the neighbor's yard
began.

He had completely forgotten about the necklace after meeting
Jimmy Surefoot yesterday. He hadn't even been conscious of wearing
it until he was getting ready for bed and noticed it in the mirror.
Then he had taken it off and studied it briefly. It had been heavy in
his hand, yet it seemed weightless when he wore it. Too tired to
ponder this curiosity, he had laid it on the bedside table and fallen
asleep.

When he put the necklace on in the morning, it molded itself to
his chest as if part of his skin. It didn't jiggle or shift around when he
walked. Rather, it flowed with his movements like some kind of
metallic liquid. The sensation was strange, but entirely pleasant. His

senses had come alive after the pendant started vibrating on the porch earlier. Now, when he pressed his hand against the pendant, nothing happened. *It's as though it has a will of its own,* he thought.

At that point, the bus arrived at school, ending Davey's contemplation. He watched the kids outside for a few minutes, hoping he wouldn't see Spike or his little gang. Regretfully, he spotted them near the bicycle racks some distance away. They were standing in the center of a group of boys. At first, Davey didn't recognize anyone else. Then the group shifted, and he saw Jimmy Surefoot in the middle. Jimmy looked angry and shook his fist in Spike's face. From Spike's shocked expression, it was clear he didn't like what he was hearing. Jimmy left a few seconds later, accompanied by six football-player types.

Davey scooted off the bus, ducked into the building, and made his way to homeroom class. A few minutes later, Amy Pigeon ran into the room and slumped breathlessly into the seat beside him.

She pulled off her backpack and stared at him. "Well look at you, hotshot."

Davey smiled self-consciously. "Yeah, I got some new clothes."

"No dummy, I mean Jimmy Surefoot. Your new clothes are definitely an improvement though. You look almost normal."

Davey rolled his eyes. "Gee thanks, but what's this about Jimmy Surefoot?"

"Come on, don't act so innocent. He told Spike to leave you alone or he'd bust him up bad. How'd you swing that?"

Davey couldn't explain it, so he shrugged. "Swing what?"

Amy let out an exasperated sigh. "How'd you get a guy like Jimmy Surefoot, who's practically the coolest kid in the whole school, to become your friend? You've only been here one day."

A wide grin spread across Davey's face. "You're my friend, aren't you? So actually, I have the two coolest kids in the school as friends."

Amy started to blush and looked away. "Hush up, here comes Spike."

Davey briefly locked eyes with him. Spike scowled and said

something to Monkey, but didn't look his way again. Davey noticed Spike had bumps all over his face. Splotches of a whitish ointment covered the bumps, making him look like a big ugly zombie with warts.

"What's that stuff on his face?" Davey whispered.

"It's Calamine Lotion. Apparently, ants invaded his house overnight. His parents freaked out and called the exterminators first thing this morning. Spike was the only one bitten, which is kind of weird. Couldn't have happened to a nicer guy, huh?"

Davey looked at her in surprise. "How do you know so much? You should publish a newspaper or something."

"That's me, Amy Pigeon, girl snoop."

Just then, the bell rang and Linda Peabody announced they would finish watching the second half of the movie, which they had started last week. She turned on the television and sat down at her desk while the movie played. The movie was *Oliver*, one of Davey's favorites, but something else required his immediate attention. He quietly eased out of his seat and walked to where Linda was sitting at her desk. "Miss Peabody, could I go to the bathroom?" he whispered.

She shook her head. "Unless it's an absolute emergency, the answer is no. See, if anyone can go to the bathroom whenever they want, it disrupts the class. Therefore, the school doesn't allow it. I hope you understand."

"I guess," he said, and returned to his seat.

A few minutes later, Linda looked up from her desk. "Davey Boehm, there's a form here for your elective class. Please take it to the principal's office."

"I did it yesterday," Davey whispered when he reached her desk.

She gave him a sly smile and winked. Then she handed him two sheets of paper. "This is a hall pass, which gives you permission to be outside the classroom, and this is the form for the principal's office. Hurry back."

Davey took the sheets and quietly left the classroom. When he was out in the corridor, he glanced at them and smiled. She had given him a hall pass and a blank sheet of paper so he could go to the bathroom. But that's not what he had in mind. He hurried to the playground and then ran to the anthill where Spike had dumped his books. A few ants were wandering on the surface of the anthill.

"There's something important I must tell the head ant," he said breathlessly.

Nothing happened for a few seconds. Then a flood of ants streamed out, at least several hundred in Davey's opinion.

"The exterminators are spraying Spike's house with poison today. If you have any friends over there, they should clear out," he told them, feeling very foolish. The ants stared at Davey for a moment and then scrambled back into the anthill. *Am I in fantasy land or what?* Davey thought as he ran back into the building.

Davey and Amy hung out together most of the day. The more he was with her; the more he liked her. He finally decided she was indeed the rarest of all commodities, a true friend. The day also passed without him having any face-to-face confrontations with Spike. *Whatever Jimmy had told him must have done the trick,* he thought. But as he soon learned, Spike had lots of mean tricks and many ways to play them.

Spike provided an apt demonstration just as English class was ending. Linda was writing sentences on the blackboard when hundreds of small marbles rolled towards the front of the room. Davey's necklace began an urgent vibration, yet he reacted too slowly. The marbles made an ominous rumbling as they clattered along the boards of the floor.

Startled by the noise, Linda turned and stepped on several marbles. Her feet looked as if she was balancing on ice for a second. Then they shot out from under her and she fell, bouncing hard on her bottom. Most of the class stared at her in stunned silence, surprised by what had happened. But Spike, Monkey, and several others broke out laughing.

Davey and Amy didn't think it was the least bit funny. They rushed towards Linda, barely avoiding the marbles themselves. Then the bell rang and the room emptied as if it were on fire. Davey and Amy stayed behind to help Linda.

"It's okay – I'm not injured," Linda said, obviously upset.

Davey saw tears forming in her eyes. *If only I had reacted quicker,* he thought.

He and Amy helped her up and then went busily around the room picking up the marbles. Upon finishing, they returned to where she was sitting at her desk. Her head was down, one hand shielding her eyes. Davey took her hand and squeezed it. "Are you sure you're all right?"

Linda nodded, but didn't look up.

"We don't like the way you're being treated and we're trying to stop it. I want you to know that," Amy blurted out angrily.

Linda managed a feeble smile. "Thank you."

Amy shook her head as they left the room. "She could have been hurt."

"Spike has to be stopped," Davey said grimly.

They stopped at Davey's locker on their way out of the building. Aunt Sally had given him a lock for the door and he wanted to put it on. But when he opened the locker, a pungent smell assaulted their nostrils.

"Gross!" Amy exclaimed as Davey lifted his jacket out. He had forgotten about leaving it there yesterday. The sleeves were shredded into strips and huge blotches of mustard and ketchup covered the fabric. Cut up pieces of his necktie lay at the bottom of the locker. Davey silently deposited them all in a trashcan and calmly locked the door.

Amy looked at him in surprise. "Aren't you angry?"

Davey shook his head. "No, I just want revenge for me and Miss Peabody."

"Good! You had me worried for a minute."

They hurried to the exit where the school buses waited. Davey was glad to see Jimmy outside the doorway. He was leaning on his bicycle, his long black hair blowing in the breeze. He looked just like the coolest kid in the school should look.

"Hop on mate, we've got places to go and things to do," Jimmy said with a grin.

"Sorry I'm late; something came up."

"No worries, now here's the plan. First, we're throwing the ole baseball for a while. Then we're going to the bicycle shop and picking you out a bike. Dad talked to your aunt this morning and everything is aces," Jimmy said.

Davey felt Amy jab him with her elbow. "Introduce me," she whispered.

"This is my friend, Amy," Davey mumbled.

Jimmy bowed magnanimously. "Ah, the beautiful Amy Pigeon, we finally meet."

Amy laughed with delight. "I'm surprised you even know my name."

"I know the names of all the pretty girls in this school," Jimmy said smoothly.

Amy felt her face turning red. "My bus is waiting. You boys have fun," she said, and then hurried towards the bus.

Jimmy pointed at her. "Is she your girlfriend, mate?"

Davey shrugged self-consciously. "We're mostly just friends."

"That's the way it starts, sport. Hey, you could do worse. She's cute and she likes you – I saw it in her eyes."

Davey climbed on the back of Jimmy's bike, lost in thought. How different his life seemed in Great Oak. A few weeks ago, he had been thrilled if a girl even spoke to him. *Now the coolest kid in school is teaching me baseball. And a girlfriend – is it possible?*

☙ Chapter 10 ❧

Heed the knowledge of those who cometh
before thee for their wisdom is great.
Thou must be an apostle of thy elders in
order to foresee the future.

— Translated from Storia Di Incanto; circa 1663

Cherokee Legends

DAVEY AND JIMMY ARRIVED at the baseball field a few minutes later. Jimmy pulled out two leather gloves and a baseball from his saddlebags and then led Davey towards the deserted field. It was like many of the places in Great Oak, old and worn out. The chain link fence had gaping holes in it, and the outfield was full of bare spots and trash.

Jimmy nodded at the field with an apologetic expression on his face. "This is where we play every Saturday. The town used to keep the field up, but it doesn't anymore. So the kids and adults who play here mow the grass, pick up the trash, and do what we can. We're fighting a losing battle though."

Davey looked around the shabby field and tried to think positively. "At least it's available. In New York, it's impossible to use a field without a reservation."

"Let's just throw the ball around for a while. We'll see how good you can catch," Jimmy said.

Davey sighed with resignation. He was embarrassed to show Jimmy how truly uncoordinated he was. "Don't expect too much. Like I said, I'm lousy at sports."

"Stand over by the backstop. That way, the ball won't get away if you miss it. And don't look so worried. This ain't the major leagues," Jimmy said with a laugh.

Davey took a position near the backstop, which was a good thing because he missed more than half of Jimmy's throws. To his surprise, Jimmy didn't seem the least bit concerned. After an hour, they had worked up a sweat and were ready to quit.

Davey felt miserable when they finished. "I warned you. I really stink."

Jimmy grinned. "Nah, you did okay; better than I expected actually. After all, it was your first time out with the pros."

Davey shook his head and wondered, just as he had yesterday, why Jimmy was so friendly. "If I didn't wear these stupid glasses, I might catch better."

They sat down on a concrete bench and Jimmy gave Davey a gentle punch on the arm. "Give yourself a fair go, mate. Just think of all the things you do better than anyone else. You're probably the smartest kid in the entire town."

"You don't know what being nearsighted is like. I just wish I'd wake up one day and be able to see without my glasses."

"Bloody heck, you'll get better with more practice. Let's come out here every afternoon and work on your game. One day, you may be the star of the team."

Davey wasn't accustomed to doing things with a friend, especially one who wasn't critical of his faults. "Are you sure you want to spend your time like this? I'm a lost cause when it comes to sports."

Jimmy only laughed. "It's no biggie. If you want to see a lost cause, wait until you start helping me with math."

Davey smiled, remembering their agreement. "By the way, thanks for getting Spike off my back."

"No worries. After what you said yesterday, Spike and I had a little knockabout this morning. It was really a hoot. I was acting mean and tough, but he had this lotion all over his face and looked so bloody stupid, I could hardly keep from laughing. Did he bother you any today?"

Davey didn't mention his vandalized locker. He couldn't expect Jimmy to solve all of his problems. "Spike didn't say a single word to me, so thanks again."

"Forget it. Let's go see my dad – I think you'll like him."

ಬಂಜ಼ಬಂಜ಼ಬಂ

The bicycle shop was located in an old storefront building on the part of Main Street, which the local residents called downtown. By modern standards, the several blocks of ancient two-story structures weren't very impressive. But they were quaint, to say the least. Bright awnings, repairs, and fresh coats of paint had rehabilitated some of the buildings, giving their old-fashioned exteriors a colorful façade. Others were in an advanced state of decay – one-step away from falling down.

Jimmy stopped his bike in front of a shop with a green awning over two large windows. *Surefoot's Bicycles* was printed in large yellow letters above the awning. Through the windows, Davey saw an interior containing bicycles of every size, shape, and style. The boys climbed off the bike, and Jimmy parked it in a steel rack on the brick sidewalk. Then he stood before the shop, his arms outspread. "Ye ole bicycle shop – my dad's pride and joy," he said, grinning.

Davey was properly impressed. "I can't wait to go inside."

Jimmy pulled Davey along the sidewalk until they were no longer in front of the store. "Before we go in, let me tell you a couple of things about my dad. He's the nicest man you'll ever meet, but kind of stubborn. Before I was born, the tribal elders were grooming him for the position of Chief, a great honor. Then he met my mother, who is not a Cherokee. He married her despite their warnings, which meant he was no longer eligible to be the chief. He's kind of sensitive

ಬಂ *94* ಜ಼

about it, so don't mention the Cherokee unless he brings them up."

"He couldn't become the chief because he didn't marry a Cherokee?"

"See, our tribe is really old fashioned. They have this rule that the chief must marry a Cherokee because women have important roles in carrying on our traditions. Dad hoped they would make an exception for him, but he was wrong."

Davey nodded his understanding. "So he doesn't let anyone change his mind after it's made up. I can relate to that."

"Couldn't have said it better myself. Dad is also a mechanical genius of sorts. For twenty years, he was the head mechanic at the town's textile mill. He almost kept the place running all by himself."

"Amy said the mill is barely open now."

"Right on, mate. The mill was an important business in Great Oak until Wally Houseman bought it. Dad hated working for him, and it wasn't just because the Housemans and the Surefoots don't get along. It was because Wally made a lot of stupid decisions, which made the mill lose money. Finally, Dad became disgusted and quit. Several years later, the mill stopped most of its operations."

"Did your dad start the bicycle shop then?"

"Not quite. He sat around the house doing nothing for a while. We lived on the money my mom made from her bakery shop, but we barely got by. After a while, people started bringing my dad broken bicycles to fix. Whenever he told them their stuff wasn't worth fixing, they'd ask him to get them something new. That eventually led him to open this shop. Now, he's making good money and we're doing fine."

"There's a reason why you're telling me this, isn't there?"

Jimmy laughed. "You catch on quick. See, my dad has become an expert on bicycles and he'll know right away what bike is best for you. If you take his advice, everything will be fine. But if you ask questions, we're in for a boring lecture on bicycle mechanics while he tries to convince you."

"I don't know anything about bicycles, so I want his advice."

"Good, now there's just one more thing. I think we should tell my dad you climbed the Great Oak."

"I thought you said we shouldn't tell anyone."

"I've been kicking it around in me noggin, mate. There's something very odd about it, especially since you're a stranger here. Ain't nobody climbed the tree in a long time, yet you do it on your first day in town. Dad knows all of the legends about the tree. We should find out what he thinks."

"Okay, as long as he won't get mad."

"Nah, Dad's cool. He tried to climb the tree himself when he was a kid."

As the two boys went into the bicycle shop, a bell on the door clanged brightly. The air inside had a faintly mechanical smell, a lingering odor of oil, grease, and paint. Davey wandered among the bicycles, examining each with curious eyes.

After a few minutes, a man hurried towards them from the back of the store. He had a generous smile on his face and his eyes twinkled with good humor. "Ah, customers, I love customers," he said, and then pointed at Jimmy. "Wait, you're not a customer – you just ask for money." He turned towards Davey and bowed with a wave of his hand. "But you're a customer. Come in, buy something, and be welcome."

Davey grinned at Jimmy's father, liking him immediately. He was a tall and muscular man with a friendly, rugged face and a thick mane of black hair pulled back into a ponytail. He wore leather boots, blue jeans, and a denim shirt. Over his shirt was a deerskin vest decorated with beautiful bead and quill designs.

I am looking at a full-blooded Cherokee Indian, Davey thought.

"Dad, this is my friend Davey Boehm," Jimmy said.

He shook Davey's hand vigorously. "Sequoyah Surefoot at your service. Jimmy says you need a bike and your aunt says okay, so pick one out and ride into the sunset."

Davey smiled as he let his eyes wander over the array of bikes. "You have so many; it's a difficult decision. Jimmy said you would help me select one."

Sequoyah nodded pleasantly. "Ah, a wise customer, I love them the best. All right, let me think." He walked around Davey a couple of times, studying him. Then he took out a tape measure and stretched it from Davey's waist to his feet. Finally, he measured his overall height. "Tell me, have you ridden bikes before?"

"Only the ones for rent in Central Park."

"Okay, so what we need is a bicycle that can be trashed and crashed, yet keeps on running. I've got just the one for you," Sequoyah said, and then hurried towards the back of the store. Jimmy gave Davey a thumbs-up sign as soon as he left.

Sequoyah returned a few seconds later, pushing a beautiful silver bike in front of him. "This is a genuine Surefoot bike, simple but eloquent. It has small fenders, tough tires, and a stout frame that can take a lot of abuse. There are five heavy-duty gears, which will easily handle the hills around here. I built it myself; it's guaranteed for five years."

As soon as Davey saw the bike, he knew it was the one for him. "Wow, it's perfect. Does it cost a lot?"

"Don't worry; I already worked that out with your aunt. If you like this bike, it's yours – the heck with profits. Special deal for my friends, eh?" He shrugged helplessly, as if he had no control over the matter.

Davey was delighted. "Thank you, I'll take it."

"See, I knew you were a wise customer. Now go, ride, return if you no like."

"Dad, there's something else we want to ask you," Jimmy said.

"What is it, son?"

Jimmy cleared his throat. "Well…see…it's kind of a secret."

Sequoyah folded his arms and puffed out his chest. "I am named after Sequoyah, the greatest chief of the Cherokee nation. I am an honorable man and can keep a secret."

"Okay Dad, but it concerns Davey, so I want to be sure."

"Your secret is safe with me. Now speak; you have my full

attention."

Jimmy looked at Davey, who nodded in agreement. "Well, it's like this. Davey climbed the Great Oak yesterday," Jimmy said abruptly.

Sequoyah stared solemnly at Jimmy and then at Davey. He repeated these back-and-forth glances several times and finally spoke. "You're joking, right?"

"No Dad, I saw him. He was way up at the top."

Sequoyah studied Davey for a few seconds. After that, he pointed towards a cluster of stools near the back of the store and motioned for the boys to follow him. They all sat down on the stools and he leaned forward, looking intently into Davey's eyes. "You have an honest face. I see courage and determination in it. Tell me, did you really climb the tree?"

Davey nodded, feeling a little intimidated.

Sequoyah gestured expressively with his hands. "The Great Oak is a tree surrounded by centuries of mystery. I don't think anyone really understands it. People have been trying to climb it for years without success. As far as I know, you are the first boy who has ever done it. I tried a couple of times myself, but could not."

"What happened when you tried?" Davey asked.

"The tree has some sort of defense mechanism. Its branches swept me off before I had time to react. I almost broke my arm the second time, so I gave up. The tree is so majestic that people feel a compulsion to climb it, yet few are allowed. Now, the fence prevents anyone from even trying."

"I think the tree helped me climb it. It seemed to want me there," Davey replied.

Sequoyah stared at Davey, perplexed. "Why do you say that?"

Davey smiled as he thought about his experience. "Well, footholds appeared in the trunk, providing places for my feet, and the limbs of the tree formed a kind of staircase, which made climbing it easy."

Sequoyah sighed. "The Cherokee tell many stories about the tree. If you believe them, and not everybody does, there is only one conclusion. A spiritual force exists there. It's easy to understand how these stories originated. My ancestors attributed many things to the spirits of nature – things they couldn't explain otherwise. The majesty and age of the tree were enough to inspire their imagination."

"What are these stories like?"

"More or less what you might expect. Children cured of mysterious illnesses, wise men receiving visions, peace treaties negotiated, that sort of thing. All of these events supposedly occurred under the branches of the tree. I have even heard that the great Sequoyah got his idea for the Cherokee alphabet after climbing the tree."

"Do you believe these stories?"

Sequoyah chuckled. "Jimmy thinks I'm skeptical about such things, but yes, I believe them. Remember, I've had my own experiences with the tree, so I know there's some kind of a force there."

"Do you have any idea why I was able to climb it?"

"This is where it gets interesting. According to Cherokee legend, an *Adinvdo*, or spirit, lives in the tree. The spirit is very benevolent and only lets those climb it who are destined to help mankind. If the spirit favors you in this way, it will also grant your wishes. Did you make any wishes while you were there?"

"Not that I recall."

Sequoyah raised his eyebrows and smiled. "Well, my young friend, if the legend is true, you have some wishes coming. Incidentally, there's a second legend about the tree that you might find interesting. According to this legend, the tree is also the home of *Yunwi Tsundi*, the Little People."

"Who are the Little People?" Davey asked, suddenly intrigued.

Jimmy's father chuckled. "Ah, they are marvelous little spirits – sort of like fairies or elves. The Cherokee believe they take human form and appear or disappear at will. They help people, particularly children who have a problem. Sometimes, they are mischievous and play tricks on those they dislike."

An idea suddenly popped into Davey's head and he asked a strange question. "Do they ever take the shape of a squirrel or bird?"

Sequoyah shook his head. "Not that I know of, but who can say? I suppose a spirit could take any form it wants. Why do you ask?"

"There was a squirrel, a very odd looking squirrel, which showed me the tree. At the time, its mannerisms seemed more like those of a person than an animal. And there was this flock of ravens flying in this triangular formation around the tree."

"Ravens…hmmm…how many ravens?"

"I think there were seven."

Sequoyah's eyes widened with astonishment – then he grinned. "You and Jimmy are making this up, aren't you? You're pulling a fast one on me."

Davey quickly shook his head. "No, it's the truth. I promise."

"Bloody heck, Dad! Davey didn't tell me any of these details," Jimmy protested.

"All right, I apologize for doubting you. Seven ravens may have great significance, that's all. It took me by surprise. To the Cherokee, the number seven represents the height of purity. It's a symbol of power. Did any other unusual things happen while you were there?"

Davey told him about the gate opening and the squirrel showing him how to climb the tree. He left out the part about the necklace. For some reason, he wanted to keep it a secret.

"Holy dooley," Jimmy exclaimed when he finished.

Sequoyah gestured for silence while he thought about Davey's words. Finally, he spoke. "There is an odd coincidence at work here, a very odd coincidence. Chief Yona, my grandfather, tells of a man who arrived in Great Oak many years ago. He was white, like you, but lived with the Cherokee for a time. According to Yona, this man climbed the Great Oak many times. Apparently, he actually talked with the spirit living there."

"Wow, tell me about him," Davey said, growing excited.

Sequoyah's eyes twinkled mysteriously. He lowered his voice as though telling a great secret. "The Cherokee called him Tsusga Gineli, which means *Friend of the Oak*. He was a magician who came to town with a traveling carnival. When the carnival left, he stayed behind and married a local woman. Many people were afraid of him. The mayor even accused him of being a witch."

"A witch? Does he still live here?" Davey asked.

"No, he disappeared back in 1937. A fierce storm descended upon the town and lightning killed a number of prominent citizens. No one saw Tsusga Gineli after that night, but his body wasn't found…he wasn't killed by the lightning."

The story captured Davey's imagination. "So what happened to him?"

"Well, that's a great mystery."

"Why haven't I ever heard this story?" Jimmy asked.

"No one knows what really happened, so they don't speak of it. Yona is the only person still around who knew Tsusga Gineli, but he won't discuss him either. They were friends, and I think the memory is too painful," Sequoyah said.

Davey smiled. "Is this one of those legends, which may not really be true?"

Sequoyah stared at Davey without expression. "Oh, the man was real, that's for sure. Otherwise, you wouldn't be here."

"I don't understand," Davey said.

"The man's real name was Antonio Sabatini. Now do you realize why your climbing of the tree is such a coincidence?"

Davey's necklace began a sudden vibration and he glanced around. *Is the necklace alerting me to something?* he wondered. He saw no sign of anything unusual and turned back to Jimmy's father. "No, why should I? Was he someone important?"

When Sequoyah heard this, he laughed heartily. "Yes, my young friend, yes indeed. Antonio Sabatini was very important. He was your great grandfather."

❧ Chapter 11 ❧

Take heed, for evil doth wear many faces. Like a thief in the night, it creepeth within the shadows, awaiting an opportunity to strike.

— Translated from Storia Di Incanto; circa 1675

The Black Pagoda Conspiracy

ON A MORNING several days later, New York's Chinatown came alive with its usual frenzy of activity. The tantalizing smell of restaurants cooking hung alluringly in the air. Shops opened, trucks unloaded, doors banged, trashcans clanged, and people scurried about getting ready for the day. Conversations in a variety of Chinese dialects, cars blasting their horns, and the rat-a-tat-tat of a jackhammer added to the veritable symphony of sound. It was New York City at its busiest.

Androf Protsky reveled in the commotion as he strode through the hustle and bustle of Canal Street. He was a tall, burly man with muscled shoulders and the blunt face of a ruffian, yet he moved with a startling grace as his long legs propelled him forward. Pedestrians stepped aside to avoid brushing against him. When his eyes met theirs, they quickly looked away. To them, he was trouble – a man to avoid.

Androf slowed while he approached the entrance of a tall building and checked the address on a scrap of paper in his hand. Satisfied, he casually continued on his way. He was an hour early for his appointment, as was his habit. A long time ago, he had learned to watch silently before making a commitment.

He spotted a small coffee shop on the other side of the street and headed in its direction. For the next hour, he sat at a table near the restaurant's window, huddling over a cup of coffee and a daily newspaper. His eyes never left the entrance of the building across the street. *Take care, Androf. You cannot afford a mistake,* he told himself.

He saw no signs of treachery during his vigil. He didn't know the man he was waiting to see or the purpose of their meeting. All he knew was that a strange set of circumstances had brought him there. *Perhaps my life is taking another turn,* he thought.

ဆာလ္ဆာလ္ဆာလ္

Androf had entered the United States three months ago as Andy Tennison, a New York citizen returning from Canada. His fake passport, New York driver's license, and Social Security Card verified his assumed identity. They were perfect imitations – they should be as he had paid dearly for them. Still, they would not withstand intense scrutiny. Any involvement with the police would cost him his freedom.

With the help of a stolen car, he had made his way to New York, seeking an old friend. His name was Ming Qin Cheng, a Vietnamese who had arrived in the city two years earlier. The man owed him a favor and Androf wanted to collect. He needed a hiding place where he could gather resources before disappearing into the vast melting pot of America.

Ming lived in a small apartment tucked away in a rickety building on one of Chinatown's back alleys. Ming had smiled ruefully when he saw Androf standing in his doorway. He had been afraid Androf would show up one day.

In Paris, three years ago, the two men had formed an unlikely alliance, a friendship of opposites. Androf was big, violent, and impulsive, while Ming was small, quick, and clever. But they had one thing in common – they were both criminals. They earned their living by bringing misery to others. In this endeavor, they found that two were better than one.

Three policemen had been chasing Ming when Androf inadvertently crossed their paths. One of the officers had seen Ming picking a man's pocket and blown his whistle. Ming took off as though he was running in the Olympics; the police followed, their whistles sounding fiercely. The three policemen were widely separated in their pursuit when Ming ducked into an alley and almost collided with Androf.

Normally, Androf would not interfere in such a matter. But he was in a foul mood and looking through the alley for something worth stealing. As Ming dodged around him, the officer closest to Ming plowed into Androf. Outraged, he knocked the policeman unconscious with one well-placed punch. The second officer arrived a few seconds later. Androf had no choice but to knock him out too. The third policeman was a short, fat man who had not yet appeared.

Ming shouted for Androf to follow him, and the two men ran through a series of alleys until they were far away from the scene of the fight. At last, they stopped and caught their breaths. Looking at each other, they burst out laughing. That moment was the beginning of a short-lived partnership.

Ming was a meticulous organizer and Androf was brash and assured. Together, they executed a series of daring burglaries of fine Parisian homes. They stole money, jewelry, and other items they could sell quickly. Before long, they had earned a sizeable amount of money. But like most criminals, they spent it foolishly, living the good life. When they needed more money, they simply committed another crime. Each crime led to more risk and eventually their luck ran out.

Ming was the one who finally blundered. The two men broke into a stately townhouse, unoccupied for a week while the owners were away. The hot summer had left the rooms stifling. Sweating profusely, Ming pulled off his mask while rifling through the drawers of a bedroom chest. He didn't notice the tiny video camera filming him from one corner of the room.

A week later, Ming's picture appeared on the walls of every police station in Paris. Upon discovering this, Ming packed up and departed the same day. Androf stayed behind, having no reason to leave. After all, his picture was not the one taken.

Six months passed before Androf heard from Ming again. Ming had made his way to New York, which Androf found amusing. He had not believed Ming would escape capture so easily. The two men talked over the telephone several times a year thereafter. Androf kept Ming's address and telephone number tucked away in his memory, certain they would prove useful.

ഇരുൽഇരുൽഇരുൽഇരുൽ

When Androf appeared at Ming's Chinatown apartment, Ming took him in without hesitation. Androf quickly learned Ming was not the same man he had known in Paris. The months of fear and uncertainty since leaving France had put their mark on him. All Ming wanted now was an ordinary life, a regular job, and peace.

After arriving in New York, Ming found employment as a clerk at a Chinese grocery. Soon, his intelligence and hard work paid off. He became the manager of the store and began to earn a decent wage. He also became friends with a young Chinese woman who lived with her grandfather down the hall. Their friendship blossomed and there was talk of an eventual marriage. Ming had grown content with his ordinary life and finally felt secure. He wanted to keep it that way.

Ming's change of attitude didn't bother Androf. His only concern was whether it posed a danger. He didn't think Ming would betray him – such an act could harm Ming as well. Nor did he intend to start up his old partnership with Ming. Upon reflection, he decided Ming was too naïve to be a good criminal. Androf promised to leave as soon as he made some money and figured out where to go.

It wasn't long before Androf concluded he liked Chinatown. He enjoyed the teaming masses of humanity and the torturously winding streets. The community had a pulsing rhythm, one like the crashing waves of an ocean on a beach. In some ways, it reminded him of Kosovo, his home. *Chinatown is a good place to be lost for a while,* he thought.

Everywhere he went, the scent of Chinese spices filled the air with fragrances more powerful than a rose garden. Colorful banners, flags, and awnings hung from the stores and fluttered in the breeze. The irregular buildings provided a constant visual surprise – the pagoda-shaped roof of a Buddhist temple would suddenly appear alongside an office building or open-air market, as if the planned order of things were actually chaos. Asians of every nationality flooded the streets, jabbering at each other in Mandarin, Cantonese, or some other language. It was enough to make Androf smile, a rare occurrence.

Androf's biggest problem was that he was too noticeable. He was a head taller than most of Chinatown's residents and his mane of blond hair attracted many stares. This forced him to spend most of his daylight hours lounging around Ming's tiny apartment. Even when he roamed the city at night, he was uncomfortable. Police were everywhere, always on the alert for someone like him. After a few months, he told Ming that he was beginning to feel like a caged lion.

Ming smiled slyly and suggested it might be time for Androf to move on, perhaps to a smaller city having fewer police. Although Androf was normally oblivious to subtle remarks, he didn't miss the innuendo. Ming was getting tired of having him around, a worrisome development. Androf was not yet ready to leave.

As fate would have it, events unfolded a few days later, which solved their problems. Androf returned to Ming's apartment late at night and found him with Pakong, his girlfriend, and her grandfather in the cramped living room. By the looks on their faces, Androf knew something was wrong.

"What has happened? Have the police come looking for me?" Androf asked, thinking only of himself.

"Don't worry; it does not concern *you*," Ming replied.

Androf shrugged. "Whatever bothers you, concerns me."

Frustration was evident in Ming's troubled face. "Perhaps you are right. A wrong has occurred, which may require your assistance. It involves Pakong, who works in the accounting section of a big department store on Wall Street. A supervisory position has become available and she is the most qualified for the job. But her boss, a Portuguese man named Alfonso Dias, will not consider her. In the past, he has denied other women such opportunities and discriminated against Asians."

"I will work there no longer. I hate Alfonso Dias and cannot bear to see him again," Pakong cried, tears running down her face.

Pakong's distress brought Ming to his feet. "She has done everything asked of her for more than three years. She works long hours and often comes home late at night. Dias should not deny her this chance for advancement."

Androf put a scowl on his face though he was inwardly pleased. Pakong's problem presented an opportunity to put Ming in his debt. If he could help, there would be no more talk about his leaving. "Return to work tomorrow, Pakong. I will make this man Dias disappear from your life. Meet me outside the store when it closes and identify him."

Silence filled the room while everyone considered what Androf had said. Finally, Ming spoke. "You cannot do this as a favor, Androf. I will pay you."

Pakong's grandfather rose slowly from his chair. "No! I am the one who must pay. She is my granddaughter and this man insults me. He takes away my respect. I can give a hundred dollars. Is it enough?"

Androf nodded gravely. "It is enough." He didn't care about the money. What he cared about was staying in Ming's apartment until he was prepared to go elsewhere. If they were all involved in a crime together, Ming could not send him away.

The next day, Androf waited alongside Pakong in a nearby alcove until she pointed out Alfonso Dias. Then Androf sent her home and followed Dias – a short, pudgy man with a black mustache and an ill-fitting blue suit. Moving with the slowness of a turtle, Dias took the subway towards Queens, stepped off the train when it stopped, and entered a bar near the station. The sign over the door read: *The Last Drink Saloon*. Androf was amused by the irony as he trailed Dias inside.

For two hours, Dias gulped drink after drink while joking with other men at the bar. Androf ordered a beer and watched from a table in the back of the room. Everyone had a good time, particularly Dias and his friends. Finally, Dias slid his bulk off the barstool and headed towards the door. Androf eased out of the bar a few seconds later, smiling grimly. His wait was over.

Dias walked on unsteady feet towards a neighborhood of small bungalow houses. Androf followed in the shadows. An occasional dog barked, but no one else was about. Before long, Dias entered a dark, secluded street. Androf quickly slipped on a pair of leather gloves and sneaked up behind his prey.

"Hey Alfonso, did you forget something?" he asked, throwing his arm around the shorter man's shoulder.

"What..." Dias said in startled reply. It was the last word of his life.

Two days later, Pakong's grandfather knocked on the door of Ming's apartment, bowed, and gave Androf an envelope containing a hundred dollars.

Androf bowed in return. "You have your respect back, Grandfather."

The old man nodded and handed Androf a slip of paper. "I have written the name and address of a man who may have work for you. If you meet him at nine o'clock tomorrow, you will honor me." Then he turned and slowly walked away.

That evening, Ming treated Androf to a night on the town. As they strolled through the Asia Market enjoying the odd mix of smells, an old Chinese woman approached Androf and began speaking in Cantonese. Her clothes were dirty and her gray hair hung down in tangled sheets from under a straw hat. She held a wrinkled pamphlet in one hand and repeatedly shoved it in Androf's face.

Androf looked with confusion at Ming. "What does she want?"

Ming laughed heartily. "Ignore her; she is a beggar. She wants you to buy a Buddhist prayer list from her." The thought of Androf buying prayers from anyone struck Ming as very funny.

The old woman was insistent. She repeatedly thrust the pamphlet in Androf's face while blocking his way. Finally, Androf lost his patience, grabbed the pamphlet from the woman, and threw it on the ground. "Get away from me, you old cow!" he shouted, knocking her down.

"Let's get out of here. There may be police around," Ming whispered, and they dashed from the building.

Androf broke into laughter once they were several blocks away. "This Chinatown is a crazy place. It suits me, Ming. Maybe I'll settle here for a while."

Ming nodded, but said nothing in return. *Androf is like a bull in a china shop,* he thought. *If he stays in Chinatown, he will eventually make trouble for me.*

৪০০৪৪০০৪৪০০৪

Androf glanced at his watch while he waited for his appointment in the building across the street. Pakong's grandfather had said nine o'clock, which was only five minutes away. There was no apparent danger, no sign of police entering the building or lurking about. He left the coffee shop, walked up a block, crossed the street, and came back towards the building. He entered without hesitation, went directly to the elevator, and punched in the number for the 12th floor. The elevator took him up without a sound.

When the elevator stopped, he stepped into a small marble-floored lobby. Two carved mahogany doors faced him. Etched into the surface of each door was an ornate pagoda, stained in black and encircled by gold metal. Large gold letters above the doorway read: *The Black Pagoda Trading Company*. Androf raised his eyebrows as he opened one of the doors.

He found himself in a small reception room paneled in fine mahogany. An exquisite oriental rug lay in the center of the floor. Facing the doorway, a beautiful Chinese woman sat primly behind an elaborately carved desk. The desk's legs were shaped like Chinese dragons, long tongues flicking out of their mouths.

"May I help you?" The woman asked, showing no emotion. The look on her face indicated she thought Androf was in the wrong place.

"I wish to see Yong Chow Lee," Androf said.

The woman frowned. "Mr. Lee is a busy man. What is your purpose?"

"Tell him his nine o'clock appointment is here," Androf ordered, sitting down in one of the several chairs in the room. He did not like the woman's attitude. *Maybe she doesn't like my broken nose. Or perhaps it's the scar,* he thought, self-consciously touching the ugly red line along the right side of his face.

The woman rose from her desk and disappeared through a door on one side of the room. Her long black hair swayed like a silk curtain as she moved. *She is beautiful, but of poor spirit. She needs a lesson in respect. Were the circumstances different, I would teach her this lesson,* Androf mused.

The woman returned a few minutes later. "You may wait in the conference room. I will show you the way."

Androf trailed her down a spacious hallway. Stunning oriental paintings accented the walls and expensive vases sat demurely on black pedestals in indented alcoves. Small spotlights highlighted the beauty of the artwork. Androf smiled at the display of opulence. Although he was a simple man, he respected the wealth it represented.

The woman ushered Androf into a large conference room and departed without further explanation, closing the doors behind her. A round conference table containing the inlaid design of a black pagoda sat majestically in the center of the room. A dozen leather chairs stood around the table. Androf sat in one of the chairs and casually inspected the room.

Wallpaper made from a blue silk fabric covered the walls. More artwork hung at discreet intervals around the room. Androf had seen this type of arrangement before, even used ones like it in Serbia. He knew cameras were cleverly hidden around the room, perhaps even in the artwork itself. Someone was watching him. He cursed himself for being so stupid and immediately thought about leaving. But it was already too late. Fate had dealt him a hand – his only choice was to play it.

A small Chinese man of indeterminate age entered the room several minutes later. He wore a black silk suit of expensive design. Underneath the suit, a collarless black shirt buttoned at his neck. His long black hair was braided into a pigtail, which trailed down his back. A thin mustache arched around his lips until it met his chin. The features of his face were an expressionless mask, but his dark eyes surveyed Androf with intensity. His left hand held a thick paper-filled file.

The man offered Androf his right hand. "Mr. Protsky, I am Yong Chow Lee."

Androf frowned, thinking Ming must have betrayed him. He was the only one who knew his true identity. "You are mistaken. I am Andy Tennison," he said, trying to sound convincing.

Yong Chow Lee calmly opened the file, took out the pamphlet Androf had snatched away from the old woman last night, and laid it on the table. Then he pulled out a copy of Androf's International Police Dossier and slid it towards him.

"I am a careful man, Androf. The nature of my business requires it. I had you photographed in the Asia Market last night and obtained your fingerprints from this pamphlet. From these, my sources obtained a copy of your police record."

"But I am Andy Tennison," Androf protested, knowing it was futile.

Yong Chow Lee shook his head. "No, you are Androf Protsky, an international criminal wanted for war crimes in Serbia. You are also wanted for robbery and murder in Germany and France. You should take comfort in the fact that I know these things."

"Why is that?" Androf growled, feeling his anger rise.

Yong Chow Lee smiled for the first time. "It will allow us to put aside our pretenses and discuss the business which brings us together. If I were the police or meant you harm, you would already be under arrest or dead."

Androf grunted his acquiescence. "What do you want of me?" He was at a disadvantage and recognized it. This man knew all about him, but he knew nothing in return. Somehow, he must make him reveal his intentions.

"I am surprised by how well you speak English," Yong Chow Lee remarked.

"I was raised in a Kosovo orphanage from the time I was five. The Catholic nuns who ran it were very strict. I hated their pious ways, but they did one good thing for their wards. They insisted we speak English as well as we spoke other languages. It helped me enter the United States without difficulty."

Yong Chow Lee nodded pleasantly. "Good, now we are talking openly. As you will learn Androf, we are in a position to help each other. I am associated with many powerful men. My associates have needs, which require individuals having certain skills. You have performed a service for a friend, the type of service I require. This is how you have come to my attention. When I saw your police record, I was pleased."

"Continue," Androf muttered.

"Before I tell you more, I must ask a few questions. If I said that I needed someone killed, would you just do it or would you ask why?"

Androf chuckled. "I would only ask how much you would pay

me."

"What if I told you the person was a woman or a child?"

Androf had never killed a woman or a child, but he shrugged, playing Yong Chow Lee's game. "All the better, they are easier to kill than men."

Yong Chow Lee's eyes gleamed. "I think you are the man I am looking for."

Androf sneered. "Why not have one of your Chinese lackeys do this thing?"

Yong Chow Lee ignored the disrespect in Androf's voice. "I need a man who looks and speaks like an American."

"And what would you have him do?"

Yong Chow Lee sat down in a chair across from Androf. "My associates have investments all over the world. They are constantly buying and selling objects of great value. Tell me Androf, do you play chess?"

"I am a man of action. I do not play games," Androf scoffed.

"Chess is a game of strategy. Each move requires advanced planning. That is the way my associates conduct their business. It is a game to them, a deadly serious one. As we speak, a sale of some factories in China is pending. If the sale goes through, they will make millions. They seek an advantage in the game, a position of influence, which might make the sale happen if the buyer shows reluctance."

Androf was puzzled. "I do not understand."

"The key to the transaction lies in the hands of a man who will evaluate the factories. He and his wife are already in China, so the game has begun. They will be there for some time, observing the factories and measuring their potential. If the man reports the factories are acceptable, the transaction will happen. If not, my clients will lose the opportunity for great profit."

"You want me to kill this man?" Androf asked.

Yong Chow Lee chuckled. "Don't be so eager, Androf. Killing is not always the answer. The man and his wife have a thirteen-year-old boy. They have sent the boy to live with his aunt in North Carolina while they are away. The boy could be a pawn in this game of chess. He may serve as a way to influence the man's decision, if necessary."

"How does this involve me?"

"You will go to North Carolina and position yourself to follow my instructions. You will do nothing, except be ready. The aunt lives in a small town and you must fit in there. First, we must make a few changes in your appearance."

Androf raised his eyebrows in surprise. "What kind of changes?"

"You look too much like the wanted criminal that you are. Your broken nose and scar are distinguishing features. I know a plastic surgeon who can fix these problems. He can also do something about your fingerprints. Your hair is too blond, too Slavic, for an American. With a little work, he can make you into a different person."

Androf nodded. He had thought about altering his appearance for some time, but he lacked the money. "I like this idea."

"It will not take long to do what is needed. You can see the doctor today. After he has finished his work, you will travel to the town where the boy lives and find a place to stay near his house. You will learn his routine and be ready to perform any action required at a moments notice. However, you must keep a low profile and act like an ordinary American doing a regular job."

"What kind of job?" Androf asked.

"I have given that a great deal of thought. You will be a salesman for an automobile parts manufacturer who is learning his way around a new territory."

"That will be easy – I know a lot about automobile repairs."

"Good! I have a utility van for your use. The name, *Vertex Automobile Supplies,* is painted on the side. It is a company owned by one of my associates; the company will vouch for you should anyone check. The rear of the van contains a cage enclosed by steel mesh. If asked, you can say it is necessary to prevent theft of your supplies. The real purpose is to have a secure place to confine the boy."

Androf scowled. "You want me to kidnap this boy?"

"That is a possibility. It may force the father to reverse his position if things aren't going well. My associates will decide when the time comes. If the transaction falls through because of the father, they may want revenge. In such case, they may simply tell you to kill the boy."

"I have no problem doing this for you, but what is my reward?"

Yong Chow Lee rose from his chair, walked towards a small credenza against the wall, and spoke a few Cantonese words into a telephone sitting there. A minute later, a thin Chinese man entered the room, bowed at Yong Chow Lee, and handed him a briefcase. Yong Chow Lee took the briefcase, dismissed the man with a wave of his hand, and pushed it over to Androf.

"Inside the briefcase are ten thousand dollars, a cell phone, and pictures of the boy. Keep the cell phone on at all times and use it only with me. The money will get you started. I will send you another ten thousand each month until the matter is finished. If my associates are satisfied with your work, you will receive a bonus of thirty thousand dollars. Do this task well and we will have other assignments for you."

"What if your associates are not satisfied?"

Yong Chow Lee's eyes narrowed into deadly slits. "They do not tolerate failure. Your role in the game is to carry out their orders. If they lose because you perform badly, you will regret it."

Androf thought for a moment. He had been on the run for a long time, barely eluding the police on many occasions. He needed money and Yong Chow Lee could provide it. Living in North Carolina for a while wasn't a bad idea. It would let his trail go cold. The crime that Yong Chow Lee wanted him to commit was not important. *I will take the man's money and decide the rest later,* he thought.

"Do not worry. I will not disappoint you," he said quietly.

Yong Chow Lee nodded his satisfaction and folded his arms across his chest. It was a signal to a man sitting at a control panel on the other side of the wall. It meant there was no need for the gas. If Androf had resisted his offer, Yong Chow Lee would have suggested he think it over for a few minutes and excused himself. The doors would have locked behind him, trapping Androf in a room filling with poisonous gas.

☙ Chapter 12 ❧

A myth is a truth covered in cobwebs and lies. Thy greatest challenge rests in discerning truth from falsehood.

— Translated from Storia Di Incanto; circa 1691

A Family History Unfolds

AS DAVEY LEFT the bicycle shop, thoughts about his great grandfather occupied his mind. He felt like a detective who had discovered a long-hidden mystery — one filling him with questions. Unfortunately, Sequoyah was unwilling to answer them.

"I apologize for saying anything. It was stupid of me, but I didn't realize you didn't know about your great grandfather. You should ask your aunt," he had said.

Davey planned to do just that, but Bupkiss was waiting for him when he arrived home — his discussion with Aunt Sally would have to wait. The dog had spent the day with the local veterinarian, whom the residents of Great Oak fondly called Dogman Dan. He had received this odd nickname because he handed out dog biscuits to every canine that he passed on the streets. Of course, this earned him quite a following — especially four-legged ones.

By all appearances, Bupkiss had received the royal treatment. Dogman Dan had given the dog a bath, sprayed him for fleas, and stitched up the deep gashes from his fight with the bear. He had also repaired a tear in one of the dog's ears and patched up a few other minor injuries. He finished by bandaging each of the dog's wounds with abundant amounts of heavy white tape. This left Bupkiss looking very much like a ragtag clown as he limped towards Davey, his tail wagging awkwardly.

The dog seemed unaware of his comical appearance, and Davey choked off the laugh rising in his throat. "Poor, banged-up Bupkiss," he said, petting him gently.

At first, Bristol seemed a bit miffed over sharing his home with another dog, particularly one getting all the attention. So Davey took him aside and spoke in the special voice he used for animals. "Bupkiss is only staying with us until we can find him a new home. Be nice, okay. He's barely more than a puppy and has been through some tough times."

Bristol showed his understanding by licking Davey's nose and then going over and sitting alongside Bupkiss. *They should get along fine now,* Davey thought.

"Davey," Aunt Sally called from the kitchen. "I spoke with your mom and dad this afternoon while you were at school." Her voice was full of excitement and Davey immediately hurried into the room.

"What did they say? Are they in China? Is everything okay? Have they seen the Great Wall?" He asked, firing out each question before she could answer the prior one.

Aunt Sally laughed at his barrage. "Calm down and I'll tell you. They reached Shanghai yesterday and are going to Kansu Province today. We didn't talk long because the telephone line was full of static, but they are safe and that's the important thing."

"I wish I could have talked to them," Davey replied. "I can't wait to tell my dad about the baseball game this Saturday."

"They'll call again upon arriving in Chiu-ch'uan, their final destination. It should be this weekend, so you can speak to them then."

Davey nodded, feeling a slight pang of guilt. So many things had happened in the last few days, he had almost forgotten about his parents. It struck him as incredibly odd. *Life is supposed to be simpler in this town, but it isn't,* he thought.

Davey spent the rest of the afternoon helping Uncle Bill clean out the tool shed. All the while, he considered ways to convince Aunt Sally to tell him about his great grandfather. He hoped she would actually discuss his ancestors instead of evading the subject like his mother had. His chance came later that evening as they sat around the kitchen table after supper.

"Do you like your new bicycle?" Aunt Sally asked.

Davey's grin stretched all the way across his face. "Yeah, it's really great. Thank you so much; it's what I've always wanted."

"Well, you're welcome. Uncle Bill and I want you to be happy here, which reminds me. How was school today?"

Aunt Sally's question gave him the opening he had been waiting for. "Fine, but I'm curious about something I heard."

Aunt Sally nodded calmly. "And what was that?"

"I heard my great grandfather lived here and that people were afraid of him. They thought he was a witch."

Aunt Sally abruptly choked on a large sip of coffee, sending a stream of liquid hurling at Uncle Bill. Luckily, he scooted out of the way before being splattered. "Whoa, settle down girl," he chuckled, acting as though she was a skittish little mare.

Aunt Sally coughed and sputtered for a few seconds and then gave Uncle Bill a withering look. "Very funny, Bill."

Uncle Bill decided a retreat was in order. "You know, it just amazes me how well these dogs get along. Davey, why don't we take them for a walk?"

Aunt Sally shook her head emphatically. "No, let's talk about this. I knew Davey might eventually hear something about his great grandfather Sabatini. He probably heard it from Sequoyah, which surprises me. He should have been more discreet."

"He thought I already knew about my great grandfather or he wouldn't have said anything," Davey replied. "Why did they think he was a witch? It's not true, is it?"

Aunt Sally sat silently for a moment, thinking about his questions. Finally, she spoke. "Unfortunately, I don't really know."

Davey frowned. "What do you mean?"

"My mother never talked about her father. He disappeared before she was born. Whatever she knew about him, she never repeated. In fact, she never mentioned either of her parents until Janie and I were older. Even then, she didn't say very much."

"Why didn't she tell you about them?"

Aunt Sally sighed in frustration. "My mother had a miserable childhood. Her parents, your great grandparents, were unusual to say the least. I think she resented her upbringing, so she put her parents out of her mind. It was as though they didn't exist."

Davey was sure she was stonewalling. "You don't know anything about them?"

"Well, I've learned a few things since your uncle and I moved here, but there are many gaps in the story. I've guessed at a lot."

Davey put on a solemn, I'm older than I look, face. Finally, he was getting somewhere. "Please tell me everything, whether it's bad or not. I have a right to know about my ancestors."

Aunt Sally hesitated, knowing her sister would not approve. Still, Janie was not there at the moment and she was. *The boy is right,* she thought. *He should be told.* The room fell silent and Uncle Bill gave her a nod of encouragement.

Aunt Sally took a deep breath, her mind made up. "All right, let's start with your great grandfather. His name was Antonio Sabatini and he was from Italy. He came to Great Oak with a carnival about eighty years ago, a secretive man who never talked about himself or his family. The carnival claimed he was the world's greatest magician, and maybe he was. I found several articles referring to him and describing his magic act in the archives of our local newspaper where I work. Apparently, he was very talented."

"Is that when he met my great grandmother?" Davey asked.

"Yes, her name was Alicia Smith. She was an orphan, so I don't know anything about her background either. The Housemans found her in a basket on their front porch when she was three months old. They treated her like a servant, putting her to work when she was five and never letting her attend school. At age twenty-one, she couldn't even read or write. That's how old she was when Antonio came to Great Oak."

"It must have been awful for her," Davey muttered.

"Bad things happened in those days, especially if the Housemans were involved. When Claude Houseman took Alicia in, he was the Mayor of Great Oak. One of his brothers was the Chief of Police and the other was the City Judge. They ruled the town with an iron fist. Anyone who challenged them soon regretted it."

At that moment, Bristol marched into the room, his water-bowl in his mouth. The dog plopped the empty bowl on the table and nudged Uncle Bill's elbow with his nose.

Uncle Bill rose from his chair. "Dogs need some water. Keep going; I'll take care of them. I've already heard all of this anyhow."

Aunt Sally nodded and continued her story. "Antonio and Alicia must have fallen in love right away because they were married in a nearby town three months later. When the carnival left Great Oak, they stayed behind. That's when the trouble started."

"What trouble?" Davey asked.

"Claude Houseman was furious about the marriage, and Antonio was an outsider in a town that didn't welcome strangers. Claude claimed Antonio had bewitched Alicia, which made everyone afraid of him. Then Antonio moved his wagon to the mountains where the Cherokee Indians lived. The tribe welcomed him, further angering the Housemans. They were feuding with the Indians and didn't want Antonio befriending them."

"So what happened next?"

"Antonio and Alicia lived at the Cherokee village for seven years. During that time, Antonio taught Alicia to read, and everyone in town more or less forgot about them. Then Antonio built a house near the park and moved back to Great Oak when Alicia was several months pregnant. Of course, Claude and his brothers were outraged and they stirred up the old rumors again."

Davey found this part of the story puzzling. "I don't get it. Why did Antonio return to Great Oak if everyone disliked him?"

"It's one of the many mysteries surrounding your great grandfather. Several months later, a church near his house burst into flames. Claude said he had seen Antonio shouting incantations at the church before the fire. Therefore, everyone believed Antonio started it, even though the fire marshal said a cracked chimney was the cause."

"I'll bet that caused more stories about witchcraft."

Aunt Sally nodded. "Antonio became a convenient scapegoat for Claude, who blamed him for all sorts of bad things from then on. It was during the years of the great depression and the town had fallen upon hard times. Any new threat was enough to alarm the people. When someone saw a few Cherokee Indians visiting Antonio at his house one night, Claude accused them of hatching a conspiracy against the town. Of course, it was ridiculous, but everyone was frightened."

"What finally happened?"

"Several nights later, lightning struck Claude, his brothers, and a number of other men when they were in the park. Antonio was never seen again after that."

"Does anyone know why he disappeared?

"Sequoyah thinks his grandfather knows something, but he won't talk with me."

"So what secret is he keeping?"

Aunt Sally shook her head. "I don't know, but let me continue. My grandmother gave birth to Celina, my mother, four months after Antonio disappeared. Apparently, the trauma of his disappearance affected Alicia's sanity because Celina practically became a ward of the community. While the neighbors treated Celina with kindness, they didn't hide their contempt for her parents. In effect, they brainwashed her against them. When Celina turned eighteen, she left Great Oak."

"No wonder your mother didn't tell you about her parents."

"Well, she eventually did. When I was eight, Mom announced we were going to visit Grandmother Sabatini; she was sick and needed Mom's help. Dad was away on a business trip, so Mom had to take Janie and me with her. We were so surprised. We didn't even know we had a Grandmother Sabatini."

Just then, Uncle Bill returned from tending to the dogs. "Looks like Bristol has taken a liking to our new pet," he announced. "Bupkiss was the one who was thirsty." Then he winked at Davey. "Did she get to the part about her witchy grandmother?"

Aunt Sally frowned. "I was just starting on that when you so rudely interrupted."

Uncle Bill grinned. "Good! I like this part best."

Aunt Sally glared at him, her eyes flashing as she continued. "I was just a kid, yet I could tell Grandmother wasn't right in the head. She had this faraway look in her eyes and barely acknowledged our presence. We stayed at her house for about a week; she hardly said a word to Janie and me the entire time."

"Don't forget all those odd things that happened," Uncle Bill interjected.

"All right Bill, stop interrupting. Who's telling this anyway?"

Uncle Bill twisted his mouth shut with his fingers. "My lips are sealed," he mumbled between his teeth.

Aunt Sally suppressed a grin and resumed her story. "I remember a weird mix of things about that trip. Grandmother and Mom argued constantly, which made us all tense. We burned candles at night because she wouldn't pay her electric bill. This made her house seem so spooky, I was afraid to sleep. The kids next door accused her of being a witch who spied on everyone. They said she could see through the eyes of birds, which flew around the town. She also had this strange obsession about the park."

Davey forced himself to remain calm. All of these details were like pieces of a puzzle. They painted a troubling picture of his great grandparents, yet he felt compelled to learn all he could. "Tell me about the park," he asked, urging Aunt Sally to keep talking.

"Grandmother insisted upon visiting this old tree in the park, despite her illness. The tree is called the Great Oak – it's the namesake of the town. I remember how crazy her actions seemed. Snow covered the ground and it was very cold outside. She was an old woman in poor health, yet every day she went to see the tree."

"Is that why she stayed here even though everyone disliked her?"

"She and Mom had a terrible argument about it. Mom wanted her to live with us in Greensboro, but she refused. She said the tree was where Antonio was and that she had to be near it."

"She thought he was buried there?"

"Who knows what she thought; her mind was so confused."

"What else did they argue about?"

"Grandmother also had an obsession about having a grandson. This really upset my mom because Grandmother showed no interest in Janie and me. She told Mom the family needed a male heir."

"Needed a male heir…why?"

Aunt Sally shook her head. "I asked Mom, but she wouldn't say."

Davey looked thoughtful for a moment. "I'm a male heir, aren't I?"

A startled expression appeared on Aunt Sally's face. "It hadn't occurred to me before, but you certainly are. In fact, you are the Sabatini's only male heir."

Davey grinned. "Maybe I'm a long-lost prince and heir to a fabulous fortune."

"You just reminded me of another odd thing. Mom said they were very poor when she was growing up. However, after my grandmother died, a man at the bank said she had an account with thousands of dollars in it. Where the money came from is another mystery."

"What did your mother do with the money?"

"Mom used it for our college educations. She thought it was a great way for Grandmother to atone for ignoring Janie and me."

"Where is Grandmother Sabatini buried? I should visit her grave sometime."

"She wasn't buried – she was cremated. She left a letter behind, asking Mom to scatter her ashes around the Great Oak. It was her final obsessive act. Joe Harrison, the park warden, unlocked the fence and allowed us to carry out her wishes. We held a little ceremony as we sprinkled her ashes there."

Davey not only found this fascinating, but his necklace also started a distinct vibration. *It's alerting me to something,* he thought, wondering what it was. "Did anyone else attend her funeral?"

"Nope, it was just our family – and the birds, of course."

Davey smiled. "The birds?"

"Yes, it was amazing. Hundreds of birds filled the Great Oak, all silently watching us. It was as if they were saying goodbye to Grandmother."

Davey was stunned. He recalled the birds outside his window on his first morning in Great Oak. The similarities were obvious. "How did you and Uncle Bill wind up in Great Oak anyway?"

"Fate, I guess. We were living in Greensboro and Bill was working as a furniture designer at a nearby factory. Then he received this great job offer from the furniture plant owned by Wally Houseman. It was too good to turn down."

"What an odd coincidence," Davey remarked dryly.

"I have often thought so. Anyway, Bill took the job and we moved here. Of course, we knew little about my grandparents at the time. We bought this old house, fixed it up, and made many new friends. A year or so later, I made the mistake of telling a neighbor my mother was from Great Oak. In a matter of days, the whole town was gossiping about me being Antonio Sabatini's granddaughter."

"What did they do after they found out?"

"Some of the old timers began staring at me in a funny way. I wondered why, so I started asking questions. Gradually, the stories about my grandparents came out. Then Wally Houseman fired Bill. He told everyone he didn't want any Sabatini kin working for him. Bill just shrugged it off and started his own company. Now, he sells his furniture designs all over the world."

"I've heard several bad things about the Housemans at school.

Nobody likes them," Davey stated.

"Wally's son is in your class, isn't he?"

"Yeah, Spike. He's a bully."

"Well, stay away from him. The whole family is mean."

"Aunt Sally, do you mind if I snoop around a bit? You know, to see what else I can find out about the Sabatinis," Davey asked.

Aunt Sally glanced at Uncle Bill and shrugged. "No, I don't mind. You can start by looking through the information I've collected about them. I have it all in an old shoebox. There are copies of the newspaper articles I mentioned and even the letter containing Grandmother's burial instructions."

Uncle Bill put his hand on Davey's shoulder. "Davey, listen to me for a minute. The Sabatini name invokes strange reactions from people in this town, so be careful who you ask."

ଔ Chapter 13 ଵ

Magick has many faces, and unknown messages may lie hidden in every enchantment. Thus, thou must learn to examine that which seems confounding.

— Translated from Storia Di Incanto; circa 1693

The Message

AFTER SUPPER, Davey sat in his room, hurrying through his homework. The bedraggled shoebox containing his aunt's research about his ancestors lay on his bed. Every few minutes, he glanced towards the box, feeling an urgent need to delve into its contents. When an amber glow appeared along its worn edges, he resisted no longer. He dumped the contents of the box onto his bed, sorted through the collection, and selected the newspaper article with the earliest date.

𝕿𝖍𝖊 𝕲𝖗𝖊𝖆𝖙 𝕺𝖆𝖐 𝕷𝖊𝖆𝖋𝖑𝖊𝖙
September 15, 1925

Magic Arrives in Great Oak

Hold onto your hats, dear readers, and hurry on down to Harrison Park where a marvelous demonstration of magic awaits you. Bingham Carnival arrived two days ago, bringing *The Great Sabatini* to our town. He is a magician of such incredible skill – I could hardly believe my eyes.

The Carnival has set up the magic show in an outside, roped-off area, not in a tent. The ten-cent admission price is well worth it, so don't miss his performance. Read on friends and you will understand why.

Before the show started, we waited on benches around a small, torch-lit platform. Suddenly, a cloud of amber smoke covered the platform and Antonio Sabatini emerged from inside the cloud. How he got there, I do not know.

He was a tall, imposing man, clothed entirely in black. Gold jewelry adorned his fingers and wrists and a magnificent gold necklace shimmered in the flickering light. Moreover, a long black cape swirled around him as though it were alive.

In a deep, melodious voice, he spoke his only words of the evening. "Ye, who believe in magical nights, marvel now at wondrous sights." The audience fell silent, entranced by his mysterious appearance.

Then a black cane, topped by a golden dragon's head, materialized in his hand. At a snap of his fingers, flames erupted from the dragon's mouth. He tossed the cane into the air and it circled above us, spouting fire and roaring like a beast.

Over the next hour, I saw things defying explanation. Lightning and fire shot from his fingers; icy gusts of air exploded wherever he pointed. Everyone gasped with surprise and delight at the unbelievable things he could do. One after another, his magic feats came so fast we could hardly catch our breaths. Then a cloud of amber smoke surrounded him again, and he was gone.

After the show, I asked him for an interview. He answered my many questions with a single remark. "As you can see, magic be, of the blood within me." If you know what that means, dear readers, let me know!

Larry Tompkins, Staff Reporter

Davey read the article two times, savoring each word. The reporter's story was so vivid, he felt as if he had actually seen his great grandfather perform. For the first time, he had heard his stage name – The Great Sabatini. His mind's eye formed a picture of his ancestor, a man cloaked in magic and mystery. *The Great Sabatini...my great grandfather...I'm starting to know you,* he mused. Of course, this only made him eager to read more and he hastily reached for the next article.

The Great Oak Leaflet

February 23, 1926

Sabatini Marries and Moves to the Mountains

This reporter's interest in The Great Sabatini continues unabated. It now appears that Sabatini has left the Bingham Carnival.

As you know, the unusually harsh winter forced the carnival to stay in our town instead of leaving as scheduled. In the meantime, Sabatini has moved his wagon up the mountain to Cherokee Indian land. How he got there, on roads covered by three feet of snow and ice, is a mystery.

The folks at the carnival said that Sabatini had occasionally cleared short stretches of snow-covered roads with his magic. Being a bit skeptical, I wanted to check things out for myself. So yesterday, I set out on my ever-reliable mare, *Tomboy*, for a good look at the mountain road. I didn't find a single sign of any passing wagon and the roads were still impossible to traverse. If Sabatini moved his wagon up the mountain, he must have flown it there. Now, that's what I call magic!

My news about this mysterious man isn't over yet. Two weeks ago, he also married Alicia Smith, the live-in maid and more or less adopted daughter of our less than perfect mayor, Claude Houseman. Apparently, she also accompanied Sabatini up the mountain to live with the Cherokee.

When I asked Claude about this, his face grew red with anger. He claimed that it was all a lie and that no marriage had taken place. Then he said that Sabatini had cast a spell over the girl, bewitching her.

Now, a little bird told me that Claude's cronies call him the Minotaur behind closed doors. If you ask me, it's because of his bull-headed stubbornness and bad temper.

Anyway, when Claude gets mad, it's always an ugly thing to see. Trust me, dear readers, when I mentioned Alicia's marriage, he carried on as if someone had stolen his favorite hunting dog.

To get my facts straight, I checked with Hal Reams, the Justice of the Peace over in Rest Easy. Hal confirmed that the Sabatinis were legally married there on February 10th.

Claude gave me one of his famous shrivel up and die looks when I told him about my conversation with Hal. Then he changed his story a bit and alleged that Alicia is not right in the head. Thus, he claims the marriage is a sham.

It's funny though, Hal Reams said that both the bride and groom appeared level headed and very happy.

Dear readers, it seems like someone is awfully confused. In case you're wondering, it ain't me!

Larry Tompkins, Staff Reporter

Smiling wistfully, Davey envisioned his great grandfather's carnival wagon flying through the air like a giant winged bird. The part about Claude Houseman reinforced Aunt Sally's opinion about the evil ways of the Houseman family, and it struck Davey as incredibly odd that a mayor's friends would secretly call him the Minotaur. What kind of statement did that make about the town's leader? Obviously, the reporter didn't like him either. He picked up the third article, intrigued by old stories of life in Great Oak.

The Great Oak Leaflet
July 18, 1926

The Great Sabatini Seen in Town

Rumors have been circulating for months about sightings of The Great Sabatini in Harrison Park. Back in February, I reported that he had moved his wagon up the mountain to live with the Cherokee Indians.

But yesterday, dear readers, I had the good fortune of encountering the mysterious magician in the park. He was standing alongside the Great Oak when I approached him. Much to my surprise, we actually had a lengthy conversation – of sorts.

Sabatini has this unusual habit of speaking in rhyme. At first, I thought this was part of his stage personality. But apparently, it's just the way he talks.

Anyway, I asked him why he was living with the Cherokee. He smiled mysteriously as he replied. "Fate has brought me to this place, and they provide nature's embrace."

Then I asked why he was in Har-rison Park. "I came to see the tree, 'tis where the spirit be," he said with twinkling eyes.

As I glanced up at the Great Oak, I was surprised at how magnificent and hardy the tree appeared. If you remember, a year ago the town council took up the subject of the tree's deteriorating health. Our infamous mayor, Claude Houseman, stated that the tree was dying. He presented a proposal for the tree's destruction; he and his tree cutting brethren would turn it into furniture – even pay the city for the wood.

Now, we all know the House-mans have hated the tree ever since the town chose it for its namesake. They still want the town named after them – Housemanville can you believe it?

I saw this as nothing more than a foolish bit of nonsense at the time, but it also filled me with curiosity. It left me wondering how far our bull-headed mayor would go to have his way. Fortunately, the mayor's proposal was defeated because the tree has made a miraculous recovery. I've never seen it look healthier than it does now.

When I told Sabatini this story, he made a very strange reply. "The tree fights the evil here and protects what we hold dear. The battle was nearly lost, but strength was gained at great cost."

Not understanding, I asked him what he meant. But he just looked at me with his expressive eyes, smiled, and walked away.

Dear readers, the man acts as though he knows some deep, dark secret about our town. Now, I'm wondering what it can possibly be!

Larry Tompkins, Staff Reporter

The contents of the article held Davey spellbound, particularly the remarks that his great grandfather made concerning the tree. *What secret did he know? Was it why he disappeared years later?* Davey's thoughts then turned to the Great Oak itself. *Was it really dying, or was that just something the Housemans said so they could cut it down?* A picture of the tree formed in his mind. It was the key; everything involved it in some way. Suddenly, an insistent tapping on his window interrupted his thoughts – a tapping with a familiar rhythm.

Davey immediately knew what was making the sound. He quickly shut the door of his room, ran to the window, and raised it. Sure enough, the oddly marked face of the squirrel from the Great Oak greeted him.

Normally, the sudden appearance of the squirrel would have amazed him because he had just pictured the tree in his mind. But so many odd coincidences had happened over the last few days, he didn't even blink. "What brings you here?" Davey asked with a smile.

As if answering his question, the squirrel leapt onto Davey's bed and scurried over to where the contents of the shoebox lay scattered. The little animal poked through the material, obviously searching for something. Then visibly excited, it grabbed a tri-folded sheet of paper and thrust it towards Davey.

After Davey's prior experience with the squirrel, there were few ways the animal could surprise him. This was one of them. The squirrel's actions suggested it could read – a ridiculous notion. Davey took the sheet and laid it back down on the bed. "If you don't mind, I'm going to finish reading these newspaper articles first," he said.

The squirrel picked up the folded sheet and thrust it at Davey, more insistent this time. Davey simply shook his head. "We'll look at it in a minute. I'll read this next article aloud so you can listen."

The squirrel let out a sigh and stretched out on the bed, its head propped up by one little hand. The squirrel's antics made Davey smile. "I could swear you're a person," he said, and began to read.

The Great Oak Leaflet
April 13, 1932

Sudden Storm Injures Leading Citizens

Late last night, a sudden electrical storm descended upon our fair town. The storm appeared without warning, as moments earlier not a single cloud was in the sky. Strangely, the storm stayed directly over the park, missing the rest of Great Oak.

A large group of men had gathered in the park at the time. Exactly why they were there is unclear, but I understand some sort of secret meeting was underway. When I inquired about the nature of this meeting, I was told to mind my own business. Dear readers, no one should speak such words to a curious reporter like me. They only make me more inquisitive!

Anyway, many of the town's leading citizens were present, including our notorious Mayor, Claude Houseman, Police Chief, Gutter Houseman, and City Judge, Bugsy Houseman. Lightning struck them all, inflicting serious injuries.

Will Smith, George Collingwood, Hank Johnston, Billy Bob Eggers, Dan Webster, Barney Jones, and Butch Evans all died immediately. The rest are now in bed at their homes, trying to recover.

The lightning was especially brutal to the three Housemans. Claude cannot hear or speak and his right side is paralyzed. Gutter has become blind, and Bugsy is in a coma. Our hearts go out to the victims of this terrible tragedy.

In the meantime, Antonio Sabatini has suddenly gone missing. Is there some connection between this and the secret meeting in the park? So far, my efforts to uncover the facts have not produced results. But never fear, dear readers, this intrepid reporter will eventually learn the truth. You shall be the first to hear it when I do!

Larry Tompkins, Staff Reporter

Davey looked at the squirrel, his eyes wide. "Seven people dead, the Housemans severely injured, and my great grandfather missing, all on the same night. And Larry Tompkins seems to think there's a connection. I wonder what it could be."

The squirrel leaped on Davey's shoulder and again thrust the tri-folded sheet in front of his face. Davey responded calmly. "Be patient! There's only one more article. Then I'll look at what you have."

The squirrel voiced its disapproval by jabbering furiously at Davey, but he hurriedly reached for the last article anyway. As he quickly learned, Larry Tompkins had not written it.

The Great Oak Leaflet
August 15, 1932

Larry Tompkins Found Dead – Reward Offered!

We mourn the passing of our popular reporter, Larry Tompkins. He died on Main Street two nights ago, the victim of a hit and run accident. Apparently, he was walking towards Harrison Park at the time.

A witness reported seeing a large truck fleeing the scene at high speed. The truck had no license plates or identifying marks. A police search for the vehicle is underway. Any person having knowledge about the incident should contact Tom Wilkins, our new police chief. A reward of five hundred dollars is available for information resulting in an arrest.

Larry had worked at The Great Oak Leaflet for the last ten years. He was a fine man and a good friend. Many of our readers have praised him for his investigative abilities and often-humorous commentaries about our prominent citizens.

A few days ago, he told me that he was about to uncover the truth behind the disappearance of Antonio Sabatini, a man whom he liked and respected. Apparently, Larry had found a witness who knew why he was missing. I believe he was on his way to a meeting with this witness when the truck struck him. Regretfully, he did not share the name of the witness with me.

Alas, we will truly miss our beloved reporter. Our heartfelt condolences go out to his family.

Jim Towns, Editor

Davey's eyes narrowed after finishing the article. He felt like he had just lost a friend. Someone had murdered the reporter, a desperate act to keep the truth out of the newspaper. He wondered who the mysterious witness was, but there were no more articles. With a sigh, he looked at the squirrel. "I guess they never found out." The squirrel returned his gaze, its eyes sad. "Okay, now what did you want to show me?" Davey asked.

The squirrel hopped into Davey's lap and thrust the tri-folded sheet of paper into his hand. When Davey opened it, he found himself staring at his great grandmother's burial request. Her handwriting was crude, and the letter contained many misspelled words. He sounded out the words, as if reading the slang from *Huckleberry Finn*.

To mye daughter Celina

I knowe I ain't ben a good mother fer yew but pleas do me this last thin. Burn mye body and spread mye ash round the Great Oak. Antonio say be near the tree and I want my ash dere. Do not wurry the pain is gone a way now and I am peace. Forgive me fer mye fault and save dis fer the heir who comes yet. It will mean some thin to him. Yer mother Alicia

An image of Alicia appeared in Davey's mind after he finished. For some reason, he didn't see her as Aunt Sally had – an old, demented woman. Nor did he see her as a witch – like the kids next door had proclaimed. Instead, he pictured the beautiful young woman who Antonio had married.

Davey looked at the squirrel, curious about why the animal had felt the letter was so important. *Was it the reference to the heir?* If he was the heir, the letter was supposed to have a special meaning, but he couldn't detect one. *It's a puzzle,* he thought, *and solving puzzles is what I do best.* "Is this important because I am the heir?" he asked.

The squirrel nodded solemnly and pointed at the letter as if Davey had missed something. He read the letter again, focusing on every word, but he couldn't find any special meaning. Then he had an idea. "Is it the ink or the paper?"

The squirrel performed a perfect double-flip and dashed around the room, winding up in front of him once more. The little animal's eyes shone with exhilaration. Davey grinned, reassured by the squirrel's actions. Apparently, he was on the right track.

Alicia had written the letter on an old sheet of parchment. Davey held the sheet under the light of the bedside lamp and examined the writing carefully. The ink was black and of ordinary thickness – there was nothing remarkable about it. He gave the squirrel a perplexed look. "I don't get it."

The squirrel calmly pulled the sheet away from him. Then the little animal turned the letter over, giving it back with the blank side up. Davey noticed the parchment had a grainy appearance. This contrasted with the front side, which was smooth. He slowly ran his fingers across the grainy surface, feeling the unusual texture.

Suddenly, his necklace began a fierce vibration and the letter came alive in his hands. The sheet started to tremble and amber sparks exploded from the surface of the parchment, spreading a tingling heat into his fingers.

"Bloody heck!" Davey yelled, using one of Jimmy's favorite oaths. He dropped the letter and leaped from the bed, suddenly frightened. The squirrel began a series of cartwheels, joyfully leaping around the room.

The letter seemed intent on following the squirrel. With a furious belching of pops, sparks, and whistles, it spun into the air and circled behind the animal, shaking and jerking. This incredible activity lasted for less than a minute, but it was filled with the squirrel's gleeful squeals and Davey's startled shouts. Finally, the letter gently floated towards the floor, landing at Davey's feet. With a final pop, it grew still, seemingly exhausted.

The reverse side of the letter was now facing him. A diagram and short passage had appeared on the formerly blank page. He prodded the paper with his toe, just to make sure its shenanigans were over. *Magic – Sabatini magic,* he mused, still somewhat stunned.

Coming out of his daze, Davey realized that the dogs were barking in the hallway. He also heard footsteps hurrying towards his room. Moving quickly, he shuffled the letter under the newspaper articles and jumped on the bed, just as the door opened.

"What's going on?" Aunt Sally asked, peering into the room.

"Uh…I was…pretending," he stammered, his face turning red.

Aunt Sally managed a grin, remembering the racket she had made when she was a kid. "I thought World War Three had started."

"I'll be quiet; I promise," Davey replied.

"Please do, Uncle Bill and I are ready for bed. You should turn in as well."

Davey nodded, hoping his aunt would leave quickly. He was afraid the squirrel would appear at any minute; its presence would be impossible to explain.

"Well, goodnight then," Aunt Sally said, shutting the door.

With a sigh of relief, Davey immediately searched the room for the squirrel, but it was nowhere to be found. Shaking his head, he sat down and gingerly picked up the mysterious letter. Then he read the message, which had magically appeared on the reverse side.

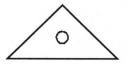

You have come at last!

And so, the end begins. Make haste, as

there is much to learn, and even more, which must be done.

Be guided by the triangle and heed its warnings. The tree will help you.

Antonio

Davey stared at the writing for a long time. He could almost hear the voice of The Great Sabatini speaking the words. They implied Davey's arrival in Great Oak was a long-anticipated event. Of course, it was not the only puzzling part of the message. He thought about the words: *And so, the end begins.* They sounded somewhat ominous. And what was he supposed to make haste and learn or do? He didn't like the sound of that either. It was almost an order. "Don't I have any say in the matter?" he asked aloud.

Davey was tempted to put the letter aside and forget it, yet the unfolding mystery was impossible to resist. "All right, but I'm not blindly taking orders from anyone. I'll make my own decisions," he said, nodding in satisfaction at his resolve.

He focused upon the rest of the message. The reference to the triangle was clear. It was the pendant of his necklace. Evidently, the pendant had the ability to give warnings and provide guidance. *Warnings and guidance about what?*

Larry Tompkins had written that Antonio wore a magnificent necklace during his magic show. *This must be the same one,* Davey concluded.

Although he had only worn the necklace for two days, Davey felt oddly incomplete without it. Removing the necklace, he examined the etchings on the chain and the pendant. *I wish I knew what these symbols stood for.* He was sure they were some form of hieroglyphic writing – if only he could interpret them. Suddenly, a big smile spread across his face. "I'll bet I can," he said.

He sat down at his computer and logged onto the internet. Then he went to the website for Google, typed in the word hieroglyphic, and clicked on search. A list of more than a dozen websites came up. As he clicked through the sites, he found one containing illustrations of hieroglyphic symbols, which were accompanied by English translations.

When Davey looked through the illustrations, his heart skipped a beat. Before his eyes was a match for one of the hieroglyphics etched on the necklace — the symbol for the word fire. Then he found another match — the symbol for the word wind. Laying the necklace alongside his computer, he hurriedly researched the meanings for each symbol. All the while, his excitement was growing.

Thirty minutes later, he had come up with a complete translation. He put the words together in a logical sequence and read what they said. The hieroglyphics on the right side of the chain described various natural forces or elements, *earth, wind, water, fire, lightning, and ice.* Those on the left side of the chain represented forms of life, *plants, trees, insects, birds, fish, animals, and humans.*

The symbols on the pendant were different. His translation of them resulted in a simple, all encompassing statement:

The Power Rules All Things!

Davey shivered as he read the words. Without his knowledge, a paradigm shift in the fabric of his life was occurring. An unknown force had entered his world. In the days ahead, he would come to know it.

Yawning, he turned off his computer and climbed into bed. His mind whirled with thoughts of what he had learned during the day. Intermixed in his musings was an image of the Great Oak, its massive branches beckoning. "The tree will help you," he murmured, recalling the last words of his great grandfather's message. His eyes closed and he fell into a troubled sleep.

☙ Chapter 14 ❧

Magick and powere are woven together.
Those with the magick skill have always
been close to powere; mysterie envelops
us, and it calls to us.

— Translated from Storia Di Incanto; circa 1701

The House Down The Street

DURING THE NEXT THREE DAYS, Davey and Jimmy spent every available hour practicing for Saturday's baseball game. This kept Davey's mind so focused on baseball, he almost forgot about his mysterious ancestors. Uncle Bill joined the boys each evening for a final session of high-speed catch in the backyard. To Davey's amazement, his ability improved each day.

This was not the only change occurring in Davey. Outwardly, he was a bit more self-assured, his personality slightly more assertive. Practically overnight, he grew an inch; within days, his muscles started to develop a lean toughness. The gawky lack of coordination, which had plagued him all of his life, was beginning to fade. But inwardly, the changes were more subtle. A unique perception was growing, a palpable awareness of the natural forces around him. It was the first of many steps in the emergence of his inherited skill.

On Friday afternoon, Jimmy declared Davey ready for Saturday's game.

A grin formed on Davey's face. "I *do* think I've gotten better."

"You definitely have," Uncle Bill said. "Some of your throws were burning my hand."

Jimmy retrieved a small package from his bicycle and brought it over to where Davey and Uncle Bill were standing. "Ta da," he said, handing the package to Davey.

"What's this?" Davey asked.

"Open it and find out, mate."

Davey ripped the package open and pulled out a green t-shirt. Lettered in gray on both sides of the shirt were the words: *Surefoot's Indians,* along with a small insignia of an Indian chief. On the back of the shirt was also his last name: *Boehm.* He felt his throat constricting. *A team jersey, one with my name,* he thought. He had never seen anything more beautiful. "I don't know what to say," he mumbled.

Jimmy grinned, pleased by Davey's reaction. "No worries, you've earned it. Dad makes them up for all the kids, just for fun. It's another one of his businesses, you know, athletic uniforms and that sort of thing."

"Well, it looks like you made the team," Uncle Bill said with a laugh. "Let's go inside and celebrate; the root beer is on me."

ഇ൚ഇൠഇൠ

Meanwhile, in another part of town, Spike and Monkey Davis sat on the expansive back porch of Spike's three-story home.

The town's residents called the old structure *Houseman's Castle,* but the name was more grandiose than the house deserved. In truth, it was a haphazard and crude castle at best. It stood in the center of an upwardly sloping eighty-acre tract located along the eastern boundary of Great Oak.

From a distance, Houseman's Castle appeared to be one large semicircular structure. Even so, it was actually a cluster of structures joined by covered walkways and limestone walls. Two forty-foot towers protruded from the front corners of the main house. Three smaller houses and a large barn completed the complex.

Rectangular blocks of limestone, laid more than one hundred years ago, formed the exterior walls of the buildings. The limestone had come from the Houseman's very own quarry on nearby Brown Mountain. Age and the black stains of mildew gave the surface of the limestone a decrepit and foreboding look, as if it were reflecting the personalities of the residents within.

Claude and his two brothers had designed the complex in 1894 from pictures of medieval castles in Europe. To Claude, it made a perfect statement about the growing Houseman dynasty. Back then, the Housemans saw themselves as feudal lords that ruled the peasants of Great Oak. After all, every feudal lord of any merit had a castle, or so they reasoned. Of course, that was before the storm in the park had extinguished their grand illusions.

Wally Houseman was the lord of the castle now. His ruthless ambition was even more malevolent than that of his ancestors. Wally envisioned a time when he and his son would rule over a vast fortune – the largest empire of wealth and power in the State's history. Naturally, Spike was not yet ready to sit at his father's side; he was only a boy of thirteen. However, he was learning the unrelenting ways of his father and proving to be an apt pupil. Soon, he would take a giant leap forward.

As if aware of his future, Spike watched from the heights of the porch as the third member of his little gang arrived. He and Monkey had been talking about what mischief they could cause at school next week. Torpedo jumped off his bike while it was still rolling and let it crash into the row of bushes underneath the porch. "You won't believe what I just heard," he shouted, running up the steps to where the other boys were.

"Well, tell us, pinhead," Spike said lazily.

"I don't like it when you call me pinhead," Torpedo replied sullenly.

Spike's eyes flared with irritation. *It's hard hanging out with idiots like Torpedo and Monkey all the time,* he thought. *They're like dogs requiring constant petting.* "Don't be such a baby, Torpedo. Are you going to tell what you heard or not?"

Torpedo was aware of Spike's nasty temper and didn't press the issue. He quickly blurted out his news. "Hambone is playing on Jimmy Surefoot's team in the game this Saturday."

Monkey's jaw flopped open, an act changing his monkey-like face into one resembling a baby hippopotamus. "Why would he pick an uncoordinated nerd like Hambone for his team?"

"How I hate that kid," Spike said.

"Which kid, Surefoot or Hambone?" Monkey asked.

"Both of them, but I hate Hambone more," Spike growled.

Torpedo looked puzzled. "He's only been here a few days. How come you hate him so much? He ain't bothering us none."

The question startled Spike. He had felt an overwhelming dislike for the kid from New York as soon as he saw him, but he didn't know exactly why. "I got instincts about Hambone. His goody-goody attitude irks me. Besides, I don't need a reason for not liking him."

"Yeah...I hate him too," Monkey agreed.

Torpedo shrugged. "Okay, so why don't we just pound on him until he goes back to New York?"

Spike shook his head angrily. Sometimes Torpedo was so thickheaded, it made him want to scream. "Don't you remember what Jimmy said about us leaving him alone? We don't want the whole eighth-grade football team after us."

"I hate the thought of playing baseball with a geek like him, even if he's only on the other team," Monkey said hotly.

Spike was silent for a moment, thinking hard. Suddenly, a malicious grin spread across his face. "I've got it! Kids get hurt all the time playing sports, don't they? The game tomorrow may give us an opportunity. It can't be obvious or look intentional, but if Hambone gets hurt by accident, who can say it's our fault?"

ഇരുത്തു

On Saturday morning, Davey stood in the backyard, absentmindedly throwing a tennis ball for Bristol and Bupkiss. The distinct smell of fall was in the air, and a cool, crisp breeze ruffled his hair. Overhead, the sun radiated warmth from a nearly cloudless sky. *What a perfect day for baseball,* he thought. He didn't notice the ravens sitting on the roof of the house and wasn't aware of them watching him intently. His mind was on the baseball game.

In a few hours, he would actually be playing his favorite sport – not sitting on the sidelines like he always had before. He longed to do this with all his heart, but anxiety filled him. Despite his increased confidence, he was afraid of making a fool of himself. That's what had happened when he tried out for the soccer team at his old school. The laughter of the other kids still rang in his ears. Still, he had promised Jimmy and was going to keep his word. He just wished Jimmy hadn't talked him into it. In Davey's opinion, not playing at all was better than playing badly.

While loading a stack of old boards onto the bed of his pickup, Uncle Bill glanced over at Davey. He knew pre-game jitters when he saw them. *Davey needs something to get his mind off the game,* he thought. "How about lending a hand over here," he yelled.

Davey gave the dogs one last toss of the ball and walked towards the pickup. Uncle Bill carried an armful of old boards from the basement and dumped them on the ground. "I'll carry them out and you stack them in the truck," Uncle Bill said.

"Okay, where are you taking them?"

"Over to Ed Nolen's house. They're leftovers from when we remodeled here. I told Ed he could have them if he wanted."

"Who's Ed Nolen?"

Uncle Bill grinned – Davey had taken the bait. "He's a friend who is remodeling an old house down the street. You might enjoy meeting him. The house is where your great grandmother once lived."

Suddenly, Davey was all ears. "Is it the house that Antonio built?"

Uncle Bill nodded, his eyes twinkling. "Yes, and Ed Nolen is a neat guy…used to be a foreign war reporter. You can come along if you want. He'll probably offer you a tour of the old house, if you're interested."

"You bet!" Davey exclaimed, forgetting the game for a moment.

As soon as the truck was full, Davey and Uncle Bill drove a short distance down the street and pulled into the driveway of a small bungalow. A thick line of juniper trees ran along the front, obstructing the view of the house from the road. Stacks of boards, piles of stone, an old hot water heater, and several mounds of construction debris littered the front yard.

A thirty-year old, ruggedly handsome man was painting the front doorway when they drove up. He waved, laid down his paintbrush, and walked towards the truck.

"I don't know whether I'm rebuilding a house or just starting a junk yard," he said, gesturing towards the clutter in his front yard.

"I brought you those old boards I told you about," Uncle Bill said. "And this is my nephew, Davey. He's staying with us while his parents are in China."

Ed beamed as if he was the official goodwill ambassador for the town. "I'm always glad to meet a new resident. Sorry about the mess – I hope it's temporary, but sometimes I wonder."

Davey and Uncle Bill climbed out of the truck and began to unload the boards. Ed joined in, and soon the truck was empty; the boards neatly stacked on the ground.

"Davey, you wouldn't know anything about eighty-year old plumbing systems, would you?" Ed asked with a chuckle.

"No sir," Davey said. He liked the relaxed and friendly way that Ed spoke.

Ed shook his head with mock sadness. "I've traveled all over the world and fixed broken pipes in the most backward of places. Despite that, the plumbing in this house defies logic. Either the plumber who installed it was insane, or the ghosts living here are tormenting me."

Davey's eyes widened. "Are there really ghosts in the house?"

Ed's face took on a serious look. "I feel their presence all the time."

Uncle Bill started to laugh. "Careful Ed, you're stirring up trouble.

Davey's great grandparents built this house and he's trying to find out more about them. With a little encouragement, he'll want to have a séance over here."

"Hey, what a great idea!" Davey exclaimed.

Ed grinned mischievously. "I was just kidding. I already knew about your relatives living here. As far as I know, there are no ghosts in the house, but come in and have a look around if you like."

"Is the plumbing really bad?" Davey asked, following Ed towards the house.

Ed let out a bemused laugh. "Yes, and the electricity, the heating system, and almost everything else. Except for what I've already fixed, of course. Some of those don't work either."

As Davey studied the house, he concluded it was a very strange structure. The front wall was made entirely of stacked rock. An elevated porch ran along its length, and the slate roof had a high pitch, which angled back awkwardly. A squat steeple stood in the center of the roof, a lookout tower of sorts. An old weathervane sat on the tip of the steeple – a triangular shaped weathervane. Four rock columns, connected by heavy log railings, supported the porch and the beams of the roof. A thick wooden door and small slotted windows provided the only openings along the front wall.

As Ed walked through the doorway, he delivered a running commentary on his remodeling efforts. "The house had a dark and gloomy feel before I started. These front windows are too small to let in much light. I didn't want to tear down the stone along the front, but I'm putting a glass door here and cutting large windows along the sides of the house. The back will be almost entirely glass after I'm finished as well."

Uncle Bill added an explanation of his own. "The house was purchased by Ed's parents after your great grandmother died. They wanted a place in the mountains for vacations, but they didn't come here very often."

"Didn't they like it?" Davey asked.

Ed shook his head. "Every time they were here, Wally Houseman came by and almost demanded they sell the house. All he wanted to do was tear it down – he said it was an eyesore. The rest of the town was somewhat standoffish too. After I was wounded in Afghanistan, I needed a place to recuperate and write my book. So I bought the old house from them and began to remodel it."

Davey had so many questions he didn't know where to start, but Uncle Bill spoke up first. "By the way Ed, how's the leg doing?"

"Getting stronger every day. I'm walking without my cane all the time now."

Davey stared at him. "You actually got shot?"

"I sure did, three times, once in the shoulder and twice in the leg. I was driving through this little village with four other people when a group of men fired at us. We didn't know why or even who they were. My photographer and two others died. The rest of us received wounds, some of them serious. I decided I'd had enough of war reporting after that."

"And now you're writing a book," Davey said, finding Ed's life fascinating.

Ed laughed heartily. "Well, it's a tossup between writing and rebuilding this house. So far, I'm not making much progress with either. After I finish the kitchen though, I'll at least be able to scramble eggs and brew coffee. Who knows, maybe I'll become a chef next. Come on, I'll show the kitchen to you. It's nearly complete."

A center hallway divided the downstairs of the house into two halves. On the right side of the hall was a large living area, complete with a massive stone fireplace. As they walked along, Davey's necklace began an insistent vibration. He peered into the living room and noticed the mantel had symbols carved into the stone.

"There's something there I need to see," Davey muttered under his breath, but Ed continued past the living room without stopping. The windowless rooms seemed dark and oppressive – more like a fortress than a home. Fortunately, the lights were on or they would have been walking in darkness. *No wonder the house spooked Aunt Sally when she was a kid. I can imagine how it looked in candlelight,* Davey thought.

"These rooms will be a lot brighter when I cut in the windows," Ed remarked, as if he were thinking the same thing.

They reached a mahogany staircase, which led up to the second story of the house. As they passed the staircase, the vibrations of Davey's necklace became even stronger. He recalled the words of Antonio's message. *Be guided by the triangle and heed its warnings.*

"What's the upstairs like?" Davey asked, hoping Ed might show it to him.

"There are two rooms and a bathroom up there. I'm using one as an office and the other as a bedroom. The bathroom is in shambles because I'm changing all the fixtures, replacing the floor, and expanding the walls. Come back in a few weeks. It's too much of a mess to show right now."

Ed led them into the kitchen and turned around proudly. He smiled at the looks of astonishment on their faces. The kitchen was light and airy, with granite counter-tops, stainless-steel appliances, and modern cabinets. Double windows let in a stream of sunlight over the sink and a large bay window offered an expansive view of the back yard. White ceramic tiles covered the floor.

"Wow, it looks like a picture out of a magazine," Davey said.

Ed grinned. "Hey, I like this kid. Bring him around more often."

Uncle Bill glanced at his watch. "Davey, we have to get going. You need to get ready for your game and we're keeping Ed from his work."

"Can we go through the living room on the way out?" Davey asked.

Ed nodded enthusiastically. "We sure can. I'll show you the most interesting thing in the whole house."

I'll bet it's the fireplace, thought Davey, and sure enough, it was. Ed stood in front of the huge mantle and pointed at the markings on the stones. "I have no idea what these symbols mean."

Davey stared silently at the fireplace. The same symbols were on his necklace, but he was keeping the necklace a secret, so he didn't say anything.

"And these words are Italian," Ed continued, indicating carved wooden letters protruding from a large stone over the mantel. The words arched above a triangle cut into the center of the stone.

Davey was certain Antonio had put the carved letters there and he had done more than just attach them to the stone. He had fused the letters into the stone somehow. *Wanted them there permanently,* Davey thought.

"The letters are made from some kind of hard wood; it's tougher than the stone itself. I've never seen wood like it before," Ed said.

Davey stood on his tiptoes and reached up to touch one of the letters. His fingertips tingled when they neared the surface of the wood, alerting him to its origin. The same tingling sensation had occurred when he touched the Great Oak. He jerked his fingers back, afraid the wood might start glowing if he touched it. Stepping back from the mantle, he read the words aloud.

LASCIARE IL POTERE TENERE IL MALVAGIO LONTANO.

Ed turned out to be fluent in Italian, so he offered an English translation. "Let the power keep the evil away."

"Sort of an odd statement to put over a fireplace," Uncle Bill said.

Ed shrugged. "Some sort of a religious invocation, I guess. Kind of makes the house mysterious, don't you think?"

Davey silently counted the number of words – there were seven. Sequoyah had said the number seven represented the height of purity to the Cherokee. Was it a coincidence, or had Antonio used seven words intentionally? Davey repeated the words aloud. "Let the power keep the evil away." *Another mysterious reference to the power,* he thought.

℘σ℘σ℘σ℘σ

A short time later, Davey ate a quick sandwich and then changed his clothes. After putting on the t-shirt Jimmy had given him, he inspected himself in the mirror. The reflection greeting him was a bit of a surprise. For the first time, he noticed that he was becoming tanned and muscular.

"Must be all the exercise I've been getting," he said aloud. Then he noticed his necklace showing above the collarless t-shirt, so he placed it in the drawer of his desk. Immediately, he felt its absence, yet there was no other choice. If anyone saw the necklace, there would be questions – ones he was not prepared to answer.

He hurried outside, climbed on his bike, and was about to leave when Aunt Sally came running out of the house.

"Stop!" she ordered, and then ran over to him. She gave him a hug and produced a blue baseball cap from behind her back. The cap had the white insignia of the New York Yankees on its front. "I bought this for you yesterday," she said.

Davey hugged her in return. "You are the best second mother anyone ever had."

Aunt Sally pulled the cap over his head. "Go get them, slugger."

With a wave of his hand, Davey pedaled away. As he rode down the hill, his anxiety over the game returned. Unseen, the ravens sitting on the roof launched themselves into the sky, following at a lofty height.

The shortest route to the ball-field led through the park. Impulsively, he chose the trail going past the Great Oak. He could only stop for a few minutes, yet he longed to see the tree. *Maybe it will calm me down,* he thought.

Davey could feel the magic of the tree, even before he reached it. And when he saw the tree, it pulled him forward like a majestic beacon. Its force was so strong he couldn't resist getting off his bike. Again, he felt the compulsion to climb its branches.

He put his hands on the gate and looked up at the limbs arching above his head. As soon as his fingers touched it, the lock clattered open and the gate swung inward. Instantly, the squirrel popped up in front of him, its eyes shining.

Davey laughed at the squirrel's presence. Once more, he marveled at the squirrel's black fur and the white circles around its eyes. "How do you keep appearing and disappearing? I was sure Aunt Sally was going to see you the other night."

The squirrel stared quizzically at him.

"If only you could talk," Davey said.

The squirrel hopped over until it was just a few inches away. Overhead, the leaves in the tree rustled softly, a gentle whisper on the wind. The sound seemed musical and Davey imagined faint words in the melody – words he couldn't quite decipher.

Davey bent down and touched the little animal. It responded by grasping his fingers, tugging them gently. A feeling of tranquility came over him and he glanced up at the tree. "I'd like to stay, but I'm due at the baseball field. I'm the newest member of Jimmy Surefoot's team and came by for a little inspiration."

The squirrel made a chattering sound, attracting his attention. With an impish look, it pointed at the tree. Then the animal covered its eyes with its small hands as if playing a game of hide-and-seek. When it took its hands away, the white circles around its eyes had disappeared.

The squirrel's actions so mystified Davey, he was at a loss for words. "Are you telling me something?" he finally asked.

The squirrel repeated the maneuver, first replacing the white circles around its eyes, next taking the white circles away. Again, it pointed at the tree as though offering an explanation.

Davey shook his head, aware of the magic, yet unable to comprehend its meaning. He stood up and gazed at the tree, feeling the presence of its benevolent spirit. For the second time that day, he recalled a passage from Antonio's message. He had written that the tree would help him. *Help me how?* he wondered.

He glanced down at the squirrel and found that it had vanished again. He was reluctant to leave, but he couldn't delay any longer. With a final glance at the tree, he climbed back on his bike. "Wish me luck," he said, and pedaled away.

✂ Chapter 15 ✂

Learn to embrace thy mystical heritage.
Use it wisely, and fate shall favor thee.
Use it selfishly, and disappointment shall
follow.

— Translated from Storia Di Incanto; circa 1713

The Baseball Game

DAVEY WAS PLEASED to see Jimmy's smiling face at the baseball field when he rode up. About a dozen kids were hanging around in small groups, and others were still arriving. Davey waved as he parked his bike and then hurried over to where Jimmy was standing.

"About time you showed up, mate. I was getting worried," Jimmy said with a grin. He quickly introduced Davey to the other members of his team.

Davey became a bit more worried as he met them. Most were athletic-looking eighth graders. He was not only the smallest, but also the youngest kid on the team. However, everyone acted friendly and seemed pleased he was there. Nobody questioned his ability – for the moment.

"We're putting you out in left field. There's not a lot of action out there, so don't nod off," Jimmy said with a laugh. "Oh by the way, the other team calls themselves the Great Oakers. If you ask me, it's a bloody stupid name for a ball team."

Davey looked over at the group of boys huddled near third base. They were the team the Indians would be playing. He frowned when he saw Spike, Monkey Davis, and Torpedo standing among them. Then he noticed a man who looked like his math teacher crouching over home plate. He was brushing dirt off the base with a small whiskbroom and acting very official.

"Is that Mr. McDonnell?" Davey asked in surprise.

"Yeah, I talked him into being our umpire. He keeps us from arguing over balls, strikes, and outs. Without him, we'd be bashing each other all the time."

Davey felt somewhat reassured by his teacher's presence, especially after seeing Spike with the other team. Mr. McDonnell was dressed in his typically outlandish fashion. Red shoes, red socks, and red sweat pants covered the lower half of his body, making him resemble a large ripe apple. A green and red striped shirt covered his upper half, which almost seemed appropriate for his umpire-like status. He glared around the field, his handlebar mustache flapping in the breeze. Then he put a large whistle to his mouth and blew, piercing the air with a shrill sound.

"All right lads, gather around," he bellowed. When everyone had assembled, he continued solemnly. "Now lads, I want a good clean fight, no low blows, and no late punches at the end of each round." Everyone was silent until he laughed heartily. "Blimey lads, wrong sport, this isn't boxing; it's baseball. Okay, same rules apply."

Davey smiled along with everyone else. An animated chatter broke out as each team began taunting the other. He caught a glimpse of Spike glaring at him, his eyes spiteful. When their eyes met, Spike spit on the ground in Davey's direction.

Mr. McDonnell held his hands up for silence. "Since the Indians batted first in the last game, we'll start with them in the field today."

Jimmy put his arm across Davey's shoulders as they walked out to the field. "Relax mate, you'll be aces."

"Right," said Davey, trying to sound confident.

High up in the sky, the seven ravens floated on the wind, their intentions unknown. When everyone was in position, Mr. McDonnell performed one of his famous ballet-twirls. "Play ball," he roared.

As it turned out, Davey's concerns were groundless. Jimmy had been right all along. Left field was an easy position to play. Not a single ball came anywhere near him during the first two innings. *Maybe I won't make a fool of myself after all,* he thought as his team ran back towards the dugout.

Davey's first challenge came when it was his initial turn at bat. Monkey Davis, who was the catcher for the other team, did everything he could to distract him. When the ball approached the plate, Monkey yelled, "swing!" Davey swung blindly at the first two pitches, missing both times.

Davey was sure he would strike out, but he forced himself to concentrate. For some reason, an image of the tree came to him and his nerves steadied. The next pitch looked like a strike and he swung with greater care. Much to his surprise, the bat caught one edge of the ball, sending an oddly looping grounder in the direction of second base.

It should have been an easy out, but both the shortstop and second baseman tried to make the play. The ball took two erratic hops, reversing direction each time. This confused the two players and they ended up colliding. The ball stopped a few feet past them as though mocking their clumsiness.

With a frantic effort, the shortstop grabbed the ball and made a desperate throw towards first base. The ball went wild and sailed over the first baseman's head. Davey rounded first and made it to second before the ball was under control again. He stood on the base and grinned as his teammates cheered.

Torpedo Jones, the shortstop who had made the wild throw, shook his head in disgust. "Luck of the geeks," he said, loud enough for Davey to hear.

The next batter hit a smashing line drive towards center field. Davey ran like a maniac until he crossed home plate, scoring a run.

Jimmy came over and pounded him on the back. "Good onya mate, good onya! The way Torpedo and Johnny tangled each other up was a hoot. Shook them up, I'll bet."

The Indians were three runs ahead at the beginning of the fifth inning, and the game was going smashingly well, in Davey's opinion. His fielding ability was still untested, but that was soon to change. The Oakers had a man on first base and there were no outs. Spike, the Oakers best hitter, stepped towards the plate and took a left-handed batting stance. He was attacking the Indians' weakest point – left field.

Spike clobbered the first pitch, and the ball soared high into the air, straight towards Davey. He ran back, but lost sight of the ball in the rays of the sun. When the ball reappeared, he panicked, realizing it was going to come down beyond him. He backpedaled furiously, stuck his glove up, and jumped. His feet seemed propelled by rockets as he sailed upwards, higher than he had ever jumped before. By some miracle, the ball landed in his glove with a resounding thump. He could hardly believe his luck when he felt the ball there.

The runner on first base tagged up and then streaked for second. As soon as Davey came down, he whipped the ball towards the second baseman. It was a quick, fluid motion, a moment of startling athletic skill. The ball flew from his hand as though shot from a cannon. With a loud whap, it landed in the glove of the second baseman, who easily put the runner out. Davey had executed a perfect double play. *How lucky can I get,* he thought as he grinned at his teammates.

"Holy dooley, bloody good show," Jimmy yelled from his position at third base. He was pleased, but also stunned. While Davey was improving, he hadn't expected anything like what he had just seen. *Where did that move come from?* he wondered.

Spike's face grew red and he pounded the ground angrily with his bat. He cursed so loudly that Mr. McDonnell blew his whistle. "Spike, you know I don't approve of those big words, especially ones I've never heard before."

The Indians all laughed heartily at his remark. On the other hand, the Oakers stared about sullenly, finding no humor in anything. They were getting frustrated.

The Indians were ahead by four runs when Davey came up to bat again. He was so relaxed; he didn't even care if he struck out. He swung hard at the third pitch and hit a solid line drive over Torpedo's head. By another stroke of luck, the ball landed between the right and center fielders, catching them by surprise. Davey made it to second base, and one of his teammates scored. He tried to look serious like a ball player should, but couldn't stop grinning. *This is the best day of my life,* he thought.

By the eighth inning, the Indians were six runs ahead and the game was all but won. The Oakers were arguing among themselves, furious over their miserable performance. They couldn't seem to hit the ball anywhere without making an out.

Spike had started pitching for the Oakers. His pitches were erratic, but he threw the ball hard and fast, striking out the first two batters. Davey was up next. While he approached the plate, Monkey Davis went out and talked with Spike. Davey watched Spike's piggy eyes glaring at him as the two boys whispered together. After a few minutes, Monkey returned to the catcher's position and dared Davey to hit the ball. Suddenly, Davey felt a slight tug on one of his shoes.

"Hey, your shoe is untied," Monkey jabbered.

Instead of stepping out of the batter's box, Davey naively looked down at his feet. Instantly, Spike wound up and threw. Davey heard Jimmy yell, but never saw the pitch coming. When he looked up, the ball was inches from his face. Pain exploded in his head as the ball struck him between the eyes; he fell to the ground with a cry.

Mr. McDonnell blew his whistle furiously. "Spike, you're through," he roared.

"It was an accident," Spike protested.

Jimmy jumped up from where he was sitting. "In a pig's eye! Monkey distracted him and you threw on purpose."

Total confusion immediately descended upon the ball field. Jimmy and his teammates piled on Spike and Monkey, their fists flying. Mr.

McDonnell repeatedly blew his whistle, trying to regain order. "This game is officially over," he shouted.

Most of the Oakers took off, not wanting any part of the fight or the rest of the game for that matter. Spike and Monkey beat a hasty retreat too, as soon as Mr. McDonnell separated the fighting boys and allowed them to escape. Then the teacher turned his attention to Davey, who was lying on the ground, unconscious. The broken pieces of his glasses had fallen in the dirt beside him. "Jimmy, help me put the poor lad in my car. I'm taking him to the Emergency Clinic."

Immediately upon arriving at the clinic, Davey was loaded onto a stretcher and wheeled into the emergency room. The nurse hurriedly telephoned Aunt Sally, while Mr. McDonnell telephoned Jimmy's dad and told him what had happened. Both parents said they would be there in a matter of minutes.

෨ଓ෨ଓ෨ଓ෨ଓ

Meanwhile, Spike, Torpedo, and Monkey regrouped a short distance from the ball field. Spike had a big grin on his face and the three boys gave each other high-fives. Spike and Monkey had taken a few lumps from Jimmy and his teammates, but not enough to prevent them from relishing what they had done.

"It worked perfectly," Spike said, his eyes gleaming victoriously.

Torpedo shook his head, still concerned. "Jimmy thinks you did it on purpose."

Monkey grinned ecstatically. "All we have to do is keep saying it was an accident. Nobody can prove otherwise."

Spike glared at Torpedo. "Where were you when they were beating up on us?"

He shrugged nervously. "By the time I got there, old man McDonnell had stopped everything."

Suddenly, a loud cawing distracted the three boys. As they looked up, seven ravens swooped down upon them. Zooming just over their heads, they vented their rage. The boys felt a rain of bird-poop striking their heads…splat…splat…splat.

"What the heck?" Spike exclaimed, wiping his head in disgust. He had received the brunt of the attack.

Torpedo held his nose as he looked at him. "Phew, you stink, Spike."

Spike wiped his hand on Torpedo's face. "Now you stink, pinhead."

"Look out, they're coming back!" Monkey cried, bird-poop dripping from his face.

Spike, Torpedo, and Monkey frantically ran for shelter as the ravens descended upon them again, but they didn't move fast enough. When the boys finally found cover, the smelly revenge of the ravens had blanketed them from head to toe.

ഇരുന്നുരുന്നു

Aunt Sally, Uncle Bill, and Sequoyah all arrived at the Clinic about the same time. They rushed inside, their faces grim. Aunt Sally carried a file containing Davey's medical records in case they were needed.

The nurse immediately led Aunt Sally and Uncle Bill into the emergency room. Sequoyah stayed with Jimmy and Mr. McDonnell in the waiting area. Sliding curtains divided the interior of the room into three treatment areas. The area with Davey in it was the only one occupied. He lay on a hospital gurney, monitor wires sticking to various places on his body, and a bulky bandage covering his forehead. A doctor stood over him, shining a light in his eyes. A nurse standing nearby watched the monitors.

Aunt Sally let out a loud gasp and tears began to stream from her eyes.

Hearing the sound, the nurse looked up. "Doctor, the boy's parents are here."

The doctor left Davey's side and came towards them. He was tall and slender, with shaggy blond hair and an unshaven face. He seemed barely old enough to be a college student, let alone a doctor. "I'm

156

Doctor Sorenson. Don't let all of this worry you," he said, indicating the monitors. "His vital signs are good and we don't think he's seriously injured. I'm just taking a few precautions."

"Precautions against what?" Uncle Bill asked.

"He received a good whack on the forehead where the ball hit him, and there was a small cut, which we stitched up. There is also some swelling, which we are controlling with an ice pack. He probably has a mild concussion, but he's been unconscious for a while and we don't like that. If he stays unconscious for long, it may indicate a serious injury."

"Can I talk to him?" Aunt Sally asked, regaining control.

"Yes, it might help him wake up," the doctor said. "First, let's remove the bandage. I want to see if the swelling has gone down."

The nurse removed the bandage and carefully lifted the ice pack from Davey's forehead. Doctor Sorenson examined him for a few seconds and nodded. "The swelling has subsided – a good sign," he said, motioning Aunt Sally towards the gurney.

Aunt Sally gently touched Davey's hair and let her fingers trail down the side of his head. Davey remained motionless at first and then twitched his shoulder. The flicker of a smile crossed his face.

"Go away, Bristol," he said slowly, his voice barely more than a whisper.

"Davey, it's Aunt Sally. Time to wake up," she said softly.

Davey's eyes opened a fraction, fluttered, and then closed. After a few seconds, they opened again, wider this time. "Aunt Sally...what are you doing here?" he mumbled, struggling to sit up.

"Lie still, you're in the hospital. A baseball hit you in the head, remember?"

Davey thought about it. "Spike did it on purpose," he finally muttered.

Doctor Sorenson stepped over and probed Davey's eyes with a small light. "Let's check his vision now. Sometimes a blow to the head can cause blurred eyesight." The doctor adjusted the upper half of the gurney, raising him to a sitting position. He pointed at an eye chart hanging on the opposite wall. "All right Davey, can you read the letters on the chart over there?"

Davey read the letters slowly, line after line; he stopped at the smallest line. "I can't read the last one."

The doctor smiled. "That's okay, neither can I." His voice had a soothing, unhurried quality, and he turned towards Aunt Sally. "He seems fine. His eyesight is better than average, almost perfect in fact. Nobody can read the last line."

Aunt Sally was relieved at first, but confusion showed on her face a second later. "That can't be right. He doesn't have his glasses on. He can't see a thing without them. Here, look at his medical records," she said, thrusting her file into the doctor's hands.

By force of habit, Davey reached up to adjust his glasses. He was still in a stupor, far from alert. "Where *are* my glasses?" he asked.

"They were broken when the ball hit you," Aunt Sally replied.

Davey looked around the room, bewildered. "How very odd," he mumbled.

"What's odd?" Uncle Bill asked.

"I can see everything perfectly," Davey said, trying to get up.

"Just lie still and let the doctor read," Aunt Sally said, her anxiety growing.

The doctor studied the file for a few minutes, mumbling as he read. When he finished, he stared at Aunt Sally. "According to these records, he has chronic myopia with astigmatism in both eyes. There's no way he can read the chart without glasses."

"He just did – you saw him!" Aunt Sally exclaimed, her voice rising.

"All right Sally, calm down," Uncle Bill said quietly.

Doctor Sorenson sighed. "Yes, I saw him read the chart and can't explain it."

"Could his injury cause his vision to improve?" Aunt Sally asked.

The doctor shook his head. "No, it's medically impossible. Head injuries can cause vision to deteriorate, but not improve." He looked thoughtful for a few seconds. "We should probably do a brain scan, just as a precaution. I'll have one of the local eye specialists come in and check him too. Nothing seems to be wrong with him, but I've never heard of anything like this."

Uncle Bill went out to the reception area and told the others that Davey had regained consciousness. Everyone smiled in relief, especially Jimmy. He felt partially responsible because it was his idea for Davey to play in the game. "Are they letting him go home?" he asked.

Uncle Bill shook his head. "Not yet, they're running a few more tests, just to be sure about his vision."

"Is he having problems with his eyesight?" Sequoyah asked.

Uncle Bill gave them a confounded smile. "No, it's the opposite. Davey can see perfectly. As strange as it seems, he read the entire eye chart without his glasses."

Jimmy and the two men stared at Uncle Bill in stunned silence. Jimmy was the one who spoke first. "You mean he doesn't need glasses anymore?"

"It appears so," Uncle Bill replied.

"Praise be to the saints and all that's glory; it's a blooming miracle," bellowed Mr. McDonnell. Everyone laughed as he did a little jig around the room.

Jimmy pulled his father away from the others. "Dad, I need to tell you something," he whispered.

"All right son, what is it?"

Jimmy had become visibly excited. "I heard Davey wish for this exact thing several days ago. We were playing catch, and he wished he'd wake up one day and be able to see without his glasses. Those were his precise words."

"Lots of people wish for things – some do it all the time. Heck, I do it too."

"Dad, you're missing the point. First Davey climbs the Great Oak, something no one else can do. Then he wishes to see without his glasses and his wish comes true. Remember what the legends say. The tree will grant the wishes of those it favors. It's too much of a coincidence, Dad."

Sequoyah started to chuckle. "Son, despite what the legends say, I've never known anyone who can honestly say the tree has granted their wishes."

Jimmy wasn't convinced. "Remember all of the unbelievable things the tree did when Davey climbed it? If it can do those things, maybe it can grant wishes too. Yona has always said the tree could. Perhaps we should ask him."

Sequoyah nodded, acknowledging the point. Yona, now in his eighties, was the chief of their Cherokee tribe and the wisest man Sequoyah knew. He thought it over as Jimmy watched him. The more he thought about it, the more intrigued he became. "Has Davey wished for anything else? If he has, and those wishes have come true, it would be meaningful."

"I don't know Dad, but I'll find out."

"You learn what you can and then I'll talk to Yona. We'll see what he thinks."

❧ Chapter 16 ❧

―――――――

*Magick and miracles are much the same.
Only those with great vision truly
knoweth the difference. But heed ye my
words! Magick is performed by men.
Miracles come from a divine source.*

— Translated from Storia Di Incanto; circa 1725

The Three Of We

THREE DIFFERENT DOCTORS examined Davey during the course of the afternoon. They evaluated the brain scan, tested his eyes repeatedly, and ran a battery of other tests. Finally, they all sat down with Aunt Sally in a small conference room. Shaking their heads, the doctors seemed mystified. Davey had made medical history. There was no scientific explanation for his improved eyesight. Nor was there anything wrong with him, except for the stitched-up cut and the purplish bruise on his forehead.

By the time Saturday evening rolled around, Davey was home relaxing in bed. He wanted to get up, but Aunt Sally was adamant. The doctors had prescribed bed-rest for the next twelve hours and she was following their instructions to the letter. She brought Davey a big plate of food and sat on the bed watching him eat – glad his appetite was hearty. In fact, she had never seen him eat so much. *Somewhat odd, considering what he's been through,* she thought.

Davey noticed Aunt Sally watching him and smiled. "You don't need to keep staring at me. I'm fine…really. Look, my eyesight is still perfect. I can even make out the small numbers on that calendar across the room." He read the numbers aloud, thrilled by the simple act of seeing without his glasses.

Aunt Sally was amazed at how untroubled he seemed. She looked at the calendar on the wall and was astonished. She could barely read the numbers herself. "You gave us a scare, that's all. If anything ever happened to you, I'd never forgive myself," she said quietly. Those words made her think about her sister. *How will I ever explain this to Janie?*

At that moment, Uncle Bill called up from the bottom of the stairs. "Jimmy Surefoot is here to see Davey. Is it okay for him to come up?"

"Yes, he's finished eating now," she hollered back. Then she stood up and took the tray with Davey's empty dishes on it. "You stay in bed like the doctors said."

Jimmy appeared at the doorway a few minutes later, a broad grin on his face. "Bloody good bruise you've got there," he exclaimed.

"I know. I can't believe I let Spike nail me like that."

Jimmy sat down in the chair at Davey's desk. "Hey, he has some bruises of his own. I got in a few good licks before Mr. McDonnell broke up the fight."

"There was a fight?"

"A short one, but we gave Spike and Monkey a good thrashing."

"Thanks for sticking up for me."

"No worries mate, besides no one is bashing our star left fielder while we're around. By the way, you did a bloody good job in the game. You made me proud," Jimmy said, beaming.

"It was just luck," Davey muttered.

Jimmy picked up the chair and moved it alongside the bed. "Listen mate, there's something I have to ask. When we were playing catch a few days ago, you said something about wishing you could see without your glasses. You know what the legends say about the tree making wishes come true. Do you think it granted your wish?"

Davey gave Jimmy a meaningful glance. "I've been thinking about the Great Oak ever since I woke up in the emergency room."

Suddenly, Uncle Bill called up to Davey again. "Amy Pigeon is on her way up."

Davey heard footsteps on the stairs, and then a timid voice called to him from outside the doorway. "Davey, is it all right if I come in?"

"Sure, Jimmy is here too."

Amy stepped into the room, looking somewhat embarrassed to be there. "I heard what happened at the ball field. Are you okay?"

Davey was both happy and surprised to see her. *There's a girl, a really cute girl, who is worried about me,* he thought. "Yep, thanks for asking," he finally said.

Amy raised her forearm to her head, covering her eyes. "Thank heavens, seeing you like this, so terribly wounded, so vulnerable, why dear boy – I think I'm going to faint," she said dramatically, collapsing to the floor. Then she bounced up, grinning. "That was my *Scarlet O'Hara* imitation, pretty good huh?"

"Perfect, absolutely perfect," Davey said.

Amy put her hands on her hips and glared at him. "You know, I should be really mad at you. I let you out of my sight for one day and you wind up in the hospital."

"How did you hear about it?"

"Are you kidding…it's all over town. Of course, ace reporters like me hear everything first. Can you actually see without your glasses?"

Davey grinned. "Want me to read the calendar over there?"

Amy turned towards Jimmy, looking thoughtful. "You know, he's not nearly as ugly without his glasses."

Jimmy laughed loudly. "Hold on now, no point in exaggerating."

"All right, shut up you two," Davey said, smiling happily. Despite his bruised forehead, he felt terrific. He had proven himself on the baseball field, and now two friends, two really good friends, were at his house because they were worried about him.

Amy glanced around the room as if wondering where to sit. She thought it might seem presumptuous to sit on Davey's bed.

As though reading her thoughts, Davey patted the bed beside him. "Listen Amy, come and sit down. I was just about to tell Jimmy something important. I want you to hear it too."

Amy sat down alongside Davey, letting her fingers find his hand. "Are you sure you're okay? I really was worried," she whispered.

Jimmy cleared his throat noisily. "Maybe we should talk later. You two act like you need some privacy."

Amy pulled her hand away from Davey's with a soft laugh, but her eyes stared straight into his.

Davey smiled; then his face turned serious. "Be quiet Jimmy and listen. You two are my best friends and I need your help figuring something out. Weird things have been happening to me ever since I arrived in Great Oak. I want to tell you about them."

"What weird things?" Amy asked, a bit confused.

"Before I start, you have to promise this stays between us?"

Amy looked at Jimmy for a second. "He's gone daffy hasn't he?"

Jimmy nodded gravely. "Humor him – the doctors said we should pretend he's normal."

"Come on you guys, I'm being serious," Davey protested.

"All right mate, just funning with you. We promise, don't we Amy?"

"Of course," she replied, wondering what was on Davey's mind.

Davey started at the beginning and told them everything – well almost everything. He held back a few of the details for later. Although Jimmy had heard parts of it before, he listened patiently to the entire story without interrupting. Davey told them about the birds outside his window, the mysterious squirrel, his climbing of the Great Oak, what he had learned about his great grandparents, and his visit to Ed Nolen's house. He concluded with his wish about his glasses.

Amy and Jimmy were both silent when he finished. Finally, Amy spoke. "So…you think the Great Oak made your wish come true? I'm sorry, but that's ridiculous."

"Actually, I made three wishes. They all came true."

Jimmy grinned because this is exactly what he had wanted to learn. "I knew it. What were the other two?"

"I made the first wish when I was sitting in the tree. I wished Spike would leave me alone. The very next day, you told Spike to stop bothering me and he did what you said. Then I made the wish about my glasses – we know how that turned out. Finally, right before the game, I went by the tree and wished for luck. You've got to admit, I had one lucky break after another on the ball field today."

Amy looked at him with disbelief. "You must be kidding. Almost everything has a logical explanation. All of it could be some sort of odd coincidence. Oh sure, the stuff about the squirrel and the tree sounds pretty strange. But to conclude some kind of hocus-pocus is occurring – that's a bit much."

"Here's another detail I didn't mention," Davey replied. He told them about the squirrel making the circles disappear around its eyes. "How do you explain that?"

Jimmy shrugged. "I don't know; tell us what you think."

"I think the squirrel was telling me what was going to happen. It pointed at the tree to make sure I knew the tree was granting my wish."

"It's too incredible. I just can't believe it," Amy said firmly.

Expecting her reaction, Davey had saved the best item for last. He motioned towards his desk. "Jimmy, will you hand me the shoebox over there?"

Jimmy brought over the shoebox and Davey took out the letter containing Alicia's burial instructions. The mysterious message from Antonio on the reverse side was no longer visible. Davey handed the letter to Amy and asked her to read it.

Amy scanned the letter and passed it to Jimmy. "You think the part about the heir means you? Okay, so what does that prove?"

Jimmy read the letter and returned it to Davey. "I don't get the point, mate."

Davey turned the letter over and showed them the other side of the page. "Do either of you see anything written here?"

They both looked at him as if he had lost his mind, but shook their heads.

"Now, watch this," Davey said, running his fingers across the blank page and laying it on the bed. *Please Antonio, don't fail me now,* he thought.

For a few seconds, nothing happened. Then the letter repeated its performance of several nights ago, emitting sparks, whistles, pops, belches, and flying about the room. Jimmy laughed uproariously, but Amy turned pale and looked as though she might faint. When the letter floated back down to the bed, Davey let them read Antonio's mysterious message.

Amy stared at the message in stunned silence. A disturbing thought had suddenly occurred to her. *What if I like Davey because of the tree?* She looked at Davey, her eyes troubled. "Just tell me one thing. Did you make a wish about me?"

Davey held up his hand as if taking an oath. "No, I absolutely did not. I didn't wish for either of you guys to be my friends for that matter."

"Hey, I'm glad we're friends – even if the tree did it," Jimmy replied.

Amy smiled faintly. "Okay, I'm convinced; something very strange is happening. What's this triangle that the message mentions?"

Davey took off his pajama shirt and showed them the necklace, which he was wearing. "The squirrel gave this to me when I climbed the Great Oak; I think it was my great grandfather's. The pendant vibrates whenever something important is about to happen, and these symbols say: *The power rules all things.*"

"The power rules all things…what does that mean?" Amy asked.

"I have absolutely no idea," Davey replied.

"This is scary. Look, I've got goose bumps," Amy said, holding out her arms.

"It's bloody awesome," Jimmy exclaimed, "science-fiction stuff."

Davey nodded in agreement. "I feel as if I'm in the middle of a bizarre mystery, one revolving around my great grandfather. The message tells me to learn and do things, but I don't know what. The tree is granting my wishes, but I don't know why. I'm really clueless."

Amy finally understood. "You want our help, don't you? That's why you told us about everything."

Davey managed a smile. "Three heads are better than one; I don't think I can figure it out by myself. But remember, it has to stay among us."

"It's the adventure of a lifetime – count me in," Jimmy said.

"Well, I can't let you boys go off on your own. You'll just get into trouble," Amy said, a tremor of excitement in her voice.

Jimmy grinned with delight. "We're forming a team, a secret pact."

"All for one and one for all; we can call ourselves The Three Musketeers," Amy replied, getting into the spirit.

Jimmy shook his head. "It's been done, little miss. What about The Brave Threesome? I like the sound of that better."

Davey had a sudden inspiration. "No, that's too complicated. Hey, I've got it. Let's call ourselves The Three of We."

"It's sort of poetic. I like it," Amy agreed.

They looked at each other and laughed. Davey extended his hand and the others put their hands on his. "To the Three of We!" Davey exclaimed. They all smiled, blissfully unaware of the dark challenges that lay ahead.

☙ Chapter 17 ❧

Hearken, oh ye magician, the future is hard to discern. Be not dismayed by the uncertainty of events. Fate shall reveal all in time.

— Translated from Storia Di Incanto; circa 1736

An Uncertain Future

LINDA PEABODY FELT as if she was on a treadmill, going nowhere fast. Over the last eight months, her life had become one disaster after another. Her fiancée had rejected her, she was a failure as a teacher, and most of her students hated her. *Why doesn't something good happen to me?* she wondered. The subject was so depressing that she crammed her time full of busywork, leaving no room for thoughts about her future – or lack thereof.

So on Saturday night, she readily agreed to help Aunt Gilda plant winter pansies in the flowerbeds the next morning. Although it meant rising before dawn, she had a hard time sleeping and her mind was especially vulnerable to sad thoughts while she was lying awake. Still, she was curious. "Why are we getting up so early," she asked.

As expected, Aunt Gilda's reasons were eccentric. "Planting at dawn is best for the flowers, dear. You see, they are barely awake then and less disturbed by the move from pot to soil. Besides, it will give you a chance to see the sun rise on Charlesville, a thrilling event all by itself."

Linda had quickly learned Aunt Gilda was an expert storyteller, a talent she had developed into a form of art. Three types of stories were in Aunt Gilda's repertoire, morsels, entrées, and desserts. According to her, a morsel was a mildly amusing bit of gossip, an entrée was a good long story with real substance in it, and a dessert was a short delightful tale. Before beginning any story, Aunt Gilda would gaily inform her listeners of the type of story she wanted to tell and then wait for encouragement. Linda was one of her better audiences – she always provided the proper enthusiasm.

Charlesville was the name of Aunt Gilda's rambling old house, and the story about it embodied the softhearted wackiness of her personality. Charles, Aunt Gilda's late husband, was a native of Charleston, South Carolina, a city filled with old southern charm. The old house in Great Oak reminded Aunt Gilda so much of the antebellum houses of Charleston that she and Charles had purchased it, even though it was more than a hundred years old at the time. That had been thirty-five years ago, and they had spent a small fortune restoring the house to its former days of glory. Unfortunately, old houses require continuous repair and Aunt Gilda's advancing age prevented her from maintaining it properly. As a result, the house was in a rather decrepit state when Linda arrived in Great Oak.

Charles had died ten years earlier, and Aunt Gilda was convinced his spirit still lived in the old house with her. Therefore, she named the house after him to make him feel welcome during his haunting days. To Aunt Gilda, it was a clever play-on-words, similar to Charleston yet different because the name was Charlesville – the place where Charles lived on instead of where he was born. Whenever she was returning home from visiting friends, she would announce she was going to Charlesville. This made her recall fond memories of her beloved husband and the spirit waiting for her there.

Linda had heard the story several times and each time she marveled at how sweetly dedicated Aunt Gilda was to the memory of her late husband. *That's what true love is about*, she angrily told herself. *It's not an opera-singing clown like Michael, who jilted me instead of being my soul mate for life.*

Getting angry over her misfortunes relieved Linda's depression sometimes, and Aunt Gilda's stories made her want to taste the joy of life again. With that in mind, Linda crawled out of bed on Sunday morning, dressed hurriedly, and rushed outside where the pansies were waiting. She hoped the activity, combined with Aunt Gilda's storytelling, would make her feel better.

Aunt Gilda was already there in the flowerbeds, digging holes in the soil with a small trowel and looking very spry for her advanced age. "You look tired, dear," she said, after glancing up when Linda appeared.

Linda sighed wearily, "I hardly slept at all last night. I kept hearing these strange thumping noises, as though someone was climbing up and down the stairs in heavy boots. I should have gotten up and looked around, but you know what a big chicken I am. If anyone was there, I would have died of fright."

"I'm sorry, dear. It was just Charles roaming around. He always acts up this time of year. His rheumatism is bothering him, and he doesn't realize how noisy his comings and goings are. I'll pour him a glass of brandy tonight. It usually settles him down."

Linda smiled, but didn't say anything as she turned her attention towards the pansies. Aunt Gilda was such a character. While Linda didn't believe Charles was haunting the old house, Aunt Gilda's way of attributing so many happenings to him was a constant source of amusement. She knew the stories would begin at any minute, which was fine with her.

"Of course, there's a possibility it might have been Henry. He makes noises like that sometimes, but usually in the spring. The rest of the time he sleeps," Aunt Gilda said, thinking aloud.

Linda's ears perked up. "You haven't mentioned Henry before."

Aunt Gilda stopped her digging for a moment. "You mean I haven't told you about Henry? He was the owner of the house before we bought it and one of our friends. Poor Henry, he fell down the stairs and broke his neck. That's an entrée of a story."

Linda smiled, ready for the tale. "Oh, do tell it, please!"

"Well all right, just give me a moment to collect my thoughts."

As typical of her approach to working in the garden, Aunt Gilda was dressed entirely in green clothing. She had even painted her fingernails and toenails with green polish and put on an emerald necklace with matching earrings. On top of her head was a green baseball cap; green canvass shoes covered her feet.

Aunt Gilda glanced over at Linda, who was carefully easing the pansies out of their pots and placing them into the earth. "Oh no, dear, I should have told you before. You're dressed all wrong and frightening the little plants. I can practically hear them screaming with anxiety. They are very sensitive and a little unsettled because of the planting, you know. The color green puts them at ease. It makes them feel as if you are a friend. Please, go inside and put on something green."

Mumbling under her breath, Linda trudged back into her room. She rummaged through her closet until she found an old pair of green jeans and a green sweatshirt. After changing her clothes, she looked at herself in the mirror. *I look awful,* she thought.

For one thing, the sweatshirt was a brighter shade of green than the jeans, which made them clash alarmingly. But in Linda's opinion, the main problem was the haggard look on her face. Aunt Gilda was right – the image staring back at her did look tired, not to mention thin, stressed-out, and generally unhappy. Her lack of sleep and poor appetite were taking their toll. Her clothes hung loosely, rather than fitting snugly as they once had, and her usually bouncy hair drooped around her face in stringy loops.

"Come on Linda, where's the old spark?" she asked the mirror, hoping for the smile that had once come easily. All she saw was a weak grin. "You are pathetic," she told her reflection and stomped out of the room.

"A definite improvement," Aunt Gilda announced after Linda reappeared in her green planting clothes.

"I guess," Linda muttered gloomily.

"Linda, what is it? I know something is bothering you. Why don't you tell me about it? It's good for the plants, you know, hearing about the troubles we humans have. They learn to appreciate their simple life – and they are not gossips. The little darlings can really keep a secret."

The last thing Linda wanted to do was talk about her problems. "I'd rather hear the story about Henry falling down the stairs. You were just starting it."

Aunt Gilda gave Linda a coy smile. "First, tell me what's bothering you, and then I'll tell you about Henry."

Linda shook her head in frustration. "I'm just worried, that's all. As if my own misery is not enough, one of my favorite students was hurt yesterday at the baseball field. He's a really nice kid, but kind of naïve and vulnerable. Some mean boys in his class are picking on him. I think they injured him on purpose."

Aunt Gilda's hand covered her mouth, her fingers trembling. "My goodness, what happened?"

"A baseball hit him in the head. I saw Timothy McDonnell in the grocery store yesterday and he told me about it."

"Is the boy all right?"

"I don't know. I guess so – at least for now," Linda said, sighing.

"Well, why don't you find out? Does he live around here?"

"Actually, he does, right down the street. Still, I don't want to intrude."

Aunt Gilda put down her digging trowel and stared at Linda in exasperation. "Linda, you know I love and admire you, but you're just too passive for your own good. You may think I'm a meddlesome old woman – and maybe I am. But getting through life and being happy requires initiative. You can't sit around moping and waiting for an invitation. Go out and get involved."

"Oh Aunt Gilda—" Linda protested, not liking the direction of the conversation at all.

"Wait Linda, I'm not finished," Aunt Gilda interrupted. "I know your fiancée let you down. For goodness sake, get over it! There are lots of fish in the sea. Go out; make new friends – recreate the happiness you once had. Great Oak can provide you with wonderful experiences, if you let it. A beautiful girl like you should be out with a man, not hanging around a worn-out, old biddy like me. Seek him out dear. He may be just around the corner."

"I *like* being here with you. Besides, you're not a worn-out, old biddy," Linda replied meekly.

"Of course I am dear, but that's not the point. You are letting the events in your life control you instead of taking charge of them. All you have to do is reverse the process."

"I suppose so, but I don't know where to start," Linda said, suddenly feeling as miserable as a dog left out in the rain.

Aunt Gilda slowly eased her body into a standing position. "Come on dear, let me help you. These little pansies will wait for a while. They are very patient, you know. Let's go into the house and discuss this over a nice big breakfast."

Linda shook her head. "I'm not very hungry."

"Hush up and listen to an old biddy. You are not eating enough, so I'm stuffing some food down you whether you like it or not. Next, I'm going to pour you a little glass of the special brandy I keep for Charles. I want you to sip it while taking a long, hot bath. It will make you feel nice and sleepy. Then go back to bed and get some rest. After you wake up, put on some pretty clothes and take a stroll around the neighborhood. Stop by the house of your injured student and ask how he is doing. You'll be surprised by how much better you feel when you return."

Linda nodded in resignation. Her life was in ruins and now she was getting advice from her wacky old aunt. Before long, even Charles would be telling her what to do. However, Aunt Gilda was right; she had to get her life going again. "Okay…I'll do it," she said, managing a smile. And for some reason, the simple decision made her feel better all by itself.

Later that morning, Sequoyah and Yona sat in the mountains overlooking Great Oak. They sat in chairs crafted by Yona from saplings many years ago. In fact, Sequoyah remembered sitting in the same chairs when he was a boy, listening to Yona speak as he was now. He found the memory comforting, a rare continuity in an ever-changing world.

The two men sat under the spreading boughs of an ancient cedar tree, which grew along the edge of a small plateau. A short distance away, the mountain fell off sharply and tapered towards the valley a thousand feet below. A squat log cabin, Yona's home for as long as Sequoyah could remember, stood nearby. Thin wisps of white smoke trailed lazily out of the stone chimney. The pleasant smell of a slowly simmering venison stew floated in the breeze.

Sequoyah sipped herb tea, Yona's favorite concoction. He waited politely for Yona to ask the reason for his visit, which he eventually would. At the moment, they were chatting about nothing in particular. Such was the unhurried way of the Cherokee. Manners were important in their life.

Yona's slow but strong voice rang out in the mountain air. "I would like to see the Vietnam War Memorial in the great Capitol so I can read my son's name on the wall. Will you take me there?"

"Of course Grandfather, whenever you wish."

"We must go there soon. I have seen a horned owl perched in the tree outside my window. It is a very old owl, old like me. The owl comes and goes, yet its purpose is clear. My time on this earth is nearly over. The owl is telling me to do what must be done before I journey to the spirit world. When the owl comes and stays, my time here will end. This is why we must go soon."

Sequoyah studied his grandfather. Over the last few years, his movements had become noticeably slower. Even so, he was remarkably healthy for an eighty-year-old man. "Perhaps the owl will not come back for a while, Grandfather. Still, I will accompany you on this trip. We will see my father's name on the wall together."

The old man smiled sadly. "You are a good grandson, Sequoyah. I should have had more patience with you. After you married the white woman, my heart wept for many moons and I took away your Cherokee birthright out of spite. This was wrong of me. I should have rejoiced at your happiness instead. Your wife is a good woman; I must atone for my behavior. I have spoken with the elders and they have agreed. If she will permit, I will hold a ceremony and make her an honorary Cherokee. Then the Council of Elders will offer you the seat of One Eyed Doya, who is now with the spirits."

Sequoyah was practically speechless. He had never heard Yona admit a mistake. In fact, he didn't think Yona made mistakes. He hastily put his thoughts aside and replied. "She will be as pleased...I am pleased as well, Grandfather."

Yona smiled, and his smile warmed Sequoyah's heart. "Good, now tell me why you have visited your old grandfather."

"I came to tell you about a boy who has arrived in Great Oak. Forgive me for speaking of a painful memory, but he is the great grandson of Tsusga Gineli. Jimmy met him the first day he was here – sitting in the Great Oak."

Yona drew in a sharp breath as his eyes took on a far away look. *Perhaps the owl was warning me about something else,* he thought, sitting in silence for a few minutes. When he finally spoke, his words seemed nothing more than random mutterings. "Can he be...Tsusga Gineli...does it begin?"

Sequoyah was instantly alarmed. He had never seen Yona act in such a manner. "Grandfather, are you all right?"

Yona waved a shaking hand and regained his composure. "Tell me about this boy. You say he climbed the Great Oak. What else has he done?"

"His name is Davey Boehm, and he has moved here from New York. He is small and scholarly, unlike Jimmy's other friends. Jimmy brought him to the shop, and the two boys spoke with me about the Great Oak. I told them the old legends about The Little People and the Spirit. In turn, the boy recited a fanciful story about a squirrel leading him to the tree and helping him climb it. He said seven ravens flew overhead in the formation of a triangle. He asked if the ravens and the squirrel could be little people."

A slow smile spread across Yona's face. "The Little People disguising themselves as squirrels and ravens? It sounds like something Tsusga Gineli would do. What else has happened, Sequoyah? Your eyes tell me there is more."

Sequoyah sighed, hoping Yona wouldn't laugh at his foolishness. "The tree may have granted three wishes for the boy. The only one I know about is quite significant. The boy had poor vision and wore thick eyeglasses. He wished to see without his glasses, and now his vision is perfect. Jimmy has taken a vow of silence and wouldn't tell me what the other two wishes were."

"Tell me about this vow of silence," Yona replied.

"Davey has asked Jimmy and another friend, Amy Pigeon, to join him in a secret pact. They think they're on some kind of a mysterious adventure."

Yona was momentarily stunned. His mind recalled a brief portion of the prophetic message delivered so many years ago by Tsusga Gineli. *He is my heir, joined by two. Young and powerful are these few.* Yona had recited the prophecy a thousand times in his head, yet its cleverness always amazed him. "How did this wish concerning the boy's eyesight come true?" Yona asked.

"He was hit in the head by a pitched baseball and knocked unconscious. When he woke up, his eyesight was perfect."

"What is the name of the boy who threw the baseball?"

His grandfather's question perplexed Sequoyah, but he provided the answer. "It was Wally Houseman's son, Spike."

Yona grew silent again and gazed across the valley at the rugged cliffs of Brown Mountain. Sequoyah waited, in keeping with Cherokee custom. Slowly, Yona pushed himself up from his chair and walked towards the edge of the plateau, studying the mountain. A few seconds later, Sequoyah followed, knowing it was what Yona intended. The old man turned to face him as he approached. "The forces are aligning."

"What forces, Grandfather?" Sequoyah asked softly.

Yona ignored his question. "What does the boy know about Tsusga Gineli?"

"Not much, for some reason his parents haven't told him about his great grandfather. When I mentioned his name, the boy didn't even know who he was."

Strength flowed into the old man. In his eyes, the keen fierceness of an eagle appeared and his posture grew erect, his back ramrod straight. He spoke not as Sequoyah's grandfather, but as Chief Yona, leader of the Cherokee. "Listen closely Sequoyah; bring the boy to me. There is danger in this thing – much harm can happen. We must move quickly before it is too late."

Sequoyah's face narrowed in concern. Yona acted as if he was preparing for a war council, his instructions sharp and decisive. Sequoyah knew questions were a waste of time as no answers would be forthcoming. He must wait until Yona met with Davey. Then he would learn why his grandfather had suddenly become so excited.

os Chapter 18 so

_Only the foolhardy attempt to alter the
natural flow of events. Be ye forewarned,
magician. Thou shalt not trifle with fate!_

— Translated from Storia Di Incanto; circa 1749

The Test Of The Tree

ON SUNDAY AFTERNOON, the Three of We gathered on Davey's
front porch. Aunt Sally had allowed Davey out of his room, but said
he couldn't leave the house. Amy and Jimmy didn't seem to mind.
They were content just sitting around and discussing what Davey had
told them last night.

As typical of older Great Oak homes, the porch where they sat was
three feet above the ground. It stretched along the front of the two-
story house, a grey slate roof overhead. Graceful, white columns
supported the roof, connected to each other by a white railing.

Jimmy lounged in a wicker chair, his feet propped on the railing.
He was throwing a tennis ball into the front lawn where Bristol and
Bupkiss waited with excitement. If he didn't throw the ball quick
enough, they both barked. A few feet away, Amy and Davey sat in a
wide swing, slowly rocking back and forth. To the casual observer, it
was a tranquil scene – one of youthful innocence.

"Got any ideas about what we should do next?" Jimmy asked.

Davey turned towards Jimmy, still marveling at how well he could
see without his glasses. "I've been thinking; we need to learn more

about The Great Sabatini. Your dad's grandfather, Yona, may be the only person who can tell us anything. Somehow, we must convince him to talk with us."

Jimmy shook his head. "Probably ain't going to happen, mate. I'll try, but I think it's a lost cause."

Amy chimed in with another idea. "There's something I've been puzzling over. How did Alicia manage to write her burial instructions on the same sheet of paper where Antonio's message was?"

"What do you mean?" Davey asked.

"Well, think about it. Alicia wrote her burial instructions shortly before she died. Antonio had disappeared many years earlier, leaving the sheet with his message behind. Therefore, she must have kept the sheet around all those years, knowing she had to use it in a way that would cause you to find it. Could a supposedly crazy person do that?"

"That's a good point," Davey replied.

Amy's excitement increased as she continued. "Maybe Alicia knew what happened to him. Maybe she was the witness the reporter was going to meet. If she was, and she wasn't crazy like your aunt thinks, maybe she confided in someone else."

Davey thought about it for a moment. "According to Aunt Sally, Joe Harrison, the park warden, knew Alicia well. He could be a good person to ask. Do either of you know him?"

"I do," Amy replied. "He's friendly with my parents and comes to our house sometimes."

Jimmy nodded. "Okay, I'll try to arrange a meeting with Yona, and you two go see Joe Harrison."

"I have another suggestion," Amy said. "While we assume the Great Oak has been granting Davey's wishes, we can't be completely sure. I think Davey should make another wish as a test. Only this time, let's make the wish about someone else."

Jimmy started to laugh. "What a bloody great idea – he can wish for Spike's nose to fall off."

Davey shook his head. "I don't want to harm anyone, even if it's a rat like Spike."

"What I had in mind was helping someone," Amy said. "That would be in keeping with the legend of the tree."

"And who is this deserving person?" Jimmy asked.

Amy stuck her tongue out at Jimmy and then grinned. "Not you, hotshot."

Davey jumped out of the swing with an exclamation. "I know who she has in mind – Miss Peabody!"

Amy smiled. "Yes, she's such a nice person and tries so hard, yet she's miserable. Her students give her a hard time and Spike constantly does nasty things to her. She deserves a break."

"You think he should wish for her to get a break?" Jimmy scoffed.

Amy glared at him. "Well, why not?"

"Come on you guys, let's not argue. We're in this together," Davey said.

"Aw, just having a little fun; didn't mean nothing," Jimmy replied.

"All right, I'll keep it simple. I'll wish for the tree to do something, which will make her happy."

The Three of We nodded, smiling at their little conspiracy. They didn't know what would happen, but they didn't see how any harm could come of it. Davey put both hands over his necklace, closed his eyes, and pictured the Great Oak in his mind. "Miss Peabody is my friend and a good person. She is deserving of your help. I wish for her to find happiness."

A strange silence fell over the porch. Suddenly, an eerie wind blew through the trees, even though the air had previously been still. Davey thought he heard the melodic rustling of the Great Oak's leaves, yet the tree was a mile away. Moreover, he imagined a whisper in the melody, a long drawn-out sigh that sounded like the word *yes*. Then his necklace began to vibrate. Even the dogs seemed to sense something unusual had occurred. They abruptly stopped chasing the ball and looked up at Davey.

After a few minutes, Jimmy broke the silence. "Can you tell if it's working?"

"I don't know…maybe…the necklace is vibrating," Davey replied.

"This is freaking me out," Amy said in a hushed voice.

"So what do we do now?" Jimmy asked.

Davey sat down in the swing again. "We wait to see what happens."

"Let's go for a bike ride," Amy suggested. "I'm getting anxious just sitting here."

"You guys can, but Aunt Sally won't let me. She said I couldn't do anything strenuous until the doctor sees me again."

"I hope we didn't harm Miss Peabody in any way," Amy said with a sigh.

Davey frowned, not liking the thought. "We're just trying to help her. Don't get cold feet on us now."

"Actually, It was a bloody good idea," Jimmy offered. "I'm just wondering how we'll know if it works?"

"I have this feeling we'll find out soon enough," Davey said.

Amy slouched down beside Davey. "I hope so – the suspense is killing me."

Bupkiss brought the ball to Jimmy and stood looking at him, chomping on it in his mouth. Jimmy pretended not to notice. When the dog realized Jimmy wasn't going to wrestle the ball away, he dropped it in his lap. Jimmy picked the ball up and threw it to Amy. "Play catch with the dogs for awhile. It'll give you something to do."

Gooey dog-saliva covered the ball and flecks of moisture sprayed over Amy when she caught it. "Gross," she said, glaring at Jimmy.

Bristol climbed onto the porch, circled around a few times, and lay down. He was tired of chasing the ball. Bupkiss, still full of energy, ran down to a spot below the railing and barked a few times, urging Amy to throw it. She responded by tossing the ball over his head; it skidded crookedly into a clump of bushes near the street. Bupkiss tore into the bushes after it, then stopped abruptly, woofed a few times, and stared intently at a figure coming towards him.

"Someone is coming," Jimmy said, standing up.

"Grab Bupkiss or he'll run out there," Davey replied.

"Bloody heck, it's Miss Peabody!" Jimmy whispered.

Amy jerked upright and halted the rocking of the swing. "I'm getting goose bumps," she said.

"Stay calm," Davey ordered. "Jimmy, please get Bupkiss before he makes a pest of himself."

Jimmy ran after Bupkiss, but he wasn't fast enough. When Linda approached the front walkway, the dog circled around her, wagging his tail, jumping up, and yelping excitedly. However, Linda surprised everyone by quickly taking hold of the dog's collar and forcing him into a sitting position. Then she knelt down and spoke to him with a soothing voice. Bupkiss responded by licking her face, causing her to laugh gleefully. Bristol, feeling left out, bounded down from the porch and joined the fun by licking her ears.

Davey and Amy ran down from the porch as well. Meanwhile, Jimmy pulled Bristol back and watched while Linda calmed Bupkiss by rubbing his ears and scratching his chest. Bupkiss rolled over with a contented sigh and put one paw on her leg.

"I didn't know you had two dogs," Linda said, looking up at Davey.

Davey smiled. "The one you're petting is Bupkiss. He's an orphan that we found in the woods. We're looking after him until he finds a home. The other one is Bristol – he's my dog."

Linda was suddenly glad she had taken Aunt Gilda's advice. Petting Bristol reminded her of how much she liked animals, and she was happy to see Davey up and about. "I just came by to find out if you're okay. When I heard about what happened yesterday, I was worried."

"He was knocked out cold," Jimmy said.

"His glasses were broken, but he can see without them now," Amy added.

Linda stared at Davey in astonishment. "I thought there was something different about you...so you don't need glasses anymore?"

Davey frowned at Amy and Jimmy, which meant for them to stop talking about his glasses. "My eyesight has been getting better and the doctor said I could see fine without them."

"That's wonderful," Linda said. She turned towards the dog beside her and cupped his face in her hands. "You're just a big baby aren't you?"

Bupkiss responded by licking her face again.

"Hey, you have a way with dogs," Davey said. An idea suddenly formed in his mind. He was going to play a role in making his wish happen.

A wistful smile crossed Linda's face. "I love dogs. I had a German Shepard just like him. His name was Zapata; we practically grew up together."

"You don't have him anymore?" Jimmy asked.

Sadness appeared in Linda's eyes. "No, he died a year ago when I was away at college. I miss him so much."

"You could adopt Bupkiss," Davey suggested. "He's a really neat dog and he likes you. You could be his new owner."

Jimmy and Amy exchanged glances, surprised at how the wish was working out. Davey's role in it was also a surprise.

Linda sat quietly for a few seconds, mulling over Davey's suggestion. With a smile, she remembered what Aunt Gilda had said about taking control of her life. *Maybe adopting Bupkiss is a way to start*, she thought. "Why, it's a wonderful idea," she blurted out. "Aunt Gilda has to agree because I live in her house, but she likes dogs. Bupkiss could keep her company while I'm away at school."

"Why don't you phone her? If she agrees, you could take him home today," Davey said.

Linda laughed. "This is so unexpected. I came by to see you, and now I have a new dog. I feel like a kid at Christmas."

Davey showed Linda into the house and hurried back to where Amy and Jimmy were waiting. "Blimey, I can't believe it," Jimmy said.

"Did you see the look on her face?" Davey beamed. "She's totally happy."

"Stop it you two," Amy scolded. "You're grinning like idiots. I'll die if she ever finds out what we've done."

Just then, Linda came out of the house, a big smile on her face. "Aunt Gilda said yes! Bupkiss, looks like you've got a new home." Bupkiss let out a little bark, aware of the excitement, but unsure of the reason for it.

Davey was both pleased and sad. Although he had only looked after Bupkiss for a short time, he had become fond of the dog. He knew Linda would give him a good home, but he wanted to make sure they were compatible. Besides, his necklace was vibrating again. He felt as if something else was going to happen.

"I've got an idea. Let's take the dogs for a walk. We can go down to the park and then circle back towards your house," Davey said.

They all agreed, and Davey went into the house to ask permission and fetch leashes for the dogs. Then they formed a little parade as they marched towards the park. Linda, Davey, and the dogs were in the middle, Amy and Jimmy on the sides. Everyone seemed to be having a good time, including the dogs. It was clear Bupkiss was smitten with Linda. For the most part, she kept him under control, even though he was constantly chasing after leaves or anything else that moved.

"I think he needs a little training," Linda said with a laugh.

"He's just excited, mainly because you're the one who's walking him. I think he really likes you," Davey replied, still sensing that something else was about to happen.

"Oh, I hope so," Linda said, laughing gaily as Bupkiss pulled her forward.

As they passed along the front of Ed Nolen's house, their peaceful parade suddenly fell into disarray. Linda and Bupkiss were out in front, and she was slightly off balance, hurrying to keep up with the dog. Abruptly, a squirrel leaped down from a nearby tree and dashed across the street in front of them. Bupkiss immediately lost all sense of mannerly behavior and took off, furiously scampering after the squirrel. With a peal of laughter, Linda followed along, unable to slow the charging dog.

"Come on. It's happening," Davey muttered excitedly.

"What do you mean?" Amy asked.

"It's the tree again," Davey whispered.

"How do you know?" Jimmy asked.

"Just come on," Davey shouted, beginning to run.

The squirrel headed straight up the driveway of Ed Nolen's house. Bupkiss followed, pulling Linda helplessly along. The Three of We came last; each wondered what was going to happen. Bristol ran too, not particularly interested in the squirrel, but watching the fun.

Ed Nolen was walking along his driveway when the strange assortment of animals and humans descended upon him. His back was turned, but he heard the racket they were making. He spun around just as the squirrel reached him. The little animal darted around his legs, Bupkiss hot on its heels.

Linda, holding onto the dog's leash, plowed directly into Ed. In turn, he wrapped his arms around her and tried to keep from falling. Meanwhile, the squirrel circled around them, staying a foot ahead of the dog. Bupkiss scrambled after it, entwining the two adults in the leash as he chased the squirrel. After circling Ed a couple of times, the squirrel headed towards the nearest tree. Bupkiss made a final lunge as it scooted by him, but only succeeded in toppling Linda and Ed onto the ground.

"Oh…oh…oh…dear me!" Linda cried as she fell on top of Ed.

Bupkiss was unable to pursue the squirrel further because he was now constrained by the leash around Ed and Linda. So he gave up and lay down, draping the upper half of his body over Linda. Bristol arrived a few seconds later and started licking her face.

For a moment, the only thing Davey, Amy, and Jimmy could do was look at each other in open-mouthed astonishment. Finally, they broke into laughter, staring at the two adults and Bupkiss, who was practically lying on top of Linda.

"Well, so nice of you to drop by," Ed said, a grin spreading across his face. Apparently, finding a pretty woman wrapped in his arms wasn't the least bit displeasing.

Linda hid her face in Ed's shoulder, trying not to laugh. "I am so embarrassed," was all she could say. Her remark only made the Three of We laugh harder. Ed started laughing too, and Bupkiss let out a few shrill barks as though proud of himself.

Linda felt her face turning red. "Children…please stop laughing and untangle us."

Davey pulled Bristol away, and Jimmy held Bupkiss while Amy unwound the leash. After they were untangled, Ed and Linda slowly stood up and brushed themselves off.

"I am so terribly sorry," Linda said, getting a good look at Ed's face for the first time. Of course, this made her blush even more because she found him very attractive.

Ed laughed heartily. "Don't be sorry. Nothing this exciting has happened to me in a long time. By the way, my name's Ed Nolen."

Linda shook his hand shyly. "I'm the awfully embarrassed Linda Peabody. Trust me – I don't usually make such a flamboyant entrance."

Davey volunteered more information. "Mr. Nolen is a foreign war correspondent. He's rebuilding the house where my great grandparents lived…and Miss Peabody is my English teacher; we were taking the dogs for a walk." Then Amy jabbed him with her elbow. "Oh, and these are my friends, Amy and Jimmy," he hastily added.

Ed bowed graciously, his eyes friendly. "Welcome to my home, one and all."

Linda found herself smiling. "So…what's a war correspondent doing in Great Oak?" she asked, suddenly interested in learning more about Ed.

"Recovering – my war reporting days are over," he replied.

"He was shot three times in Afghanistan," Davey stated.

"How terrible. Why does someone get into such a dangerous profession?" Linda asked. She was curious, but also wanted to keep the conversation going.

"It happened by accident, or stupidity, depending on your perspective. I started working for the *New York Times* as an assistant editor on the foreign affairs desk. Things were fine until one of our reporters in France died in an automobile accident. They sent me over to take his place because I'm fluent in several languages. Then the Bosnian War broke out, which is where the stupid part begins. I volunteered for an assignment in Serbia. I was there for almost five years and didn't get a scratch. From there, I went to Afghanistan. Within three months, I was nearly dead."

"I could never be where there's fighting. I can't even watch war movies on television," Linda said.

Ed gave her a grim look. "I don't watch war movies anymore either. There are too many painful memories."

"I suppose being a war correspondent doesn't leave much time for marriage and children," Linda said. As soon as the words were out of her mouth, she regretted them. *You're such an obvious fool,* she thought.

A faraway look crept into Ed's eyes. For some reason he felt a sudden need to tell Linda about his past. "I met a photographer in Serbia, a French woman named Chandra. We were together throughout the war and got married when we returned to France. Then we went to Afghanistan, young, foolish, and thinking we'd live forever. She was killed when out caravan was attacked."

Linda's heart went out to Ed. "I'm so sorry. You must have been devastated."

"Yes, I was. The doctors operated on me three times, but I couldn't seem to get well. Then one night, I had a dream about Chandra. We were back in our old apartment in Paris and she was on her knees beside the bed, praying for me. The doctors were astonished when they examined me in the morning. My wounds were healing and I was finally out of danger. Sounds kind of crazy, doesn't it?"

The story made Linda want to cry. "No, it doesn't sound crazy at all. It sounds wonderfully romantic. A tribute to the love you felt for each other."

"Mr. Nolen is writing a book about it," Davey said, knowing the rest of his wish was now being fulfilled.

Ed grinned sheepishly. "My book isn't going very well. It's a lot more difficult than writing newspaper articles."

Amy was watching this exchange with growing excitement. "Maybe Miss Peabody could help. She's the best English teacher in the whole world."

Ed's face lit up. "Well, maybe she could. That is, if her boyfriend wouldn't get jealous of her spending time with such a handsome author."

Linda offered a bemused smile. "I'd be happy to try. As for the boyfriend part, I'm in the same situation as you. I was engaged, but it didn't work out. It didn't end tragically like your marriage did, despite how I felt at the time. To be honest, he left me standing at the altar."

Amy's mouth flew open. *So that's why she's been so sad*, she thought.

Ed smiled. "He must be a fool."

"That would be my opinion," Linda replied, suddenly feeling a bit lightheaded.

Ed studied her for a few seconds. "Listen, I just finished remodeling my kitchen and I'm dying to cook something. Would you consider coming over for dinner tonight? I could tell you my ideas about the book and bore you with war stories."

Linda felt the old familiar smile forming on her face – the one she thought she had lost forever. "I'd like that."

Ed gently took Linda's hand. "Come on, I'll give you a brief tour of the house. You kids can come along if you wish."

"You go ahead. We'll stay here with the dogs," Davey said. He could see what was happening and wanted Linda and Ed to spend some time alone.

As soon as they disappeared into the house, Amy spoke up. "They're so perfect for each other, it's scary."

"Bloody amazing – you think it was the tree?" Jimmy asked.

Davey nodded. "Incredible, isn't it? Think of the series of events that just occurred. Each one played a part in bringing them together."

Amy was full of doubts. "How can you be positive it was the tree? I can't believe anything could make all of this happen."

A big grin flashed across Davey's face. "Remember the squirrel, which ran in front of Bupkiss? The same squirrel gave me the necklace."

C3 Chapter 19 ଓ

Fear ye well the forces of conceit and malice. They dwell in darkness, seeking to make puppets from corrupt hearts!

— Translated from Storia Di Incanto; circa 1758

Like Father, Like Son

LATER THAT AFTERNOON, Wally Houseman stood at the windows of his study. He was watching the sun fill the sky with brilliant layers of orange and red as it slipped behind the jagged ridges of Brown Mountain. Sunset was his favorite time of day, a symbolic supplication of light to darkness. Soon, night would fall over his castle, and the forces attuned to him would come alive.

During the night, the mysterious lights would appear over Brown Mountain. They had become increasingly active recently. The locals had seen the lights for centuries, and no one knew what caused them. They told stories about ghosts flying above the mountain or alien spacecraft landings, but Wally only laughed at such tales. He knew the source of the lights and his knowledge thrilled his black heart.

Wally's study was located in one of the towers of Houseman's Castle. The room had an ignominious history – it had been the study of his father, Melvin, and his grandfather, Claude, before him. Many nefarious schemes were born inside its walls. Now, it was Wally's private domain. As he glanced about the room, he was pleased with the statement it made about him.

When Wally took over the study, he removed all traces of his father from the room. Wally felt no remorse over his death, even though he had died of a mysterious illness at a relatively young age. In Wally's opinion, the Housemans were better off without his father. He was a weak man, unable to embellish his grandfather's legacy.

Nevertheless, Wally left a large portrait of Claude, his grandfather, hanging over the stone fireplace. He also kept the walls dotted with the stuffed heads of wild animals, old hunting rifles, animal skins, and other trophies collected by Claude. To these, Wally added his own peculiar treasures – hideous weapons of war from the middle ages. The combination of items gave the study an ominous appearance, one dedicated to the violence of past generations.

Wally was a big man with an uncanny resemblance to his grandfather. He had the same brooding face, the same arrogant demeanor. In his flights of fancy, Wally pictured himself at his grandfather's side as he led his hooded followers.

Ah, to have been there in those days, Wally frequently thought. Although Claude had died twenty years before he was born, Wally felt like he knew him through the writings Claude left behind. When reading them, Wally sometimes sensed the spirit of his grandfather in the study. It was an evil force; one that Wally welcomed.

The study was a vast circular room, which took up the entire fourth level of the tower. Massive oak beams arched high above the thick floor-planks to support the peaked roof of the ceiling. Six equally spaced windows along the limestone walls offered views of the countryside from every angle. As Wally surveyed his domain, he sighed contentedly. Soon, very soon, his plans would come to fruition. Then he would assume his grandfather's title. The Minotaur would return after many years of sleep.

A massive table stood in the center of the room. On it was an architectural model of Wally's plan for the downtown area of Great Oak. Wally had spent the last eight years laying the groundwork for his project – one that would make him fabulously wealthy. He had bribed the town's officials and greased all of the wheels. *Nothing stands in my way now*, he thought, laughing aloud.

In a series of real estate transactions, Wally planned to tear down the school buildings, the town park, the textile mill, and various other structures, combining the land into one large tract that he controlled. Clusters of high-rise apartments, hotels, restaurants, shops and entertainment facilities would take their place. Great Oak would become a tourist's haven, bringing a flow of new dollars into his family's coffers.

As for Wally, he would collect a hundred million dollars for his efforts. The money would launch his campaign for governor. From that position, he would foster corruption throughout the Southeast. Equally as important, his project would destroy the ancient tree – the so-called Great Oak.

The tree had stood in his family's way for much too long, an albatross thwarting their plans. Wally's eyes gleamed as he pictured a bulldozer ripping the tree from the earth. When the tree was gone, the forces of darkness would be at Wally's disposal.

Of course, there were still a few remaining obstacles. Wally had strained the family's resources to the limit; he was running out of money. Several more bribes and under-the-table deals required funding, but Wally had ways of reaching into hidden pockets if necessary. If he had calculated everything correctly, there would be more than enough to meet his needs until the payoff came.

He had to deal with another annoyance as well. The Save the Trees Committee, a paltry group of local citizens, opposed his plan. Sally Winston, a newcomer in Great Oak, led the disorganized fools. She was the granddaughter of Antonio Sabatini, the man who had caused Claude's downfall.

Wally did not see Sally as a formidable opponent. She was young and inexperienced, lacking the skills of her illustrious ancestor. If she caused too much trouble, he would simply remove her. She didn't realize the force of his resolve – his willingness to do unspeakable things. Wally smiled maliciously as he considered everything. *He was close, so very close.*

Wally's musings ceased at the sounds of heavy footsteps on the stone staircase. He turned as Spike entered the study.

"Sineous told me to come up," Spike said nervously.

Sineous Crop was Wally's personal servant. He also kept track of everything Spike did. Spike was understandably anxious over the summons to his father's study. Trouble and pain usually followed.

Wally sat down in the leather chair behind his immense, claw-footed desk. "You've been making trouble for me, haven't you?"

Spike stood in front of the desk, trembling. "What trouble, Dad?"

Wally's deep voice rumbled like distant thunder. "You hit a kid in the head with a baseball yesterday and sent him to the hospital. What did I tell you about such things?"

Spike sighed in resignation. "You said I shouldn't get caught."

Wally picked up the black cane lying on his desk and casually admired the handle, an ornate dragon's head. The cane had been one of his grandfather's trophies. Now, it belonged to Wally. He carried it in his hand wherever he went, thinking it projected an image of ominous authority. With a flash of movement, he slammed the length of the cane on the desk. A sharp crack echoed throughout the study, the high ceiling magnifying the sound. "Right," he bellowed. "I said you shouldn't get caught!"

Spike assumed a posture of innocence. "It was an accident, Dad."

Wally's grey eyes glimmered like liquid pools of silver. "Lying is a mistake. I can see right through you."

Spike felt like kicking himself. He was a fool to hide things from his father. It only resulted in more pain. "Okay, I hit him on purpose. Monkey and I cooked it up. I couldn't help it – I hate this kid."

Wally studied his son, not revealing his true feelings. He wanted to be stern and angry, but he couldn't. *Spike is just like me*, he thought. Deep inside Wally's black heart, a feeling of pride surfaced. "You shouldn't be making trouble right now. Who is this boy that you hate?"

"He's a nobody Dad, just a nerd from New York who moved here last week. I made it look like an accident, so I don't think there will be any trouble." Spike was stretching the truth because there had already been a squabble with Jimmy Surefoot and his friends. He hoped his father didn't know about it.

Wally had a network of spies around town, which kept him informed. "I didn't hear about a family moving here from New York."

"He's Sally Winston's nephew or something. I think his mother is her sister."

Wally's face turned ugly. "What are you saying? Is this boy a Sabatini?"

Spike fidgeted helplessly, feeling like a fly caught in a spider's web. He knew about his father's hatred for the Sabatinis. "I don't know anything about him being a Sabatini. His name is Davey Boehm. All I know is that he's living with the Winstons while his parents are in China."

"Just what I need," shouted Wally, slamming the cane down on the desk again. "Don't you understand? Sally Winston is a Sabatini. If this boy is her sister's son, he's also a Sabatini."

Wally rose from his desk and walked towards the window overlooking Brown Mountain. He was confounded by this unexpected turn of events. Abruptly, three wavering yellow lights shot up above the mountain. Wally was sure they were a warning. *Why is another Sabatini suddenly here?* he wondered.

Spike watched his father for a few minutes, afraid one of his fits of anger was about to begin. He started inching his way towards the stairs. "Dad, can I go now?" he asked meekly.

Wally wheeled about and quickly strode towards his son. After a few hurried steps, he stood in front of him, glaring down. Spike raised an arm across his face, waiting for the blow that was surely coming. To his surprise, nothing happened.

Instead, Wally reached behind his head and unfastened the leather thong around his neck. Hanging from the thong was a smooth, flat disk. The surface of the disk was black and polished, yet it absorbed light rather than reflecting it. He put the necklace around Spike's neck and secured the clasp. "Wear this from now on. Never remove it, not even when you sleep."

Spike held the disk up to his eyes, admiring it. The surface seemed impenetrable in its blackness, but then a strange thing occurred. From somewhere deep inside the disk, a yellow, lizard-like eye blinked open. The eye stared at him intently, and Spike felt something very cold probing his mind. An icy shiver ran along his spine and his knees began to shake. Then the eye slowly closed and the feeling was gone. Spike glanced up at his father. "It's from the cave, isn't it?"

Wally's voice was low and full of cunning. "Yes, I was saving it as a present for your birthday. I wanted you to wear it on the day of your first venture into the cave. How does it make you feel?"

A fierce grin appeared on Spike's face. "I feel powerful...like I can crush anyone in my way."

Wally nodded his approval. "That's how it should be. Now, listen very carefully. Stay away from this Sabatini boy. I need time to figure out how to deal with him and his aunt. You can have your way eventually, but not until I give my permission."

Spike breathed a sigh of relief. His session with his father was apparently over and he was escaping without any bruises. "Okay Dad, I promise."

Wally's face suddenly grew angry. "Remember what I told you about promises. They are weak words, which are easily broken. Tell me what I want to hear," he shouted.

Spike snapped to attention. "I swear it at the risk of pain."

Wally grinned, the words giving him pleasure. "Now, go downstairs and fetch Sineous for me."

As Spike left the study, Wally opened a drawer in his desk. A dozen black disks similar to the one he had just given Spike lay inside. Each was of a different size and attached to a leather thong. Some had three deep grooves along the surface – marks resembling the talons of a claw.

Wally selected one of the larger disks and placed it around his neck. He braced himself as an icy cold rushed through his body. After a few minutes of agony, he picked up his cane and walked towards the architectural model in the center of the room. He had a lot to consider.

Sineous Crop entered the study a short time later, carrying a silver tray. He was a tall, dour-faced man older than Wally was. However, he had the strength of a man twice his size and one-third his age. His head was completely bald and he walked with purpose. Beneath his white shirt, he wore a black disk like the one around Wally's neck.

Sineous was a valued servant at Houseman's Castle. He had lived there his entire life; he was the only person Wally trusted. Sineous knew all of the secrets swirling through Wally's twisted mind. This was because evil had intertwined their souls.

The Crop's servitude to the Housemans began back in 1887. That was the year when Dalton Crop, Sineous's father, started work as a laborer at the Houseman's limestone quarry on Brown Mountain. Like many who came there, Dalton just showed up one day, looking for work. Although Dalton wasn't well educated, he had the kind of bold instincts that make some men leaders. Within three years, he became the foreman of the quarry.

One day, as Dalton was inspecting the terraced layers of the quarry, a thunderous rockslide erupted above him. He escaped injury by diving under an overhanging ledge while a river of rock poured down the mountain. Some of his workers were not so fortunate. Five men lost their lives when the avalanche swept over them.

After the rockslide ended, Dalton rushed out from his shelter and inspected the carnage. Below him, the cries of injured men made the quarry sound like a disaster zone. Dalton was not a harsh man at the time, but his first concern was damage to the quarry. As he looked up, he saw a startling sight. Near the top of the cliff, a small black hole had appeared. Dalton felt himself inexplicably drawn towards the strange opening.

Dalton hastily arranged for the rescue of the injured and then picked his way through the rubble until he reached the black hole. As he grew near, he realized it was the entrance to a cave – a cave with a distinctly odd opening. Despite the bright sun overhead, no light penetrated into the cavity. When Dalton cautiously thrust his hand into the opening, it was as though he had reached into a pool of frigid black water. His arm completely disappeared from sight at the point where it entered. Then his fingers touched something inside the cave – something floating in the air. An icy force rushed through his body, propelling him backwards. His mind went numb, and he collapsed into darkness.

An hour passed before Dalton regained his senses. He woke up lying in the rubble, moaning and weeping. Those who heard his cries thought the landslide was the source of his grief, but they were wrong. An evil force had flowed into Dalton from inside the cave. It was the power of the force, a sense of goodness lost, which had overcome his emotions. For the rest of his life, he would never feel compassion again.

Dalton immediately went to work. He procured a large tarpaulin from the supply shack and fastened it over the mouth of the cave with iron stakes. Then he selected two of his most trusted men, gave them rifles, and told them to keep everyone away from the area. After that, he saddled his horse and rode to Houseman's Castle.

Dalton Crop and Claude Houseman were inseparable from that day forward. Claude put him in charge of managing the affairs of the Castle, but his real job was harnessing the force inside the cave. Each night, the two men sat in Claude's study, planning and scheming. They frequently visited the cave together; over the years, they gradually came to understand the ominous force existing there.

Now, forty years later, Sineous was managing the affairs of Houseman Castle. Before he died, Dalton had trained his son to take his place and revealed the many secrets of the Housemans. Of greatest importance, Dalton told Sineous everything he knew about the evil inside the cave.

Without speaking, Sineous placed the silver tray on Wally's desk and began preparing a fire in the fireplace. On the tray, two snifters of brandy sat waiting. When the fire was burning brightly, he spoke to Wally. His voice possessed a low hissing quality. "The fire is ready, master."

Although aware of his presence, Wally acknowledged Sineous for the first time. "Bring the brandy and sit with me. I am troubled about something."

Sineous picked up the tray and waited for Wally to take his place in one of the large chairs. Then he presented the tray, letting Wally take his pick of the glasses. Only when Wally was satisfied did Sineous sit down.

Wally took a sip of his brandy and nodded. "Sineous, another Sabatini has come to town, a boy of Spike's age. This has happened just as we are on the verge of destroying the tree. Do you think it's a coincidence?"

Sineous remained silent for a moment. When he finally spoke, his voice was grave. "We must treat this as if it is not a coincidence. As you know, your grandfather had been trying to kill the tree for many years and the tree was gradually dying. Then Antonio Sabatini came to Great Oak and put a stop to what Claude was doing. My father believed the tree somehow summoned Sabatini here to help it. Now, you are about to destroy the tree and two more Sabatinis have come. Thus, the tree may have turned to the cursed Sabatinis once more."

A look of distress suddenly crossed Wally's face. "Am I in danger? Will the tree try to kill me like it killed Claude?"

Sineous shook his head. He had explained this to Wally countless times, but Wally still didn't understand. "Master, the tree did not kill Claude. The tree's spirit is too benevolent to take a life. The residual effect of the magic that Sabatini cast in the park caused Claude's death. My father did his best to heal Claude and his brothers after the lightning struck them, but his efforts were in vain. They were too badly injured."

"Why wasn't your father also in the park that night? I thought Dalton was always at Claude's side."

"Your father, Melvin, was very ill at the time; Claude ordered

Dalton to stay in the castle to look after him. Of course, Claude miscalculated, being unaware of the extent of Sabatini's power. Claude had his brothers and many other men with him; he believed there was nothing to fear. He thought Sabatini was merely an entertainer, a carnival trickster who pretended to perform magic. Nevertheless, the fact that Dalton didn't accompany him turned out to be a stroke of luck. Otherwise, there would have been no one to cover up the attempted hanging of Sabatini. Dalton even killed the reporter, Larry Tompkins, to protect the Houseman name. After that, he killed one of Claude's minions who wanted to tell what he knew."

Wally's eyes gleamed at the thought. "Dalton was a great man, a loyal friend to the Housemans. You have never told me the details of his death. I know he had many enemies and I have always wondered about his accident."

"I didn't want to worry you, master. Now, it is a subject that we must discuss. My father made two promises to Claude before he died. First, he promised to ensure the survival of the Housemans. Second, he promised to revenge Claude's death. Melvin was the only Houseman left after Claude and his brothers died. Despite Claude's legacy, Melvin was unable to shoulder much responsibility, so Dalton had his hands full with the first promise for many years."

"I remember Dalton teaching me when I was a boy," Wally replied.

Sineous nodded, recalling Dalton's excitement when Wally was born. "My father was surprised when Melvin sired a son, and he was pleased when you grew into a robust child. When Dalton began your training, he was measuring you – testing your ability to rebuild the Houseman dynasty."

Wally smiled at the memory. "He said I was just like my grandfather."

"After Dalton was satisfied that you could lead the family, he turned his attention to the second promise. Knowing his task was risky, he trained me to carry on in his absence, as I was an adult at the time. Then he implemented his plan for revenge against the Sabatinis.

That was what killed him."

"So…his death was not an accident?"

"He was murdered. You see, after much thought, Dalton decided the best revenge for Claude's death would be the death of Celina Sabatini."

Wally recognized the cleverness of this. "She was Sabatini's only child."

Sineous offered a snake-like smile. "His reasoning was simple. Her death would prevent any more Sabatinis from being born."

"He died while trying to kill her?"

"No, he died *before* he could try. Celina was a young woman who worked in a downtown store at the time. My father planned to hit her with his truck as she walked home in the dark. He killed the reporter the same way, you know. There was only one problem; he forgot about the magic of the Sabatinis."

"But The Great Sabatini was dead."

"Apparently, that didn't matter. On the day of Dalton's planned attack, a flock of ravens flew inside the window of his truck as he was driving down Brown Mountain. The birds distracted him so much that he drove off the mountain. His truck exploded in a ball of fire on the rocks below."

Wally was puzzled. "Whose magic sent the birds?"

"I think they were sent by the witch, Alicia Sabatini. Somehow, she summoned the birds to protect Celina, and thus preserve the Sabatini bloodline."

"And Dalton was no longer able to carry out Claude's revenge."

"No, but I was. I attempted nothing while Alicia was alive. The old witch lived for a long time, and I was afraid of her powers. But after her death, I learned Celina was living in Greensboro. Then I arranged for an automobile accident, which killed Celina and her husband. Regretfully, their two daughters were not with them."

"Why haven't you told me of this before?"

"It was many years ago. You were not ready to hear of such things."

Wally's face showed his appreciation of his servant's boldness. "Excellent Sineous, you have done well! Now, it is time for us to continue Claude's revenge. This boy and his aunt give us a perfect opportunity. They are naive – no match for our cunning. Moreover, they show no signs of having the powers of their ancestors. With the help of the cave, we will wipe them out."

Sineous shifted in his chair. "This is why I have told you about my father's death. We must not take the Sabatinis lightly or assume they have no powers. They are here for a reason, as their magic links them with the tree. It is strongest when they are near the Great Oak. If we can lure them away, we can attack them successfully. I was able to kill Celina because she was in another place."

"How far away do they have to be?"

"As far as possible, master. Remember, there are two of them."

Wally nodded. "As always Sineous, you have provided good counsel. Some ideas are already forming in my mind, but we must move quickly. I want these Sabatinis eliminated before they cause trouble."

⚘ Chapter 20 ⚘

Many fear that which cannot be understood. Yea, heed this truth. Knowledge that thou art feared is useful against thy enemies.

— Translated from Storia Di Incanto; circa 1772

A Taste Of Fear

THE TRIP FROM NEW YORK to Great Oak took Androf Protsky a full day. He drove the entire route at a speed below the legal limit, intent on avoiding notice by the police. Yong Chow Lee had provided him with a beat-up white van; its engine strained and surged like an old farm tractor. Still, it carried him to Great Oak without breaking down, so Androf had no complaints.

Painted on each side of the van was the logo of Vertex Automobile Supplies. The same logo appeared on the back of Androf's uniform and above the front shirt-pocket, along with the name, *Andy Tennison, Sales Representative*. All of Androf's fake identification used the same name as well. *It's a clever deception,* Androf thought, confident in his ability to fool anyone in a small town.

The uniform was Androf's idea and it pleased him. Particularly after Yong Chow Lee said Androf's attention to detail was impressive. That was important because the Chinese man was the one funding the kidnapping scheme in North Carolina. Androf wanted to make sure the money kept flowing.

Androf spent his first night in Great Oak at a cheap motel on the outskirts of town. Nobody paid him the slightest bit of attention. He ate dinner at a greasy truck stop located along the highway near the motel. The truck stop was a busy place, full of boisterous men drinking beer and shoveling steak and potatoes into their mouths. The food did not suit Androf, but he accomplished his purpose – learning how to fit in.

He watched and listened to those around him for several hours, his mind recording everything. In order to avoid attracting attention, he must become like these ordinary men. He had to learn their mannerisms and way of speaking. After lingering over his meal for as long as possible, he walked out the door. On his way, he picked up a copy of the local bi-weekly newspaper, *The Great Oak Leaflet*, and carried it back to his room.

The newspaper, or rather what Androf read in it, contained a bit of luck. When Androf scanned the advertisements, he found a garage apartment for rent at 256 Elm Street. By Androf's reckoning, it was only a couple of houses away from the address Yong Chow Lee had provided – the place where the boy lived. Androf figured there was a good chance the apartment was still vacant since the newspaper had yesterday's date on it. He decided to make the apartment his first objective and went to sleep.

As Androf drove along Elm Street the next morning, he located the house of Bill and Sally Winston. Then he found the house where the garage apartment was for rent. He had been right – the apartment was across the street and three houses away from where Davey Boehm lived.

He pulled the van into the driveway and checked his appearance in the rear-view mirror. The marks of his recent plastic surgery had all but disappeared and his mane of blond hair was now short and brown. The long scar along one side of his face was gone and his broken nose was straighter and less prominent as well.

Androf smiled at himself in the mirror. He didn't look much like the Androf Protsky wanted by the police. The only unchanged features were his hard, threatening eyes. He forced a big grin onto his face and the eyes lost some of their malice. The face in the mirror looked about right now. He was just a friendly country-boy, struggling with a new job in an unfamiliar town.

Androf climbed out of the van and walked purposefully up the front steps of the house. He wore his worker's uniform and carried the copy of the newspaper. He put the country-boy smile on his face and rang the doorbell. After a few seconds, he heard movement inside the house. Moments later, the front door opened a few inches, a safety chain attached. Two beady eyes peered out at him from thick bifocals.

"Go away, I don't need whatever you're selling," said a harsh female voice.

Androf did his best to imitate the country dialect overheard at the truck stop. "Morning ma'am, I was wondering 'bout the garage apartment. Still got her for rent?"

"What? Oh, the garage apartment. Why…yes it is. You surprised me; I just put the ad in the paper and didn't expect anyone so soon," said the voice, a little less harshly.

The door closed and Androf heard the woman release the safety chain. When the door opened again, Androf found himself looking at a plump elderly woman. Swirls of curler-wrapped, grey hair sat atop her head, making her look somewhat foolish. She wore a faded blue housecoat overlaid with a floral design. Fluffy pink slippers covered her feet. Androf guessed her age at about seventy-five.

"I don't recognize you, young man. Are you from around here?" she asked.

Androf pointed at the embroidered nameplate on his chest and put the friendly grin on his face again. "Name's Andy Tennison, just moving into town."

The woman stared at Androf for a few seconds taking it all in, the friendly grin, the worker's uniform, the embroidered nameplate. Then she managed a small smile. "Well, I'm Alice Silversmith. Excuse my appearance – I was getting ready for my bridge club meeting. We meet every Wednesday, you know. Why don't you come in and I'll tell you about the apartment."

Androf followed the woman into a large living room. He noticed the furniture was old and threadbare, the nap of the carpet badly worn. The woman was having a hard time making ends meet. He stored the information away, thinking it might come in handy.

Alice motioned for Androf to sit down and positioned herself primly in a chair some distance away. She looked nervous – not completely at ease around him.

"Oh dear, where are my manners. How about some coffee?" she asked.

"Thank you kindly, but I done had my fill. Hope I ain't disturbing you none. See, I'm looking for a place right soon."

Alice perked up on this bit of news. "I've never rented the garage apartment before, so I'm new at this. My husband died last year, and now I need a little extra income. My daughter fixed the apartment up, and her husband moved some old furniture up there. Mind you, it's nothing fancy, but it's clean and efficient. It will suit a single man, if that's what your needs are."

Androf kept the friendly grin on his face. "I'm single all right and it sounds mighty fine. See, Mrs. Silversmith, I'm kinda down on my luck. My wife done run off with my best friend and we got divorced. She took every darn stick of furniture we had, which weren't much anyhow, but it left me with nothin. So…I'm mostly starting over. Got this new job and all, which is why I'm in Great Oak." Androf looked down, seemingly embarrassed to discuss such things.

"Why bless your heart. I hope there weren't any children," Alice said.

Androf tried to look pious, no easy feat for a man like him. "No, thank gosh. I'd be all torn up if we'd had kids."

"What kind of work do you do, Andy?"

Androf smiled when he heard her use his first name. She was buying his story. "I ain't got much schooling ma'am, but if there's one thing I know – it's car engines. Heck, I done fixed half the cars in

Backbend, Ohio at one time or the other. That's where I'm from. Anyway, after the divorce I just had to get away. I seen an ad for this here job selling automobile parts. The job was in Akron, but they done filled it by the time I got there. Then this manager fella says I'd be perfect for a territory they was setting up in North Carolina. I got nothing keeping me in Ohio, so I says bring it on, brother. Course, I knew the man upstairs was looking after me when it happened."

"What exactly does a person do in your job?"

"Well, see there's all them independent type gas stations and body shops in little towns around everywhere. I go see them and talk over the products my company sells. Stuff like carburetors, distributors, water pumps, that kinda thing. We got good quality parts and cheap prices. With the help of the almighty, I oughta do okay."

"You sound like you're a church going man," Alice stated.

"Go as often as I can ma'am, as often as I can."

Alice smiled in satisfaction. "Why don't you call me Alice? After all, if we're going to be neighbors – we should be friends."

"Shucks Alice, you kinda remind me of my dear old mama."

Alice felt like her luck couldn't get any better with this man for a tenant. "You seem nice, Andy. The rent is two hundred dollars a month. Is that okay?"

"Yes ma'am, I can sure afford that. While I ain't gonna make much starting out, my boss says I can earn a lot if I work hard and get my customer base going. Maybe I can do some handyman stuff around the house too. Course, I wouldn't charge you nothin. Just do it cause it's the neighborly thing."

"You're a credit to your mother, Andy Tennison. Come on, I'll get the key and you can have a look at the apartment."

Androf followed Alice down a long hallway towards the back door of the house. The key to the garage apartment hung on a peg near the doorway. She handed him the key and pointed out the back door at a building behind the house.

"The staircase is on the outside. Hope you don't mind if I don't come with you. I don't climb stairs much anymore because of my arthritis. Take your time and just knock on the back door when you're finished."

Androf followed her instructions, but he was only going through the motions. He intended to rent the apartment even before stepping out of the van. The location was ideal, and the fact that the old woman couldn't climb stairs was a bonus. She wouldn't be bothering him or snooping around when he was gone.

However, when Androf opened the apartment door, he was surprised. The big room was larger than he had expected; windows on each side made it appear light and airy. The front half of the room made up the bedroom and the back half contained a kitchen on one side and a bathroom on the other. Everything considered; it was perfect.

Androf returned to Alice's house in only five minutes. "It's a right nice little place. If it's okay, I'll move right on in," Androf said when Alice reappeared.

"Well, that's wonderful, but I promised my daughter I'd discuss it with her before I made a decision about anyone."

Androf pretended not to hear. Instead, he held up twelve fifty-dollar bills fanned out in front of her face. "I done got three months rent here. That way, you ain't got to collect more anytime soon. When three months is done, I'll fetch you the same amount again. I ain't gonna be the least bit of trouble for you, Alice."

Alice couldn't take her eyes off the money. She let it stay in Androf's hand for a few seconds before gently plucking it away, her fingers trembling. "You go ahead, Andy. My daughter will be thrilled I've found someone as nice as you."

Androf gave her his country-boy smile. "Thank you, Alice. I'll just keep this here key, okay."

"All right – welcome to the neighborhood."

"I'll run along now cause I got me some calls to make on them body shops. See, my boss done give me this here list of places all over the mountains. Starting at the top and working my way down. Won't be back for a while, then I'll unload my stuff."

Androf walked to the driveway and climbed into his van. The next order of business was to pick up some things he needed. He figured a distance of a hundred miles would be about right for that purpose. *There's nothing like furnishing a new home,* he thought, whistling a little tune as he drove away.

Androf drove south along the highway for several hours and then stopped at a rest area and changed his clothes. Now, he was no longer Andy Tennison, auto parts salesman – he was Androf Protsky, car thief. He scooted behind the wheel and continued along his way, heading for the city of Hickory.

When Androf reached the city limits, he began driving around until he came across a large shopping mall. He drove through the parking lot until he found an area behind the mall containing two-dozen cars. He decided this was the parking area for the employees working there, people who wouldn't notice if their cars were missing for a few hours. Then he parked the van in the main lot and left with a small bag of tools.

In a matter of minutes, Androf was back at the employee parking area and sitting in a sedan, which the owner had foolishly left unlocked. A short time later, he drove the sedan onto the highway and began searching for a house in a quiet neighborhood. It didn't take him long to find what he wanted – a modest house with an attached garage. The house was a distance away from other homes and somewhat screened from the street by trees and bushes.

Androf pulled into the driveway and waited in the sedan for several minutes. There was no sign of activity in or around the house. He stepped out of the sedan, walked up to the door, and rang the doorbell. If anyone answered, he would pretend to be lost and ask for directions. As luck would have it, no one was home.

Androf grabbed his bag of tools from the sedan and put on a pair of leather gloves. Even though the doctor had removed enough skin from his fingers to make his fingerprints hard to detect, he wasn't taking any chances. The lock on the back door was easy to pick and he was inside the house in seconds. He hurried through the house, raised the garage door, and quickly drove the sedan into the garage. Then he closed the garage door behind him. So far, he had been at the house for about five minutes.

He found several large garbage bags and moved through the house collecting things. Sheets, towels, blankets, pillows, pots, pans, knives, forks, spoons, plates, cups – they all went into one of the bags. He located a decent television, video recorder, and small stereo system; he put them all in the sedan. Then he took the other plastic bag and went back through the house gathering other things, a coffee maker, desk clock, food, and two bottles of wine.

Androf laughed while he worked, enjoying his little shopping spree. It wasn't the first time he had set up housekeeping in this way. He was accustomed to leaving places in a hurry and frequently left most of his belongings behind. Why anyone bothered to keep stuff when it was so easy to acquire replacements was a mystery to him. After all, he was a criminal. His mind held a disturbing concept of right and wrong. To Androf, right was anything he wanted – wrong was anything in his way.

After Androf had put everything into the bags, he carried them out to the car. One last trip into the house yielded three other items, a large picture of some ducks flying through the air, an oriental carpet, and an old shotgun. He thought they would add nice touches to his new apartment.

Androf had only been at the house for thirty minutes when he backed the loaded sedan out of the garage and headed towards the shopping mall. He returned the sedan to its parking place and walked back to his van. Then he drove the van over to the sedan and transferred the stolen items into the van's storage compartment. Two hours after entering the city limits of Hickory, he was back on his way to Great Oak.

At ten o'clock that evening, Androf telephoned Yong Chow Lee. As instructed, he used the cell phone, which the Chinese man had given him. Their conversation was short, their words carefully chosen. Anyone overhearing them would discern no particular meaning in the few short sentences.

"I am at a good location – close by," Androf said.

"Have you seen him?" Yong Chow Lee asked.

"I am going tonight," Androf replied.

"Call me tomorrow," Yong Chow Lee snapped, and then hung up.

Dressed in black clothes, Androf eased down the steps of his garage apartment a few minutes later. The night was dark, and rain clouds moving across the sky made it even darker. A steady breeze picked up leaves from the ground and blew them towards him. A storm was coming – he could smell it in the air. *It's a good night for prowling,* he thought.

Androf stayed in the darkness of the trees as he crept along the street. A cluster of tall pines stood directly across from the house where Davey Boehm lived, and he darted into the blackness between the pines and watched the house for a while. Not another person was outside in the night; the entire town was his for the taking.

Despite Androf's belief, he was not the only one watching Davey's house on that night. Upon the highest peak of Aunt Sally's roof, seven ravens maintained a silent vigil. The birds had been there every night since Davey arrived in Great Oak, their presence and purpose unknown to all but themselves. Their black feathers didn't stand out against the night sky, nor were their dark shapes distinguishable from the shingles of the roof.

Oblivious of the watchers around him, Davey was doing his homework in his bedroom. Androf could not see him, but he knew someone was in the room because the lights were on and an occasional shadow moved across the window. He wondered if the boy was there and felt a compulsion to find out, to get a look at his target.

Androf noticed a tall elm standing alongside the house, and it gave him an idea. The trunk of the tree rose past the window of the bedroom; its branches appeared sufficient to support his weight. Androf figured he could see inside the room from midway up the tree – maybe even get into the house that way when the time came to kidnap the boy. *It's worth checking out,* he thought. He crossed the street, moving cautiously in the darkness.

The ravens on the roof shifted their bodies into readiness as Androf left the shelter of the pines. Their yellow eyes glowed warily as they watched him approach the house. A few seconds passed, and then they launched their bodies into the air, floating like black ghosts in the night sky.

After reaching the tree, Androf looked up at the lit window. It was open and the curtains fluttered in the breeze, inviting him to inspect the window closer. *This is almost too easy,* he thought with a smile. Glancing at the tree, he found a branch within his reach and pulled himself up. From there, the climbing was not difficult; he quickly made his way up to a point opposite the open window.

As Androf climbed, the ravens circled above the tree, an unseen force in the darkness. The birds studied him intently, waiting until he reached a vulnerable position. They flew in the shape of a triangle, prepared to attack.

Unaware of the ravens above him, Androf sat in the tree and watched Davey through the open window. He could see the boy clearly, and the sight filled him with exhilaration. The boy was small, no match for his own massive strength; Androf was so close, the windowsill so easily within his reach that he could be inside the room in seconds. A thick branch arched towards the window and Androf crawled along it, testing its strength in preparation for when he would kidnap the boy. However, this put him in a defenseless position. As soon as the ravens saw Androf on the branch, they hesitated no longer. Filling the air with furious shrieks, they dove straight towards him.

Androf froze as the screeching cries of the birds reached his ears. Their horrible sounds sent chills along his spine, and he searched about in the darkness with alarmed eyes. He was completely exposed, his body in a precarious position. Suddenly, the birds were upon him, a vicious mass of slashing beaks and tearing claws that stuck with deadly precision. They tore at his ears, neck, face, and hands, each strike afflicting pain and confusion. He scrambled back towards the trunk, swinging at the ravens with frantic movements of his arms. Muted screams of pain rose in his throat as he unsuccessfully tried to defend himself. The birds floated in the air around him, black shadows that struck his exposed flesh without restraint.

Androf had never encountered an enemy such as this. He began a hasty retreat, trying to get out of the tree as quickly as possible. When he was two-thirds of the way down the trunk, the ravens launched another attack. In a coordinated maneuver, they came at him from different directions. One landed on his head, digging into his scalp with pointed claws and pecking angrily at his forehead. Another grabbed onto his shoulder, repeatedly jabbing a razor-sharp beak into his neck. The others engaged in equally damaging forays, making mincemeat of his fingers, ears, and even finding the tender flesh of his ankles.

Androf screamed, but the sound was lost in the wind. He shifted his weight, warding off the birds by swinging an arm and leg at the same time. It was a foolish effort that doomed him to further injury. His jerking movements made his grip slip and he fell the remaining ten feet to the ground. He landed on his neck and shoulders with an impact that jarred every bone in his body. The air whooshed out of his chest, accompanied by a loud moan of anguish. Involuntarily, his knee jerked forward with the force of the fall, striking his face and splitting his lip. It was a heavy blow, and he lay like a rag doll, fighting to stay conscious.

The angry barking of a dog from inside the house brought Androf out of his stupor. *Get away; get away,* his brain screamed. Whimpering in pain, he rolled to his feet and scurried towards the pine trees across the street. He hid deep inside the shadows there, his breath coming in ragged sobs as his eyes searched for his attackers.

The ravens, satisfied Androf was no longer a threat, didn't pursue him. They resumed their positions on the roof, invisible once again in the blackness of the night. After a time, the rain began. A few sporadic drops fell at first, but then it came down in torrents.

Under the cover of the rain, Androf limped back to his apartment.

A sharp pain surged through his chest whenever he took a breath and one foot barely supported his weight. The fall from the tree had broken one of his ribs, his ankle was sprained, and his face and hands were a mass of bruises and cuts, many requiring stitches. He knew his face would be a black and purple mess tomorrow. Days would pass before the cuts would heal, the bruises gone. Until then, he would have to stay out of sight.

Androf had been in many fights before, but none that had left him with such feelings of inadequacy. He could deal with the pain – it was something real. But an enemy had attacked him without reason, an unprovoked enemy. *Why would birds attack humans?* It was beyond his comprehension.

Paranoia had always lurked about in Androf's mind. It was only natural, considering his dangerous way of life. He had enemies in many places – he never knew when one would show up, yet his experience with the ravens was something new, something bordering on the supernatural. It was enough to make him have crazy thoughts. He could feel his grasp of reality slipping. For the first time in his life, he had tasted fear – true fear.

ᦟ Chapter 21 ᦞ

---

*Thou shalt find stories within stories,
and truths within truths. Lo, the wise
magician creates certainty from mystery.*

— Translated from Storia Di Incanto; circa 1784

The Park Warden

AUNT SALLY TOOK DAVEY back to the doctor on Monday morning. The doctor smiled and shook his head again, unable to comprehend why Davey could see without his glasses. Still, he gave Davey a clean bill of health.

For his part, Davey expected nothing less. He had awakened full of confidence, his blood pulsing with vibrant energy. Overnight, more muscles had appeared and a new quickness had developed in his coordination. He felt like the proverbial ugly duckling, turning into a swan.

Aunt Sally looked at him in surprise when he came down for breakfast. "I can't believe how much you have grown. Why, the clothes I just bought you hardly fit anymore."

Uncle Bill stood alongside Davey, measuring his growth. "The boy is sprouting up like a weed. He'll be bigger than me soon."

Davey laughed, pleased by their remarks; his imagination wasn't playing tricks on him after all. He *was* getting taller. Moreover, he was experiencing other mysterious changes – strange new talents were making themselves known.

Davey first became aware of these changes while sitting alone at his desk last night. He was thinking about how much he missed Bupkiss when Bristol suddenly ran into the room. The dog sat down beside him and put his paw on his leg as if reminding Davey of his presence in the house. Davey had the uncanny feeling he had somehow sent out an unspoken message to Bristol.

A short time later, another startling event occurred. Davey was reading his history textbook and came across an intriguing passage about Hannibal bringing his army of elephants across the Alps. He wanted to mark the passage, but he couldn't find his yellow highlight-pen anywhere. "Come out, come out, wherever you are," he said aloud, picturing the pen in his mind and trying to remember where he had last seen it. To his surprise, the pen came rolling out from beneath his bed.

Davey thought about this strange occurrence for a while and then decided to experiment. He laid the pen on his desk and placed his hand a short distance away from it. With his mind focused on the pen, he consciously willed for it to move towards his hand. Sure enough, the pen rolled across the desk until it touched his fingers. He performed the exercise several more times, and the same thing happened. *How very odd,* he thought, somewhat in shock.

Davey's last experiment with the pen was happening at precisely the same time that Androf was fighting with the ravens in the tree outside his window. The wind carried away the sounds of their struggle, so Davey was blissfully unaware of the battle. Soon, that changed.

Abruptly, a loud thud from outside the window broke Davey's concentration. Bristol jumped up and began barking, and Davey felt his necklace start an urgent vibration. Glancing about the room, he noticed the curtains of his open window flapping in the wind. He peered out the window, feeling a tinge of anxiety. Threatening rain clouds hung heavy in the night sky, but he saw no sign of danger.

With a shrug, Davey shut the window and walked back towards his desk. *Just the wind,* he thought, as if it explained why his necklace was vibrating. Had he known about Androf, he would have been terrified.

The mental effort of moving the pen had made Davey's head throb and he suddenly felt very tired. *I'll experiment more tomorrow,* he decided, yawning as he climbed into bed. When he closed his eyes, a pleasant image of The Great Sabatini formed in his mind. The magician was performing his magic show in the park, and objects were flying in the air around him. Soon, Davey was fast asleep.

ഇൽൽ൝൝൝

When Davey arrived at school after seeing the doctor, everything seemed different. The word had gotten around about his grand performance in the baseball game, and kids he didn't know suddenly started speaking to him. On the other hand, Spike, Monkey, and Torpedo ignored him completely. Moreover, they stopped making snide comments behind his back.

At lunchtime, while Davey was sitting with Amy behind the large column in the cafeteria, two cute girls approached their table. The girls, one blonde and the other brunette, nodded curtly at Amy and immediately turned their attention to Davey.

"We're wondering if you'll try out for the seventh-grade basketball team," Allison Chambers, the dark-haired girl said, smiling flirtatiously.

Cindy Albertson, the blonde girl, picked up the conversation as if the two girls were speaking as one. "We're asking because we're cheerleaders for the seventh-grade and the basketball team needs better players. We think you might be a good addition."

"See, we'd like a winning season," Allison interjected.

"And we like having players who are worthy of our cheers. There's nothing worse than cheering for a bunch of losers," Cindy added.

Davey almost laughed when he heard this. *Obviously, they haven't seen me on the basketball court,* he thought. "Well, I'll consider it," he finally said, looking serious.

"Oh good," the girls said in unison. Then they turned and jauntily walked away.

Amy, who had watched this brief exchange with a somewhat spiteful expression, began to chuckle. "Maybe you should form a fan club."

Her remark caught Davey off guard. *She is actually jealous,* he thought, surprised and a bit amused. "The only fan I care about is you," he hastily replied.

"Oh?" Amy muttered, her eyebrows rising. But the grin appearing on her face indicated her unspoken pleasure.

Finally, it was time for English class. Davey kept a close eye on Linda, hoping no adverse effects from his wish would appear. To the contrary, Linda grew progressively happier as the class went along, and her students treated her with a new sense of respect. She even laughed at Spike's disruptive behavior, which turned out to be an excellent strategy. His face grew red and he swelled up like an angry bee, unable to interrupt further until he calmed down again. The class was over by then.

"The tree is still doing things to make her happy," Amy whispered as she and Davey approached Linda after class.

"How are you and Bupkiss getting along?" Davey asked.

Linda's face lit up like a Christmas tree. "I can't thank you enough for letting us have him. Bupkiss is such a joy – we can't stop laughing at his antics. Aunt Gilda wants you to come for a visit so she can thank you properly."

Davey smiled in response. "I'll bring Bristol. He and Bupkiss can play together."

Amy was eager to learn how Linda's dinner with Ed Nolen had turned out. Of course, there wasn't any way she could come right out and ask. Such subjects were off limits between teachers and their students.

However, Linda solved Amy's dilemma by bringing up Ed's name herself. "Ed is wondering if you guys will help him with some chores this weekend. He'll pay you for your time."

Davey and Amy glanced at each other and then they both nodded. Davey was thinking about the upstairs portion of the house. His necklace had indicated there was something important up there. *Maybe I'll have a chance to look around*, he thought.

Linda's question also gave Amy an opportunity to satisfy her curiosity. "So…are you helping Mr. Nolen with his book?" she asked casually.

"We started working on it last night."

Amy grinned, her eyes twinkling. "Hmmm…are you two becoming an item?"

Apparently, Linda didn't mind the question in the least. An auspicious glow appeared on her face and she returned Amy's grin. "Maybe," was all she said, yet it was enough. Davey and Amy filled in the rest from the way she said it.

After school was over, the Three of We gathered briefly at the bicycle racks. Davey gave Jimmy a report on Miss Peabody, and he blurted out his own good news. "Yona has agreed to meet with you. I got all wigged-out when my dad told me about it."

"That was quick work!" Amy exclaimed, taken by surprise.

Jimmy broke into a laugh. "Actually, it wasn't my doing. Dad went to see Yona on Sunday for one of their regular powwows, and Dad told him about Davey climbing the tree. Yona has always been fascinated by it and said he'd like to meet Davey. He wants Dad to bring him to the Council House for a visit. Amy and I are invited as well."

"Great! How soon can we go?" Davey asked.

"We should do it quickly – before Yona changes his mind."

"Friday is a teacher work day, so we don't have school. Maybe we can go then," Amy suggested.

"I'll see if Dad can set it up," Jimmy replied.

"Amy and I are going over to the park. We're hoping to talk with Joe Harrison. Why don't you come along?" Davey asked.

A frown formed on Jimmy's face. "I can't, mate. I'm helping Dad in the shop this afternoon. We're taking inventory." Jimmy's deepening frown indicated that taking inventory was not his idea of a good time. "Let me know if you learn anything."

Thirty minutes later, Davey and Amy were standing in front of the Great Oak. They had searched the park for Joe Harrison without success, finally winding up at the tree. Amy had seen the tree many times, yet never experienced the sense of awe that she felt now. Of course, her thoughts about the tree had changed considerably during the last few days.

"I still have a hard time believing a tree can make wishes come true," she said, her voice barely more than a whisper.

"Yeah, but you saw what happened with Miss Peabody."

"I know...I know," Amy replied, feeling bad for still having doubts.

"Let's see if the gate will open for us," Davey suggested.

Amy was a bit spooked, unsure of how she would feel if the locked gate actually opened. "Uh...we really should keep looking for Mr. Harrison."

"Oh, come on," Davey said, pulling her forward.

Abruptly, a voice sounded from behind them. "A magnificent sight, isn't it? Can you believe anyone would destroy such a tree?"

Amy and Davey nearly jumped out of their skins. They twirled around to find a small, grey-haired man standing a few feet away. Somehow, he had come up behind them without making a sound.

"Oh hello, Mr. Harrison," Amy stammered, her heart pounding. "This is my friend, Davey Boehm. He just moved here."

Joe looked keenly at Davey, his eyes crinkling as a smile spread across his face. "Your aunt told me about your arrival; she's a good friend, you know. I knew your grandmother, Celina, and great grandmother, Alicia, too," he added with a chuckle. "In fact, the only Sabatini that I didn't know was your great grandfather."

The man's sudden appearance and his fortuitous news stunned Davey so completely that he was briefly at a loss for words. He simply looked at the man, his mouth open as he tried to think of what to say.

Sensing Davey's surprise, Amy filled in the silence by asking a question. "What did you mean about someone destroying the tree?"

Joe acted as if the very thought of something happening to the Great Oak was painful. "The Housemans have been trying to kill it for more than a century, but my family and others have been preventing it. I've learned most of what I know about these things from my father and grandfather. After I became the park warden though, I caught one of them at it."

"You actually caught a Houseman harming the tree?"

"Well, it was Sineous Crop, a fellow who works for them, so I figured they were the ones behind it. See, I was patrolling with my shotgun at night. There had been some vandalism in the park and I was doing my job – protecting my wards so to speak. Anyway, I saw Sineous throwing these black rocks into the tree. They had big leather loops attached to them, and he was trying to snag the loops on the branches. Funny thing – as soon as one of those rocks touched the tree – they disintegrated into ashes. It was mighty strange."

"Why was he doing that?"

"Oh, he came up with some nonsense about the rocks helping the tree, but I knew he was lying. He's too nasty a fellow to be doing something helpful. I said he'd get a belly full of buckshot if I caught him around the tree again, so he grabbed his bag of rocks and ran off. A few weeks later, I put the fence around the tree. Nobody messes with the Great Oak without my permission."

While Amy was having this exchange with the warden, Davey was busy studying him. He was a spry, elderly man, barely as tall as Davey. A mane of grey hair crowned his head, and a rather shaggy mustache and goatee covered the lower part of his face. His eyebrows were great furry things that wiggled across his brows like caterpillars when he talked.

"Did you say you knew my great grandmother?" Davey asked.

Joe's eyes twinkled merrily. "I sure did. Alicia and I were good friends. We talked every day when she came to the park. She was a very *unusual* woman."

"I'm trying to learn more about her," Davey said.

Joe laughed gleefully. "I've been expecting you, young man. As soon as I heard you were in town, I knew we'd meet before long."

"Why is that?" Davey asked, immediately astonished.

"Alicia said so, and she had a way of predicting things. She said a male Sabatini heir would show up one of these days, asking questions. You see, her daughter and I were childhood friends; we practically grew up together. I've been involved with your ancestors for nigh onto fifty years. I was mighty upset when Celina left Great Oak. We were both sad about it for days."

"I thought Celina hated Great Oak," Davey said.

The old man lowered his voice. "That was just for appearances sake. See, I know some things no one else does, not even your aunt. She'll be disappointed if she finds out I've kept them from her, but I promised Alicia I'd only tell you."

Davey looked at him. "Is it okay if Amy hears?"

"I reckon so, since she's with you, but she has to keep it to herself."

"I promise," Amy said earnestly.

The old man nodded. "Everyone thought Alicia went crazy after Antonio disappeared; she kept up the ruse her entire life. There are forces in this town that hate the Sabatinis, and she thought this would protect her and Celina. It did for many years, but when Celina was older, Alicia sensed she was in danger and sent her away. Alicia never told anyone where Celina was, except me. Celina and I talked often by telephone, and I helped her look after her mother from afar."

"Did Alicia ever mention Antonio, or what happened to him?"

"No, not very often. The only time she mentioned his name was when she spoke to the tree."

"She spoke to the tree?"

"Yep, she came here every day and sat under the tree, talking to it."

"Was that to make everyone think she was crazy?"

"Well maybe...but I had the feeling she enjoyed it."

"Was there anything else that she wanted you to tell me?"

The old man looked startled for a moment, then chuckled. "Well of course there is; I almost forgot the important part. Alicia wanted you to know that things – objects of some kind – have been left here for you. Apparently, they will come to you in unusual ways as part of your birthright. She said this was inevitable, similar to my role in helping you fulfill your destiny. Kind of mysterious, huh? That's the way Alicia was. Yes sirree, mighty mysterious!"

Joe's words left Davey shocked. The necklace had appeared in an unusual way, so there was some truth in what he said. "Did she say what my destiny was?" he finally asked.

Joe chuckled again. "According to Alicia, you are destined to save the town. That's it, pure and simple. She didn't say how or from what. Maybe it will become apparent, like everything else."

&)(&)(&)(&)(&

At the kitchen table that evening, Davey's conversation with Joe Harrison preoccupied his mind. Aunt Sally and Uncle Bill chatted amicably, each poking fun at the other in their humorous way. Finally, Aunt Sally looked over at Davey. "You seem unusually quiet. Did everything go okay at school today?"

Davey was still lost in thought. "Uh…sure…I talked with Miss Peabody. Bupkiss is doing fine," he stammered.

"Hey, I've got some news to share. Guess who called me today," Uncle Bill interjected.

"Judging from the look on your face, it must have been the President of the United States," Aunt Sally replied.

"Not even close," Uncle Bill said smugly.

Davey's necklace began a sudden vibration, and he was instantly alert. "Who was it?" he asked, his voice abnormally loud.

"Well, if you must know, it was Wally Houseman."

Aunt Sally's face narrowed into a frown. "What did that jerk want?"

Uncle Bill puffed out his chest and smiled. "Actually, our conversation was quite pleasant; he was as nice as pie. He apologized

&) 222 (&

for firing me last year and praised my work. Then he explained why he was calling. He wants to adopt some of the more modern techniques used by the furniture factories on the West coast. He asked me to go there and study them."

"You must be joking," Aunt Sally replied.

"Nope, he's offering me a lot of money. He's even willing for us to go out to Seattle and find a temporary place to live at his expense. We can keep the house here and return when the job is finished."

"Surely, you're not considering this," Aunt Sally scoffed.

Uncle Bill shrugged. "Well, business is a bit slow and we could use the money."

Davey's necklace was vibrating furiously now. "Don't do it!" he said, jumping out of his chair. "It's some kind of a trick."

"A trick…what are you saying!" Uncle Bill exclaimed.

Davey's mind was working overtime, trying to come up with a reason why they shouldn't leave Great Oak. "Why would other furniture companies let you copy what they're doing? My dad says the furniture industry is fiercely competitive."

"Apparently, Wally has everything arranged. He named the factories and said they had all agreed."

"Davey is right. Wally's competitors wouldn't give away their secrets," Aunt Sally said.

"Well, I have some friends in those factories – even sold them some furniture designs. I can make a few calls and check out Wally's story, but why else would he pay for us to live there?"

Aunt Sally had to think about that. Then she rose from the table, suddenly furious. "Wally just wants us out of Great Oak. His proposal is coming before the city council next month. He knows my Save the Trees Committee will oppose him and doesn't want me stirring everyone up."

Uncle Bill started to laugh. "That's a bit far-fetched, don't you think?"

"Nothing is far-fetched when it comes to a devious rat like Wally. You call your friends and check things out. If Wally is telling the truth, I'll be dumbfounded."

At that point, Davey sat quietly while Uncle Bill and Aunt Sally continued their debate. He was no longer listening, his mind having shifted to his own concerns. *I can't leave Great Oak now. I have things to do here – important things.*

⚘ Chapter 22 ❧

---

*Much can be gained from the wisdom of
ancient ones. Thou shalt embrace their
truths. Ye may grow trees of knowledge
from the tiniest of seeds.*

— Translated from Storia Di Incanto; circa 1796

The Council House

ON FRIDAY MORNING, the Three of We piled excitedly into the
front seat of Sequoyah Surefoot's pickup; each wondered what new
experiences the day would bring. Sequoyah was curious as well – eager
to learn why Chief Yona had seemed so anxious to meet Davey. A
spirit of adventure hung in the air as the truck made its way through
Great Oak and then turned onto the highway heading west.

The ride to Greyhead Mountain was smooth for the first few
miles, and the three kids filled the pickup with animated
conversation. Just as their incessant chatter was getting on Sequoyah's
nerves, he turned off the main highway and onto a narrow, unpaved
road. Soon, everyone was holding on for dear life as the pickup
lurched through deep ruts. Sequoyah sighed in relief. The bouncing
of the truck had jarred his passengers into a blessed silence.

"Got to pave this road one of theses days," Sequoyah grunted as
the truck shuddered through another big bump.

Davey silently agreed, hoping they would arrive at their
destination in one piece. The lull in their conversation allowed him to

reflect upon the outcome of Wally's proposal to send his uncle to Seattle. Davey grinned as he thought over last night's scene in the family room.

Uncle Bill had sheepishly explained what his further investigation had revealed. "My friends at the factories laughed at the idea of me studying their methods. When I told Wally about their reaction, he called me a fool and hung up."

"Davey and I were right. It *was* a trick to get us out of town!" Aunt Sally had exclaimed triumphantly.

"Yes, Sally dear, your wisdom should never be questioned," Uncle Bill had muttered, seemingly baffled over the entire matter.

Another bone-jarring pothole brought Davey back to the present. The road had taken on an upward slant, which made it even more treacherous. Their destination was Chief Yona's village, one of the many Cherokee settlements that had once inhabited the Blue Ridge Mountains. Of those remaining, only a few preserved the old ways of their ancestors. Yona's village was one of them.

"Listen kids," Sequoyah said as the truck bumped along. "Although this is an informal meeting, take it seriously. The Council House rarely receives visitors from Great Oak. Generations ago, the Council of Elders passed a formal edict that barred outsiders from the village. Their edict still exists, so be polite and don't expect a warm welcome."

"But we were not involved in those things," Amy protested.

Sequoyah smiled. "They know that, but edicts of the elders enjoy a long life. They made this decree in 1838 after thousands of Cherokee from Georgia and Tennessee died on a forced relocation to Oklahoma. We call it the *Trail of Tears* – a shameful chapter in American history. The Cherokee in those states were driven from their homes because gold was found on their land."

"I read about it in a book…it made me cry," Amy said.

"My ancestors saw it as a great truth about the white men who had come upon their land. Nothing has happened in Great Oak over the years to change their minds."

Davey found this perplexing. "Why did Chief Yona invite us?"

Sequoyah smiled. "I think he is curious. Your great grandfather was his friend, and he is intrigued by your climbing of the Great Oak."

"Will he tell us about him?" Davey asked.

"I think he has something like that in mind," Sequoyah replied.

Amy shifted her position in the seat, pressing against Davey. The touch of her leg made him acutely aware of her nearness. "Uh...I hope he isn't mad about anything," he stammered.

Sequoyah shook his head. "No, but that reminds me – this meeting requires a certain protocol. You must show great respect, so no loud talking after you enter the Council House. Act as if you are in a church. Never interrupt Yona when he is speaking and ask questions only when invited to do so."

"I'm surprised Aunt Sally let me come without her," Davey said.

"I'm glad she did; there would be no meeting otherwise. Yona has been unwilling to discuss your great grandfather in the past, even among members of the tribe. I think it violates the edict against involvement with outsiders, but you are just kids, a fact which allows him to bend the rules if he chooses."

"It's a little scary though, being at the Council House when you are an outsider," Amy said.

"Don't worry; while Yona may seem stern, he is not. Underneath his pretenses, he's just a nice old man."

"Dad, tell them how Yona got his name," Jimmy interjected.

Sequoyah nodded, happy to tell one of his favorite stories. "It helps me explain the ways of the Cherokee. You see, my people have always respected nature. Every day, they thank the sun for its blessing, the trees for their wood, and the animals for their meat and skins. All natural events deserve consideration – their meanings recognized. That is how Yona got his name. He was an unnamed baby when his mother went into the river to wash, leaving him in a cradle on the bank. Suddenly, a large bear came out of the woods and sat down beside the cradle. The bear sat there for a long time, listening to the baby babble, and then ambled away without harming him. After the chief heard the story, he named the boy Yona, which means bear in Cherokee. He said the bear's spirit had blessed him."

"You should also warn them about Yona's storytelling," Jimmy added.

Sequoyah chuckled. "Yona loves to tell stories, regardless of whether anyone wants to hear them. If he starts telling a story, we must politely sit and listen. Inside the story, there is usually an important message."

At that moment, the truck reached a fork in the road; Sequoyah fell silent as he eased it towards the right. After another series of jarring ruts, they proceeded slowly as the road climbed along the edge of the mountain. They were traveling through thick woods now, tall trees surrounding each side of the truck. The sun shown brightly overhead, yet the sunlight barely penetrated through the branches. Occasionally, a gap appeared between the trees, and they could view the countryside from their lofty position. In the valley below, Great Oak appeared as a tiny, picturesque town.

Finally, the pickup stopped at two massive boulders forming a natural gateway; a pair of heavy log doors stood between the boulders. Carved into the surface of the doors was the unmistakable image of a running wolf. Jimmy and Sequoyah jumped out of the truck and pulled on the doors; the metal hinges screeched loudly as they swung open. Amy grabbed Davey's hand, squeezing it hard. "I'm getting goose bumps," she whispered.

Jimmy and his father climbed back into the truck, and they were on their way again. A vast clearing appeared before them as the truck passed through the gateway. In the center of the clearing stood a large, circular building, made from logs and stone. There were no windows in the squat building, but open space was visible between the dome of the roof and the walls. At the top of the roof was a large smoke hole.

Sequoyah pointed proudly towards the building. "That, my young friends, is the Council House, a building constructed two-centuries ago without modern tools. It has seven sides, each side representing one of the Cherokee clans. We repair it occasionally, but it's the original structure. There is no electricity or running water inside; the latrines are in the woods. Use them now if you feel the need."

Amy grimaced. "I'll bet they're full of spiders."

Jimmy grinned. "They don't smell too good either."

"Gross," Amy replied.

"Maybe later," Davey suggested.

They climbed out of the pickup, each feeling a sense of awe as they approached the front doors of the Council House. Carved into the doors was the same wolf image that had appeared on the gates. The handles on the doors were made of deer antlers, held in place by thick leather straps. When Sequoyah pulled on one, the door opened easily and they all stepped inside.

Shards of sunlight spilled through the openings in the roof, providing a scant illumination. They found themselves in a cavernous, theater-like chamber having a recessed floor. Stone steps separated the tiered levels of the chamber into sections, each section filled with split-log benches. At the bottom of the steps, twenty-feet below where they stood, was a circular earthen floor. A fire burned in a stone-lined pit in its center.

"Wait here," Sequoyah said. He went around the room lighting oil lanterns attached to the beams supporting the ceiling. As he did, the lower part of the chamber took on a cheerful glow, but the upper part remained in shadows. Then Sequoyah led them down to the earthen floor, pointed at a bench, and they sat down together. Across from where they sat, a stone platform jutted out. A curved table with elaborate carvings along its thick edges rested on the platform. Seven brightly painted chairs sat behind the table.

"How will Yona know we are here?" Davey whispered.

Sequoyah smiled. "Don't worry; watchers have informed him of our progress as we drove up the mountain. We must be patient. Custom requires he keep us waiting. After all, he is the chief."

While they waited, Davey studied the room. Huge logs formed the beams of the ceiling, supported by posts made from tree trunks. Black soot rimmed the smoke hole and many of the ceiling planks. He pictured the room filled with painted men, imagining the sound of drums and hearing the cadence of Cherokee songs rising and falling. He felt a stirring in his blood, a longing to partake in the ancient traditions of the chamber.

Sequoyah stood up and began a detailed explanation of the Council House. "The room is divided into sections, each reserving places for the seven Cherokee clans. These clans are the Bird Clan, Deer Clan, Paint Clan, Wolf Clan, Blue Clan, Long Hair Clan, and Wild Potato Clan. Insignias for each clan are on the walls behind their respective sections. Before us is the sacred fire; it is always kept burning. The wolf insignia on the door indicates that Yona is from the Wolf Clan. It will change, depending upon the clan of the next chief."

Amy pointed towards the table across from them. "Is that where the elders sit?"

Sequoyah nodded. "Each elder represents one of the seven clans. An elder has recently died, and Yona has asked me to take his place. When this happens, I will represent the Long Hair Clan because the Cherokee are a matrilineal society and that was my mother's clan."

Suddenly, the sound of flutes interrupted Sequoyah's words. He hurriedly sat down as seven Cherokee musicians slowly descended the steps from different parts of the chamber. Each musician was dressed in the ceremonial garments of a different clan and played a drum, flute, or rattle. Their combined voices sang the Cherokee greeting song. Expressions of joy showed on their faces, and their music rose into a crescendo when they reached the floor. Then it stopped, and silence filled the room.

The Three of We glanced at each other in astonishment. They had not expected a fancy ceremony. Sequoyah raised his eyebrows in appreciation, also a bit surprised. *Why is Yona putting on such a show?* he wondered.

Five elderly men silently emerged from the shadows behind the council table. The men wore buckskin robes, beautifully decorated by beads, fur, and quills. Two had feathers in their hair; the others did not. The men sat down in the chairs behind the council table, leaving the chair in the center vacant for Yona. The chair of the elder who had recently died was also empty.

As soon as the elders had taken their places, the singing started again. The song was similar, but of a different cadence. It announced the arrival of the chief. As the song ended, he came down the steps.

Yona was dressed entirely in white buckskin. A thick band of beads and quills lined the outer edges of his robe, interspersed with strips of silver that gleamed in the flickering light. A necklace of bear claws hung from his neck; a beaded headdress of eagle feathers held his white hair away from his face. Four stripes of red war paint crossed his nose and extended towards each ear. He used a carved wooden staff for support, yet his stance was erect, his eyes keen and intense.

He's actually more frightening than a bear, Davey thought.

Yona glared down at his visitors, his face stern. Then his mouth formed a slow smile. "Sequoyah...we thank you for bringing us these warriors before their coming battle. We pray to the spirits for their success."

Amy glanced at Davey. "What is he talking about?" she whispered.

"Maybe he's speaking in metaphors," Davey muttered.

Sequoyah rose from his seat and offered a warm smile. *I don't know what Yona is up to, but his words explain the war paint,* he thought, bowing respectfully. "We greet you, oh great chief, with our thanks for sharing your wisdom on this day."

Yona nodded and made a slight motion of his hand. At his signal, the seven musicians faded into the shadows, and he began to speak. "You are here on a matter of great importance. Before I explain, I would ask the great grandson of Tsusga Gineli a question."

Sequoyah turned and motioned Davey forward. Upon reaching Sequoyah's side, Davey smiled timidly at the old chief.

Yona studied Davey for a few seconds. At last, he spoke, his voice commanding. "The Great Oak has granted your wishes and allowed you to climb it. Another thing also happened when you were there. Will you speak of it?"

Davey instinctively knew the chief referred to the necklace. He stared into the old man's eyes as he pulled it from inside his shirt. "A squirrel gave me this," he said. "I think it was my great grandfather's."

Without comment, Yona sank resolutely into his chair and sighed heavily. After a moment, the elders began talking among themselves. Yona hadn't told them the reason for their meeting; they were becoming increasingly curious.

"Be silent," Yona ordered. "Have we become like crows cackling in the cornfield?" Instantly, the room grew quiet. Yona reached towards Davey, fingers trembling. "Will you let me hold it?" he asked gently.

Davey took off the necklace and gave it to Yona. The old man ran his hand across the surface of the pendant, touched the opaque jewel with reverence, and then handed it to the elder beside him. Silence filled the room as the elders passed the necklace around. Finally, they all put their heads together and a low conversation followed in Cherokee. After a short discussion, Yona returned the necklace to Davey, who immediately put it on again.

Yona nodded as if satisfied. "Tsusga Gineli gave it to me before he disappeared. I buried it beneath the Great Oak at his request. Over the years, I had begun to doubt if I would ever see it again; now it hangs from your neck. I am curious about one thing. When Tsusga Gineli touched the jewel, it came alive. Does it do so for you?"

Davey held the necklace up and touched the jewel on the pendant. It glowed brightly as amber currents swirled inside the stone.

"So…it speaks to you, just as it did to him!" Yona exclaimed.

"May I ask a question?" Davey inquired.

Sequoyah, who was still at Davey's side, cringed inwardly. He had told Davey not to ask questions unless invited to do so.

However, Yona did not mind. "Ask all the questions you like."

Davey quickly blurted out the question that had been on his mind since receiving the necklace. "Do you know its origin – the source of its magic?"

Yona smiled wistfully as he considered the question. He had wondered the same thing many years ago. "Your great grandfather was a skilled artisan and made many magical objects, including the necklace. As for the source of its magic, I asked him once, but could not comprehend his answer. That was sometimes the case."

"What do you mean?"

"He often spoke in verse. Understanding his meaning was like solving a puzzle. Since I do not write well, I sometimes committed his words to memory so I could later ponder their meaning. If what he said seemed important, I wrote it down when I had more time."

"Do you remember what he said when he gave you the necklace?"

"Yes…it was impossible to forget. These were his exact words."

The heir who comes after me,
Travels a path of discovery,
Bury this beneath the tree
And he will make recovery.
When the necklace again you see,
You must explain the mystery!

"But…I don't understand. How did he know I would find it?"

Yona chuckled, remembering the mystical powers of his friend, Tsusga Gineli. "Aah – your great grandfather was a *didanvwisgi* – a great shaman. He could read the stars and see things others could not. The ability to predict the future was one of his talents."

"Well then, what mystery was he referring to?" Davey asked.

Yona's eyes took on a faraway look as he pictured the hooded men surrounding Tsusga Gineli, their torchlight flickering upon his bound figure. More than sixty years had passed, yet the image was still clear in his mind. "At your great grandfather's request, I took a vow of silence regarding his disappearance. For many long years, I have kept my promise, awaiting the return of the necklace. Now, you have showed it to me. At last, I can speak of what took place…and why it happened."

Ꮳ Chapter 23 Ꮔ

---

*Yea, only the great magicians can foresee
the whims of fate. For ages, our magick
skill hath foretold the fall of nobles and
kings. Be thou not a false prophet lest ye
be judged as such.*

— Translated from Storia Di Incanto; circa 1803

Ustiwaya

YONA MOTIONED for Davey and Sequoyah to sit while he gathered his thoughts. "Perhaps I should start at the beginning," he finally said. "The Cherokee's friendship with your great grandfather began after he saved the chief's son, Cui, from certain death. Cui and several braves were crossing a frozen river when Cui fell through the ice. Suddenly, your great grandfather appeared and pulled him from the river. Cui was shaking with cold and nearly dead, but Tsusga Gineli warmed the boy with magic, restoring his health. After that, the chief declared him a hero and invited him to live in the village."

"Did he receive his Cherokee name then?" Davey asked.

"No, the chief named him after he brought his wagon to the village and we came to know him. The tribe felt blessed by his presence; he shared our love of nature and our beliefs in the spirits. In turn, we offered our friendship and gave him the name, Tsusga Gineli, which means *Friend of the Oak*."

Davey remembered how Yona had received his name and asked

with a smile. "Why was that name chosen?"

"It was an obvious choice. The chief soon learned that the Great Oak fascinated Tsusga Gineli. He spent many long hours climbing the tree, sitting in its branches, and talking with it. He even believed the Great Oak had summoned him to these mountains. One day, I asked him about it, and this was his answer."

The spirit of the Great Oak tree,
Inspires wonder and majesty,
Fate has caused my soul to be
Linked to its great sovereignty!

For centuries the tree has stood,
As goodness and a guiding hand,
Yet evil seeks to harm the wood
Protecting all in this fine land.

From overseas, I heard my name,
The calling voice was in great pain,
At last, I saw from whence it came
And with the tree, I will remain!

Davey thought about the meaning of the poem. *Could the tree have summoned me as well?*

A brief pause followed, and then Yona resumed his story. "Our friendship was a gradual thing. After Tsusga Gineli moved to the village, I followed him around at a respectful distance, a young and curious boy. He saw the admiration in my eyes, and we began to talk. Soon, we were taking walks and going on hunting trips together. From then on, we became like brothers. I taught him about the Cherokee, our history and way of life. In return, he told me about himself and explained his magic skill. He came from a family of powerful magicians – the magic was in his blood."

Davey's heart was pounding; he was finally learning the truth about his ancestors. "Will you tell me about his family?"

Yona nodded gravely. "His clan endured a life of many hardships in the great land across the sea. They wandered endlessly from place to place, entertaining with magic and fortune telling. Centuries earlier, they had angered a powerful enemy, who constantly hunted them. Their enemy was evil and relentless, killing his relatives whenever they could. It was like a blood feud."

Davey was eager to learn more, despite the unhappy story. "So…everyone in his family was a magician?"

"No, just the men were magicians. You see, it was not a learned skill, but an inherited trait that only male children could use. Still, both men and women in the bloodline were able to pass the trait on. As they did, the skill increased from one generation to the next. In 1892, the enemy caught up with the family and slaughtered them. Tsusga Gineli was the only survivor, leaving him as the family's sole heir."

Davey suddenly understood. "So he came to Great Oak, married Alicia, and tried to rebuild the family in a safer place."

"Yes…Tsusga Gineli believed that meeting Alicia was also part of his destiny. They were a perfect match. Not only was she beautiful and kindly; she had magic skills of her own. She inherited them from her Cherokee father."

Davey stared at Yona with astonishment. "I thought she was an orphan."

"Only the Cherokee were aware of her true heritage. Alicia was the love child of a Cherokee brave, Yonvadisi, and a white girl, Mary Johnson. She was the oldest of five children in a poor family living in the woods, and he was from a Cherokee village west of here. They kept their romance a secret, intending to run away and marry, but Yonvadisi died in a rockslide before they had the chance. Mary was pregnant with his child, and she died in childbirth six months later. Her family did not want the baby, so they abandoned the child on the doorstep of Houseman's Castle and moved on."

"What kind of magic skill did she have?" Davey asked, thinking he already knew the answer.

Yona studied Davey carefully. *This day holds many surprises for the boy,* he thought. "Yonvadisi was the son of Kanagagota, a Cherokee chief having the ability to call deer and other animals. The skill was legendary within his tribe, and Yonvadisi inherited it. They say a flock of birds circled overhead, warning Yonvadisi of the rockslide before he died, but he could not escape in time. The people of his village thought Yonvadisi would be their next chief. He was popular and his skill greatly benefited the tribe. Thus, when Yonvadisi died, they were sad for many reasons."

"Did they find out about the baby?"

"One of Yonvadisi's friends eventually told them about it. The tribe sent a delegation to the Johnsons, hoping they would let them raise the baby, but the family had already moved away. Months later, the tribe learned that the Housemans had the child. Knowing their efforts would be futile, they made no attempt to claim her."

Davey had a sudden thought. "Did Tsusga Gineli know about Alicia's magic skill when he married her?"

Yona shook his head. "Alicia knew nothing about her parents until Tsusga Gineli brought her to the village, and we told her about them. Then we arranged for an old shaman from Kanagagota's tribe to train her. Soon, birds flew around her wherever she went, so our chief gave her the name Tisqua Ada, which means *Bird Woman*. I remember Tsusga Gineli's delight when he learned she was with child. I asked him if his child would have both magic skills, and this was his reply."

> *When two magic bloods combine,*
> *It may make a stronger line,*
> *But only time will tell this tale*
> *Depending if the child be male!*

"I must have both skills! I have a way with birds and animals, and I can make the necklace come alive," Davey exclaimed.

Yona nodded. "Tsusga Gineli's prophecy said you would have great power."

Surprise showed on Davey's face again. "What prophecy?"

"As I said before, Tsusga Gineli could see into the future. He would stare at the stars as though in a trance, unmoving for hours. Then he would consult his magic cards and interpret what the stars had revealed. He did not always tell what he learned, but just before he disappeared, he delivered a prophecy about you."

"A prophecy about me…what was in it?" Davey stammered.

Yona paused again, choosing his words carefully. He had waited many years for this moment to arrive. He took a deep breath and continued.

"Tsusga Gineli and his wife lived with the Cherokee for seven happy years. Then one day, he received a message from the stars; the Great Oak was in danger. To protect it, he built a house near the tree and watched over it. Six months later, the stars sent another message; he would enter the spirit world during a terrible confrontation with the Housemans. He said that an heir with stronger powers than his would finish what he had begun."

Davey was stunned. *Did he mean me? How can I possibly have stronger powers? I know nothing about magic.* Then he put the thought aside and asked. "When did this confrontation occur?"

Yona's eyes shown with anger and his voice rose, seeming to fill the chamber. "It happened in 1937, the year of my twelfth birthday. I was staying at Tsusga Gineli's house when Claude Houseman and his men came for him, wearing hoods over their faces. They bound him with ropes and took him to the Great Oak, proclaiming that they were going to hang him and burn the tree. Tsusga Gineli had already informed me of their intentions and instructed me not to interfere, but I followed the men and watched from the shadows. He delivered this prophecy as he stood before them, a rope around his neck."

Hear me now, oh wicked men,
You have no cause to harm me,
Abandon all your ways of sin
And do no ill to this great tree!

Look at me, ye men and see,
Remain here and incur my wrath,
Be forewarned that my decree
Informs you of great aftermath.

A plague dwells within this town,
Filled with evil Housemans be,
Claude will never wear the crown
And shatter will his dynasty!

In this town, there is a war,
Evil has been here too long,
But I have come here from afar
To help the tree fight the wrong.

Years from now, the ending be,
When one comes who has the power,
To face hate and make men free,
I speak of him in this dark hour!

He is my heir, joined by two,
They stalk the evil in its lair,
Young and strong are these few,
Their arrows will pierce the air!

As for you, ye men of sin,
These dark clouds reveal your fate,
Your retreat should ye begin,
Lest ye enter hell's hot gate!

Davey could hardly believe his ears. Tsusga Gineli had known he would come to Great Oak and had foreseen the forming of their pact – the Three of We.

"What happened next?" Davey asked immediately.

Yona resumed his story. "For a brief moment, the hooded men lost their nerve, but Claude Housemen rallied them and they continued their foolish plan. Then Tsusga Gineli called down lightning from the sky, and it struck the men repeatedly. It was a fierce sight to behold."

"What became of my great grandfather?"

Yona glanced upward, as though consulting the spirits. "Over the years, I have given much thought to this question. Perhaps the force of his magic consumed him, but I believe otherwise. The stars did not reveal how he would enter the spirit world or in what form. I believe his spirit fused somehow with that of the tree. This powerful force is watching over you as we speak."

Initially, Davey thought Yona's explanation was pure fantasy, but it was as believable as anything else that had happened. *I'll think about it later,* he decided, and asked another question. "What did he mean about us stalking the evil in its lair?"

Yona rose from his chair and descended the steps towards the earthen floor. "Tsusga Gineli left something at the village, which will help me explain. Before I show it to you, I will conduct the naming ceremony. Cherokee warriors must have tribal names! Sequoyah, will you bring them to the sacred fire?"

"Can I have a name too?" Amy blurted out.

Yona smiled, thinking a surprise was in store for her as well. He had looked into her heritage. "You have an ancestor, a woman named Morning Dove. She was from the bird clan in our tribe. Many years ago, she married an Englishman and moved to Virginia. In deference to our customs, her husband assumed her maiden name, but used the English form. Thus, Pigeon became your family's surname."

A bright smile flashed across Amy's face. "I knew about my Virginia relatives, but not about the Cherokee part."

Yona gave a signal, and the Cherokee musicians filed down the steps again, singing the naming song as they came. When they reached the earthen floor, they circled around the small group beside the fire pit, moving in measured steps and playing their instruments. In the meantime, Yona put a cedar log onto the fire, and the smoke swirled around them.

When the song was finished, Yona stepped towards Davey. He gently fanned a wisp of smoke towards the boy and placed his hands upon his head. "Hear us, oh Great Spirit. Let the sacred smoke give this brave the speed of the swiftest animal. Let him have the courage of the great Wolf Clan in battle. I name him Ustiwaya!"

"What does it mean?" Davey asked.

"It means *Little Wolf*."

"Ustiwaya…it's a good name," Davey muttered.

Yona stepped up to Jimmy next, fanning the smoke towards him. "I have known you since your birth. You are kind, loyal, and have great skill with the bow. When you were a boy, I named you Hawk because of your keen eyes. Now, you will fight a great enemy and your strength with the bow will be important. You need a warrior's name, so I change your name to Uhusti Gatlida."

Jimmy bowed his head. *My name is now Strong Arrow,* he thought with a smile.

Finally, Yona fanned the smoke towards Amy. As she looked into his fierce eyes, she felt goose bumps along her arms. *If I faint now, I'll just die,* she thought.

"You are wise like an owl, yet you have the cleverness of a panther. You see what others may not. This can turn the tide of battle. I name you Ugugu Tivdatsi Digadili."

"It means *Owl With Panther's Eyes,*" Sequoyah whispered.

Amy grinned with satisfaction. "Thank you," she said softly.

Yona rapped his staff on the ground seven times; the naming ceremony was over. Joyous cries rose from the musicians as they danced around their new brothers. Yona stood tall and stared at the Three of We. Pride filled his eyes, along with a strange fury. "Come Sequoyah, let us show these warriors our greatest treasure," he said.

⊛ Chapter 24 ⊛

Lo, ye must knowe that spirits live. Some shall aid ye, and some shall cause ye harm. They dwell in the secret places of the earth, and thou must take care around them.

— Translated from Storia Di Incanto; circa 1815

The Magic Wagon

AFTER THE NAMING CEREMONY, Yona led the Three of We out of the Council House. They formed a line, Yona in front and Sequoyah bringing up the rear. "We are going to the edge of the mountain," Yona announced and took off in determined strides, his route taking them through the village.

Sequoyah was surprised at his grandfather's pace. Despite his advanced age, the old man moved with agility and speed. Sequoyah smiled as he hurried to keep up. *Yona has been invigorated by this,* he thought.

The historic sights of the old Cherokee village filled Davey's eyes while they walked. He saw many log homes scattered along the terraced ridges of the mountain above them. As his gaze drifted upward, Davey realized the clearing where the Council House stood was only two-thirds of the way up the mountain. "Does the tribe own all of Greyhead Mountain?" he asked as they continued on their way.

"It was Cherokee land long before the first white men came,"

Sequoyah replied. "The British recognized our claim in many treaties, and we became their allies during the Revolutionary War. After the war, the Colonial Government declared our treaties invalid, so our tribe purchased the mountain for two-hundred dollars. My ancestors did this, even though the land had always been ours. Years later, the Housemans tried to cut timber on the mountain, claiming we did not have title. We took them to court, and they lost after a long and bitter struggle. No one has questioned our ownership since then," Sequoyah said proudly.

"Good!" Davey exclaimed. He had developed an intense dislike for the Housemans since arriving in Great Oak.

As they progressed through the clearing, Davey noticed several large open-air buildings decorated with colorful feathers, animal skins, and woven blankets. Water wells and fire pits for cooking stood nearby. Four women and two men were tending a large fire, over which five cast-iron pots bubbled merrily. Their cooking imbued the air with intriguing smells, and Davey realized he was getting hungry.

Yona stopped for a moment, as though sensing Davey's interest in the food. "We will return later and have lunch with the tribe. You can sample our Cherokee cooking at that time," he said, and then continued his purposeful trek.

They passed a small school building, which stood on a neatly manicured plot. Just ahead was a split-railed corral, holding more than a dozen horses. Davey saw several men busily forking hay and putting grain out for the animals in a barn next to the corral. Outside the barn, a lone man sat on a blanket tooling leather bridals.

"May we come back and ride the horses sometime?" Amy asked, glancing wistfully at the corral.

"You have Cherokee names now, and Yona has welcomed you into the tribe. You may come here whenever you want," Sequoyah replied.

Davey and Amy felt like they had stepped back in time, witnessing things that few outsiders had ever seen. They were beginning to feel a sense of pride in their newly found heritage. The man sitting on the ground cried out "osiyo!" when they passed. Amy asked Sequoyah what he meant.

"He is saying hello to his new kin," Sequoyah explained. "News travels quickly in the village."

Davey and Amy returned his greeting, smiling cheerfully. They instinctively knew these people were their friends and hoped to visit the village many more times in the future. From then on, they said "osiyo" to everyone they met.

Yona turned onto a narrow trail at the edge of the clearing, and soon they were scrambling up a steep incline. Sequoyah expected Yona to slow his pace, but he used his staff for support and climbed effortlessly as the trail wound its way higher. Finally, they reached a fork in the path and Yona stopped. Two stakes marked the left side of the fork. Each stake was taller than their heads and decorated by swirls of white paint.

Yona pointed at the stakes and explained their meaning. "The paint forbids passage along this trail unless accompanied by the chief. However, you have my permission to come here without me in the future. You will understand why when we reach out destination." Then he took the left fork without further comment.

They walked for over a mile, each step taking them towards the edge of the mountain. At last, the trees grew scarce and they arrived at a flat, rocky precipice. Immediately, Davey's necklace began to vibrate, and he found himself looking out over open space.

A large stone platform stood in the center of the precipice, covered by a high thatched roof. Stout wooden posts supported the roof, but the structure was open to the air on all sides. Resting on the platform was a large carnival wagon. Painted in bold letters along its sides were the following words.

The Great Sabatini

The World's Most Astonishing Magician

The wagon glittered in the sunlight, its surface bright and shiny. Colors of green, red, blue, and yellow decorated its various parts, yet there was something distinctly odd about it. Wrapped around the lower part of the wagon were the thick boughs of a tree. The boughs formed the skeletal shape of a boat's hull, but it was not solid, merely an outline. The large spoked wheels of the wagon protruded beyond this clumsy looking fame, giving the impression of a boat, which could travel on land.

Attached at intervals along the upper sides of the wagon were round woven shapes, two feet in diameter. They were shield-like objects made from the same wood as the boughs, though of thinner branches. There were six of these shields, three on each side of the wagon. Yona stepped aside while Davey, Amy, and Jimmy hurried towards the wagon with cries of astonishment.

"It's my great grandfather's wagon! How did it get here?" Davey exclaimed. He walked around the wagon and let his fingers touch the boughs encircling its base. As he did, his fingerprints left glowing marks along the surface of the wood. Davey looked at Yona in surprise. "These branches are from the Great Oak."

"Yes," Yona replied simply and began to explain. "Tsusga Gineli brought the wagon to the village shortly after we gave him his Cherokee name. One morning, we found it resting in front of the Council House with Tsusga Gineli and his wife asleep inside. Two feet of snow covered the ground, yet the wheels left no tracks in the icy surface. When the chief asked him about this, he answered with this poem."

> *When one travels in the sky,*
> *It's easy to stay warm and dry,*
> *So I flew in from up high*
> *And landed here, by the bye!*

"He flew it," Davey proclaimed, an image of the flying wagon filling his mind. "Perhaps I can do it one day," he added.

Yona's eyes seemed full of intrigue. "Perhaps you can do it now," he replied, wanting to test the boy's skill.

Davey shook his head. "I don't know how."

Yona recalled when he and Tsusga Gineli had ridden in the wagon together. "Tsusga Gineli did not use magic words to make the wagon fly. The power was within his mind. Try to move it a few inches with your thoughts – it will be a start."

"The branches from the tree must serve a purpose," Amy said. "Maybe they help it fly."

"Have a go at it," Jimmy suggested.

Each night during the week, Davey had practiced moving the highlight pen with his mind. His ability improved until he could make the pen fly through the air. Nevertheless, the wagon was so much larger – moving it seemed impossible. Still, he decided to try.

He focused his mind and willed for the wagon to rise. Nothing happened at first, but he concentrated on the branches and pictured the wagon as a boat, bobbing along a sea of clouds. Suddenly, the branches around the wagon began to creak and tremble. Then the entire mass lurched a few feet into the air. It hung suspended for a few seconds like an ungainly bird and then banged noisily back onto the platform.

"Bloody heck, you did it!" Jimmy exclaimed.

"I can't believe it," Amy said. "I've got goose bumps."

Davey slumped down on the platform, momentarily exhausted. "Amy is right. The branches provide some sort of lifting power."

"Let's look inside the wagon. Maybe Tsusga Gineli left something important in there," Amy said.

Davey's ability had pleased Yona, yet he held up his hand to halt them. "Wait," he commanded. "Ustiwaya can make the wagon fly, but only practice will keep it in the air. First, let me explain why it is here."

He motioned for them to follow him towards the edge of the precipice. After they had gathered around him, he pointed at another mountain about a mile across from them. "That is Brown Mountain.

Study it Ustiwaya, and tell me what you feel."

Davey stared silently at the mountain for a moment. As he did, his necklace began an urgent vibration and an abrupt chill ran along his spine. "There is something evil there," he said, shivering. "It's a dangerous thing."

"Yes," Yona replied gravely. "Sit now, I wish to tell you a story." When they had each found places around him, he began to speak again.

"Tsusga Gineli learned many things from the spirit in the Great Oak. The spirit was very old, older than time itself. It spoke of a period when many spirits roamed the earth. These spirits were mystical creatures, formed by bundles of leftover energy when the earth was created. Some were benevolent, like the spirit in the tree, and some were evil. Whenever these opposite spirits confronted each other, a great upheaval occurred. Floods, volcanoes, or violent storms resulted, destroying both spirits and causing great damage to the surrounding land. After this had happened for many centuries, only a few spirits remained."

"How was he able to speak with the spirit?" Amy asked.

"He used his magic skill. Through it, he established a unique form of communication with the tree. The spirit did not speak in words, but made pictures appear in his mind. He was able to interpret the meaning of these pictures."

"He must have found it fascinating," Davey remarked.

Yona nodded and then continued his story. "According to the spirit, when man came upon the earth, the remaining spirits ceased their roaming and found sanctuaries in which to exist. These sanctuaries were natural formations like waterfalls, caves, and towering trees. They were places where energy trickled up from the earth's core to nourish the spirits."

"What happened if a sanctuary ran out of energy or was destroyed?" Amy asked.

"Aah, that brings up an important point. The spirits initially moved easily from one sanctuary to another, but over time, their ability to travel diminished. Today, if a spirit has to find another sanctuary, it may wither away and die before it has the chance."

Davey found this intriguing. "How long has the spirit lived in the Great Oak?"

"The spirit did not measure time by days or years, but by memories of events. The spirit told Tsusga Gineli of many things, which had occurred beneath the tree. Judging by those events, it took sanctuary in the tree long before the white man came to this land. Ever since then, the spirit caused the tree to emit an aura of peace and prosperity. At first, good things happened, but then another influence came, and the tree began to die."

"Did the spirit know the tree was dying?" Jimmy asked.

"Yes, and it eventually summoned Tsusga Gineli for help. You see, many years after the spirit selected the Great Oak as its sanctuary, a strange coincidence occurred. An evil spirit took sanctuary in a cave on Brown Mountain. Why this evil spirit selected a sanctuary so close to the Great Oak is unknown."

"Perhaps the evil spirit wanted to challenge the tree's influence," Amy said.

Yona nodded. "This may be. At any rate, the evil spirit immediately began its dark work. It inspired a renegade group of Indians living on the mountain to worship it. Soon, they began to kill innocent people and ravage the land by setting fires in the forests and attacking nearby villages. Fortunately, we captured one of their leaders and learned of the evil spirit. We assembled an army, drove the renegades away, and threw burning logs into the cave, which forced the spirit into its deepest cavern. Then we blocked the entrance of the cave with many stones, sealing off the spirit from the outside world. This allowed the tree to spread its benevolence over the land once more."

"It was a legendary battle in the history of our tribe," Jimmy added. "The elders tell stories about it, but do not mention the evil spirit."

"It is bad luck to speak of this evil," Yona said. "You are learning about it out of necessity."

"What do you mean? Has the spirit escaped from the cave?" Amy asked.

Yona shook his head. "No, but the cave is no longer sealed. As the Housemans expanded their empire, they purchased the portion of Brown Mountain where the cave is located and started a limestone quarry. However, they didn't plan their excavation carefully enough. One day, a landslide occurred, and the stones blocking the cave slid down the mountain. This permitted the evil spirit to exert its influence again."

"When did this happen?" Davey inquired, wanting to get the sequence of events fixed in his mind.

"About a hundred years ago. This time, the evil spirit sought to attack the Great Oak. It did not confront the tree directly. Such an act would destroy them both. Instead, it incited the Housemans to do its bidding. They were an easy target, a malicious family that had always hated the tree. Before long, the tree's health was in danger. That was when the spirit in the tree summoned Tsusga Gineli."

"And he healed it!" Davey exclaimed.

"Yes, although he never explained how."

"Why couldn't the spirit in the tree defend itself?" Amy asked.

"Tsusga Gineli said the spirit was filled with great kindness. It could not harm any entity, even the evil spirit in the cave. All it sought from Tsusga Gineli was protection. However, Tsusga Gineli knew he would not live forever, so he consulted the stars for guidance and they revealed his fate. His role was to guard the tree. It was his heir's destiny to kill the evil spirit."

"But his magic was so powerful…why didn't he do it?"

"There was a dark secret in his past of which he spoke little. All I know is that he had allowed evil to enter his heart when he was young. For the rest of his life, he atoned for that mistake. In a sense, protecting the tree purified him, yet he was afraid to go near the cave. Only one who has not felt evil can resist the spirit's influence."

At last, Davey understood why he was in Great Oak. Of course, it was incredible. Still, there was no doubt in his mind. He glanced at Amy and Jimmy. "Can we do this?"

"The prophecy spoke of us. If we don't, who will?" Amy replied.

"It's a far, far better thing than we have ever done," Jimmy said stoically.

Davey and Amy stared at him, shocked by his version of the famous line from *A Tale of Two Cities.*

Jimmy grinned back at them. "Hey, I read too!"

Davey turned towards Yona. "All right, what should we do?"

The boy's magic skill had impressed Yona, but he knew it was not yet strong enough to confront the evil spirit. "You must practice until you can make the wagon soar like an eagle. Start by searching it; Tsusga Gineli left items there that only you can find." Then he looked at Amy and Jimmy. "And you must learn to think and act as one, so you can help Ustiwaya in ways that do not require magic."

"You haven't told us why the wagon sits on this cliff," Davey said.

"This spot is directly across from the cave on Brown Mountain. Tsusga Gineli infused the branches and shields on the wagon with magic and painted it with a varnish made from the sap of the tree. They help the wagon fly, but also serve another purpose. Their magic exudes an aura, which protects us from the evil spirit's influence. If you fly the wagon to the cave, its aura will protect you as well."

Davey turned his attention to the wagon. He walked around it, searching for a door, but found none. "There is no opening."

Yona smiled. "Tsusga Gineli sealed the wagon with magic. You must open it with your mind. Use your skill, Ustiwaya. You must practice until it becomes second nature to you."

Davey focused his mind, thinking hard. *Where is the most logical place for a door?* he wondered. He decided it would be at the rear of the wagon and pictured an opening in the wooden panel. Slowly, the barest outline of a doorway appeared in the wood. Smiling, Davey touched the panel. With a sudden creaking sound, a door flew open. After that, three steps flopped down towards the ground. Davey gave Amy a bemused glance, walked up the steps, and peered inside.

At first, the interior seemed shrouded in darkness, but as soon as Davey stepped inside, a faint glow appeared along the walls. He found himself looking into a small room, barely large enough for one person. His weight caused a slight shifting of the wagon, and he braced himself against its sides. When he touched the wood, his fingertips began to tingle, the glow became three times brighter, and the walls moved outward until the room doubled in size.

Davey stuck his head out the doorway and looked down at Amy. "Did you notice the wagon changing shape?"

Amy shook her head, puzzled by his question. "I've seen no change."

Davey smiled and focused his attention again on the interior of the wagon. *Sabatini magic,* he thought, while examining the space. The room seemed completely empty at first, the walls bare. Even so, as he touched various surfaces, furniture began to appear. A bed flopped down on one side, and a table and bench unfolded in a corner. Painted murals spread themselves along the walls, and Italian words danced across the ceiling. As this happened, a swooshing sound filled the air, and amber sparkles of magic dust flew everywhere.

Each time something appeared, Davey let out a soft cry of surprise. Then the outline of three small doors became visible on the far wall, and a glorious painting of the Great Oak splashed across the wall's surface. Davey's necklace began to vibrate, and he knew what he sought was there. He hurried forward and touched the wood. When he did, the doors opened and he saw three deerskin-wrapped bundles.

Davey carried the bundles outside and laid them on the ground. Amy and Jimmy gathered around him, their eyes dancing with excitement. Yona and Sequoyah were equally as curious, but they watched silently from a distance.

"Blimey mate, let's open them!" Jimmy shouted, reaching eagerly.

"Let Davey do it," Amy said. "They were intended for him."

Jimmy grinned. "Right you are…as usual."

Davey sat down, selected one of the bundles, and opened it. As the deerskin wrapping fell away, a graceful oak bow came into view. The wood was polished and etched with hieroglyphic symbols. Tiny amber jewels dotted the bow, each similar to the stone on his necklace. As soon as Davey touched the wood, he knew his great grandfather had made it from a branch of the Great Oak. He also felt a surge of energy when his fingers brushed along the tiny jewels.

The bow was unstrung, but Davey found a smaller pouch inside the deerskin wrapping, which contained a coiled bowstring. When Davey pulled out the bowstring, the pouch changed into a flat piece of leather and a message appeared on its surface amid a shower of amber sparks. After the words became clear, he read the message aloud.

> *The one with you who is strong,*
> *Will use this bow to right the wrong,*
> *The bowstring sings a magic song,*
> *And arrows fly straight and long!*

"Let me hold it; I'm the one named Strong Arrow!" Jimmy exclaimed.

Davey gave the bow to Jimmy and he immediately tried to string it; the wood was like a piece of iron in his hand. "Bloody heck, I can't even bend it," he said after several tries.

Davey took the bow and slowly ran his fingers along its carved surface, sensing its magic. "I feel your power, let me harness it," he whispered. Abruptly, the bow turned into a pliable piece of wood, and Davey quickly attached the string at both ends. He handed the bow back to Jimmy with a smile. "All it takes is a little magic."

The next bundle was three feet long. An ornate leather quiver filled with arrows lay inside the wrapping, each arrow made from the wood of the Great Oak. Along the pointed ends of the shafts, tiny amber jewels glittered from small holes in the wood. *There is magic power in these arrows,* Davey thought. He handed the quiver to Jimmy, who slung it over his shoulder with a grin.

The final bundle was a small, square package. When Davey

opened the wrapping, he uttered a cry of awe; two magical items lay inside. The first was a green scarf, decorated with hieroglyphic pictures in blue, red, and yellow. The second was a pair of gold bracelets, studded with large amber jewels. As soon as Davey removed the objects, another message appeared on the surface of the leather. Once again, he read it aloud when the writing was finished.

The scarf holds a wisdom spell,
Use it and be wise as well,
Truth will cause a ringing bell
Lies produce an ugly smell!

The bracelets are for my heir,
Their power rules the very air,
With cold, or hot, or forces fair
Wield them all with greatest care!

Davey handed the scarf to Amy. "You should wear this."

Amy took the scarf and wrapped it carefully around her neck. "Thank you; I am honored." Then a wide grin spread across her face. "I heard the slight tingle of a bell because I told the truth," she exclaimed.

Jimmy's face broke into a grin. "I thought you always told the truth."

Amy wrinkled her nose. "Phew, I smell dirty socks. You told a lie!"

Davey laughed and began to examine the bracelets in his hand. Each bracelet was a coiled rope of woven gold, consisting of seven loops. Amber jewels, a half-inch in diameter, decorated the loops at intervals. He silently counted the jewels – there were fourteen. *There is a lot of magic power here,* Davey thought, slipping one of the bracelets over his hand.

The golden coils immediately flowed along his wrist, similar to the way the necklace had shaped itself to his body. He felt a dizzying sensation as the power rushed through him. He took a deep breath and steadied himself against the ground.

Amy watched him with concern. "Are you all right?"

Davey answered in a strained voice. "Yes…I'm just getting used to its power." He slipped the remaining bracelet over his other wrist. Once more, he braced himself while the magic surged through him. After several minutes, he rose on shaking legs. He suddenly felt lighter than before and jumped forward, testing his strength. His leap carried him across a span of five yards.

Yona's eyes opened wide as he watched him. "Ustiwaya, you must use care in trying out your new skills. Take little steps at first."

Davey bowed his head, feeling foolish. "Yes, I promise."

Yona patted the boy on the shoulder. "Good, let us return to the village now and eat lunch with the tribe. We can try out Tsusga Gineli's bow and arrows afterward."

Davey stopped and glanced back at the wagon as they left the precipice; the wagon stood unmoving, its door open. *When I come here again, we will fly together,* he thought. Then he focused his mind and willed for the wagon to seal itself. Instantly, the deerskin coverings flew into the wagon, the door slammed shut behind them, and the doorway disappeared from view. With a satisfied smile, he hurried to join the others.

⊗ Chapter 25 ∞

Nature hath a way of warning when evil comes anon. Thus, when nature seems amiss, ye should be wary.

— Translated from Storia Di Incanto; circa 1819

A Sudden Storm

THE THREE OF WE sat alongside Sequoyah and Yona in one of the open-air pavilions near the Council House. Bowls of corn, venison stew, smoked pork, kale, mushrooms, and turnips were stacked before them. *There is enough here for an army,* Davey thought as he piled food upon his plate.

More than a hundred members of the tribe sat at the tables surrounding them. The villagers talked and laughed in subdued tones, casting frequent glances at their guests. Whenever Davey's eyes met theirs, curious smiles greeted him.

After everyone had eaten their fill, Yona gave a signal, and a line of seven elegantly dressed women approached their table. They wore robes of white deerskin; ornate feather and bone necklaces hung from their necks. An elderly woman led them, wearing a radiant tunic of red, blue, and yellow beaded sunbursts.

"She is Elogi Ugithisa, the high priestess of the Ani-Wodi," Sequoyah explained. "Her name means *Aunt Daylight*…the other women are her assistants. The Ani-Wodi are shamans and keepers of the tribe's sacred paint. They are members of the paint clan and hold positions of great authority."

A rhythmic beating of drums soon began, and Elogi Ugithisa and her assistants broke into song as they marched around the table. She carried a pot of red paint and marked the foreheads of the Three of We with a single stripe as she passed. The women who followed her sprinkled pollen dust over their heads and shook bone rattles. They circled the table four times, repeating the process until their song was finished. After that, shrill cries of celebration filled the room.

Yona rose from the table, gave a nod of thanks to the Ani-Wodi, and began a short speech. "We have welcomed our new brethren into the tribe and given them Cherokee names. Out priests have called upon the Great Spirit to strengthen their courage and anointed them with the sacred war paint. These warriors follow the path of our friend, Tsusga Gineli, and undertake a great quest. I ask each of you to greet them and offer any help they require."

For the next hour, the men, women, and children of the village crowded around their table. They clasped the hands of the Three of We, patted them reassuringly, and the younger children gave each of them fierce hugs. Many villagers uttered words of admiration for the magnificent bow carried by Jimmy, as well as the bracelets and scarf worn by Davey and Amy. Despite their curiosity, the villagers did not ask any questions about their coming quest.

"I feel like a celebrity," Davey whispered to Jimmy.

"Yeah, ain't it great!" Jimmy exclaimed.

"I know they are curious, yet no one has asked why we are here," Amy said.

"It is not the Cherokee way to ask questions about personal matters. We believe a person must invite such a conversation first. Otherwise, it is considered bad manners," Sequoyah replied.

After the villagers had departed, Yona's face broke into a broad smile. "Come warriors, let us try out Tsusga Gineli's bow," he said. Once again, they followed him through the village. This time, he headed towards the other side of the Council House.

"He's taking us to the tribe's archery range," Jimmy announced.

The archery range was a long, open area, surrounded by thick woods. Wooden targets shaped like panthers, bears, wolves, and deer stood at the far end, and several bird-shaped targets hung from the trees. Yona halted at the end of the range and looked at Jimmy. "Can you hit a target from this distance?" he asked, smiling mysteriously.

"I can shoot an arrow that far, but not accurately," Jimmy replied.

"He speaks truthfully," Amy said, still intrigued with her wisdom scarf.

"Shoot an arrow and let's see what you hit," Yona commanded.

Jimmy notched an arrow in the bowstring and slowly took aim. His muscles bulged from the effort, but he managed to draw back the string completely. As he released the arrow, a faint musical sound filled the air. The arrow streaked towards the targets, passing above them and eventually striking a tree at the edge of the range.

"Blimey, what power this bow has!" Jimmy exclaimed.

"Shoot another arrow, but pick the smallest target. This time, I want Ustiwaya to focus on the target and make the arrow hit it," Yona instructed.

"Okay," Jimmy said. "I'll aim at the duck hanging from the tree."

Davey focused his mind and pictured the arrow hitting the duck. When he was ready, he nodded at Jimmy. The arrow soared through the air, faster than their eyes could follow, and struck the duck in its center.

"Unbelievable, good onya!" Jimmy cried in a surprised voice.

Jimmy and Davey repeated the experiment until the quiver was empty. They picked a different target each time; every arrow hit its mark. Amy cheered enthusiastically as each arrow struck, and Yona nodded at Sequoyah when they were finished. "They are a good team," he said quietly.

Suddenly, the sound of distant thunder reverberated across the mountains. Sequoyah glanced at the sky with a frown. He had been absorbed in watching Jimmy and hadn't noticed the weather changing. Now, he saw dark clouds rolling across the western sky with black and threatening underbellies. "Gather your arrows," he said. "A storm is coming and we must leave."

"Darn, I wanted to see the horses again," Amy said.

"Sorry Amy, there isn't time. The road can be treacherous in a rainstorm," Sequoyah replied.

As soon as the arrows were gathered, they bid Yona goodbye and hurried towards the pickup. The trip down the mountain went faster than on the way up, despite the same jarring bumps in the road. While Sequoyah concentrated upon the winding road, the Three of We sat in silence. In the rearview mirror, Sequoyah caught glimpses of the sky behind him. The clouds had thickened, and the entire western horizon had turned into a churning mixture of black and purple.

"Here it comes," Sequoyah warned as a long streak of lightning flashed overhead. A deafening roar of thunder quickly followed, making everyone cry out in alarm. Within seconds, rain flooded the windshield and the truck began to fishtail along the road.

"Blimey, that was close," Jimmy muttered.

Amy squeezed Davey's hand as more lightning and thunder boomed around them, but said nothing. Davey's necklace vibrated furiously, and he wondered if the evil spirit was somehow responsible for the storm. He glanced at Amy and knew by the look on her face that she was thinking the same thing.

At last, the truck pulled onto the highway and Sequoyah grinned with relief. He had seen the village road completely wash out in heavy rains, had witnessed trucks tip over as they skidded down the road in storms like this. *Nothing better than getting home safe,* he thought.

ஐ✺ஐ✺ஐ✺ஐ✺

Wally Houseman watched the approaching storm from the windows of his study. The flash of lightning and din of thunder gave him a thrill, despite his foul mood. His mind conjured up more devilish schemes when such fury surrounded him.

Wally and Sineous Crop were discussing Bill Winston's refusal of

Wally's offer of employment. Wally grew irate as he though about how quickly his plan had fallen apart. "I can't believe he checked up on me!" he yelled angrily.

"He outsmarted you, that's all. Your plan was not a good one," Sineous replied, sounding somewhat superior. "I have a better idea."

Wally laughed, as if Sineous was a mindless idiot. "Very funny, *you* have a better idea."

"You'll understand when you see this object. It's out in the woods, so I have to go get it," Sineous said, and then quickly left the study.

After fifteen minutes, Wally grew impatient. "Where has the fool gone?" he shouted, pacing around like an angry bull. A short time later, Sineous trudged noisily up the stairs. He backed into the study, dragging a burlap-wrapped object by a short rope. "I dug it up this afternoon," he said breathlessly. "My father buried it in the woods."

Wally sensed the presence of something evil and hurried towards Sineous. "Unwrap it!" he shouted, his curiosity getting the best of him.

Sineous pulled the object upright and slowly removed the burlap covering, careful not to touch what lay inside. As he did, a large, black stone came into view. The stone had the shape of a hideous mouth, screaming in pain. Wally reached out to caress the stone, but Sineous pushed his hand away. "Touching it will make you sick," he said.

"Where did it come from?" Wally asked, his eyes devilish.

"My father found it in the cave many years ago. To test its power, he placed it beneath a small house where the quarry workers slept. They all became violently ill."

"I like it," Wally said, smiling fiendishly. "What else has it been used for?"

"You could say that it saved your grandfather's political career back in 1910. There had been talk about Ralph Harrison running against Claude in the next election. He could have been a formidable opponent, but my father snuck into the basement of Ralph's house and hid the stone among some old boxes. After a time, Ralph went crazy."

Wally yelled exuberantly. "Sineous, this is great – tell me more!"

Sineous smiled broadly. "The stone causes a variety of illnesses. In the case of the Harrisons, the illness was depression. It permeated the family's blood and subsequent generations inherited the tendency. As a result, they have all led miserable lives. Joe Harrison, the park warden, is the only one left. He has never married and has no heirs."

"Are other stones like this one available?" Wally asked, imagining all sorts of wicked things that he could do with them.

"My father found six similar stones, all smaller than this one. He buried them in a circle around the Great Oak, and the tree began to die. Then Antonio Sabatini showed up and healed the tree. When my father dug up the stones later, they had all become ashes. Somehow, the roots of the tree destroyed them."

Wally laughed heartily. "The Great Sabatini protected the tree, but he is not here now to protect Sally Winston and her nephew. What if we placed this stone in the basement of her house? The same thing that happened to the Harrisons might occur."

Sineous smiled maliciously. "My thoughts exactly."

Wally's eyes gleamed. "Don't wait another minute, do it tonight!"

"Master, there is a bad storm coming."

Wally raised his arms towards the sky, practically howling with delight. "It's perfect, don't you see? No one will notice you on a night like this."

⁐⁐⁐

Linda Peabody barely reached Ed Nolen's house before the storm hit Great Oak. She had spent the entire day in a workshop conducted by Eunice Bluestone, an event dreaded by every teacher at the school. However, she felt so lighthearted after the workshop ended that she ran the entire way to Ed's house, which kept her from getting soaked.

Linda had been worried about the workshop because of Eunice's reputation for singling out teachers and making fun of their mistakes. Linda couldn't remember making any terrible blunders, yet she was still concerned. When she heard Eunice call out her name halfway through the afternoon, she was understandably mortified.

Eunice's voice seemed almost friendly, making the other teachers smile in anticipation. This was one of Eunice's favorite ploys. She acted sweet as sugar and then let you have it with a kidney punch.

Linda stood up at the back of the room; she had been hoping to escape notice there. "I'm here," she called out, wincing as if Eunice was about to hit her.

Eunice continued, as nice as could be. "I'm putting you in charge of the Scholar's Team this year. Please create a plan for selecting the team members and have it on my desk by next Friday. Will you do that for me, dear?"

Linda nodded, so surprised she couldn't speak. She knew Eunice was desperate to win the Scholar's Team competition; a winning football, basketball, or baseball team meant nothing to her. The competition was between all twenty middle schools within a three county region. Great Oak had finished at the bottom for almost ten years. Each year, Eunice picked her favorite teacher as the team's coach. The results were always the same; Great Oak came in last.

"I guess we know who her new pet is," Emily Watson snorted.

"It's because of Davey Boehm. Linda hasn't done anything except luck into being his home room teacher," Pamela Dickson replied smugly. She was the type of person who was happiest when running someone else down.

Linda just smiled when she overheard them. They were right, of course, but she wasn't going to let that fact diminish her enjoyment of working with the Scholar's Team. Besides, there was something else lifting her spirits – being able to share her happiness with Ed Nolen.

଼୪ଈଓ୪ଈଓ୪ଈଓ

Androf Protsky sat in his apartment, brooding as the storm rolled into Great Oak. Five pain-filled days had passed since his encounter with the ravens. A need for revenge had boiled inside him the entire time.

The morning after falling from the tree, he could barely walk. His ankle hurt, agony racked his neck and back, and he had two cracked ribs, which throbbed painfully whenever he took a breath. His face, neck, and hands festered with infection from the deep gashes inflicted by the ravens. When he looked at his bloody and bruised face in the mirror, he cried out angrily, but that only made the pain worse. *I have to get out of here before Alice sees me,* he thought. *She might call the police.*

Androf had received many injuries over the course of his wicked life, but his need for secrecy prevented him from seeing a doctor like an ordinary person. Thus, he had become good at doctoring himself, even though he had no medical training. Everything he needed was available at a local drugstore. As soon as he found one, Doctor Protsky would be in business again.

Despite his injuries, Androf managed to leave the apartment before dawn. All he took with him were a few clothes, his cell phone, and the old shotgun from the house in Hickory. He left a note on his apartment door saying that he'd be back in a few days. The note was for Alice, his landlady, in case she came snooping.

Androf drove the white van away from Great Oak until he reached a little town called Rest Easy. Normally, he would have found this name ironic. No town could rest easy while he was about, but he just wanted a place to hide out for a time. He found a drugstore, bought the medical supplies that he needed, and purchased food at a nearby grocery store. Androf stumbled along the aisles, knowing he was a pitiful sight. He wore a cap pulled down low, a pair of dark glasses, and avoided looking at anyone. Still, nobody paid him any attention.

On a narrow highway heading east, Androf came across a run-down motel with a dozen small units. A faded sign in front proclaimed that it was the Harmony Inn. The shabby little buildings had the shape of log cabins, a style popular some fifty years ago. Hardly any cars were in the parking lot, confirming its third-class status. Androf rented a cabin, paying for four days in advance. He kept his face hidden from the stooped old man who took his money, but his precautions were unnecessary. The old man was partially blind and almost deaf.

"The maid comes on Mondays, Wednesdays, and Fridays," the old man said.

"Tell her to stay away. I just want to rest," Androf grumbled.

"Eh, what's that?" The old man asked, cupping his ear.

Androf yelled his comment again, which made his injured face hurt.

"Suit yourself, the rent's the same," the old man said, turning away.

When Androf was inside the cabin, he telephoned Yong Chow Lee.

"Did you see the boy?" he asked immediately.

"I went to his house, but there was a problem," Androf mumbled.

"Speak up…I can barely understand you!" Yong Chow Lee barked.

"I am injured. I climbed a tree to look through the boy's window and was attacked by a bunch of birds."

"What nonsense, birds do not attack men," Yong Chow Lee said.

"Come to North Carolina and climb this tree. We'll see what you say then," Androf replied angrily.

Yong Chow Lee was silent for a moment. *Have I made a mistake by hiring this fool?* he wondered. Finally, he spoke, "I don't understand this business about the birds."

"It was night and the birds attacked when I was near the boy's window. In the confusion, I fell from the tree. When I recover, I will go back again."

"How bad are your injuries?" It was a practical question. Yong Chow Lee just wanted to know if Androf could still do his job.

"Broken ribs, that sort of thing – I should be okay in a few days."

"Do not linger," Yong Chow Lee said coldly before he hung up.

Androf was developing a feeling of hatred for the Chinese man, yet he kept his emotions under control. He needed to heal for his own reasons, not because of what Yong Chow Lee said. He had a score to settle with the ravens; he needed to prove that he was not afraid of them. For the next two hours, he stitched up the cuts on his face and put tape around his broken ribs, cursing profusely all the while.

Androf spent the next four days in the little cabin, sleeping, cleaning the old shotgun, and thinking about how to get even with the ravens. On the afternoon of the fourth day, he checked his face in the mirror and decided he could return to Great Oak. Although some of his wounds were still painful, the bruises and swelling were gone. He stopped at a sporting goods store on the way back, purchasing shotgun shells, a crossbow and arrows, a black motorcycle helmet, protective pads for his body, binoculars, a goalie's facemask, a baseball bat, a waterproof jogging suit, and three canisters of pepper spray.

"Mister, this is a mighty odd collection of stuff," the chubby girl behind the checkout counter said.

"Mind your own business," Androf snapped.

She finished tabulating the cost of his items in silence. As he left the store, she stuck her tongue out at his back.

Before long, Androf was back in his apartment, planning his next move. *Birds want a war, they'll get one,* he thought, looking through his new gear. Just then, the storm blew into town, changing his plans. He doubted if the birds would be out in such weather – his war would have to wait. The prospect of putting off his revenge filled him with anger. He paced his apartment until the rain eased, giving him a chance to search for his enemy. If he could just find one bird to kill, he would be happy.

When Androf stepped out into the night, the force of the howling wind shocked him. Even though the downpour had slowed, the wind was blowing the remaining raindrops with a pummeling force. He smiled as he heard them striking his body, yet felt nothing. The motorcycle helmet covered his head and the black goalie's mask shielded his face. Under his waterproof suit, assorted baseball, football, and hockey pads were in place. Heavy gloves were on his hands and his right fist carried a baseball bat. The new binoculars and a canister of pepper spray were inside his pockets, and the crossbow hung across his back. He felt ready for any adversary.

Under the cover of the night, Androf reached the pine trees across from Davey Boehm's house. He settled into the deep shadows and pulled out his binoculars. Inch by inch, he scanned the roof of the house and the tree alongside the window. There was no sign of a bird anywhere. Disappointed, Androf sat down to wait. He had only been there a short time when the sound of laughter reached his ears. A man and woman came into view, struggling against the wind as they walked along the street. The man had his arm around the woman, and they huddled together under a flimsy umbrella. They were so absorbed in each other; the wind and rain didn't bother them.

Androf inspected their faces with his binoculars. The woman was young and pretty, the man tall and handsome. He felt a sudden tinge of envy. Many months had passed since he had enjoyed the company of a woman. He inspected the man's face again and a distant memory flickered inside his brain. *This man looks familiar, but where could we have met?* Androf decided to follow them while he thought about the familiarity of the man's face. He kept in the shadows with his baseball bat ready, but left his crossbow hidden among the trees.

Linda and Ed were oblivious to the black figure following them. They had enjoyed a leisurely dinner at Ed's house and romance was in their hearts. Of course, their mood would have been different had they known about Androf stalking them.

Androf followed Ed and Linda until they reached Aunt Gilda's rambling old house. His eyebrows rose as he took in the sight. Inside such houses were many items of value, precious treasures waiting for a thief's hand. He found a hiding place behind a clump of large bushes and watched the man and woman talking on the porch. His binoculars stayed mostly on the face of the man, but he also scanned the front of the house looking for ways to get in. He kept thinking about where he had seen the man before. *If we have met, it must have been a long time ago,* he decided.

The thought took Androf back to his years in Serbia, to the time when he commanded his own unit in the militia. His position allowed him to take whatever he wanted, whenever he wanted it. There was only one man whom he answered to in those days. His name was Josef Ubeck, a man with the cunning of the devil himself. Ubeck was Androf's supreme commander, but he was more than that; he was Androf's God.

It was Androf's recollection of Ubeck that finally allowed him to remember who the man on the porch was. About ten years ago, Ubeck had met with several war reporters in Serbia, boasting of his control of a large territory. Androf had stood at Ubeck's side as the reporters asked insulting questions about issues like human rights. The man on the porch had been the most insolent of these reporters. Later, the man had written a scathing article about Ubeck, which had appeared in many newspapers.

Androf remembered how angry he had become at the reporters' obvious disregard for Ubeck's accomplishments. He had wanted to beat the men until they begged for their lives. However, Ubeck had only laughed at the reporters, telling them that they must not hold human life in such high regard for they showed little concern for their own. Then he gave them a warning. Since they were fools, he would allow them to leave. They would receive no such consideration should he catch them in Serbia again.

Androf had always thought Ubeck's generosity back then was a mistake. Allied forces captured Ubeck a year later and put him on trial before a War Crimes Tribunal. Many of the statements he had made to the reporters became evidence against him. The man on the porch had been the most damaging witness. The Tribunal sentenced Ubeck to life in prison, and he died in an attempted escape shortly thereafter. Androf had fled Serbia to avoid a similar fate.

The fact that this same reporter was now standing a short distance away seemed incredible. He and Androf had met halfway around the world, yet they were now together in this strange little town. The reporter was a threat; he knew of Androf's association with Ubeck. Should he recognize Androf, he would surely notify the police. Androf smiled as his mind explored the irony in these circumstances.

Chance has brought me here to exact revenge for Ubeck, he thought. *I will enjoy killing this troublesome reporter.*

Androf followed Ed when he finally left Linda's house. The wind blew forcefully and the rain had resumed, pouring down as if the heavens had burst. Androf fought the temptation to bash him with the baseball bat. It would be so easy – the noise of the wind and rain would cover the sounds. But Androf quickly discarded the idea. He didn't want the police investigating a murder close to where he lived.

As soon as Androf saw Ed's house, a better way of killing him surfaced in his mind. Old houses were notorious for electrical problems while being rebuilt. Wires were crossed, circuits overloaded, gas pipes developed leaks. These careless errors caused fires a sleeping man could not escape.

Androf decided to think it over, yet he was sure this was the answer. He could easily arrange for a fire without raising suspicions; he had done so several times in the past. *Just another tragedy in good old Great Oak,* he mused, smiling as he headed back towards Davey Boehm's house. His immediate objective was killing some ravens.

❧ Chapter 26 ❧

---

*Be not alarmed by the lingering soul of
one who has passed. Good shall remain
good and evil shall remain evil in the
hereafter. Thus, fear not ghosts who seek
ye out unless they traveled evil paths.*

— Translated from Storia Di Incanto; circa 1826

Forces In The Night

AS DARKNESS APPROACHED, Yona stood alongside the magic
wagon and watched the faint projectiles of light rising above Brown
Mountain. Wind and rain pelted his body, yet he stayed warm and
dry inside a thick goatskin coat and old felt hat. He was sure that the
lights were the probes of the evil spirit, searching for ways to influence
his people. Even so, he smiled as the wagon's aura extinguished the
lights before they reached Greyhead Mountain. "You cannot come
here, evil one. Tsusga Gineli protects us!" he shouted into the night.

Yona had returned to the rocky precipice after Sequoyah left the
village with the Three of We. He stayed at the precipice for the rest of
the day, letting his mind enter a trance-like state. Yona had a unique
ability. Occasionally, he could link his thoughts with the spirits of the
bears living in the mountains.

This mystical process occurred while Yona did the Cherokee
stomp dance and uttered bear-like growls. For hours, he had danced
around the magic wagon, invoking the protection of the bears for the

sake of his young warriors. Inside his mind, he heard the bears answering his call. Finally, when he was too tired to continue, he stopped and began a silent vigil above the village. He had done what he could.

ಬಂಧ

Meanwhile, Davey sat in his bedroom, listening to the fury of the wind and rain. He hadn't experienced such a storm while in New York City. High up in his parent's condominium, the weather was more of a distant thing, but as his aunt's house creaked and groaned around him, the storm seemed like a live and violent force. Outside his window, the branches of the tree lashed against the side of the house, adding to the night's fierce agitation.

Bristol lay on the floor nearby, hoping Davey would stop what he was doing and play with him. However, Davey had focused his attention upon his great grandfather's bracelets. He held them in his hands, examining each carefully. The bracelets had made him feel light as a feather earlier in the day. The message on the deerskin had said they ruled the air, and he thought about what that meant. Antonio had also etched the hieroglyphic symbols for fire, ice, wind, and lightning along the undersides of each bracelet. *Can I wield these powers when I wear them?* Davey wondered.

He placed the bracelets on his wrists and felt them gliding along his skin. The sensation was like the faint tickling of a feather, an entirely pleasant feeling. Immediately, the amber stones on the bracelets turned translucent and emitted a soft glow. His necklace reacted in turn, the large stone growing brighter and the pendant beginning a gentle vibration.

Davey recalled the newspaper article about The Great Sabatini's magic show. It reported that fire, lightning, and icy gusts of air had shot from Antonio's fingers. He rose from his chair, held his hands in front of him, and said the word fire. Nothing happened.

Bristol thought playtime was beginning, so he stood up and

ಬ 269 ೞ

wagged his tail. Perplexed, Davey ignored the dog and sat down. With a sigh, Bristol stretched out on the floor again and closed his eyes.

Davey let his brain analyze the problem. According to Yona, Antonio had made the wagon fly with his mind. "The same principle could apply here," Davey muttered and stood up again. This time, he decided to try lightning instead of fire. He pointed at the closed door of his room, formed a picture in his mind of a lightning bolt streaking across the sky, and willed it to shoot from his fingers. Abruptly, a crackling sound filled the room and a thin stream of electricity shot from his hand. The lightning hit the door with a bang and sputtered along its edges until its force dissipated. Startled, Bristol jumped up and barked, unsure of what had happened. A few seconds later, Davey heard footsteps in the hall; then the door of his room opened.

"Is everything okay in here?" Uncle Bill asked, peering into the room.

"Uh…sorry, Bristol and I were just playing," Davey said sheepishly, concealing his hands so the bracelets weren't visible.

"Keep it down; your aunt is asleep," Uncle Bill said.

"Is it all right if Bristol stays in here tonight?" Davey asked.

"As long as you're quiet," Uncle Bill replied, shutting the door again.

Davey rushed towards the door and inspected it. Fortunately, there was no damage. "Bristol, did you see what I just did?" Davey whispered.

"Woof," barked the dog, bounding over to where Davey stood. He was sure playtime had arrived, but Davey just rubbed the dog's ears. "I'd better practice outside from now on," he said softly, a smile spreading across his face.

഑)ഓ഑)ഓ഑)ഓ഑)ഓ

Androf had returned to the pine trees across from Davey Boehm's house and sat in the darkness, searching for the ravens again. He knew from experience that his enemies would not expect an attack during the storm. In Serbia, he had chosen nights like this to cross into enemy territory. Often, he did it for the simple thrill of being in harm's way.

Now, Androf felt like he was back in Serbia, preparing for such a sortie. After the lights in the boy's room went out, he signaled for his troops to get ready. When he realized no one was there to follow his orders, he grinned fiendishly. He had become a one-man army.

One hundred feet separated Aunt Sally's home from her neighbor's house; thick bushes and large trees marked the boundary between them. In a crouch, Androf zigzagged across the street and into the trees between the houses. He moved warily as he scurried towards the thicker woods in the back. His eyes surveyed the sky and the rooftops, searching for the ravens. One hand carried his crossbow and the other held his baseball bat, but he saw no sign of the enemy. *The fools have abandoned their posts, giving me a chance to find another way into the house,* he thought with elation.

Unbeknownst to Androf, the ravens didn't leave Davey unguarded; three grey wolves, an alpha male and two females, patrolled the woods around the house. The wolves had only a vague sense of why they were there. It was a matter of instinct, a primitive need to protect their own. Despite Androf's careful maneuvers, the wolves sensed his presence immediately. They kept their bellies low to the ground, the two females following the alpha male as he stalked the intruder.

Androf had a clear view of the backyard from his position in the woods. Across the yard, he saw a large, two-story garage with an outside staircase. As Androf examined the structure, he decided it offered a secure place for studying the back of the house. Staying hidden among the trees, he cautiously headed towards the garage, stopping when he was halfway there. He slung his crossbow across his back, took out his binoculars, and scanned the roofline of the garage. *No ravens are sneaking up on me tonight,* he thought.

Behind Androf's back, the three wolves crept into position. The alpha male crouched, readying for his attack. The two females angled to each side, waiting for their leader to spring.

Androf heard the snarling of the wolves just before they came at him. In alarm, he dropped the binoculars and turned, swinging his baseball bat. The alpha male's body was in the air, its fangs aiming at Androf's throat. Simultaneously, the two females attacked his legs, trying to bring him down. Androf managed to hit the alpha male with the bat, knocking the wolf back. The animal scrambled to his feet, but it was stunned. One of the females bit into Androf's ankle, but his shin guard deflected the animal's teeth. The other wolf was more successful, finding his unprotected thigh. Androf screamed in pain as the wolf's teeth dug into his flesh.

Androf realized the baseball bat was useless in the close quarters confronting him now, and he threw it away. Frantically, he reached for the pepper spray in his pocket. By some miracle, he found it quickly and shot a stream at the alpha wolf to keep it away. The smell of the spray filled the air; the wolf reacted by backing up and shaking its head.

The wolf biting into Androf's thigh yanked on his leg, almost making him fall. Androf screamed again, held the pepper spray inches from the wolf's face, and sprayed. The animal yelped and immediately retreated as the spray bit into her eyes. The third wolf grabbed onto his left forearm, and the weight of the animal pulled him over. Crying out in pain, Androf sprayed the third wolf, and it scrambled away as well.

After that, Androf didn't waste any time getting out of the woods. He scooted backwards along the ground while shooting bursts of pepper spray towards the wolves. In a few seconds, he reached the open spaces of the backyard, struggled to his feet, and searched fearfully for his attackers. As soon as he put weight on his injured leg, an intense pain racked his body and he fell again. Practically hysterical, he shot a long blast of pepper spray towards the woods. This time, the wind picked up the spray and blew it back into his face. The pungent odor permeated his eyes and mouth, and tears streamed from his eyes as he began to choke.

Crying and retching, Androf staggered towards his apartment. Agony filled each step, and he sobbed with frustration as he thought about his narrow escape. For the second time in a matter of days, he had known fear.

ᎦᏣᎦᏣᎦᏣ

An hour later, Sineous Crop entered the wide band of woods stretching behind the houses along Elm Street. The black stone from the evil spirit's cave rested on his back, held in place by leather straps and wrapped in a thick blanket to protect him from its deadly effects.

Sineous let out a string of curses as the wind whipped at his clothing and the rain flew in his face. "Why did Wally make me do this on such a miserable night?" he muttered bitterly to himself.

Using a small flashlight to light his way, Sineous trudged along a path beside a rocky ravine that was rapidly filling with runoff water from the storm. Burdened by the weight of the stone, his steps were slow. He cursed again as he fell in the slippery mud on the path, but the rushing water in the ravine covered the sounds of his foul oaths. Similarly, it drowned out the noises made by the lumbering figure following him.

When Sineous was halfway to Aunt Sally's house, he stopped to rest. As he leaned against a large boulder, he noticed a faint movement among the trees on his left. The night was so dark; he assumed it was his imagination, but then the sound of something tearing through the brush alarmed him. His worst fear was realized when he pointed his flashlight towards the sound. A large bear was heading his way.

In a panic, Sineous hurriedly retraced his steps along the path. He hadn't traveled more than twenty feet before another bear appeared in front of him. Sineous turned, flashing his light about in every direction. Bears were approaching him on all sides, and behind his back were the swirling waters of the ravine.

ᔪ 273 ᭖

Sineous screamed as the first bear attacked with a powerful swipe of its paw. The blow broke his arm and sent him sprawling backwards into the ravine. He fell a distance of ten feet, landing on a large, barely submerged boulder. The black stone on his back shattered into a thousand pieces when he hit, inflicting even greater pain. Then the rushing water swept him away, eventually dumping his body into the New River a mile downstream.

❧❦❧❦❧❦

A strange noise woke Linda Peabody from a deep sleep. Bupkiss stood alongside her bed, whining as his cold nose nuzzled her hand. Outside, gusts of wind whistled around the corners of the old house and sheets of rain splattered against the windows.

"Bupkiss, let me sleep," she groaned. "I was dreaming about Ed."

Bupkiss whined again and licked her hand. Linda shook herself awake, reached for the lamp beside the bed, and flicked the switch several times without success. She fell back into the bed with a sigh. *The electricity must be off*, she thought.

Bupkiss put his paws on the bed, wanting to cuddle with Linda. She assumed the noises of the storm were making him anxious; she was feeling a bit anxious herself, especially when the wind abruptly rattled the windows of the house. "You are not getting on the bed," she said firmly. She rubbed the dog's ears and gave him a hug. "Now, go back to your own bed and lie down."

At that moment, Linda heard a loud thumping noise and realized that the noise was why Bupkiss had awakened her. Bupkiss whined again, more urgently this time. Linda knew he would start barking soon, and she didn't want Aunt Gilda to wake up. "All right, I hear it too," she said quietly. She took a flashlight from her bedside table and beamed the light on her alarm clock. It was three in the morning. The loud noise sounded again…thump…thump…thump.

Linda climbed out of bed and pulled a robe over her pajamas. Bupkiss danced around her, filled with excitement. As soon as she

❧ 274 ❧

opened the door, he dashed into the hallway; Linda followed, shining the flashlight along the walls until they reached the stairway. Then they stopped and peered cautiously into the dark foyer below.

The thumping noise was louder now; it seemed to be coming from somewhere below the staircase. Linda felt a chill running along her spine. Bupkiss, unable to restrain himself any longer, started barking fiercely.

Linda hushed the dog, screwed up her courage, and began inching down the stairs. Bupkiss stayed beside her, keeping his body pressed against her legs. Suddenly, Linda heard a creaking sound behind her. With a gasp, she turned to see Aunt Gilda standing on the landing a few feet away. Bupkiss let out an excited bark and ran up to greet her.

"Linda dear, what's going on?" Aunt Gilda asked. She wore a long-sleeved nightgown decorated with cartoon characters and carried a ceramic candleholder with a glass chimney. The flame of the candle threw shadows on the wall behind her, increasing the eeriness of the moment.

Linda held up her hand for silence. "Listen," she whispered.

Thump…thump…thump, came the noise from below the stairs.

"Oh my," Aunt Gilda said in a low voice. "Do you think it's Charles? I forgot to put his brandy out for him."

Linda was growing weary of Aunt Gilda's habit of blaming her late husband for every noise in the house, but she didn't say anything. "I don't know, but I'm going to find out," she whispered, starting down the stairs again. Bupkiss watched her, his tail wagging. After a second, he let out a high-pitched bark and scrambled down the stairs to catch up. Aunt Gilda followed at a slower pace.

Linda waited until they were all together on the staircase; then they held on to each other as they descended the rest of the way. Bupkiss stayed between the two women, growling protectively, but mostly getting in the way. The thumping grew louder as they neared the lower floor. Finally, they reached the foyer, stopped, and listened for the thumping to get a sense of its direction. When they heard it again, Bupkiss barked shrilly, and Linda clamped her hand over his muzzle to hush him.

"Come on, it's this way," Linda said, pretending to be brave.

They inched their way along the foyer, heading towards the rear of the house. The thumping sounded continuously and when they reached the closet under the staircase, Linda abruptly halted. It was obvious that the thumping was coming from behind the closet door. Moreover, a faint amber light shown on the floorboards underneath the bottom edge of the door.

"Oh dear me," Aunt Gilda said.

"What do you keep in there?" Linda asked.

"Just some old things, which belonged to Charles. I haven't looked in there for years."

"The electricity is off, so what is making that light?" Linda asked, pointing at the bottom edge of the door.

"I don't know, dear. Maybe Charles is doing it."

Linda rolled her eyes. If Aunt Gilda said another word about Charles, she was going to scream. They stared at the door for a short time until the thumping stopped. Finally, Linda reached out and twisted the door handle. The knob turned, yet the door wouldn't budge. "It won't open," she said, her voice trembling.

"It's locked, dear. The key is right here," Aunt Gilda said, sounding somewhat amused. She opened the drawer of a small table against the wall and produced a tiny skeleton key.

Linda stuck the key into the keyhole and unlocked the door. She took a deep breath and looked at Aunt Gilda. "Should we open it?"

"Go ahead, dear. If it's Charles, he wants out," Aunt Gilda said.

Linda turned the handle, and an amber glow spilled out as the door swung open. Linda felt something cold brush across her face and jumped back with a shriek. Then she retreated down the foyer, pulling Aunt Gilda with her. Bupkiss scrambled to stay behind the women, his claws clicking furiously on the wooden floor.

An odd silence filled the house for the next few seconds. Even the wind and rain seemed strangely diminished. Then, ever so slowly, the amber light grew brighter as it moved towards the closet doorway.

After a few seconds, a glowing box floated into view.

"Oh my goodness," Aunt Gilda said, clutching at Linda.

The box hovered in the air, four feet or so from the floor, then floated slowly towards the two women. Linda watched the object in shock, unable to move. "What is it?" she gasped.

The strange apparition didn't seem to perturb Aunt Gilda in the least. "It's just a box that Charles had. I've never seen it act like *this*."

The box reached a point several feet from the two women and hovered in the air, no longer moving towards them. Linda backed further down the foyer, dragging Aunt Gilda along. Bupkiss stayed with the women, baring his teeth and growling at the box.

Aunt Gilda trembled with excitement. "Don't be afraid; it's Charles! I sense his presence," she exclaimed.

Linda nearly screamed in response. "Aunt Gilda, please! I'm too frightened to think about Charles."

Aunt Gilda began to giggle. "Smell the air, dear. It's his favorite cologne. I always smell it when he's around."

Linda was sure Aunt Gilda had finally lost her mind, but then, much to her surprise, she smelled the cologne too. She recognized the smell because Aunt Gilda sprinkled it around her bedroom to remind her of Charles. She didn't know whether to laugh or cry.

The box was on the move again, following the women while they inched backwards along the wall. Linda let out a little moan as she watched it.

"Don't be such a sissy," snapped Aunt Gilda. "Everything is perfectly clear. Charles is bringing the box to us. He wants us to have it."

Linda didn't like being called a sissy, even though she felt like one at the moment. "Aunt Gilda, if it's Charles, why can't we see him?"

"Because he's a spirit, dear," Aunt Gilda replied, as though she was explaining a very logical thing to a very illogical child. "Let's go into the living room and sit down." Then she addressed the ghost. "Charles, please bring the box in there."

The two women hurried into the living room and sat down

together on the sofa. Bupkiss watched the glowing box with a wary eye as he hopped onto the sofa and wedged himself between them. Normally, Linda would have made him get off the furniture. However, these were special circumstances and she hugged him instead.

"Charles, we're waiting," Aunt Gilda called gaily, glancing at the archway connecting with the foyer. Sure enough, the box came floating into the room a few seconds later. It circled over to where the two women sat and gently settled onto the table in front of them. Linda shrank back into the cushions, unable to speak.

"Thank you dearest," Aunt Gilda said, as though a perfectly normal thing had just happened.

Linda drummed up her courage and inspected the box. She felt less frightened now because it was no longer floating in the air. It was wooden, about a foot square, and less than a foot high. The shape was elegant, with curved sides and carved pedestals for feet. After a while, she felt brave enough to reach over and touch it. The surface was smooth and she felt no ill affects from the amber glow.

"What's in it?" Linda asked.

"I don't know, dear. Charles never told me."

"Let's open it and find out," Linda said, suddenly growing bolder.

A simple latch held the lid closed. When Linda opened it, she discovered that the source of the amber glow was not the box, but the object inside it. She lifted the object out and held it in her hands. It was heavy and she wondered how it could have floated in the air, yet there was no denying that it had.

The object was shaped similar to the box and was obviously some sort of container. Four silver bands, each about one inch wide, encircled its golden surface at equally spaced intervals. Along its top and sides were hieroglyphic symbols etched in black. As Linda examined the object, she wondered what was causing the amber glow around it. She also wondered why there was no lid or other apparent way to open it.

Aunt Gilda finally broke the silence. "I do remember something about this now. Charles showed it to me a long time ago. He was keeping it for someone, but I don't remember who."

"It looks like it might be valuable. Perhaps we should put it away," Linda suggested.

"No...leave it out in plain sight. If I keep looking at it, I'll remember who it's for."

"The way it floats around, it could be anywhere by tomorrow," Linda muttered.

Aunt Gilda replied with calm assurance. "Charles won't move it again. Now that he's brought it to our attention, the rest is up to us."

⳦ Chapter 27 ⳧

All ye with magick skill, knowest thou this. Magick shapes the events around ye, whither thou makes it so. Magick bends the threads of fate; nothing is simple coincidence.

— Translated from Storia Di Incanto; circa 1829

A Hole In The Roof

THE NEXT MORNING, Davey climbed out of bed with a head full of ideas. Surprisingly, he wasn't thinking about his experiences at the Cherokee village or his coming quest. He was thinking about Halloween and his costume for the annual party in the park next Friday.

The Halloween party was a long-standing tradition in Great Oak. Practically everyone in town, adults as well as children, showed up wearing a costume. Bands played music, booths offered a variety of food and games, and judges awarded prizes for the best costumes. The kids at school had been discussing it with great anticipation.

More than a week ago, Amy had announced that she was wearing a homemade witch's costume; she had been putting bits and pieces of it together for some time. According to Amy, it would be the best witch's costume in the history of Great Oak. Jimmy, in keeping with his heritage, was going as a Cherokee War chief, complete with a genuine war bonnet.

Davey hadn't decided about his costume until this morning, the idea popping into his head upon awaking. He was going to dress like a magician – a particular magician known as The Great Sabatini. Collecting what he needed would require some quick work, since he hadn't started yet. The first thing he did was pick up the telephone and call Jimmy. Sequoyah answered on the second ring, and Davey thanked him again for taking them to the Cherokee village.

"You thanked me three times yesterday, Ustiwaya. No more thanks are necessary," Sequoyah replied.

Davey paused, momentarily startled. "Ustiwaya…uh…I guess it'll take me a while to get used to my Cherokee name," he finally said.

Sequoyah laughed heartily. "A good Cherokee never forgets his name. Hang on, I'll fetch Jimmy."

Jimmy's voice came on the line a few seconds later. "Bloody heck of a storm, eh mate?"

"Yeah, I'm glad we made it back before it really got bad. Listen, Amy and I are helping Mr. Nolen at his house this morning. Afterwards, we're going downtown to see if we can find some stuff for our Halloween costumes. Want to come along?"

"My costume is done, but I'll come with you. Have you decided about yours?"

"I'll tell you about it this afternoon. Let's meet at the Great Oak around one o'clock. I want to show you something." Davey smiled as he imagined the look on Jimmy and Amy's faces when he shot lightning from his fingers.

A short time later, Davey joined his aunt and uncle at the breakfast table. He and Uncle Bill filled their plates with blueberry pancakes and immediately began to eat. "I'm as hungry as a bear, and this is exactly what I wanted," Davey said between mouthfuls.

Uncle Bill, his mouth so full he could hardly speak, nodded in agreement. "She makes the best pancakes in town," he mumbled.

Aunt Sally, who ate in a more dignified manner, laughed. "Slow down; I feel like I'm sitting between two pigs."

Bristol sat under the table, waiting for bits of pancake to fall on the floor. Uncle Bill and Davey accommodated him by letting a bite *accidentally* slip from their forks a few times. Bristol gobbled them up noisily and then went around licking the floor.

"All right, now stop doing that. You're teaching him bad habits," Aunt Sally complained.

The phone rang and Uncle Bill left the table to answer it. Bristol eyed his unprotected plate, but Aunt Sally grabbed the dog before he could launch an attack. "See, this is what happens when you feed him at the table," she said, giving Davey a knowing glance.

Davey nodded, but heard little of what she said. His necklace had begun to vibrate and he was listening to Uncle Bill's conversation instead. He overheard only a few words, but they were enough to make him concerned.

Uncle Bill returned to the table a few seconds later. "A tree fell on Ed's house during the night; he needs help getting it off."

"Good grief…did it do any damage?" Aunt Sally asked.

"He thinks it punched a hole in the roof, but we won't know until we climb up there. I'm bringing my ladder and chainsaw over."

"I'll come too. I'm supposed to work for him this morning," Davey said, certain that another strange event was unfolding.

Uncle Bill stuffed the rest of his pancakes in his mouth, put his plate full of crumbs and syrup on the floor, and stood up. Bristol immediately lapped at the plate, pushing it along the floor.

Aunt Sally frowned. "I hate it when you do that."

Uncle Bill gave her a hug. "I know, but he's a good dog and deserves a treat sometimes." Then he turned towards Davey. "Eat fast; Ed is waiting on us."

"Bill, I don't want Davey using the chainsaw," Aunt Sally said firmly.

"Right you are, old girl. I won't even let him touch it."

Davey finished eating, rose from his chair, and carried his plate towards the dishwasher. "Those pancakes were great," he said, grinning at Aunt Sally and then glancing over at Bristol.

"Don't you dare!" Aunt Sally exclaimed.

A short time later, Davey and Uncle Bill loaded the pickup and headed over to Ed's house. The storm had blown itself out during the night, leaving the sky clear and sunny. Despite the bright morning, the damage inflicted by the storm shocked them as they drove along. Tree limbs, leaves, and other debris littered the street and sidewalks. The force of the wind had even toppled over a few trees, making their roots stick up like ugly wounds in the earth.

"What a mess," Davey said, feeling a sudden sadness.

"Happens sometimes when a storm comes through," muttered Uncle Bill. "The rain softens the ground and the roots have less holding power. If the wind gets the limbs whipping around just right, the force pulls the tree over. Darn shame to lose a tree that way."

"I hope all the trees in the park are okay," Davey said, suddenly worried about the Great Oak.

"The park is sheltered by this hill, so the wind doesn't hit it as hard. I've never seen much storm damage there," Uncle Bill said, pulling the truck into Ed's driveway.

Davey immediately noticed the tree, which lay on the back portion of Ed's roof. It was tall and slender, with stubby branches that protruded from its upper half. Fortunately, the tree had not fallen a great distance, but rather leaned against the roof, its trunk forming a sixty-degree angle with the ground. Davey and Uncle Bill carried the ladder along the outside of the house and found Ed in the backyard, staring up at the roof.

"How do we go about this?" Davey asked.

"First, we need to inspect the damage. Let's set the ladder up and take a look," Uncle Bill replied.

When the ladder was in place, Ed scrambled up to the top rung. "Looks like a limb has punched through some of the shingles," he shouted. "I'm going to climb on the roof for a better look."

"Wait Ed, those old slate shingles are brittle and break really easily. Let's send Davey up there; he's lighter than we are," Uncle Bill suggested.

"Good idea," Ed replied.

As soon as Ed was back on the ground, Uncle Bill tied a rope around Davey's waist and looped the other end across his own shoulders. After that, they went up the ladder in tandem. When Davey reached the roof, he inched his way across the shingles and Uncle Bill let the rope play out as Davey progressed. Before long, Davey reached a place where a branch had crashed through the shingles. The resulting hole was several feet in diameter.

Davey peered into the hole, but everything was dark inside the opening. However, the pendant on his necklace was vibrating like crazy. *Something important is in there,* he thought. Then he looked over at Uncle Bill. "A tree branch has punched through the roof here. The hole is pretty big, and I think the branch split when it went in. Parts of it look like they're caught inside," he said.

"Okay, I see where that branch connects with the trunk. We'll have to cut it lose before we pull it out. First, crawl further up and look for other places where the shingles are broken."

Davey climbed higher, inspected the roof where the tree lay, and shouted. "I don't see any other holes."

"Good, come back to where the roof is broken and hold on to the tree trunk. I'll cut that branch loose and then you try to pull it out. I can reach it with the chainsaw from where I am," Uncle Bill said.

Ed climbed up the ladder and handed the chainsaw to Uncle Bill. Soon, the shrill whine of its engine filled the air as the saw bit into the branch. In a matter of minutes, the blade severed the branch from the trunk, and Ed took the saw back down the ladder.

"Davey, try to get the branch out now," Uncle Bill said.

The branch had split into a vee as it punched through the shingles. Gradually, Davey worked it around until he was able to pull it out of the opening. Several more shingles broke in the process, enlarging the hole. He slid the broken branch along the roof towards Uncle Bill and looked into the opening. Sunlight spilled into the hole making the interior visible.

"There's a little room under here," Davey said, his voice excited.

Uncle Bill grabbed the broken branch and pulled it towards the edge of the roof. He looked down, made sure Ed was out of the way, and pushed the limb off. As he did, he felt a tug on the rope wrapped across his shoulder. Immediately, he turned back towards Davey, but didn't see him anywhere.

"Davey, where are you?" Uncle Bill yelled.

"I'm inside the hole – in this little room," Davey shouted back.

Uncle Bill was suddenly frantic. "Did you fall? Are you hurt?"

"No, I jumped. There's some stuff in here that I wanted to see," Davey said calmly.

"Well, get out of there!"

Davey stood on his tiptoes and stuck his head out of the hole. The edge of the roof came right up to his eyes and he could barely see Uncle Bill. "It's not dangerous; there's flooring in here and the walls are paneled, but I can't climb back out or find a doorway. Some stuff is stored in here though, so there must be a way in."

"All right, I'll go ask Ed where the door is. Keep the rope tied around your waist in case we have to haul you out and don't move around." Uncle Bill climbed down the ladder, muttering all the way.

"What's going on?" Ed asked.

"Davey jumped into this little room below the hole. Now, he can't get out. Kids…you never know what they'll do."

"What kind of little room?"

Uncle Bill shook his head and shrugged. "I don't know, but he says stuff is in there. There must be an access door somewhere."

"That part of the roof is over the master bedroom. There may be some crawl space under the eaves, but I don't know of any door," Ed said, somewhat puzzled.

The two men hurried into the house, climbed the stairs, and entered the bedroom. The room was rectangular, large, and airy, its pointed ceiling angling up to exposed beams that supported the roof. The exterior sides of the house formed two of the corners, the wall between the corners containing a long bank of windows. Each corner had been walled into a four-foot square section, which jutted into the room. The front walls of these sections consisted of built-in bookcases facing the doorway.

"Davey, can you hear me?" Uncle Bill shouted.

Davey's muffled reply came from behind one of the bookcases. "Over here!"

Ed hurried over to the bookcase in the right corner of the room and knocked on the wooden backing. Immediately, he heard an answering voice from behind the wall. "That's it – I'm right behind where you knocked!" Davey yelled.

"This bookcase must come out somehow," Ed said, pulling it forward. Despite his efforts, the bookcase refused to budge. Uncle Bill came over and they both pulled on the bookcase, but it still wouldn't move.

"There's a bookcase here, but we can't budge it," Uncle Bill shouted.

Davey inspected the wall inside the little room carefully. As he brushed clumps of dust and cobwebs away, his fingers touched a metal latch. "There's a latch holding it in place. I'm going to release it."

The men in the bedroom heard a low clicking sound. Then the bookcase moved sideways an inch or two. The squeaking sound of turning metal filled the room.

"Pull on it! I think there are wheels on the bottom," shouted Davey.

The two men pulled on the bookcase and it slowly slid open. After the bookcase was sufficiently ajar, Davey scrambled out through the opening. Dust and cobwebs covered his head, shoulders, and arms, and he had untied the rope from around his waist.

Uncle Bill's face broke into a grin. "We're not telling your aunt about this."

"A trunk and two wooden crates are in there," Davey exclaimed. "They have Sabatini nameplates on them."

The men rolled the bookcase until the opening was several feet wide. The wheels under the bookcase fit into metal tracks embedded in the floor, which only allowed it to move parallel to the exterior wall. The opening revealed a small storage area; many years worth of dust and grime covered the objects inside.

"Come on, lets get them out," Davey said cheerfully.

"Slow down – they need to be cleaned before we drag them into Ed's bedroom," Uncle Bill said.

Ed nodded. "Good thinking. I'll get my vacuum cleaner and some rags. Davey can clean them while we finish with the tree. Then you can take them over to your house and surprise Sally."

"Davey, don't open them. I want Sally to do it," Uncle Bill said.

"I already tried; they're locked."

Uncle Bill grinned at Ed and shook his head. "No one ever asks permission anymore," he muttered. Then he examined the interior of the bookcase, curious about how it worked. *Got to be a way to open it from inside the room,* he thought. After a few seconds, he found a small door cut into the back of the bookcase. The door was cleverly hidden and just big enough to permit the passage of a hand. Behind the door was the lever that freed the latch. He smiled as he pulled the lever. "Ingenious, isn't it? You simply slide the bookcase across the wall until it latches into place. Pull this lever and it opens again. The molding around the bookcase fits so tightly, it seems part of the wall. You'd never know about the storage area behind it."

"Unless a tree punches a hole in your roof," Davey added.

"I wonder what's in the trunk and crates," Ed said.

"Must be something worth hiding," Uncle Bill replied.

Davey suddenly noticed the bookcase in the opposite corner of the room. It was just like the one they had opened. "Maybe there's another storage area behind it," he exclaimed.

They all hurried towards the bookcase and Uncle Bill began searching for a hidden door along its back panel. He quickly found the door, pulled the lever, and then they rolled the bookcase away from the wall. Three wooden crates and another large trunk sat inside the storage area behind it. Each had Sabatini nameplates on them as well.

"You know Ed, all of this stuff technically belongs to you since it's in your house," Uncle Bill said.

Ed shook his head. "They belonged to Sally's grandparents, so she and her sister are the rightful owners now."

"I'm not an attorney, but I think the law considers them abandoned, which means you can claim them."

Ed laughed. "They aren't mine. If the law says I own them, then I'll abandon them on Sally's doorstep."

At that moment, they heard Amy's voice calling from the bottom of the stairs. "Hello…is anybody here?"

"We're upstairs, come up and join us," Ed shouted.

Amy appeared at the doorway a few seconds later. "What's all this?" she asked when she saw the bookcases.

"Davey will fill you in," Uncle Bill said. "Ed and I are going outside to cut up the tree."

After the two men left, Davey explained what had happened, and then he and Amy cleaned everything with Ed's vacuum cleaner. From outside, the angry buzzing of the chainsaw reached their ears while they worked.

"I hate that sound," Davey said after a while. "It's so destructive."

Amy nodded. "By the way, what did you tell your aunt about our visit to the Cherokee village?"

"I did what Chief Yona suggested."

"You said nothing?"

"Well, I had to say something, so I talked about her grandfather's friendship with Yona, and her grandmother being half Cherokee, which seemed to satisfy her. What did you tell your parents?"

"Something similar, mostly about our Cherokee ancestor, Morning Dove. I didn't tell them about our quest or any of the other stuff."

Just then, the sound of Ed and Uncle Bill coming up the steps interrupted their conversation. "Did you get the tree off the roof?" Davey asked.

"Yep, it's all cut into firewood, and we covered the hole with an old tarpaulin," Uncle Bill said.

"Gives me something else to fix," Ed added with a sigh.

Uncle Bill laughed. "I'll come over and help you tomorrow."

That decided; the two men began carrying the trunks and crates down to Uncle Bill's pickup. Each trunk was identical, about two feet high and three feet long. The five wooden crates were smaller than the trunks, but much heavier. Made out of oak planking, each crate had thick rope handles that stuck out on the sides.

"Darn thing must weigh nearly a hundred pounds," Ed said, as he and Uncle Bill struggled under the weight of the first crate. "What could be in it that's so heavy?"

"Come over and find out. It's almost time for lunch, and Sally has some honey-baked ham," Uncle Bill suggested.

"You're invited too," Davey said to Amy.

Ed smiled. "Thanks, but Linda is bringing over a picnic lunch. We're spending the afternoon on my book. You can tell me later what you find."

Amy couldn't resist a question. "Don't you think she's nice?"

"Just about the nicest thing that's happened to me in a while," Ed said.

Uncle Bill grinned. "Looks like you're smitten."

Ed chuckled good-naturedly. "Go on, get out of here."

A short time later, Uncle Bill's pickup pulled into the driveway of their home. Davey leaped out and ran into the house. "Aunt Sally, come see what we've got," he shouted.

The old chests and boxes sitting in the back of the pickup flabbergasted Aunt Sally. She was even more astonished when she heard about the secret storage rooms in her grandmother's old house. Nevertheless, what truly amazed her was the spectacle created when one of the wooden crates fell onto the driveway as they were lifting it out of the truck. The crate split open with a loud crash, and hundreds of gold coins spilled out, glittering in the sunlight.

ℭℨ Chapter 28 ℬℭ

Evil seeks the dark mind, as it doth easily turn to madness. Be forewarned that those consumed by evil hath not normal thought.

— Translated from Storia Di Incanto; circa 1833

The Man Who Wasn't There

FOR MOST OF THE NIGHT, Androf tossed and turned as the storm battered the sides of his garage apartment. His body throbbed with pain from the wounds inflicted by the wolves, and images of his cowardly retreat flashed repeatedly in his mind. *How did it happen? I was so careful,* he kept wondering. Eventually, his paranoia led him to an irrational conclusion. Unknown forces sought his destruction – dark forces, which were impossible to understand. The more he thought about it, the more delusional he became.

Around four o'clock in the morning, Androf heard a voice in the darkness. The voice spoke softly, consoling him on his misfortune and soothing his troubled mind. He recognized the voice immediately; it belonged to Josef Ubeck, his commander in Serbia. Androf believed Ubeck sat beside his bed, but didn't consider how such a thing could happen. Had he been more rational, he would have remembered that Ubeck was dead. As it was, Androf accepted Ubeck's presence as real.

Do not worry. I am here to help you, the voice said.

"My enemies are inhuman – you cannot help!" Androf cried out.

Remember this. No one can beat Androf and Ubeck when we stand together.

Androf managed a smile. "I have missed you, Ubeck."

The voice grew louder and seemed to echo along the walls of the apartment, even though it came from inside Androf's head. *You are alone no longer, Androf.*

Their imaginary conversation continued until Androf finally fell into an uneasy sleep. He dreamt of running alongside Ubeck through burned-out buildings on a war-torn street. Their long blonde hair streamed behind them as they hunted their enemies, two fearless warriors lusting for battle. The engine of a tank roared nearby, made even more real by the grating noise of Uncle Bill's chainsaw. Androf woke to the sound and immediately heard Ubeck speak.

Get up Androf, the enemy is about!

Androf pushed the voice away with a feeble wave of his hand. "Leave me be, Ubeck. I am injured and must rest."

You can rest later, now you must spy on your enemy.

Androf opened his bleary eyes and crept out of bed. The injury to his thigh was so painful; he could barely stand. Still, he forced himself upright to show Ubeck his resilience. Balancing on one leg, he peered out the window; he could see into Ed Nolen's yard, two houses away.

At first, lack of sleep clouded Androf's mind. He couldn't comprehend what he was seeing – a man and boy on the roof of the house. *What are they doing?* he wondered. Then he saw the man cutting away the branch of a tree that had fallen on the house. In the yard below, he recognized the reporter who he had followed last night.

"I wish the tree had fallen on him instead," Androf growled.

You should have killed him back in Serbia.

"It was you who stopped me," Androf complained.

A man of conviction cannot be stopped.

Androf was concentrating upon a reply when the boy on the roof turned in his direction. Immediately, he recognized the face of Davey

Boehm. Androf's lips curled into a snarl. "So…the boy and the reporter are allies. I should have suspected as much."

They don't know you are watching. Learn from their mistakes.

Just then, Androf saw the boy pull the tree limb from the hole in the roof. A few seconds later, he watched the boy disappear through the hole. "Look!" he shouted. "The boy has shown me a way into the reporter's house."

The tide of battle is already turning, Ubeck replied smugly.

⊰⊱⊰⊱⊰⊱

Despite their shock and bewilderment over the floating box, Linda and Aunt Gilda went back to bed. "Would you and Bupkiss like to sleep in my room until morning?" Aunt Gilda asked as they climbed the stairs together. "I'm a little unsettled over seeing Charles and would enjoy the company."

In truth, Aunt Gilda wasn't the least bit perturbed by what had happened. She found the whole episode exhilarating – one making a great entrée of a story. Even so, she thought Linda looked rather upset and didn't want her to be alone.

Linda readily accepted Aunt Gilda's offer. The floating box had really spooked her, and she didn't relished the idea of returning to her own room. Before long, the two women were sound asleep in Aunt Gilda's king-sized bed, leaving Bupkiss to guard the door. The dog waited until they were slumbering peacefully, then crept onto the bed and curled up between them.

When Linda woke up again, Aunt Gilda and Bupkiss were nowhere in sight. She stretched, rubbed the sleep from her eyes, and listened as the grandfather clock in the hallway chimed nine o'clock. *I'm late for school,* she thought, jumping frantically from the bed. Then she laughed, remembering that it was Saturday. She pulled on her robe, fluffed her hair in the mirror, and smiled gleefully. The Linda Peabody of old had definitely returned.

Linda found Bupkiss and Aunt Gilda sitting at the kitchen table.

ಶಿ 292 ೞ

As soon as she saw them, she burst out laughing. Aunt Gilda sat on one side of the table and Bupkiss sat in a chair opposite her, his long tail brushing the floor. They were intently watching the strange box, which had been floating before their eyes during the night.

Aunt Gilda offered a beaming smile when she heard the sound of Linda's laughter. "Good morning! You were sleeping so peacefully; we decided not to disturb you."

Bupkiss added his own greeting by hopping down from his chair and dancing towards Linda, his tail wagging furiously.

Linda gave the dog a hug and grinned. "Did I interrupt something?"

"I've recalled what Charles told me about this box and was just telling the story to Bupkiss. Shall I start over?"

"Oh, please do. Would you like a cup of tea first?" Linda asked.

Aunt Gilda looked very pleased. "A wonderful idea...and bring over those sweet rolls on the counter that I just made. This story is an entrée, so let's all get nice and comfortable."

Linda sat down at the table a few minutes later, and Aunt Gilda began her story. "Charles and I came to Great Oak in the year 1953. His family had purchased the Timberland Bank, and Charles was sent here to run it, you see."

"I didn't know Charles was the president of a bank."

"Oh yes, he became the president when we moved here. Great Oak was a nice little town when we first arrived, and being president of the bank was something quite prestigious. Of course, that was before Wally Houseman started running things."

"What does that have to do with the box?" Linda asked.

Aunt Gilda chuckled. "I'm sorry, I've let my story get a bit off track. The point I was trying to make about Charles being the president of the bank is that people trusted him. Once everyone found out what a good man he was, people sought him out for special needs. That's how this box came into his possession."

"The box was somebody's special need?"

Aunt Gilda frowned. "I'm afraid I'm not telling this very well.

Anyway, about five years after we moved to Great Oak, Charles received a visit from a Cherokee Indian. This was a great surprise, since everyone said the Indians wouldn't do business with the bank. As it turned out, the man had come to ask Charles for a favor." Aunt Gilda's eyes twinkled and she grew silent, letting the suspense build.

"Keep going, this is interesting," Linda said.

"Well, there was this woman, Alicia Sabatini, who was a friend of the Cherokee. She was a recluse and had some gold coins that she wanted to sell, so Charles went to see her. Then he established an account at the bank for her and sold the coins. After that, Alicia and Charles developed an odd sort of friendship. She would give him more coins from time to time, and he would sell them and put the money in her account. Whenever Alicia needed money, Charles would bring it to her."

"How nice of Charles," Linda remarked.

Aunt Gilda smiled. "Charles was such a dear man; he was always willing to help. One Saturday, Alicia came to our front door carrying this box. I hadn't met her before, but everyone in town said she was a witch. Of course, that was a lot of nonsense. Anyway, Charles took Alicia into his study and they talked for a long time. When she finally left, the box remained behind. I asked Charles about it afterwards, but he only smiled at me in his special way. That meant it was a secret."

"So what happened next?"

"Well, Alicia died sometime later. When her daughter came to collect Alicia's things, Charles gave her the money in her mother's account."

"Why didn't Charles give her the box?"

"That's not what Alicia wanted. I didn't find out about this until Charles had his heart attack and was very sick. He told me there were some matters I needed to look after for him. One of them was disposing of this box."

"But you still have it. What were you supposed to do with it?"

"According to what Alicia told Charles – nothing. One of her relatives, her first male heir, is going to show up on my doorstep.

When he does, I'm supposed to give him the box."

"Sounds rather improbable," Linda remarked.

"I thought so too, but Charles woke us up and carried the box out of the closet last night. I think he was telling us that someone will come for it soon."

഑ൽ഑ൽ഑ൽ഑ൽ

Silence hung in the air of the family room at Aunt Sally's house. The gold coins from the broken crate were stacked on a low table in the center of the room. Beside them were the other crates, their lids pried open to reveal more gold coins. Amy, Davey, Aunt Sally, and Uncle Bill, all sat in a circle around the crates, staring at the coins without speaking.

"There must be thousands of them," Davey finally said.

Aunt Sally kept her eyes fixed on the glittering coins. She was so mystified she could barely speak. "What are…I mean…who do…they belong to?" she stammered.

Uncle Bill laughed. "Well, they obviously belonged to your grandparents. Since you and your sister are their heirs, they belong to both of you now."

"How much are they worth," Davey asked.

Uncle Bill picked up one of the coins and hefted it in his hand. It was a fifty-dollar gold piece minted in 1895. "Well, I don't know much about these things," he said, scratching his head. "We'll have to get them appraised to know for sure, but the weight and look of them tells me they're genuine. I wouldn't be surprised if there's several million dollars sitting here."

Aunt Sally looked at him in astonishment. "You've got to be kidding."

"Nope…looks like I married me a wealthy woman," Uncle Bill said, grinning happily.

They sat in silence looking at the coins for a few more minutes, each lost in their own thoughts. Bristol rolled over with a sigh,

഑ 295 ൽ

pawing the air for a little attention. Amy squatted on the floor beside him and scratched his stomach.

"Hey, we've forgotten the trunks!" Davey exclaimed.

Uncle Bill undid the leather straps and examined the lock on the lid of the first trunk. "Since we don't have the key, we'll force it open," he said, reaching for the large screwdriver, which he had used on the boxes earlier.

"Try not to damage them," Aunt Sally said. "They're the only things I have that belonged to my grandparents."

"Except for the fortune in gold coins," Uncle Bill chuckled.

Davey watched Uncle Bill stick the screwdriver between the lid of the trunk and the latch of the lock. *Something unexpected happens here every day,* he thought.

With a bang, the lock came lose and the lid flew open. Everyone crowded around the trunk, looking into its interior. Even Bristol's curiosity was piqued, and he came over and sniffed at the contents. A piece of black cloth covered the top layer of the trunk. Pinned to the center of the cloth was a short note, printed in crude script. Aunt Sally pulled the note out and read it aloud.

To Celina

I put dese thins away for yew, mye daughter, as dey pain me to see em. Save em fer the heir who comes yet, and know that I love yew. Yer mother, Alicia

Davey noticed the note was on a sheet of parchment similar to the letter containing Alicia's burial instructions. The gentle vibration of his necklace told him that it contained a message from his great grandfather as well, so he avoided touching the sheet. *No point in having it flying about the room,* he thought with a smile.

"Would it be okay if I looked at what's in the trunk?" Davey asked.

"I think you should let your aunt do that," Uncle Bill said.

"Let's all do it together," Aunt Sally replied.

Davey removed the black cloth from the trunk, looked inside, and saw a variety of bundles, each wrapped in additional pieces of black cloth. He pulled them out separately and passed them to Aunt Sally for her inspection. The bundles offered a parade of images, brief glimpses of the life of Antonio and Alicia Sabatini. They were old photographs, framed and covered by heavy glass.

For the first time, Davey was able to look at the face of The Great Sabatini. He was a tall, slender man of fierce appearance. Dark eyebrows, a mustache, and goatee adorned a strikingly handsome face with intense eyes. In many of the photographs, he wore a long black cape and black top hat. Rings adorned his fingers and he held a long cane with a massive, dragon-shaped head. Visible around his neck was the necklace, which Davey now wore under his shirt.

The photographs showed him alone, or with others in a variety of circumstances. Some of the pictures seemed posed, as though made for publicity. In one, he stood before the camera, his outstretched hand cradling a ball of fire. In another, he was in front of his carnival wagon, shooting lightning into the sky.

Other photographs created a gentler impression, such as Antonio and Alicia laughing together as they walked along, or Antonio in casual clothes, smiling at the camera. A final picture showed him with his arm draped across the shoulders of a young Cherokee boy, each holding a bow and a quiver of arrows. Davey smiled as he recognized the distinctive features of Chief Yona. *I will present a copy of this to him,* he thought.

At the bottom of the trunk were two leather-bound journals. Each was very old and written in a language Davey couldn't read. On the front page of each journal, a title appeared, written in flowery script. The first was *Fandonie A Magico,* the other, *Storia Di Incanto.* Davey immediately knew the journals were important. He glanced at Amy, and her upraised eyebrows indicated her agreement.

Uncle Bill began to work on the latch of the second trunk with the screwdriver. Soon, the lock banged open and the lid flew up. Once again, Davey peered into the trunk expectantly. It contained all of the clothes that Antonio wore for his magic act.

To Aunt Sally and Uncle Bill, the old clothes were nothing more than a curiosity, but to Davey, they were a great discovery. Everything that he needed for his Halloween costume was there. At the very top was Antonio's long black cape, adorned by a high collar and ornate gold clasp. Below it, he found a black top hat, knee-high boots, black vest, trousers, and white silk shirt. Davey realized many of the items were too large for him, but with a little help from Aunt Sally, maybe they would fit.

Davey looked wistfully at her. "Can you make these clothes fit me?"

She laughed merrily. "I'll do what I can."

ஐ⚭ஐ⚭ஐ⚭

Later that afternoon, two men were carrying their fishing rods along the banks of the New River. The river had risen above its normal level, but the men knew of a backwater where the catfish retreated when the waters were rough. When the men reached their destination, they saw a man lying on the bank. As they examined the battered and bruised body of Sineous Crop, one of the men spoke. "He's hurt bad, George. You stay here with him, and I'll go for help."

That evening, Wally fetched Sineous from the emergency clinic. His arm was broken in two places and covered by a thick plaster cast. Angry welts and bruises dotted his swollen face and the rest of his body. Moreover, his long nose was twice its normal size.

As soon as Wally loaded Sineous into his car, he glared at him. "Did you place the stone in their basement?"

"Never got the chance; bears attacked me before I reached their house."

"Where is the stone then?"

Sineous shook his head. "It was smashed when I fell onto the rocks in the ravine." He didn't mention the shards that had penetrated his

ஐ 298 ⚭ *

body when it shattered or the strange crawling sensation, which he now felt under his skin.

Wally was furious. "You clumsy fool! I was counting on the stone to weaken the Sabatinis."

"Think of something else," Sineous snapped, and his eyes suddenly took on an angry, lizard-like appearance.

⚬ Chapter 29 ⚬

---

*Hearken magician and know that
magick worlds may be reached by thee.
These places are rife with mystery and
danger.*

— Translated from Storia Di Incanto; circa 1837

The Thoughtful Hat

SPIKE BEGAN HIS annual campaign of terror five days before
Halloween. His father had told him to stay out of trouble, but Spike
couldn't resist. After all, Halloween was a special occasion to him. For
several years, he had been playing an escalating series of mean tricks
before the big day arrived. Now, he saw his meanness as a tradition,
one worthy of intensification. He had been gathering supplies for
weeks, things like rotten eggs, rats, snakes, stink bombs, and
firecrackers. Anything that would bring misery to others went into his
collection.

Of course, Spike was cunning in his trickery. However, Davey's
developing awareness alerted him to the danger right away. It was an
intangible feeling, something akin to a prickling of his skin whenever
Spike was around. Davey was sure Spike was reserving something
truly horrendous for him and Amy. He could feel it coming, but he
didn't know what it was.

Spike's campaign started on Monday morning. During homeroom
class, Linda Peabody opened a drawer in her desk; three rats leaped

out, squealing and baring their teeth. She uttered a startled gasp, jerked her hand away, and retreated towards a far corner of the room as the rats spilled out onto the floor. Linda's quick reaction saved her from receiving a nasty bite.

Naturally, the classroom turned into chaos when this happened. The rats ran around the room while the students stood on their chairs, yelling and throwing books at them. Finally, Davey opened the door and the rats made a beeline for the hallway. Spike and his little gang were practically berserk with laughter as they watched. Amy glared at them in disgust, but her scorn only increased their delight.

Many students suffered during the week as well as the teachers. Stink bombs exploded in the hallways, glue randomly covered the seats of classroom chairs, and unseen hands threw rotten eggs at unwary backs. Spike and his goons were always around whenever these things happened, but no one confronted them. In the minds of the students, such an act was tantamount to suicide.

Davey and Amy stayed together during the week, knowing they were on Spike's hit list. As each day passed, they became increasingly wary, wondering when he would strike. On Wednesday, Davey's necklace signaled a warning while he opened his locker door, and he watched with dismay as a small copperhead snake slithered around among his books. Amy looked on in stunned silence. Copperhead snakes, even small ones, were poisonous. Somehow, the snake had gotten in through the vents in the door.

A minute later, Spike and Monkey strolled by. "I wonder how that got in there," Spike said, his piggy eyes gleaming.

Amy turned on him, consumed by anger. "Someone is going to get hurt if you don't stop," she shouted.

"Wooga, wooga," screeched Monkey Davis, going into his orangutan routine.

"I don't know what you're talking about," Spike said, feigning innocence.

At that moment, Amy lost her cool; she was wearing the wisdom scarf and knew Spike was lying. "You stinking liar," she screamed, her voice echoing along the hallway.

Monkey drew back his fist and walked towards her. "Shut up or you'll be the one who gets hurt," he said menacingly.

Davey rushed forward, driving his shoulder into Monkey's chest with surprising force. His actions caught Monkey off guard, and he stumbled back against Spike, knocking them both to the floor. An odd cracking sound occurred when they fell, and the smell of rotten eggs suddenly permeated the hallway.

Amy began to laugh. "I knew you were stinking liars."

Spike and Monkey glanced quizzically at each other. Then they realized the rotten eggs in their backpacks had shattered. Spike glared angrily at Davey, but he knew the smell coming from their backpacks meant trouble. If a teacher caught them, they would face suspension, so he and Monkey hastily scrambled to their feet and ran through the nearby exit. "You haven't heard the last of this," Spike yelled over his shoulder.

"That was probably a mistake," Davey said, after they were gone.

A bright red blush was spreading across Amy's face. "I couldn't help it; I'm sick of their childish pranks." She didn't know whether it was the act of standing up to Spike or the thrill of Davey defending her that was making her blush.

Davey turned towards the snake in his locker. It had coiled up on one of his books and was calmly watching him. "Alright, no one's going to hurt you," Davey said, taking a plastic ruler out of his backpack. He eased the tip of the ruler under the snake's body and gently lifted it into the air. The snake lay draped over the ruler, unmoving. Amy eyed the snake unhappily and kept perfectly still.

"Be right back," Davey said, and then slowly marched down the hallway to the exit. When he reached the door, he walked outside, careful not to jar the snake from the ruler. There was no sign of Spike or Monkey, so he lowered the snake to the ground. "Go home and please don't hurt anyone on the way," he whispered.

Amy had a wide grin on her face when he returned. "Wow, I'm

impressed."

"It was just a baby," Davey replied, his mind still on what Spike had said. More trouble was headed their way – he could sense it.

Thursday was the most unpleasant day by far. The teachers had reached their limits and were speaking out against the escalating danger posed by the pranks played against them. In fact, Mr. McDonnell spent the entire class ranting about the unknown students who had thrown eggs at his red Ford Mustang; the car was a thirty six-year old classic, which he maintained in prime condition. Everyone knew it was his pride and joy.

Mr. McDonnell's tirade resulted in a vicious ambush that afternoon. When he left the school, a barrage of rotten eggs hit him while he walked alone towards his car. Three eggs caught him right in the face, coating his glasses with gooey egg yolk. He never had a chance to spot his attackers, let alone pursue them.

"You little brats!" he yelled, twirling around in the parking lot and waving his fist. He shook his head, grumbling to himself as he pulled a red kerchief from his pocket and began wiping egg from his glasses. "Bloody stinkers are taking all the fun out of Halloween!"

෨෯෨෯෨෯෨෯

Androf Protsky hadn't left his apartment since his encounter with the wolves. Five days had passed before he could put weight on his wounded leg – days during which his tormented mind teetered on the verge of insanity. Finally, the coddling of Ubeck's soothing voice allowed him to function more rationally. By Thursday evening, he felt ready to confront his enemies again.

Unfortunately, getting inside the reporter's house by way of the hole in the roof was no longer an option. Earlier in the week, Androf had watched angrily while Uncle Bill and Ed replaced the broken shingles and repaired the hole. "The enemy anticipates my every move," Androf muttered bitterly.

Ubeck's voice was less perturbed. *Don't worry; there are many ways to enter a house.*

Finally, Androf was ready for another foray into the night; his primary mission was to find a different way into Ed Nolen's house. Just as he was walking out the door, his cell phone rang. Androf had completely forgotten about Yong Chow Lee during his five days of anguish. He hesitated, not wanting to speak with the Chinese man, but Ubeck was insistent.

Tell him to send more money.

As soon as Androf answered, he heard Yong Chow Lee's haughty voice. "Why haven't you called me?"

"There was nothing to report," Androf replied deceitfully.

"No more bird attacks?" Yong Chow Lee scoffed.

Don't tell him about the wolves.

"I have complete access to the boy; I can take him anytime," Androf lied.

"Stay close. Things are at a delicate point in China," Yong Chow Lee ordered.

Ask for more money!

"I need more money," Androf blurted out.

"I will send it next week. Call me in three days; I'll have new orders for you then," Yong Chow Lee snapped.

"He is lying to me about this boy, but I don't know why," Androf grumbled after he hung up, his mind filled with paranoid thoughts.

When the money comes, we will leave this cursed town.

Androf snuck out of his apartment a few minutes later. A full moon had risen over the horizon and the sky was clear. Stars twinkled overhead like tiny diamonds on a black velvet cloth. He felt invigorated as he crept over to Ed Nolen's house and then began a cautious search of the perimeter. He was soon disappointed; the house was like a fortress with few windows. The newly installed doors had double locks, which were difficult to pick.

We will dispose of the reporter in a different way, Ubeck said.

"I want to go to the boy's house and spy on my enemies," Androf whispered, feeling a sudden boldness.

Be mindful of their trickery.

Androf stalked along Elm Street, a dark figure darting between the trees. When he reached the pines across from the house, he eased into the deep shadows and began scanning the roofline. Immediately, he spotted more than a dozen ravens perched upon its peaks, their black shapes visible in the moonlight.

Androf's body began to tremble. "There are so many," he muttered, his boldness turning into fear.

Time to retreat, Ubeck said.

"I am not ready. I want to stay out in the night," Androf growled.

Go to the woman's house. Perhaps you will find something to steal.

Androf liked the idea and immediately headed towards the house at the top of the hill. He was careful to stay in the shadows of the trees and search for ravens and wolves along the way. When he reached the house, he hid in the bushes and settled in to watch.

The windows were dark; Androf saw no sign of movement, but he waited for almost an hour before going closer. Finally, he crossed the lawn and crept onto the wide veranda along the front of the house. Crouching low, he moved from window to window, peering into the interior. When he arrived at the kitchen window, he stared in surprise at what he saw. A wooden box sat on the breakfast table with its lid open. Inside the box, Androf saw a beautiful golden object. The surface of the object glowed intriguingly.

It seems valuable, yet it sits unprotected.

"I will steal it," Androf whispered.

Find a way in and be quick.

Androf left the veranda and circled to the back of the house. He found himself in a landscaped garden with an ornate fountain in the middle. A brick staircase led up to a narrow patio that ran along the back of the house. He smiled, remembering a similar house in Paris where he had stolen many things. His eyes spotted an exterior door leading into the kitchen from the patio. Seeing no signs of danger, he moved quickly up the steps to the doorway. The lock on the door was easy to pick, and he was inside the house in a matter of minutes.

The room that Androf entered was a small sun porch adjoining the kitchen. From there, he crept into the kitchen until he reached a three-foot high island in the center of the room. The only sound was the loud ticking of a clock in another part of the house.

The way is clear. Take the box and leave.

Androf slowly stood up and surveyed the room. The box sat on the breakfast table five feet away, and he quickly stepped towards it, his hand reaching for the open lid. Just as he was about to touch it, the lid abruptly slammed shut. Startled, Androf jerked back, bumping against one of the chairs at the table. He steadied himself, took a deep breath, and reached for the box again. Suddenly, something very cold slapped his face. Then the box rose into the air and flew away on an erratic course.

Androf watched the box, too stunned to move. He wiped his eyes, thinking he was seeing things. Several seconds later, the sound of a menacing growl brought him back to reality. The growl came from the opposite end of the room, from an area shrouded in darkness. Androf shuddered, thinking of only one thing – wolves!

Treachery is afoot, shouted Ubeck.

Androf fumbled for the pepper spray in his pocket while he stared at the box darting across the room. It was moving away from him, heading towards the dark corner where the growling seemed to be. He couldn't seem to take his eyes from it.

Forget the box and get out.

Androf ducked behind the island of cabinets and held the pepper spray in his fingers. Then he cautiously raised his head, pointing the canister at the corner. His hand was shaking so badly, he couldn't hold it still enough to take aim. Abruptly, the floating box flew at his face, smashing into the bridge of his nose. The blow was so powerful that he almost lost consciousness, and he fell backwards, hitting the floor with a loud thud. Tears flooded his eyes and blood gushed from his nostrils. On his right, the snarling of the wolves grew closer.

Unbeknownst to Androf, there were no wolves in Aunt Gilda's kitchen. Bupkiss was the only animal growling in the darkness, but in

Androf's mind, the same three wolves that had attacked him before were in the kitchen with him.

"Ubeck, help me," Androf cried, his mind numbed by pain.

Run for your life!

Androf staggered to his feet and ran blindly towards the door. When he passed Bupkiss, the dog lunged at his legs, making him stumble as he went through the doorway. His momentum propelled him over the railing along the upper patio, and he fell into a clump of thorny bushes ten feet below. Letting out a scream of pain, Androf rolled through the bushes and scrambled to his feet. Soon, he was running mindlessly down Elm Street, unable to stop until he was back in his apartment. Then he crawled into bed, pulled the blanket over his head, and lay there, shaking violently.

Your enemies laid a trap for you, Ubeck said in disgust.

"Oh, shut up," Androf muttered, covering his ears.

੧੦੪੧੦੪੧੦੪

Earlier that evening, Davey stood in his room, admiring himself in the mirror. He could hardly believe his eyes. Aunt Sally had done a terrific job of altering his great grandfather's clothing; the result was a fabulous magician's costume. The black cape draped neatly over his body until it nearly touched the floor. The gold clasp holding the cape closed was another piece of magic jewelry; it had the shape a dragon's head, amber stones forming the eyes.

Uncle Bill had stuffed some tissue paper along the inside of the top hat, making it fit snuggly around Davey's head. With three pairs of thick socks on his feet, the leather boots fit as well. He also wore the white shirt and black vest, which he had found in the trunk.

The final touch had been Aunt Sally's idea. She had found some thick black yarn at one of the downtown shops, combed out the coils, trimmed the material with scissors, and fashioned it into eyebrows, a mustache, and a goatee. Then she had stuck them on Davey's face with cosmetic glue.

Davey selected one of the old photographs of The Great Sabatini and compared it to his own image in the mirror. The resemblance was astonishing, so much so that Davey felt like he had suddenly become the great magician. He twirled in front of the mirror, liking the way the cape fluttered around his body. Suddenly, he heard a familiar tapping and ran towards the window beside his bed. Upon opening it, the squirrel from the Great Oak streaked into the room.

"How do I look?" Davey asked, delighted to see the mysterious animal.

The squirrel studied Davey for a moment, its tail twitching rapidly. Then it did a triple flip in the air, which Davey took for a sign of approval, and leaped onto Davey's shoulder. Immediately, the squirrel scurried along the cape and disappeared into its interior folds.

"Hey, where are you going?" Davey asked, laughing. He opened the cape and looked for the squirrel, but he couldn't find the little animal anywhere. When the squirrel didn't reappear after a few minutes, Davey took off the cape and spread it out on the bed. He saw no telltale lumps or pockets along the inside of the cape where the squirrel might be hiding. Slowly, he smoothed out the cloth with his fingers. As he did, the surface of the material changed, and a large black opening appeared in the center of the fabric.

The two-foot opening was unlike anything Davey had ever seen before; its oblong shape crinkled and waved eerily. While he stared at it, Davey felt like he was peering into the vortex of a dark cloud. Ever so cautiously, he touched his fingers to the vortex. The surface had an odd consistency, as if it were a strange mixture of air and water. He felt no ill effects from its touch. In fact, it felt rather pleasant. Finally, with a resolute sigh, he plunged his hand into the opening.

Immediately, Davey felt a gentle pressure on his hand and realized unseen objects were slipping onto his fingers. When he removed his hand a few seconds later, five gold rings were there. Amber jewels, the trademark of his great grandfather's jewelry, adorned each ring. He repeated the process with his other hand, and it emerged with five rings as well.

Davey sat on the bed and closed his eyes while the dizzying force of the rings rushed through his body. When he opened them again, the squirrel was sitting in the center of the cape, and the vortex had disappeared. "Thank you for the rings," Davey said softly. Then he looked wistfully at the squirrel. "I wish you could tell me about the opening in the cape."

The squirrel's eyes twinkled mysteriously, and it rushed across the room to where the old photographs from the trunk were stacked on Davey's desk. The letter, which Alicia had pinned on the cloth covering the items, was stuck between them. In his excitement over the magician's costume, Davey had completely forgotten about it.

The squirrel returned with the letter, and Davey knew exactly what to do with it. He brushed his fingers across the backside of the sheet, and a message from his great grandfather immediately appeared.

To my heir,

Magic and mystery infuses these items. As your skill grows, you will learn how to use them. Wear them well and in good health. The hat shares many thoughts, and the cape provides a gateway to strange and unknown places. Perhaps my boots will take you there!

The squirrel performed another triple flip, obviously pleased. Then the little animal popped over to the window and sat on the sill, peering back at Davey. It seemed to be waiting for something.

"Okay…what now?" Davey asked.

The squirrel pointed at the magician's hat lying on the bed and motioned for him to put it on. He did as the little animal suggested, and then looked at the squirrel expectantly. The squirrel assumed the unmistakable posture of a person thinking; its legs crossed and one little hand under its chin.

At first Davey was puzzled, but he eventually understood.

Antonio's message had said the hat shared many thoughts. Maybe the squirrel was telling him the hat would let him read its mind. He focused his thoughts on the squirrel and concentrated on what the little animal was thinking. A brief moment later, Davey heard a tiny gleeful voice.

The Great Sabatini is proud of you, the voice said. Then, with an affirmative nod, the squirrel disappeared.

❧ Chapter 30 ☙

***

The bloom of magick is a thing of beauty, yet heed these words. Use of thy powere requires care lest it overwhelm.

— Translated from Storia Di Incanto; circa 1850

The Halloween Party

ON FRIDAY AFTERNOON, the Three of We met at the entrance to the park, each wearing their homemade Halloween costumes. Smiles quickly turned into laughter when they saw each other's costumes for the first time. What an odd sight they made: a magician, a witch, and a Cherokee war chief, grinning at one another in mutual admiration.

Davey thought Amy's costume was unbelievably cool. She had fashioned a crooked nose and pointed chin from papier-mâché, glued them in place, and smoothed the edges with cosmetic putty so they weren't noticeable. Pea-green makeup covered her skin and highlights of black eyeliner added wrinkles to her face. A stringy grey wig and pointed hat concealed her blonde hair. The rest of her costume was equally witch-like: black dress, black shoes with curled toes, striped knee socks, skinny green fingers having pointed fingernails, and a straw broom made from a tree branch.

It was the first time Davey had seen her without her glasses. Even in her witch's costume, he thought she was extremely cute. However, he didn't tell her that. "You are positively the most dreadful looking witch ever," he said instead.

"Come closer; I'll put a curse on you," she replied, cackling like an old crone.

Jimmy's costume was equally as magnificent. A Cherokee war bonnet, resplendent with eagle feathers and colorful beads, rested on his head. Buckskin moccasins and leggings covered his feet and legs, and a bearskin vest adorned his chest. Hanging from his neck was an elaborate necklace of animal claws, which rattled ominously when he moved. He carried a six-foot long spear with a wicked-looking point affixed at the end.

As much as Davey liked the war bonnet, he thought the war paint was the best part of Jimmy's costume. Designs in black, white, red, and yellow decorated every part of his exposed skin. Red paint covered the lower half of his face and white paint covered the upper half, accentuated by vivid black circles around his eyes and yellow stripes across his forehead.

"You look absolutely ferocious," Davey said admiringly.

Jimmy beamed in agreement. "Yeah, bloody mean looking ain't I?"

"You'd better be careful with that spear; it looks dangerous," Amy cautioned.

Jimmy reached up and bent the point of the spear with his fingers. "Genuine rubber, little miss. Can't hurt a blooming thing."

Amy grinned at the two boys. "Your costumes are awesome. I'm proud of you guys, especially you, Davey. You only started last week."

"Aunt Sally and Uncle Bill helped a lot," Davey said, smiling.

"You seem so much taller than me now," Amy remarked.

"It's the boots, but they're a little big for my feet."

Amy noticed the rings on Davey's fingers. "Where did those come from?"

Davey hadn't told them about the rings, nor had he said his costume made him feel like a different person – almost as if it was haunted. He had examined the rings last night after the squirrel left and found they had the same symbols along their surfaces as the bracelets. "They were hidden, but you won't believe where," Davey replied, thinking about the cape.

"Do they have magic powers like the bracelets?" Jimmy asked.

"Yes, and so does the cape and hat."

"Come on, we need to get over to the pavilion for the costume contest," Amy said, pulling Davey by the hand. "You can tell us about them while we're walking."

When they arrived at the clearing where the open-air pavilion was located, Davey stopped and took in the sight. True to Amy's prediction, the Halloween party was quite a spectacle. The clearing was about the length of a football field, but shaped like an oval. At one end, a group of local musicians, *The Great Oak Wingdings,* were tuning up their instruments in a covered bandstand.

The pavilion sat at the opposite end, featuring a long judges' table facing the clearing; six adults sat at the table in folding chairs. Davey recognized three of them as teachers from his school. One was Eunice Bluestone, the principal, and the other two were Timothy McDonnell and Emily Watson.

A variety of colorful booths were scattered around the edges of the clearing, selling food, drinks, and candy. Other booths offered games to play or provided platforms for political speeches. Overhead, ghost-shaped lanterns and colorful flags hung from wires stretched along high wooden poles. Carved, candle-lit pumpkins completed the party-like atmosphere.

A large crowd of adults as well as kids had already gathered; others were arriving steadily. Almost everyone wore a costume of some type. The kids entering the contest were lining up near the bandstand where a woman took names and handed out numbered tags. About twenty kids already had tags, and Davey, Jimmy, and Amy dutifully took their places in the line.

"What exactly do we do in this contest?" Davey asked.

Amy explained, talking fast because of her excitement. "Everyone gets a number and puts it on their sleeve; then we all parade around in a big circle. When we pass in front of the judges, we're supposed to act like the character that our costume represents. The judges pick the kids with the best five costumes, and they become finalists. The finalists do the parade thing again, and the judges award prizes for the top three costumes. Last year, I was a finalist, but I didn't win anything."

"What was your costume like?"

Amy smiled at the memory. "It was a really neat butterfly with big wings on the back. Every time I moved, the wings flapped."

"I remember that. It was a good costume, but not very scary," Jimmy said.

Amy nodded. "My mom said it was why I didn't win, so I decided to be a witch this year. I loved that costume though."

"What are the prizes?" Davey asked.

Amy grinned. "The prizes are donated by local shops. First place is a new bicycle from Jimmy's dad. I'd really like to win it because my old bike is falling apart."

"Second place is a snowboard, and third place is a video game. I'd like either one of those," Jimmy interjected. "Hey, a thought just occurred to me. Maybe Davey could wish for us to win."

Amy punched Jimmy on the arm. "That would be cheating. If I win a prize, I want it to be because of my costume, not anything else."

Jimmy started laughing. "Just kidding, little miss." Then he pointed at the judges table. "Look, Spike's dad is one of the judges. We know who *he'll* vote for."

"Which one is he?" Davey asked, suddenly curious to see the man who he'd heard so many bad things about.

"He's the big dude sitting alongside Eunice Bluestone."

Davey's eyes focused upon a man who was more or less a larger version of Spike. He had the same piggy eyes and ruddy complexion, but his hair was longer and combed in an elaborate pompadour. Davey though he looked more like a professional wrestler than the patriarch of the town's wealthiest family. While Davey watched him, his necklace began to vibrate. *It's warning me about him,* he thought.

Just then, they came to the woman who was handing out the numbered tags. They each gave their names, received a tag, and joined the line of kids ready to parade. Jimmy studied the costumes of the other kids as they waited. "Bloody heck, I think we've got the best costumes; we just might win," he muttered.

"Which other ones look good?" Davey asked.

"Clyde Jones has a neat pirate's outfit, and Johnny Anderson is a good mummy. Only he used toilet paper for the wrappings and pieces are tearing off every time he moves. There may not be much left when he reaches the judges," Jimmy said, grinning.

"I hope he's wearing clothes underneath," Amy remarked.

Spike and Monkey Davis were wandering along the line, making snide remarks about everyone's costumes. Davey thought Spike's costume was rather pathetic. He was wearing a rubber werewolf's mask and a sweatshirt with the words *Wild One* across the front. But Monkey was wearing an impressive gorilla's suit. "Monkey's costume is cool," he muttered.

Amy made a face. "Yes, but it's not home made or very creative; both of those things count. Besides, he's a jerk."

Spike sneered as he passed Davey, "Hambone as a magician – now that's scary."

"Wooga wooga!" screeched Monkey, pawing at Amy with a hairy gorilla hand.

Amy quickly ducked behind Davey and Jimmy, and the two boys glared at him as they closed around her.

"Leave her alone or I'll smash your ugly nose," Jimmy said.

Monkey screeched and ambled away, flapping his arms. "Catch you later," Spike said, and then howled like a wolf.

Amy gave the two boys a glance of appreciation. "Have you decided what you're going to do when you pass in front of the judges?"

"I'm performing a Cherokee war dance," Jimmy said.

"I'm pretending to put a witch's curse on them. What about you, Davey?"

Davey hadn't even thought about it, but after what the squirrel had showed him last night, he had a sudden idea. Looking around, he noticed several ravens sitting along the branches of a tree at the edge of the clearing. "I'll be right back," he said, leaving the line and running towards the tree.

"Hey, we're almost ready to start," Amy shouted, but Davey didn't stop. He circled behind the tree so nobody could see him, brushed his fingers across the mysterious gateway inside his cape, and focused his mind on one of the ravens. *Do you think you could hide in here?* he wondered, using his thoughtful hat.

After a few seconds, he heard an answering voice inside his head. *You are the one,* the voice said. Then the raven flew down and perched on Davey's shoulder.

Davey gently placed the bird into the opening of the cape. *Please don't come out until I call you, okay?*

You are the one, the raven said again.

Davey quickly rejoined Amy and Jimmy. "I'm doing a magic trick," he said.

Amy wasn't the least bit surprised. "What kind of trick?"

Davey grinned. "Wait and see. It'll be great, if it works."

At that moment, the band started playing the tune from *The Sorcerer's Apprentice.* The music had just the right spookiness for a Halloween parade, and the kids circled around the clearing, spaced about ten feet apart. Several hundred adults watched as the kids passed, shouting words of encouragement. Each costume invoked laughter and applause when its wearer stood before the judges and mimicked its character.

Amy and Jimmy both performed flawlessly and received enthusiastic applause from the crowd. When it was Davey's turn, he nervously walked in front of the judges, twirling so his cape would billow around his body. "A magic trick for your amusement," he announced, extending his arm towards the judges. Immediately, the raven poked its head out of the cape and strolled along Davey's arm until it stood on his wrist.

The bird froze in place, as it were not a real bird at all. It made no effort to fly away or even flutter its wings. Davey moved his arm around and twisted his wrist, but the bird held on tight, even when Davey held it upside down. A gasp went up from those watching, and five of the six judges smiled broadly. Wally Houseman, the only judge not smiling, scowled instead.

"Let the bird fly!" Davey finally exclaimed, and the raven leaped into the air, flew around his head a few times, and then streaked away. A round of applause rose from the crowd as Davey bowed, twirled, and marched away.

When everyone had performed their routines and completed the parade, the contestants stood around near the bandstand awaiting the judges' decisions.

"That was a great trick," Amy said, grinning.

Davey twirled his mustache. "Just a little magic, my dear."

Jimmy nodded towards the pavilion. "Look…Wally and Eunice are arguing."

When Davey glanced their way, he noticed Wally was not only arguing with Eunice, he was arguing with all of the judges. Then he stood up and stormed away.

"I wonder what that was about," Davey said.

Jimmy laughed. "He probably wanted Spike to be a finalist, but the other judges wouldn't agree."

"I missed the whole thing because I don't have my glasses on," Amy complained.

A short time later, Mr. McDonnell walked across the clearing and stood in front of the contestants, a clipboard in his hands. "Good job everyone! We have selected the finalists, and they are Monkey Davis, Clyde Jones, Jimmy Surefoot, Amy Pigeon, and Davey Boehm. I'd like for them to follow me for the next round."

The Three of We exchanged grins when they heard their names called. Then Davey ran behind the tree again and returned after a few minutes, catching up with the others as they headed towards the judge's pavilion.

Amy looked at him in exasperation. "You're making me nervous. Why do you keep running behind that tree?"

"I was just getting my next trick ready."

"It better be awesome. Monkey and Clyde have good costumes," Jimmy said.

"But not as good as ours," Amy reminded him.

This time, each finalist put on a more elaborate act in front of the judges. Jimmy thrilled the crowd with a wild and furious war dance, thrusting his spear at unseen enemies. Amy received thunderous applause when she pretended to fly in on her broom, cackling, and then melting like the wicked witch in the *Wizard of Oz*. Monkey Davis acted like a crazed gorilla and shocked the judges when he climbed onto their table. This amused the crowd, but didn't seem to please the judges. And Clyde Jones was a convincing pirate, making wisecracks to the stuffed parrot on his shoulder. Unfortunately, the parrot fell off before Clyde finished his routine, which made everyone laugh.

Finally, it was Davey's turn. He walked in front of the judges, swirling his cape around his body. Then he stopped and glared fiercely at them. "Would you like to see more birds?" he asked in a mysterious voice.

"Yes!" the judges replied, their faces smiling.

"Then let there be birds," Davey said, holding both arms straight out from his sides. Suddenly, seven ravens stalked out of his cape, each one taking its place on his outstretched arms and staring at the judges. After a moment, he sent them flying. They circled above him in the formation of a triangle, cawing loudly, but making no effort to leave. "Be gone birds!" he finally shouted, and the birds swooped away in response to his command. The crowd roared its approval as Davey bowed, his cape fluttering around him.

After a brief consultation, the judges awarded the prizes. They called Jimmy's name first as the third place winner. He did a little war dance as he ran towards the judge's table and accepted a certificate for the video game. Next, they called Davey's name, and he walked proudly to the judge's table for the snowboard certificate.

"You'll have to teach me how to use it," Davey said, grinning at

Jimmy.

"No problem, all we need is some snow," he replied, pounding on Davey's back.

The band did a little drum roll before the first place winner was announced; Amy felt like she was going to faint from anxiety. Then she heard her name announced. She rushed towards the judges table, forgetting to act witch-like and shrieking with girlish laughter instead.

Sequoyah stepped forward and presented her certificate. "Come to the store tomorrow and pick out your bike," he said with a smile.

Monkey showed his opinion of the winners by pulling a water balloon from his pocket and throwing it at the judges' table. Then he ran into the crowd, screeching crazily. The balloon almost hit Eunice Bluestone, but she ducked calmly and it sailed past her head.

ଽ୦ଠ୪ଽ୦ଠ୪ଽ୦ଠ୪

Androf Protsky was one of the many adults observing the costume judging. He had learned about the Halloween party from an article in the local newspaper, but he was afraid to attend – afraid that Ed Nolen might be there and recognize him.

You can wear a mask. Perhaps the boy will be there and we can observe what he does, Ubeck said.

"What about the wolves and ravens…they will attack me," Androf replied with a shudder.

They will not attack in the daylight.

"How can you be sure…my enemies are relentless?"

Trust me; you will be safe.

Finally, Androf had donned the black goalie's mask and stalked down the hill to the park. When he saw Davey perform his tricks with the ravens, his suspicions were confirmed. "See how he controls them. He is a demon and controls the wolves in the same way," Androf said.

You must learn the source of his power. Then you can defeat him.

"I will follow him," Androf muttered, nodding his head.

Just then, a plump woman wandered past Androf and smiled. "Are you speaking to me?" she asked in a friendly manner.

"No, I was speaking to Ubeck," Androf replied curtly.

The woman saw no one nearby. "But you are alone," she said.

"Shut up," Androf growled, and then turned away.

∞୧ଈ୧ଈ୧ଔ

"What shall we do now?" Davey asked, as he, Amy, and Jimmy walked among the booths at the Halloween party.

"Eat cotton candy," Jimmy said.

"And celebrate winning the contest," Amy added.

"What about trick-or-treating?"

"That comes later," Amy said.

They came to a large white tent with open sides. In front of the tent was a sign that read: *Progress for Tomorrow.* Six architectural drawings, highlighted by spotlights, stood on easels inside the tent. Wally Houseman was talking loudly to a handful of people gathered around him.

"What's going on in there?" Davey asked, stopping for a moment.

"Wally is promoting his scheme for turning Great Oak into a tourist attraction," Jimmy said.

Amy frowned. "The City Council is voting on it in two weeks, and the School Board has already approved it. Before long, we won't have a park anymore."

Jimmy shook his head. "The Save the Trees Committee is totally against it."

"Yeah, but my dad says Wally has the thing wired," Amy replied.

"Why won't we have a park anymore?" Davey interjected.

"If the city agrees to his proposal, he's going to convert the park and the other land around here into condominiums, a hotel, and a shopping center," Amy said solemnly.

"What will happen to the Great Oak?" Davey asked, suddenly concerned.

"That will be up to Wally, since he'll own the land if the deal goes through. We should be worried about it; the Housemans aren't known for saving trees," Amy replied.

Davey felt a sudden chill as he watched Wally. He seemed supremely confident as he stood before his admirers, explaining his plan. His boisterous voice was full of promises, yet Davey sensed the treachery in the man.

"I know how we can prevent it. I can make a wish," Davey said.

"Why didn't I think of that?" Amy exclaimed. "Let's go see the tree right now!"

"We can stop by the tree when we leave to go trick-or-treating. First, let's get hot dogs, cotton candy, and play games," Jimmy said.

Davey nodded in agreement. "It won't hurt to wait for an hour."

Amy let out an exaggerated sigh as the two boys pulled her towards a booth serving hot dogs. "You guys need to get your priorities in order."

They didn't notice that two others were watching them closely. The first was Androf Protsky, who observed them from a distance. The second was Torpedo Jones – a skull mask and army helmet concealing his features. He stood behind them while they were at Wally's tent, overhearing their conversation. Then he hurried away, smiling.

Just after sunset, the bandleader made an announcement in a jovial voice. "Okay folks; make sure someone is at home to give out candy because it's time for the kiddies to begin trick-or-treating. Everyone else can stay here and wingding with us until midnight."

"Come on, let's go see the tree now," Amy said.

Jimmy led the way through the park, guided by the light of the moon. Everyone else had departed through the exit near the pavilion, leaving them alone as they headed towards the Great Oak. Amy skipped along the path merrily, still elated about winning the costume contest. Jimmy let out an occasional war cry, sharing in her happiness.

When they were halfway there, Davey stopped to adjust his boots. "Walk slow, I'll catch up," he called out. He took off his hat, sat down on a bench, and began straightening out the socks that had twisted into a lump on his foot. Jimmy and Amy disappeared along the path ahead. A moment later, Davey's necklace began to vibrate.

Suddenly, Davey heard several muffled explosions, followed by Jimmy's shouts. Then a cloud of smoke billowed out from where Jimmy and Amy had disappeared. Amy screamed several times, each scream more terrible than the one before; Davey pulled on his boot and ran as fast as he could. As he neared the smoke, he saw Jimmy coming towards him, carrying Amy, who was trying hard to catch her breath. A brownish liquid covered them both. The putrid smell of rotten eggs floated in the air, making it obvious what the brown liquid was.

Davey could hardly believe his eyes. "What happened?"

Jimmy put Amy down and wiped his face with his hand. "Spike, Monkey, and Torpedo ambushed us. They threw smoke bombs and balloons filled with some kind of rotten egg mix. They got us bad, Davey. Hit us four or five times."

"My costume is ruined, and the smell is making me sick," Amy cried, tears running down her face. Then she leaned against a tree, gagged several times, and began to throw up.

Davey was so stunned, he couldn't speak. "Where's her hat?" he finally croaked. It was the only thought that he could verbalize.

Jimmy shook his head. "Don't know, I guess they got it."

A terrible anger came over Davey. Along with the anger, a pulsing flow of energy surged through his body. "I'm getting her hat," he said grimly.

"Wait. I'll go with you," Jimmy said.

"No, you stay with Amy!" Davey yelled, and then disappeared into the cloud.

The smoke along the path was thick; Davey couldn't see anything clearly. Without conscious thought, he stretched out his hand and a gust of air shot from his fingers, pushing the smoke away. A shadowy figure loomed up in the bushes, clearly visible now. Davey recognized Torpedo's grinning face, no longer covered by his skull mask.

"Hambone…Hambone," Torpedo chanted. "Here's your prize." In his hands were two balloons filled with the rotten egg mix, his arms drawing back to throw.

Davey reacted instantly; he pointed at Torpedo and a blast of ice crystals exploded from his fingers. The powerful stream caught Torpedo in the chest, almost lifting him into the air. His body tumbled backwards into a series of summersaults; the balloons in his hands exploded as he involuntarily squeezed them, covering him with the stinking mixture.

Seconds later, Monkey appeared on Davey's right, coming towards him. He acted like a gorilla on a rampage, carrying a bucket of the smelly mixture. "Wooga wooga," he screamed, preparing to toss its contents at Davey. This time, a stream of lightning shot from Davey's fingers, sending Monkey into a convulsive dance. The bucket flew from his hands, propelled upward by his jerking arms. Davey seized control of the bucket with his mind, centering it above Monkey's head and overturning it. As the stinking liquid poured over him, Monkey collapsed in a daze.

Davey charged forward, searching for Spike. He saw him twenty feet ahead, wearing Amy's hat. Apparently, Spike didn't realize the fate of the others in his little gang; he grinned fiendishly when he noticed him coming. Davey ran so fast his movements were almost a blur, reaching Spike before he could react.

Abruptly, Davey snatched Amy's hat from Spike's head and glared into his eyes. Then he tossed the hat aside, grabbed hold of Spike, and lifted him above his head. The force of his magic was so strong Spike's body seemed weightless.

"You stinking rat," Davey shouted, letting the fury of his magic surge into the boy. Spike jerked spasmodically as an amber web encircled his body and an eerie howl escaped from his lips. After a moment, Davey threw him like a beach ball, tearing away the black disk hanging around his neck as he did. The disk turned into ash in Davey's hand, consumed by the force of his magic.

Spike landed against a tree five feet away, staring in horror as

Davey came towards him again. Davey stopped when he saw the fear in Spike's eyes. *What is happening to me?* he wondered. *I'm out of control.* As his anger drained away, he watched the hapless boy.

"Look at me," Davey ordered.

Spike did as Davey instructed, incapable of resisting.

Davey's voice bore into Spike's mind, demanding obedience. "You will not hurt my friends again or continue your evil ways. I want no more of this. Do you hear me? NO MORE!"

Spike nodded, unable to speak.

"Leave then, and never forget my words," Davey commanded, moving away from Spike and pointing at a bucket of the rotten egg mix on the ground nearby. "And take this with you," he added, motioning with his arm. The bucket sailed into the air and flung its contents into Spike's face.

Spike staggered to his feet, gasping as he wiped the foul liquid from his eyes. For a moment, he seemed uncertain of his whereabouts. Then he tenuously ambled away. As he disappeared into the darkness, Davey heard him retching and gasping for air.

Davey looked around for Monkey and Torpedo, but they had already fled, stinking of rotten eggs as well. With a sigh, he picked up Amy's hat and returned to where she and Jimmy were waiting. He had only been gone a few minutes, but it seemed like hours to him.

Jimmy had found a nearby water fountain, and he and Amy had done what they could to wash the putrid mixture from their skin and costumes. Still, the smell lingered around them as though they had crossed paths with a skunk.

Sadness filled Davey's heart as he watched Amy. "I'm sorry about your costume. Are you okay?"

A fresh tear rolled down her face. "Just embarrassed at being sick in front of you and Jimmy," she mumbled, looking very pale and fragile.

Davey managed a small smile. "That's nothing to be embarrassed about. By the way, I have your hat."

"Thank you," she said softly.

"How'd you get it?" Jimmy asked.

"I lost my temper," Davey replied without further explanation. Then he took Amy's hand. "Come on, Amy. Jimmy and I will walk you home."

ප Chapter 31 ව

Certain people can be guided by the mysterious forces of magick, even though they have no magick skill. They are often worthy of great trust.

— Translated from Storia Di Incanto; circa 1854

A Trust Fulfilled

THE NEXT MORNING, Davey went to see the Great Oak. The gate opened immediately when he appeared, and the squirrel greeted him with gleeful summersaults. They climbed the tree together until they reached the platform near the top. The air was chilly, yet the rays of a brilliant sun kept Davey warm as he looked silently down at the town below. *How my life has changed,* he thought.

Davey's mind was in turmoil. He had slept fitfully during the night, repeatedly awakened by images of Spike cowering in fear. When he finally climbed out of bed in the morning, he was full of despair. *Is the power changing me into someone who hurts others?* The thought filled him with dread.

Davey sat in the tree without speaking for a long time, letting its benevolent aura soothe his troubled feelings. The squirrel curled up in his lap as if sensing his pensive mood. At last, Davey felt his spirits rise and began to explain why he had come. "I became violently angry when Spike and his gang attacked Amy and Jimmy. I was wearing my great grandfather's magic jewelry, and its power overwhelmed me; all

I could think about was revenge. Fortunately, I regained control before anyone was seriously hurt."

Davey stopped for a moment, and the squirrel watched him intently. "I left my hat in the park last night, so I can't hear your thoughts. Do you understand what I'm saying about the power?"

The squirrel nodded and indicated Davey should continue, so he did. "When I first felt the power, I was excited about it. I didn't think about where it came from or what it does. Now, I realize it can be dangerous, so I came to make a wish. Will you and the tree help me learn what this power is and how to control it?"

The squirrel grinned, and the tree signaled its own agreement in an unusual way. A faint breeze ruffled its leaves; the breeze was too weak to move the huge limbs of the tree, yet they began to sway. As the branches and leaves rubbed together, they caused a medley of sounds, each having a distinct tone. The sounds were not random; soon Davey heard a definite tune. *The tree is singing,* he thought with a wistful smile.

The tree's song had a hypnotic effect. As Davey sat back and listened, his normal state of optimism returned and last night's violence faded into a dim memory. It was a healing process, and when the tree became motionless again, Davey felt refreshed. He was sure the tree would grant his wish.

With renewed energy, he began speaking once more. "There's another reason why I came. Wally Houseman is trying to buy the land in the park. If he succeeds, he will cut down the trees and erect buildings here. So please, will you help me stop him?"

Davey's request received no response from the squirrel or the tree. He had thought the little animal would become excited and leap around the branches, yet it sat motionless in front of him. The tree stopped its swaying as well. "You don't think this is a problem?" he asked.

The squirrel stared at him without the slightest concern on its face. *Maybe I'm not explaining it right,* Davey thought. He tried again, reciting the details of what he had seen at Wally Houseman's tent and the remarks made by Amy. Nevertheless, the squirrel reacted as if the problem didn't exist and the tree remained still.

"I guess you can't help me with this," Davey muttered. He stayed in the tree for another hour, thinking about what else he could do to thwart Wally's plans. The longer he stayed there, the less worried he became. When he finally climbed down to the ground, he was sure things would work out somehow.

After leaving the tree, Davey began a search for his hat. He had hoped to find it where he had sat down to adjust his boots last night, but it wasn't there. Then he retraced the route to the pavilion, looking everywhere along the way without success. When Davey arrived at the pavilion, he saw two men removing lanterns from the posts, while three others picked up trash around the clearing. Joe Harrison, the park warden, stood nearby, apparently the man in charge. Davey walked over to him and said hello.

"Well, if it isn't the magician," Joe replied, grinning.

Davey returned the smile. "Does the park have a lost and found department?"

Joe laughed heartily. "That would be me. What did you lose?"

"A black hat...part of my magician's costume. It belonged to my great grandfather."

"Uh-oh, every magician needs a hat. Where did you leave it?"

Davey shrugged. "I left it on a bench near the Great Oak, but it's not there now."

Joe nodded. "I've already been through the park, looking for lost stuff. I found lots of things, but no hat. I'll keep my eye out though and call your aunt if I find it."

"Thanks, I'd hate to lose it."

Joe's eyes twinkled knowingly. "I'm sure it will turn up. Remember what your great grandmother said about those magic items – they'll find *you*. By the way, watching your performance with the ravens yesterday reminded me of her. Birds were always following her around and doing her bidding."

"I guess it runs in the family," Davey replied.

Joe chuckled. "I'd say so, young man. Yes sir, I'd say so."

Meanwhile, Androf Protsky sat in his apartment, glaring at Davey's hat. He had followed Davey, Amy, and Jimmy after the Halloween party. When Davey left his hat on the bench, he ran over and grabbed it. Then he crept through the woods and watched as Davey shot what looked like lightning into the boy in the gorilla suit.

"He could do the same to me," he muttered to himself.

A few seconds later, he stared in shock as Davey flung Spike into the air. *The boy is a demon. I dare not battle him,* he thought, scurrying away through the trees.

Ubeck was strangely absent from Androf's mind for the rest of the evening, which made Androf feel lonely and anxious. Every small sound fueled Androf's paranoia, and he repeatedly called Ubeck's name without result. The next morning, as Androf was glaring at the hat and wondering what he should do with it, Ubeck suddenly spoke.

The Chinese man has played you for a fool!

"Ubeck, you have returned," Androf shouted, happy to hear Ubeck's voice inside his head. "But…why are you calling me a fool?"

Don't you understand? The boy is like a cat toying with a mouse. You are the mouse Androf, one sent by the Chinese man.

Androf's eyes narrowed into malicious slits. He slammed his fist on the table where the hat sat, sending it tumbling to the floor. "The Chinese man has tricked me, but why?" Androf asked.

He appeases the boy by offering you as a sacrifice.

"I don't understand – what should I do?"

Let me take charge. I will protect you.

Androf readily agreed, no longer thinking rationally anyhow. He picked up the hat and placed it on his head. "I have the demon's hat. Its power is mine now."

Finding it was a stroke of luck. We will use it against him.

Aunt Sally was waiting for Davey when he returned from the park that morning. "Linda Peabody telephoned a few minutes ago. She has invited you to her aunt's house for ice cream; she wants you to bring Bristol with you. I said you would be there around three o'clock, okay?"

"Sure, we talked about it at school."

"You'll need to get cleaned up. I can still smell that rotten egg stuff on you."

Davey had told Aunt Sally about Spike and his gang attacking Amy, but he hadn't mentioned his part in the fight. She had wanted to call the police, but Davey had talked her out of it. Now, he had something else on his mind. "Can we talk about Wally Houseman's condominium project? He's going to cut down the trees in the park."

Aunt Sally smiled. "Don't tell anyone, but I've already solved that problem."

Davey frowned gloomily. "Amy said he has it wired with the City Council. The School Board has already approved it."

Aunt Sally just smiled again. "Things are not always as they appear. Now, go get cleaned up."

Davey took a shower, ate lunch, and found that he had an hour to spare. He made a quick trip to Ed Nolen's house, carrying the two journals from the Sabatini trunks. Their words were Italian, and he wanted to find out if Ed could read them.

"Can you help me translate them?" Davey asked, showing the journals to Ed as soon as he arrived.

Ed smiled brightly. "Sure, but I'm awfully busy right now. It might be a while before I can get to it." Then he noticed the disappointed look on Davey's face. "Wait, I've got a better idea," he said, and ran upstairs.

Ed returned after a few minutes and handed Davey a piece of paper containing an internet address. "This is a website, which offers a shareware program for translating Italian into English. It's free, so you can download it and do your own translating. I've used it before and found it very accurate."

"That *is* a better idea…thanks!" Davey exclaimed, and hurried back home.

Exactly one hour later, Davey was sitting on the wide veranda of Aunt Gilda's house. Bupkiss and Bristol were running back and forth in the front yard, fighting over a rubber toy. Every so often, Bupkiss glanced up at the veranda, checking on them.

"Bupkiss seems totally happy. I'll bet he follows you around everywhere," Davey said.

Aunt Gilda laughed. "Oh, he certainly does. When Linda is at school, he won't leave my side. He even gets upset if I go into another room and shut the door."

"His first owners left him behind, so he probably gets a little insecure when he's alone. I'm sure he'll get over it," Davey replied.

"We can't thank you enough for letting us have him. He makes me feel like I'm sixty years old again, and that's saying something," Aunt Gilda said with a chuckle.

"Shall I get the ice cream?" Linda asked.

Aunt Gilda rose from her chair. "No dear, I'll get it. I already have everything laid out on a tray. All I have to do is take the ice cream from the freezer."

When Aunt Gilda went into the house, Bupkiss immediately dropped the rubber toy and ran onto the veranda. The dog stood at the screen door, whining as he anxiously peered inside. Linda walked to the door, opened it, and Bupkiss streaked through. Bristol stared at the rubber toy lying on the grass for a few seconds, then trotted up to Davey and lay down with a sigh.

Linda smiled at Davey as she returned. "Thank you for coming over. Aunt Gilda doesn't get out much anymore, and it's good for her to have company. We both want to express our gratitude; Bupkiss means a lot to us."

"You've helped me a lot at school, so I'm the one who should be saying thanks," Davey said, feeling a bit embarrassed.

"Speaking of school, there's something I want to ask you. Eunice Bluestone has put me in charge of the Scholar's Team. Will you try out for it?"

"What's the Scholar's Team?"

"It's a small group of students who compete on a variety of academic subjects against students from the other schools in the area. It would be a feather in my cap if we made a decent showing."

Davey liked the idea. "Sure, what would I have to do?"

Excitement filled Linda's voice as she explained. "First we'll have tryouts, which will involve the taking of some achievement tests. The six students having the top scores will make the team, and then we'll compete against the other schools on a double elimination basis. The final match between the two best teams will be on television."

Just then, Aunt Gilda reappeared on the veranda, carrying a big silver tray loaded with ice cream, strawberries, chocolate sauce, whipped cream, and cookies. Bupkiss followed her out the door, prancing as though everyone had been waiting for him.

"Well, here we are," Aunt Gilda said, putting the tray in front of them. "Linda says you're not from Great Oak," she remarked, glancing at Davey as she shoveled scoops of ice cream into glass bowls.

"I've been here for several months. New York is my home, but I'm staying with my aunt and uncle while my parents are in China. I also have some other relatives who lived here a long time ago."

Aunt Gilda was immediately curious. "Oh, who are your aunt and uncle?"

"Sally and Bill Winston, they've lived here for several years."

Aunt Gilda looked thoughtful for a moment. "I don't know them – did you say that you had other relatives here?"

"Yes, but they're all dead now."

Aunt Gilda handed out the bowls; ice cream, strawberries, and chocolate syrup filled them to the brim. Then she continued with her questions. "What were their names? Maybe Charles and I knew *them*."

Davey's mouth was full of ice cream, so he didn't reply immediately. "My great grandparents were Antonio and Alicia Sabatini," he finally said.

Linda suddenly looked at Aunt Gilda. "Wasn't Alicia Sabatini the woman who came to see Charles?"

"Oh my…oh dear me," Aunt Gilda said, her voice trembling.

Her reaction surprised Davey. "Did I say something wrong?"

Linda began to laugh. "No, but you have solved a mystery for us. We have something for you – a box that was entrusted to Aunt Gilda."

"Wait dear, we must be sure he's the right one," Aunt Gilda said.

Davey's curiosity was increasing by the second. "What right one?"

Linda leaned forward, staring at Davey. "If you don't mind, we need to ask you a question. Do you know who Alicia Sabatini's heirs are?"

Davey was perplexed, but saw no reason not to answer. "Alicia Sabatini had one child, Celina. Celina had two daughters, my mom, and Aunt Sally. I'm the only grandchild so far."

"So you are Alicia's first male heir?" Linda asked.

Davey smiled brightly. "That's what they say."

Aunt Gilda clapped her hands with delight. "How wonderful! It's just like Charles predicted. This will make a great story – an entrée, to say the least."

Linda glanced at Aunt Gilda. "Shall I get the box?"

Aunt Gilda rose from the table. "No dear, Charles asked me to do it, and I never disappoint him."

While she was gone, Linda told Davey the story about the box. She made it seem comical, even though the floating box had terrified her at the time. Davey found the story incredible, particularly the part about the ghost of Aunt Gilda's late husband. Still, he didn't question its veracity. *Strange things are always happening here,* he thought with a smile.

Bristol put his head in Davey's lap, wagging his tail because everyone was laughing. His eyes kept drifting towards the dish of cookies sitting on the table. Linda told Davey to give him one, so he did. Bristol wolfed it down and then sat alongside Davey, hoping for another. Bupkiss, who stood at the door and whined because Aunt Gilda was inside the house, didn't notice. But Linda called him over and gave him a cookie, which placated him for the moment.

Aunt Gilda returned, carrying the wooden box and laughing. "Charles is so thrilled you have come for it," she announced, handing it to Davey.

He opened the box and inspected the strange gold and silver container inside it. "What is it?" he asked, not letting on that he recognized it as another one of his great grandfather's magic items.

Linda and Aunt Gilda exchanged fanciful glances. "Davey dear, if you find out, please let us know," Aunt Gilda whispered gleefully.

☙ Chapter 32 ❧

The hands of fate form historie as the potter shapeth clay. The magician foresees these hidden forces in trances and dreams. Yea, all cometh forth as the threads of time unwind.

— Translated from Storia Di Incanto; circa 1862

The Twenty-Fifth Magician

DAVEY WAITED UNTIL his aunt and uncle were asleep before beginning his examination of the object inside the wooden box. He had carried the box up to his room without them seeing it, still wanting to keep his great grandfather's magic items a secret.

The object was a square container about a foot long and six inches high. Its surface was made of gold, except for four bands of silver equally spaced along the top. Tiny amber stones dotted the bands at intervals, glowing softly in the light of the room. The stones turned translucent at Davey's touch, and the object vibrated as if something inside wanted out. However, it had no lid or other apparent opening.

Davey focused his mind and willed for an opening to reveal itself, but nothing happened. He put the object down and racked his brain for a solution. "Maybe I need more magic power," he muttered, hurrying towards the closet where he stored his other magic items.

Bristol followed him, his tail wagging, but after he saw Davey putting on his rings and bracelets, he crept under the bed. He wanted to be out of the way in case lightning started flying across the room.

As energy from the jewelry surged through his body, Davey picked up the object again. Focusing his mind, he willed for it to disclose its contents. This time, the top began to bulge like an overfilled balloon. He quickly placed the object on the bed and watched while the upper half swooshed off. It spun in the air for a second and then returned to the bed, the contents of the object now revealed.

A velvet-wrapped bundle lay inside the lower half of the object. Davey removed the wrapping and found two items. The first was a belt of twenty-five interlinked gold squares, five amber jewels studding the surface of each square. The second was a small leather-bound journal; its pages blank. He placed the belt around his waist, gasped as more energy rushed through his body, and then turned his attention to the journal. When his fingers touched the pages, words appeared amid a flurry of sparks. After reading the first few lines, he smiled. The tree had granted his latest wish.

The Journal of Antonio Sabatini

I, Antonio Sabatini, wrote this journal to tell you my story. Through it, you will learn about a power, which is now yours to command. Take heed and discover your birthright. It will serve you well.

I entered the world in 1892, the twenty-fourth magician in a family with a remarkable heritage. My mother, despondent over my father's earlier death, barely survived my birth. When she died soon thereafter, I became an orphan. Fate put me in the hands of my mother's brother, Giusto Rozzano. He was a kindly guardian who cared for me with a loving heart.

Giusto raised me on a remote farm in the Italian countryside. He taught me to read, write, and make fine jewelry, as he was a jeweler by trade. We lived a simple life and kept to ourselves because Giusto feared the prying eyes of strangers; I learned why many years later.

Even as a child, I knew there was something different about me. I discovered what it was when Giusto gave me two old books on my tenth birthday. The first, *Storia Di Incanto*, set out guidelines for the study of magic. The second, *Fandonie A Magico*, taught magic spells and their uses. They were a compilation of what my ancestors had learned throughout the years. Moreover, they told me about my inherited magic skill.

I saved these books for you, as they are part of your birthright. Study them, and you will learn much about magic. They are written in Italian, but don't worry; a way to translate them will mysteriously appear. Such things will happen often during your life; they are part of the Sabatini mystique.

After reading these books, I asked Giusto why he did not use magic. Until then, I did not fully understand the importance of being a Sabatini. Giusto explained that he was my mother's brother; he was not a Sabatini by blood and thus did not have our magic skill. At first, I felt sorry for him; even the elementary spells were useful around the farm. Giusto jokingly said it was why he kept me around.

Thereafter, I often asked him about the Sabatinis, as he knew their history well. He waited until I turned thirteen before telling me about them. We sat in candlelight on the night of my birthday, the light flickering against the walls. Oh, how mysterious his tale seemed! I relate it now, exactly as he told it to me.

Giusto began with Pietro Sabatini, the first of the family's great magicians. He was born in the fourteenth century – a time when evil lurked in many dark places. At an early age, he demonstrated an ability to predict the future, and a patron provided for his education. He grew up to be a skilled soothsayer whom wealthy nobles came to for advice.

As Pietro's fame increased, the Odisas, a cruel Spanish family, heard about him. Over several centuries, they had established a dynasty in Granada and built a massive fortress known as the Alhambra. Its walls surrounded many palaces containing rare books and works of art, all plundered from the people they conquered.

One dark night, six men attacked Pietro as he returned home and bound him with ropes. Three weeks later, he found himself staring at the high walls of the Alhambra; he had become a prisoner of Felipe Odisa, the Caliph of Granada.

Over time, Pietro became a trusted advisor to the caliph. At first, he only forecast the outcomes of battles, as the Odisas had countless enemies and were always at war. Nevertheless, Pietro had an amazing talent, and soon the caliph sought his advice on other matters. Pietro complied willingly, despite his unhappiness over being a prisoner. Life was short for those who refused Felipe Odisa.

Pietro lived in the Alhambra for three long years. He was allowed to wander freely inside the fortress as long as he didn't try to leave its gates. During this period, he became acquainted with Sarina, the caliph's youngest daughter. She was a kind and beautiful young woman, different from her father in every way. Before long, Pietro and Sarina were spending many hours together.

Regardless of his forced servitude, Pietro found the Alhambra to be a place of opportunity. Many ancient treatises on magic, alchemy, and astronomy became available to him; he read them all. Thereafter, he consulted the stars concerning his destiny. At last, fate sent him a message; something important would soon happen.

The following week, the caliph summoned Pietro to his chambers and showed him a golden, symbol-covered artifact. The foot-high artifact consisted of two separate and distinct shapes, the bottom half a pyramid, the top half a sphere of equal size. The two shapes were not attached, but a mysterious force held the sphere at the apex of the pyramid. Pietro felt a sudden dizziness in its presence, yet he hid his discomfort from the caliph, who seemed unaffected.

The caliph explained that one of his agents had stolen the artifact from a sealed catacomb beneath the Vatican; it had remained there for centuries beside other forgotten plunder of the Crusades. A scroll with the artifact claimed it was a cherished possession of Unas, last pharaoh of Egypt's fifth dynasty. Clearly intrigued by the strange object, the caliph charged Pietro with the task of unlocking its secrets.

Pietro began his research on the next day. At first, he focused upon the symbols on the artifact's surface, but he was unable to discern their meanings. Then he screwed up his courage and touched the sphere, an act he had previously avoided. Instantly, an amber glow surrounded it and a force of pure energy rushed through his body. After repeating this many times, he detected an odd phenomenon; he could now cast spells and move objects with his mind.

Several weeks later, Sarina rushed into his quarters, sobbing as though her heart would break. The caliph had announced her betrothal to the Governor of Palma. The news left Pietro stunned; he couldn't imagine being separated from her. As it turned out, Sarina felt the same way. She declared her love for Pietro and implored him to take her away from the Alhambra. He thought about nothing else for days and finally conceived a plan. The artifact was the key – he would use it to deceive the caliph.

The next day, Pietro implemented his plan. He showed the glowing sphere to the caliph and declared that it had given him a vision of a great victory. For almost a year, the caliph's army had struggled with a siege of Ciudad Real, an important trading city in Spain. Pietro said that the city would fall if the caliph went there and led his army. Convinced by the amber glow, the caliph quickly left for Ciudad Real.

Pietro continued his plan on the following night. Using his new skills, he filled glass bottles with chemicals and sent them flying at the main gate. When they shattered, the guards became unconscious, and he and Sarina escaped on swift horses. They took the artifact with them.

Many weeks passed before they reached San Remo, Pietro's home in Italy. A great celebration ensued, for his family had given up hope that he was alive. Then he and Sarina married, rested a few days, and hastily moved on. Pietro's family accompanied them, fearing the Odisas would soon come to San Remo.

The caliph flew into a violent rage when he learned of Pietro's betrayal. His agents scoured the land, but Pietro and Sarina were nowhere to be found. Moreover, he suffered a terrible defeat at Ciudad Real, followed by other disasters in battle. He was sure that Pietro's theft of the artifact had cursed him; he died ten years later, a bitter man. On his deathbed, he made his sons and daughters swear to exact revenge and recover the artifact. Each new heir renewed this vow.

Thus, the long years of wandering began for the Sabatinis. They knew the Odisas searched for them, yet evaded capture by constantly changing their name and moving from place to place. During this time, they recognized that Pietro's magic skill was an inherited trait. His three sons had his ability, and although his two daughters did not, their male children were even more talented. Furthermore, the magic skill of each new generation increased.

The Sabatinis credited this fact to the artifact, yet they also puzzled over its true purpose. Fate had brought it to them for a reason; they were sure of that. Was it to strengthen their skills, prevent the evil Odisas from using it, or something else? The debate lasted for many years, yet nothing was resolved. The artifact remained an enigma.

For over three centuries, the Sabatinis earned their living as a wandering band of magicians, barely escaping the Odisas many times. While they loved to entertain, any notoriety alerted the enemy of their whereabouts. Finally, the Sabatinis grew tired of their perilous life. They gave up magic, became farmers, and settled in Switzerland. Then a curious thing happened; over the next fifty years, few children were born. It appeared that the practice of magic was necessary for the continuance of their bloodline. In 1847, Alfredo Sabatini remained as the family's sole heir. He took up the name Toreno, moved to France, and resumed the magic act.

Fortune smiled on Alfredo thereafter. He sired two sons, Giovanni, and Cosimo, and made an important discovery; his magic was stronger if he held the artifact when casting spells. This gave him a chance to use it for the good of humanity. A drought had devastated the farms throughout France, and while the Sabatinis had never been successful with rainmaking spells, holding the artifact made Alfredo's spells work. Upon noting this, he traveled the countryside, secretly bringing rain and ending the drought.

The next thirty years were happy ones; Giusto became the family's manager, the Sabatinis enjoyed prosperity, and Giovanni married my mother. They believed the Odisas had forgotten them, but always used the Toreno name. It was a new era for them, one prompting less caution. They performed their magic act many times and secretly helped the farmers wherever they went. Then disaster struck.

An army of Odisa agents ambushed the family when they were traveling to a distant town for a performance. All of the Sabatinis died in the bloody battle that followed. By a quirk of fate, my mother and Giusto had stayed home because of her pregnancy. After my mother died, Giusto bundled me up and we left for Italy. The survival of the magic skill depended upon me, a tiny baby, and Giusto was determined the Odisas would not find us. We finally settled on our remote farm where he felt we would be safe.

Thus, Giusto concluded his story. Since it was my birthday, he asked me to leave the room while he prepared my present. When I returned, the artifact sat before me, gleaming in the candlelight.

Over the next three years, my magic skill grew ten-fold. I used the artifact as Alfredo had, holding it in my hand while casting spells. Before long, I could summon rain, lightning, and hail from the sky. From then on, Giusto jokingly called me The Great Sabatini.

I also experimented by rubbing the artifact against the farm animals when they were sick, but this had no affect. Then I tried sleeping with it, and suddenly my dreams began to tell a progressive story. In one, I saw the earth during its creation. In another, meteors streaked across the sky, and in a third, primitive tribes danced around large pieces of rock. Finally, a dream came that was unlike the others.

In this dream, colorful spheres circled above my head. Each sphere spun towards me, but when I reached out to touch it, the sphere split in half and soared away. The dream was so vivid; I woke up. Entranced, my eyes landed upon the sphere at the top of the artifact; I wondered if it was supposed to spin. Focusing my mind, I pictured it turning. To my surprise, a slight rotation occurred. While I thought about what this might mean, I fell asleep again.

The next morning, I repeated the exercise – the sphere rotated a little more. From then on, I performed the exercise daily. Soon, I could make the sphere spin faster than the eye could see. Then the part of the dream in which the spheres split in half came to mind. Surely, this was something I should try as well. Lo and behold, the sphere divided when I formed the image. The bottom-half stopped its rotation, and the top-half floated six inches above it, still spinning.

Giusto and I were completely astonished when this happened. We stared at the artifact, cautiously watching it from a distance. Finally, we inched closer and peered into the bottom of the sphere. A viscous amber liquid shimmered inside. This prompted a new experiment. A wooden fork lay nearby, and I thrust it into the liquid. Instantly, the fork burst into flames, yet the liquid itself gave off no heat.

Filled with curiosity, I took a narrow strip of gold that we used for making jewelry and stuck it into the liquid. Unlike the wooden fork, it did not catch fire or melt, and I extracted a tiny drop of the liquid on it. By chance, I had trapped a rat yesterday in a small cage. I stuck the strip into the cage and the rat licked greedily at the liquid, only to explode seconds later. My eyes grew wide as I realized the same thing might happen to me if I weren't careful.

Extracting a larger drop of the liquid, I placed it in the center of a newly made gold bracelet. I willed for the liquid to bond with the metal, and it immediately fused with the gold and hardened into a jewel. This suggested the liquid would obey my commands.

After this extraordinary series of events, Giusto and I discussed the symbols on the artifact. Giusto believed some scholar in Rome might interpret them, as many studies of archaic writings had occurred since the days of Pietro. We decided he should go there and find out; he often sold his jewelry in Rome and knew his way around the city. The next day, Giusto copied the symbols onto a sheet of parchment and left. I stayed behind with the artifact.

Giusto was gone for thirty days. We had never been apart for such a time, and I cried when he returned. He laughed at my foolishness, yet I saw tears in his eyes as well. That evening, he told me about a professor at the Gregorian University who had translated the symbols; they were actually Egyptian hieroglyphics, which described a power that an ancient race had discovered inside a meteor. According to the translation, this power could command the forces of nature.

I knew at once that the amber liquid was the power described by the hieroglyphics. The thought made me recall the drop of liquid I had placed upon the bracelet. When I wore it, energy rushed through me. What if I wore many such pieces of jewelry? Would my spells be stronger than those cast while merely holding the artifact? Would they allow me to command the forces of nature? As it turned out, the answers were yes.

Over the next six months, I created fifteen pieces of jewelry bearing stones made from the liquid. As I created each piece, I cast magic spells onto the stones before the liquid hardened; they absorbed the spells and took direction from them. For example, in the jewel on my necklace, I infused a warning spell. This makes it vibrate whenever something important is about to happen.

Giusto was amazed at my power when I wore the jewelry, yet his awe was short lived. As we soon discovered, the professor in Rome had betrayed us. He had written to the Odisas, and they were on our trail. We learned of this by chance. A friend from a nearby village told us of armed men who were searching for Giusto. These men were camped outside his village and heading our way tomorrow.

Giusto and I were instantly alarmed; we had to flee. We spent the night gathering provisions and loaded our horses at dawn. Just as we saddled up, a dozen men came galloping towards us. Rifle shots rang out, and Giusto fell from his horse, mortally wounded.

When I saw blood soaking Giusto's shirt, a terrible rage came over me. The power in my jewelry magnified my rage and took control of my mind; all I could think about was revenge. I quickly made the earth liquify under the men's horses, and while they floundered in the muck, I brought down lightning and hailstones upon them. Neither man nor beast survived my punishing storm of magic. I let it continue for an hour; such was my fury.

Giusto died in my arms a short time later. I buried him behind our farmhouse, placed a cross upon his grave, and then turned my attention to the bodies of the men who had attacked us. One man had papers inside his tunic that identified him as Juan Odisa, the reigning head of the Odisa family. Using magic, I created a pit and let it swallow their corpses. They did not receive the sanctity of a marked grave.

At this point, let me interject a word of caution. Remorse over the men that I killed still haunts me. I had learned a terrible lesson. The power of the artifact magnifies emotions as well as magic skill, so heed my warning. Use it benevolently and you will remain pure of heart; use it in anger and evil will likely result.

I left the farm on the next day. For many months, I wandered across Europe, alone and without purpose. During this period, the image of a magnificent tree appeared in my dreams – a tree that was beckoning to me. A second version of the dream revealed a large city. The message seemed clear; I was supposed to go there. I didn't know where the city was, but in Paris, I found a library that had pictures of New York. These pictures matched with my dream, so I headed for New York.

While on my long journey, I supported myself by gambling. Perhaps the magic in my blood brought luck for I arrived in New York with trunks full of gold coins; I had become a wealthy man. I spoke little English, so I hired a tutor to instruct me. He fancied poetry and taught me the rigors of speaking in rhyme. It added mystery to my words, which I found pleasing.

Thereafter, the tree appeared in my dreams every night. This time, images of wagons were included. One of the wagons had *The Great Sabatini* painted upon its side. Then I met a man who was seeking acts for his traveling carnival. When I showed him an example of my magic, he begged me to join him. I couldn't say no; fate was guiding me, so I purchased a wagon and left with the carnival. A few weeks later, the images of a small town appeared in my dreams and I saw the name Great Oak, North Carolina, on a sign. I persuaded the owner of the carnival to make it one of our destinations.

As soon as we arrived in Great Oak, I recognized the tree. Not only was it a dominant landmark, but a benevolent aura surrounded it. My friends at the carnival could not see the aura, which reminded me of the story about Pietro and the caliph. Like the artifact, the tree was emitting a magical force that only I could detect.

During their many years of wandering, the Sabatinis had developed a strong belief in the spirits of nature. A few chapters in *Storia Di Incanto* describe their encounters with these mystical beings, and so, when I touched the tree, I sensed a spirit there. At first, I was delighted, but then I became troubled; the tree was dying.

Initially, I tried healing the tree by casting spells upon it. After two weeks of effort, I detected no improvement. Then an odd thought came to me. Perhaps the artifact could heal the tree. While this hadn't worked on animals, the tree was different; its nature was mystical. That very night, I buried the artifact near the tree's roots, intending to recover it later. Thereafter, the tree's health improved steadily.

While the tree flourished, other things did not go well in Great Oak. A malicious family, the Housemans, ruled the town with an iron fist. They reminded me of the Odisas, and I took pleasure in thwarting their evil plans. Then thieves broke into my wagon and took my most magical item – a dragon-headed cane filled with the artifact's liquid. Thereafter, I sealed the wagon so that only magic would open it.

Let me briefly digress and tell you about the cane. I cast many spells on the liquid in its head, which give it tremendous power. It seems an inert object, but comes alive when it feels the presence of our inherited skill. As a light draws the moth, it will find you. Then it will acknowledge you as its master and obey your commands. Let me also mention my friends, the Cherokee. They live in the mountains and revere nature as I do. Find Yona, who became the brother I never had. He awaits your coming.

When my cane disappeared, I immediately knew who had taken it. The thief was Claude Houseman, the Mayor of Great Oak. I could see and hear through the dragon's head while it was away from me, so I let him keep it. By spying on him in this way, I learned of another spirit in a nearby cave.

This second spirit was thoroughly evil. It had taken control of the Housemans and was influencing them to kill the tree. This puzzled me greatly. It seemed strange that two spirits, each opposite in nature, would be in this place. It was a classic struggle between good and evil, and evil was winning. Had fate brought me here for this reason? Was I entering the battle? It seemed like the answer was yes.

The snows came early that year, forcing the carnival to winter in Great Oak. I was not sure I would ever leave; the tree had enthralled me, and I had met Alicia, who soon became my wife. Therefore, I had many reasons to stay.

One night, the aura of the ancient oak shown so brilliantly, I knew the artifact had healed it. I also sensed that something extraordinary had happened. After searching under the tree, I found the artifact surrounded by the tree's thick roots. Moreover, the sphere was open; the roots had completely absorbed the amber liquid! As I pondered this, I began to laugh. A benevolent spirit now possessed the power of the artifact; it was finally safe from the Odisas. I focused my mind and looked up at the tree. The power flowing through its sap allowed me a rare insight. I would become the tree's protector.

Over the next seven years, I communicated with the spirit in the tree through a form of mental telepathy. I found it to be childlike in its innocence; it could not comprehend evil and only wanted to help others. As I came to know the spirit, the mission of the Sabatinis became clear. Benevolence is a force, which we are destined to protect. In contrast, we must seek out and destroy evil. The power in my magic items is for this purpose – use it accordingly.

As I write this, the evil spirit grows bolder. I cannot destroy it, as my past leaves me vulnerable to its influence. You must accept this challenge for you are pure of heart. The stars have revealed a more appropriate role for me; I will join the spirit in the tree and protect it throughout time. This will happen during a terrible battle with the Housemans. I wish it were not so, but fate has spoken.

As for you, my heir, much lies ahead. You are the twenty-fifth Sabatini magician. Take pride in this fact for fate has honored you. Your burdens will seem heavy, but others will stand with you in your fight against evil. Ask the tree for help when you are in need and it will respond. I will be there as well to heed your call.

ΩΣΣΩΣΩ

Davey closed the journal with a satisfied smile. At last, he understood everything, incredible as the story was. The power was not something to fear if used for worthy purposes, much to his relief.

He wondered if his great grandfather had actually joined the spirit in the tree and decided the truth would eventually become clear. His immediate task was more daunting. He had to find a way to destroy the evil spirit.

☙ Chapter 33 ❧

Lo, thou shall not cast away thy dreams lest their meanings be lost. Seek ye the messages hidden therein, as magick speaketh oft to the subconscious mind.

— Translated from Storia Di Incanto; circa 1874

Battle Plans

THE THREE OF WE returned to the Cherokee village on the next day. Davey wanted to tell Yona about the recent happenings and seek his advice. He also wanted to try flying the wagon while wearing his newly acquired pieces of jewelry. Sequoyah had matters to discuss with Yona regarding his position on the Council of Elders, so he was glad to take them there.

Bright sunlight filled the sky, yet an autumn chill was in the air. Before long, winter winds would come streaming across the Blue Ridge Mountains, bringing snow and ice. Davey felt a vague sense of urgency; he wanted to complete his quest before the weather became an obstacle.

The Three of We chatted quietly among themselves as Sequoyah's pickup made its way towards the village. Sequoyah concentrated on easing the truck through the ruts in the road, which had become bigger since last week's fierce storm. He grumbled in disgust, his comments more animated than those of their last trip.

Amy seemed to have put the matter of her ruined Halloween

costume from her mind, which pleased Davey and Jimmy. Yesterday, Sequoyah had helped her pick out the bike that she had won, cheering her up considerably. Still, Davey didn't mention the confrontation with Spike and his gang, not wanting to upset her again.

Sensing his reluctance, Amy brought the subject up herself. "I'm a little confused about what happened when you went to get my hat."

Amy's remark gave Jimmy a chance to express his own curiosity. "What *did* happen, mate? You disappeared into the smoke, and then I heard Monkey, Torpedo, and Spike screaming. A few minutes later, you returned with the hat, but wouldn't say how you got it."

"Let's talk about it after we reach the village," Davey said. "Yona will want to know, and there's a lot of other things to discuss as well."

Amy smiled and squeezed his hand. "I noticed you brought your backpack."

"I have some new magic items to show everyone."

"Bloody heck, let's see them now," Jimmy replied impatiently.

At that moment, Sequoyah slammed on the brakes and the pickup skidded to a halt in front of a huge, water-filled hole stretching across the road. Outcroppings of large boulders rose along both sides of the road, so there was no way around it.

Sequoyah climbed out of the pickup, found a long branch, and circled the hole, testing its depth with the branch. Davey watched briefly and then also stepped out. "Can we get through?" he asked.

Sequoyah shook his head. "I'm not sure. It'll take hours to get the truck out if we get stuck in the mud under there."

Davey recalled how Antonio had opened a pit beneath the men who shot Giusto and wondered if he could reverse the process. "Would you mind if I tried something?" he asked, opening his backpack and putting on his magic jewelry.

Sequoyah looked at him with surprise, but shrugged and backed away from the hole. Then Davey focused his mind, pictured the road flat and smooth, and felt the power surge through him. Soon, clouds of steam filled the air along with a sloshing sound as the mud churned around until it hardened. The entire process took about five minutes.

A wide grin spread across Sequoyah's face after the hole had repaired itself. He walked towards the center of the hole, stomping on the ground as he went. "You're mighty handy," he said, looking at Davey in amazement.

"Wow," Jimmy yelled from the truck, wide-eyed.

Amy gave Davey an admiring glance when he climbed back inside. "I guess we *do* have a lot to discuss," she said, taking his hand again.

Upon their arrival at the village, Yona convened an impromptu war council. Elogi Ugithisa, the leader of the Ani-Wodi Clan, joined their little group because of her spiritual insights and traditional role in preparing braves for battle.

When everyone had assembled in the Council House, Davey summarized the events of the week. He told them about receiving the rings through the opening in the cape, using the magic hat to hear the thoughts of the squirrel and ravens, and losing his temper and almost severely injuring Spike. He concluded by reading Antonio's journal aloud. After he finished, the room grew quiet.

Yona glanced at Elogi Ugithisa, and she began a low chant to invoke the wisdom of the spirits. As her chanting broke the silence, Yona rose from his chair and began shuffling around the ceremonial fire in rhythm to her cadence. When she finished, Yona spoke. "Let us discuss what we have learned."

Sequoyah responded first. "There was no mention of the cape or hat in the journal. Grandfather, did you ever see Tsusga Gineli use these items?"

Yona smiled, recalling an old memory. "When he was living in the village, I went to his lodge one day and found his cape spread across the floor. His voice called to me from the cape, yet he wasn't there. A short time later, he stepped out of the cape as if climbing a staircase. When I asked him where he had been, he said his magic allowed him to access many places outside the realm of reality; he added that finding his way back was sometimes a challenge."

"So this is not something for Davey to try," Amy said, giving

Davey a stern look.

"Not until he becomes much more skilled."

"What about the hat?" Sequoyah asked.

Yona reflected briefly and then spoke. "Tsusga Gineli did not wear his hat often, but he always wore it when he visited the tree."

Amy suddenly became excited. "Maybe that's how he talked with the spirit in the tree. Perhaps Davey can do the same, or even speak with Tsusga Gineli himself, if he has joined the spirit like he wrote in his journal."

Davey replied haltingly as thoughts flooded his mind. "Initially, I thought the squirrel acted for the spirit in the tree…it opened the gate and showed me how to climb up…but it also gave me my great grandfather's necklace and rings…then it said the Great Sabatini was proud of me."

Yona listened while Davey puzzled it out. "What does this tell you, Ustiwaya," he prodded, using Davey's Cherokee name.

"Of course…that's it…the squirrel acts for the spirit *and* my great grandfather…he *must* have joined the spirit."

Yona smiled at the thought. "Amy's suggestion is a good one. Perhaps you can confirm it by using the hat."

"There's only one problem. I forgot the hat after my fight with Spike, and someone took it."

Yona's smile faded. "This is a setback. Who could have taken it?"

"I don't think it was Spike or his goons; they're probably afraid to touch anything of mine now. Joe Harrison looked through the park and didn't find it, but I had the feeling it was somewhere nearby this morning."

Yona frowned, worry showing in his eyes. "Be on your guard. The spirit in the cave has probably felt your presence; it may even be why Spike attacked you. Perhaps the evil spirit is influencing other *unknown* enemies. We must find out who has it."

"I learn many things from my dreams," Elogi Ugithisa said. "Since Tsusga Gineli had this ability, Ustiwaya may have it as well. Have your dreams revealed anything?"

Davey shook his head. "Not that I can recall."

"It's worth trying," Yona added. "Wear your magic jewelry when you sleep tonight and ask the tree to send you a dream message. But you must write down your dream as soon as you wake. Otherwise, the message may be lost."

"What about the cane, which Tsusga Gineli described? I have seen Wally Houseman carrying a similar cane," Sequoyah said.

"You make an excellent point. Since Claude Houseman stole it, Wally surely has it now. If Ustiwaya can get near the cane, it should acknowledge him as its master," Yona replied.

"Then I can spy on Wally with it!" Davey exclaimed.

Yona nodded his agreement. "A good strategy."

Amy offered a new idea. "Since the tree absorbed the liquid from the artifact, its power must now flow in the tree's sap. That's why the bark of the tree glows when Davey touches it and its branches help the wagon fly."

"Right," Davey interjected, continuing the thought. "That's also why Antonio made the letters over his fireplace from the wood of the tree. The words invoke the power, so the tree's wood *must* contain it."

Jimmy added his own thoughts. "He also painted his wagon with a varnish made from the sap of the tree and put shields on it woven from the tree's branches. As a result, the wagon's aura protects those living on Greyhead Mountain from the spirit in the cave."

"And what does this tell us?" Yona asked.

The Three of We simultaneously reached the same conclusion. "The sap of the tree repels the influence of the evil spirit," they exclaimed in unison.

A smile spread across Yona's face. "Yes…it tells us how to fight the spirit."

"Tsusga Gineli's bow and arrows were made from the wood of the tree," Sequoyah remarked.

"Blimey Dad, I have an idea. If we can get more branches from the tree, you and I can make additional weapons. You know, stuff like spears and shields."

"If you collect long, slender branches, the Ani-Wodi will weave them into armor and cast blessings upon them," Elogi Ugithisa offered.

"Davey is the one who will have to get them. Only he can climb the tree," Sequoyah remarked.

"Okay, I can do that. The two books, which I found in the trunk, have magic spells in them. If I can translate them, perhaps I can place spells on the armor too," Davey said.

Amy shook her head. "Your time should be spent on practicing your magic. Give me the books and I will do the translating."

Yona's smile showed his approval. "Good! Our battle preparations are underway. Now, let us speak of when you will confront the spirit in the cave. How soon can we be ready?"

Sequoyah related the brief story of how Davey had repaired the hole in the road. "His magic skill is increasing. We can have our other preparations complete within a few weeks. Then we can go forward."

Yona smiled at Davey. "So…are you ready to fly the wagon?"

"I'm ready to try," Davey replied.

The Three of We spent the rest of the day at the Cherokee village. After several attempts, Davey made the wagon leap into the air and was able to steer it with his mind. Then Jimmy and Amy climbed aboard and they felt the exhilaration of floating in it over the village. Davey kept the wagon near the ground, just in case he lost control. From below, the villagers greeted them with astonished cries as they soared above their heads.

Yona and Sequoyah watched the flying wagon with wonder. "Unbelievable that a young boy can do such things," Sequoyah said.

Yona nodded solemnly. "Future legends will speak of it."

Later, while Jimmy and Davey practiced with the bow and arrows, Amy rode the horses. To her, the thrill was almost as great as that of flying in the wagon.

እ)ርጌእ)ርጌእ)ርጌ

እ) 352 ርጌ

Meanwhile, a radically changing Sineous Crop stalked into Wally Houseman's study. The shards of black stone, which had entered his body when he fell into the ravine, were causing a bizarre transformation. His eyes seemed haunted, and hairy spikes sprouted randomly from his previously bald head. Moreover, his teeth were slowly becoming fangs, and his broken arm had healed in three days.

Other changes were also occurring throughout his body. Sinews of muscle had formed in places were muscle didn't ordinarily exist. They were not the muscles of a normal person, but rather those of some weird creature. And his finger and toenails grew so rapidly, he had to cut them daily. They had the texture of steel; only metal-cutting shears would work.

Sineous hid these changes by shaving his head twice a day, wearing loose-fitting shirts, and keeping the plaster cast on his arm. His desire to hide them from Wally was the most startling change in him; he was now serving a different master.

Wally greeted him with a slam of his cane. "I have been waiting!"

"What's on your mind, great one?"

Wally glared at Sineous, briefly wondering why he was acting so oddly. "Spike has been in a fight with Davey Boehm. It gives me a reason to have the Sabatini boy expelled from school. Then he'll return to New York and we'll be done with him."

Sineous snorted derisively. "We won't get rid of him that easily."

"And why not?"

"Magic protects him. It will keep them from doing anything."

"Don't forget that I'm on the School Board. Eunice Bluestone will do exactly as I wish!" Wally shouted.

Sineous leaned across the desk and glared at him. "Something more devious is required – something brutal. I have a plan, which will rid us of the Sabatinis permanently. After it's done, you and I are going to be partners."

Wally had been telling lies for so long, his response came without a moment's hesitation. "Haven't I always treated you like a partner?"

Sineous stood up and headed for the stairs. "Go ahead and try your foolish scheme, but we will start doing things my way when it doesn't work." As he left the study, Wally noticed his slithering gait for the first time.

ಬಂಬಂಬಂ

That night, Davey followed Yona's suggestion and wore his jewelry while he slept. Before closing his eyes, he asked the tree to send him a message. The resulting dream was so frightening; he woke up before it was over.

In it, he was high in the sky, flying the magic wagon; he could feel the air blowing his hair and see the earth below. Then a dark cloud appeared in the distance. As the cloud came closer, he realized it wasn't a normal cloud, but rather a strange collection of black spots. Soon, it swarmed around him like a mass of angry bees.

The wagon began to fall, yet he was powerless to stop its descent. Just as he was about to hit the ground, a flock of ravens came streaking through the cloud. Two of the ravens landed on his shoulders and spoke to him. *You are the one...*the first bird said...*whom we protect,* the second added.

Suddenly, his eyes opened and the dream was gone. He staggered to his desk, jotted down a few notes, and then returned to his bed. *How very odd,* he thought and went back to sleep.

ಬಂಬಂಬಂ

Spike, Monkey, and Torpedo were absent from homeroom class on Monday. When they didn't show up by second period, rumors began spreading about Davey's fight with them in the park. His classmates asked him about it all morning long, but Davey just shrugged and said nothing. Naturally, his silence made everyone believe the rumors.

By lunchtime, ridiculous stories were circulating; Spike was in the hospital; Monkey had disappeared; Torpedo's legs were broken. The stories had become more far-fetched as time went on. Then Linda

Peabody approached Davey while he was eating lunch with Amy.

"Eunice Bluestone wants to see you," Linda said quietly.

"What's going on?" Amy asked.

"All I know is that it concerns Spike."

"I was involved, so I'm going too," Amy said firmly.

Linda shook her head. "No, she just wants Davey. You'll have an opportunity to tell what you know if anything comes of this."

Davey rose from the table and glumly followed Linda. The cafeteria grew silent when they marched through the room. He could feel everyone's eyes on his back and wondered what they were thinking.

Eunice Bluestone sat behind her desk, waiting for them. A few minutes later, Aunt Sally arrived, her face troubled. After that, Spike and Wally entered the room. Wally gave Davey an angry look, but Spike kept his eyes downcast.

Eunice signaled her readiness to begin. "Please sit down. I've asked you here because of a complaint made by Spike's father. Linda has joined us since she's the homeroom teacher of these boys."

They sat in chairs strategically placed around the room. Wally and Spike were on one side; Aunt Sally and Davey were on the other. Linda sat in the middle of the room – a peacekeeper of sorts.

"All right Wally, you have the floor," Eunice said.

Wally stood up and pointed his cane at Davey. "I want this boy expelled!"

The appearance of the cane immediately distracted Davey. The eyes in its dragon-shaped head became a bright amber, and a silent message appeared in Davey's mind. *Command me master!*

Davey focused his mind and sent the cane a mental response. *I will send for you later. Until then, be my eyes and ears.* The cane reacted by letting its eyes become blank, and Davey quickly turned his attention to what Eunice was saying.

"Wally, as a School Board member, you know that only the Disciplinary Committee can expel a student. We're here to learn the facts. I'll decide if there's sufficient cause for the committee's involvement."

Wally glared at her. "The boy attacked Spike at the Halloween party for no reason. Spike was so upset we had to take him to a doctor. Look at him – he's still not himself."

As Wally spoke, Davey glanced over at Spike. *He doesn't seem like his usually mean self,* he thought.

"Dad…it wasn't…like that," Spike stammered.

Wally cut him off with a wave of his hand. "Shut up Spike; I'll handle this."

"Wally, there's no need to interrupt anyone. Now, please sit down and let me ask a few questions," Eunice said calmly.

Linda raised her eyebrows in surprise. She had never seen Eunice handle herself in such a polite and diplomatic way. Usually, she just ordered everyone around.

Eunice looked at Davey. "What about this? Did you attack Spike for no reason?"

Davey felt his face turning red. "No…Spike has been bullying me ever since I arrived in Great Oak. He threw my schoolbooks in an anthill and ruined my jacket. Then he hit me in the head with a baseball. Last week, he put a poisonous snake in my locker."

Eunice frowned. "Why haven't I heard about these things?"

Once Davey got started, he didn't stop. "That's not all. He rolled marbles under Miss Peabody's feet, made her fall during class, and put rats in the drawer of her desk. He's also the one who threw rotten eggs at Mr. McDonnell and his car."

"Oh?" Eunice asked, her frown deepening.

Davey continued without responding. "As for what happened at the Halloween party, Spike was the one who attacked me. He and his little gang threw balloons filled with rotten eggs at Amy Pigeon, ruining her costume and making her sick. Then he tried to dump his rotten egg mix on me. I was just defending myself, that's all."

Eunice looked over at Spike. "Is Davey telling the truth?"

Wally jumped up. "I told you what happened. The boy is lying!"

Aunt Sally couldn't keep quiet any longer. "Don't call my nephew a liar!"

Eunice rolled her eyes in exasperation. "I want to hear from Spike."

Suddenly, tears started to run down Spike's cheeks. Then he began to speak, and his voice rose to a crescendo as he did. "Yes, I did all of those things, but I will not hurt his friends again or continue my evil ways. Do you hear me? There will be no more of this. NO MORE!"

Davey stared at him in astonishment. *Spike is telling the truth and repeating exactly what I told him in the park,* he thought.

Wally Houseman slapped Spike on the head several times. "I told you to shut up and let me handle this," he growled, his teeth clenched.

Aunt Sally started to rise. "Stop hitting that boy," she shouted.

Linda stepped between them. She had just gained an insight as to why Spike was always causing so much trouble in class. "Please, let's all calm down," she said.

Wally drew back his cane, as if intending to strike Linda and Aunt Sally. However, Davey quickly sent the cane a silent command, and it froze in mid-air. A comical scene ensued as Wally struggled with the cane in front of everyone. When Davey finally released it, Wally fell back into his chair, breathing hard. Davey hid the grin forming on his face while everyone else stared at Wally, completely bewildered.

"Are you going to expel this boy or not?" Wally finally shouted.

Aunt Sally stared angrily at Wally. "Can't you hear? Spike is the one who should be expelled. He's admitted what he did."

Eunice pounded on her desk with a beefy hand. "For Pete's sake, everyone shut up! You adults are worse than the kids in this school."

Her commanding voice had the desired affect. After a few seconds, the room had grown quiet again. She glanced around, daring anyone to say another word while she thought about how to deal with Wally. Finally, she spoke, her voice soothing. "Wally, we've been friends for a long time; let me offer you some advice. If the Discipline Committee takes up this matter, they *will* expel Spike. He has promised to behave from now on, so I suggest we just forget about what happened."

Wally's face instantly turned ugly. His eyes narrowed into tiny slits, focusing on Aunt Sally. "You nasty witch! You put a spell on Spike, didn't you? The Housemans ran the Sabatinis out of this town once before, and we'll do it again, mark my words."

Eunice stood up. "That's crazy talk, Wally. This meeting is over."

Wally turned towards her, his eyes blazing. "This meeting may be over, but I'm not done with you – you're fired!"

"You can't fire me; only the School Board can do that."

Wally grabbed Spike by the collar and propelled him towards the door. Before he stomped out of the room, he pointed at Eunice. "Remember this moment. I'll be president of the School Board next year – probably be mayor too; then you'll be history."

Everyone exchanged embarrassed glances after Wally left. Davey sat quietly in his chair, feeling sorry for Spike. He also felt like giving Aunt Sally a hug, but he didn't think it was the time or place for such a display of affection.

At last, Linda broke the silence. "He's not very nice."

"I'm so sorry; I shouldn't have lost my temper," Aunt Sally said, rising to leave.

Eunice offered a wry smile. "No need to apologize. A fool like Wally can make anyone angry."

❧ Chapter 34 ☙

Hearken thou magician; consider the prickly pear that hides its fruit with thorns. Peel away the layers and a treasure lies within.

— Translated from Storia Di Incanto; circa 1877

The Boy Who Changed

SPIKE, MONKEY, AND TORPEDO were back at school the next day. Spike sat in the front row, paid attention, and remained quiet unless a teacher called upon him. In fact, he acted like a model student. Outside of the classroom, he kept to himself. If Monkey or Torpedo approached him, he turned his back and walked away. Everyone wondered about the change in Spike, but nobody complained about it – nobody except his former gang members, who were totally confused by his change of attitude. As a result, they didn't cause any trouble; they were lost without their leader.

"What's up with Spike?" Amy wondered aloud as she and Davey left English class. "He was actually nice to Miss Peabody today."

Davey had already told Amy about his bizarre meeting in the principal's office. "Maybe Spike meant what he said. Maybe he's changed."

Amy didn't believe Spike had changed without a reason. "He's acting so different. Maybe what you told him in the park is influencing him in some way."

Davey had wondered the same thing. "It did seem stuck in his head."

"You mean…like some kind of a mental command?"

Davey shrugged. "I guess – something like that anyway."

"It's scary to think you can change people by what you say."

"Yeah, especially when I'm not consciously doing it."

"Well, I should be finished with the translation of the Sabatini magic books soon. Maybe they will tell us if you inadvertently put a spell on him. In the meantime, don't issue any commands to anyone."

"Aye, aye sir," Davey said, saluting smartly.

For the rest of the week, Davey and Amy tutored Jimmy in math. The Scholar's Team tryouts were on Friday, and they desperately wanted him to make the team. But on Thursday, Jimmy tried to skip their last session. "Leave me be, mates. My blooming head is so crammed full of numbers, I can't think straight," he complained.

"Not until we go over the algebra problems you missed yesterday," Amy said firmly.

Jimmy looked mournfully at Davey. "Bloody heck, if she ain't a bossy one!"

Davey laughed. "Come on, be a sport. This is your last day of torture."

On Friday afternoon, The Three of We met outside the room where Linda Peabody was conducting the tryouts. When they arrived, Davey saw Spike pacing the hallway, an anxious look on his face. This gave Davey a sudden inspiration and he turned towards Amy. "Do you have the wisdom scarf in your backpack?"

"As a matter of fact, I do."

"Good, put it on and let's go talk with Spike. Maybe we'll learn something."

Jimmy's face clouded. "Do it without me; I might bash him."

Spike saw Davey and Amy coming, and he began edging along the hall in the opposite direction, his eyes downcast.

"Hey, wait up," Davey said, hurrying towards him. "Are you

trying out for the Scholar's Team?"

Spike nodded without looking up. "I know you guys don't want me, but I'd like to be on the team. Probably won't make it anyway."

Amy watched Spike intently, yet said nothing.

"Go for it. You're smart enough," Davey said.

Spike glanced at Davey; his face showed no sign of hostility. "Thanks, I guess it won't hurt to try."

"Good luck then," Davey replied, and turned away.

Spike grabbed Davey's arm, restraining him for a moment. "Listen Davey, I'm sorry for what I did to you and Amy. It wasn't my idea to have you expelled either. I'd actually like to be friends."

Davey gave him a brief smile. "Come on, let's go inside."

They walked into the room together. Spike took a seat in the front row, and Davey and Amy plopped down beside Jimmy several rows away. "Well, what do you think?" Davey finally whispered.

"According to the scarf, he's telling the truth."

"Even the part about being friends?"

Amy nodded solemnly. "Even that."

Davey thought it over as Linda handed out the aptitude tests. Finally, he reached a decision. With a smile, he pictured the Great Oak in his head. Then he made a silent wish.

ဆာ၄ဆာ၄ဆာ၄

Androf Protsky saw Alice Silversmith waving at him when he pulled his van into the driveway. "I wonder what the old biddy wants," he muttered.

Act nice, Ubeck ordered from inside Androf's head.

Alice tottered over towards the van, smiling broadly. "The mailman delivered a package for you, Andy. Will you come in and have a cup of coffee while I get it?"

"Sure enough," Androf replied, slipping into his friendly, country boy routine. He followed her into the house and sat down in the kitchen. Alice walked into another room and returned after a few seconds with the package. "I hope its something good. I love getting surprises in the mail. It makes me think of Christmas."

Androf looked at the package and grinned; it was from Vertex Automobile Supplies. He knew at once that it contained the money from Yong Chow Lee. Alice watched him eagerly, hoping he would open it.

"Ain't nuttin much, just some reports from my boss," he said.

Disappointment registered on her face. "Oh, how's the job going?"

Androf managed a friendly smile. "Mighty fine, got me lots of customers and all – should be making some good money soon."

"I'm so glad. I hope you like living here, Andy. Having a nice man like you around makes me feel secure. Made any friends yet?"

Androf did his best to seem timid. "Shucks, I'm the shy type."

"Why don't you get involved in the community? There's a big political fight going on right now, and everyone is choosing sides. It's a good time for newcomers to meet people."

Androf's ears perked up. "A big fight?"

"Oh yes! See, there are those who support Wally Houseman and those who don't. He wants to build condominiums and hotels in the park, but a lot of us old timers don't care for the idea. Maybe it's because we don't like the Housemans very much. They've been running this town forever, and we're fed up with their shenanigans."

Androf nodded. "I done heard about it at the Halloween party."

"The City Council will vote on it next week. Why don't you attend the meeting? It will be exciting."

Androf grinned. "Why, I just might do that, Alice. I just might."

When Androf was back in his apartment, he opened the package and dumped the contents on his bed. Ten thousand dollars, wrapped in bundles of fifty-dollar bills, spilled out over the sheets.

"We've got the money, Ubeck. We can leave whenever you want," Androf said.

I'm thinking about what the old lady said. Maybe we'll stick around for a while. There's opportunity when trouble is brewing.

Linda Peabody was dressing for dinner when the telephone rang. Ed Nolen was on his way over, and she wasn't nearly ready. *I hope it's Ed and that he's running late,* she thought. Then she smiled, remembering that Aunt Gilda liked him. She could keep him busy with a story or two while he waited.

Aunt Gilda called upstairs to Linda. "It's for you, dear. It's a man, and it's not Ed," she said, giving her a disapproving look.

Puzzled, Linda picked up the phone.

"Linda, it's Michael," a voice immediately announced.

"Michael who?" Linda asked, even though she knew who it was.

"You know, your opera singing clown," Michael said, somewhat unsettled.

"Oh *that* Michael," Linda replied dryly.

So far, their conversation wasn't going like Michael had hoped. "Uh…Linda, I've been thinking…I'd like to see you," he stammered.

"Are you bringing your new girlfriend along?"

Her sarcasm shocked him. "Of course not – that's over now. I made a mistake, a terrible mistake. You were the one for me all along. I'd like to patch things up."

Linda grew quiet, savoring the moment.

Her silence made him even more anxious. "Linda, say something."

Over the last six months, Linda had often fantasized about this moment. That had been when she was laying awake at night, crying her eyes out. Now, Michael's phone call brought clarity to her feelings. She took a deep breath and began to explain. "I'm sorry Michael, but you're too late. I've met someone else, a wonderful man who makes me happy. I love him and he loves me." Linda felt almost giddy when she said the words.

"Is there anyway I can change your mind?" Michael asked sadly.

"No, but at least we can finally move on. Goodbye Michael; good luck with your life," Linda said, and then quickly hung up.

Aunt Gilda wasn't eavesdropping, but she realized Linda was

speaking with her former boyfriend and overheard her say a rather firm goodbye to him. She hoped Linda's life wasn't going to be in turmoil again. "Is everything okay, dear?" she asked timidly.

Linda's smile had never come easier. "Things are fine – no, that's not quite right. Things are wonderful," she replied.

⊱⊰⊱⊰⊱⊰⊱⊰

Sineous and Wally had all the details worked out. After Wally's disastrous meeting with Eunice, he had returned to Houseman's Castle in a terrible mood. Since Wally acted that way most of the time, the degree of his anger was hardly noticeable.

Sineous hadn't wasted any time gloating over Wally's failure. Instead, he quickly laid out his plan for getting Aunt Sally and Davey out of Great Oak. Despite his foul mood, Wally liked the idea. It was so fiendishly evil, so totally brutal, that he thought of little else for the rest of the week.

Of course, putting all the pieces together wasn't easy. However, Wally had connections with people who would do anything if he met their price. As far as Wally was concerned, eliminating the Sabatinis made it worth what they asked.

Sineous implemented the plan on Saturday afternoon by calling Aunt Sally's house. He used a telephone line that was impossible to trace, or so he believed. When Aunt Sally answered, he launched into his story. He put on an upper class accent, which sounded perfect. Of course, this had taken a lot of practice. Moreover, he had memorized the script that he and Wally had written.

Sineous's voice had just the right tone to be believable. "Mrs. Winston, this is Ronald Fairchild with the American Embassy in Shanghai," he began. "Sorry to be the bearer of bad tidings, but I have unfortunate news. You see, there's been an accident."

Aunt Sally's heart began to hammer. When she heard the word Shanghai, she knew something awful had happened. "Is it my sister? Oh please, say she's all right."

ജ 364 ⊶

"Actually, it's Mr. Boehm who is injured – some sort of industrial accident, I believe. I'm calling on *behalf* of your sister. She and her husband are flying back home as we speak. Their plane will arrive in Los Angeles this evening, and they will immediately proceed to Gilead Hospital where a team of doctors is waiting for them."

Aunt Sally was crying now. "How badly is he hurt?"

"Sorry, I don't know the details. I'm afraid it's rather serious though. It's the reason for my call, you see. Your sister would like you to bring her son to Los Angeles as soon as possible. I wouldn't tell the boy this, but it may be his last chance to see his father alive."

This remark really tore Aunt Sally up. She began to cry louder.

"I've already made all the arrangements," Sineous continued. "If I'm correct, Greensboro has the closest major airport to you."

This time, Aunt Sally mumbled a reply. "Yes, it's two hours away."

Sineous had timed his call so she wouldn't have a moment to think, let alone check on his story; all she could do was pack a few clothes and leave. "Good, I'll have tickets for you, your husband, and the boy waiting for you at the United Airlines counter. Just give them your names. The flight leaves at four o'clock, so you'll have to hurry. Can you make it?"

"Yes," she gasped, practically choking.

"A man from the State Department will meet your plane in Los Angeles. He'll have a sign with your name on it, and his car will take you straight to the hospital."

"I didn't realize the Government helped out like this."

"Oh yes, we take great measures to look after our citizens when they are abroad. When special circumstances like this arise, we step in and take charge. Hurry now, Mrs. Winston. You don't want to miss your flight."

"Yes…thank you."

After Sineous hung up, he grinned at Wally. "She bought it. Could you hear her? She was blubbering like a baby."

Wally's eyes gleamed. "The stupid witch – this will teach her."

Sineous hoped Wally had done his part. "Do the men meeting

their plane know what to do?"

"They're trained killers. The Sabatinis don't stand a chance."

Meanwhile, Aunt Sally was running around in a panic. It took ten minutes of searching the house to find Davey and Uncle Bill. As she looked, she grabbed up clean clothes and stuffed them haphazardly into a large overnight bag. Finally, she just collapsed on the floor and started sobbing, unable to continue.

Naturally, Uncle Bill and Davey were alarmed. They crowded around her, trying to figure out what was wrong. At first, Aunt Sally was crying so much, they couldn't make sense of her words. When they finally got the gist of her story, they were shocked.

"It's a lie," Davey blurted out, his necklace vibrating furiously. During the last week, he had called upon his great grandfather's cane several times. Each time, the cane responded by letting him see through its eyes and hear through its ears. The images were fuzzy and the sounds muffled, yet he had seen Wally and another man talking and heard the word *Shanghai* spoken twice. They were involved in this; he was sure of it. He also knew Aunt Sally and Uncle Bill would find his story unbelievable.

Davey closed his eyes and pictured the Great Oak in his mind. *I need your help,* he thought desperately. He concentrated with such intensity that his face turned red.

Uncle Bill watched Davey with concern. He thought the boy looked like he was about to come unglued and walked over and hugged him. "Pull yourself together, son. It may not be as bad as it sounds. We need to get ready and leave."

Davey hoped the tree had heard his urgent request. He had a strange feeling something awful was going to happen if they left Great Oak. "But Uncle Bill, it isn't true," he insisted.

At that moment, the telephone rang. Aunt Sally rushed towards the phone, thinking it was the man from the Embassy again. This time, she heard a different voice.

"Sally, it's your favorite sister," the voice said cheerfully.

"Oh Janie, thank goodness you called. How is Walter? We're all terribly upset here," Aunt Sally said, beginning to sob again.

"What do you mean? Walter is fine – we're both fine."

"But Janie, I thought he was injured. The man from the Embassy said—"

Janie interrupted immediately. "What man?"

"Ronald Fairchild, he's with the Embassy in Shanghai. He said Walter was hurt and you were flying to Los Angeles. We were supposed to meet you there."

"What nonsense…I've never spoken to him and Walter is standing right beside me. I called to tell you that we might be leaving China soon. I can't say more, but things aren't going very well here."

"Speak with your son for a minute," Aunt Sally said, handing the phone to Davey. Then she rushed into the kitchen, blew her nose, and tried to compose herself.

Davey talked for a while with both of his parents. After that, he returned the phone to Aunt Sally, who spoke with Janie for a very long time indeed. Eventually, even Uncle Bill managed a hello. Finally, after everyone had spoken with everyone else, the call ended. Aunt Sally seemed confounded by the series of events. "So…who was the man that called?" she asked shakily, still traumatized.

"Well, it obviously wasn't someone from the American Embassy," Uncle Bill replied.

"It was one of Wally's tricks," Davey said, his voice firm.

Aunt Sally's face darkened. "If that's true; he will soon regret it."

☙ Chapter 35 ❧

Let thine enemies believe magick be an illusion and nothing more. Thus, gain advantage with the art of surprise.

— Translated from Storia Di Incanto; circa 1884

Wally's Big Surprise

AUNT SALLY spent the next day investigating the mysterious telephone call from the American Embassy. She began with the State Department in Washington, D.C. After a seemingly endless wait, she learned what she had already suspected; Ronald Fairchild was not an employee of any American Embassy, let alone the one in Shanghai.

Next, she contacted United Airlines and checked on the flight, which he had told her to take. Indeed, there was such a flight from Greensboro to Los Angeles, and three pre-paid tickets had been waiting for them at the airport. Despite this, no one could tell her who had purchased the tickets.

Aunt Sally was becoming increasingly irritated. Someone had put a lot of effort into their mean trick, but who was the culprit? Finally, she spoke with Miriam Ward at the telephone company – a friend from the *Save the Trees Committee*. Aunt Sally asked Miriam if she could find out who had called her house yesterday. Unfortunately, Miriam said a court order was required before the company could disclose the names.

Then Aunt Sally told Miriam the entire story, including her

suspicion that Wally was trying to get her out of Great Oak before the City Council meeting. Miriam was aghast when she heard the details; she already disliked Wally because he had fired her husband at the furniture factory last summer. She agreed to look into the matter – off the record, of course.

Miriam called Aunt Sally back several hours later, whispering as if she was involved in an illegal conspiracy. "I know where your phone call came from, but promise me you won't say anything. I'll get fired if they find out I told."

"I promise, Miriam. I just need to know who did it."

"You were right! Mind you, I don't know who actually made the call, but it came from an unlisted and very private number at Houseman's Castle. These private numbers are kept in confidential records, but I managed to access them."

"You're a genius, Miriam."

Miriam giggled at the thought. "Well, I've worked here for twenty years. I should know a thing or two by now." Then Miriam asked a very logical question. "Why would Wally trick you into going to Los Angeles when you could just turn around and come back? You'd be here in plenty of time for the meeting; it's three days away."

When Aunt Sally thought about it, she reached a scary conclusion. Something was supposed to happen in Los Angeles, which would prevent her from coming back. And it was going to happen to Davey and Uncle Bill as well. She was seething by the time she hung up with Miriam. For the rest of the day, she walked around the house imagining all sorts of bad things – things that sent chills down her spine. In fact, she hadn't been so terribly frightened in her entire life.

Somehow, Aunt Sally's fear triggered a dormant trait within her body. After all, she was Alicia Sabatini's granddaughter, and Alicia had inherited some very unusual abilities from her Cherokee father. Although Aunt Sally wasn't thinking specifics, she desperately wanted to punish Wally for what he had tried to do. Her desire was so incredibly strong that the animals in the forests around Great Oak felt it. Unbeknownst to Aunt Sally, they responded to her need.

A few students stood around the bulletin board at Great Oak Middle School, talking in hushed tones. The bulletin board was where items of interest typically appeared. Linda Peabody had posted the list of Scholar's Team qualifiers, and there were a few surprises on it.

The students had expected both Davey and Amy to be on the list, so no mystery there. Jimmy had also qualified, which was a bit curious. While everyone liked Jimmy, he wasn't a particularly good student. However, Spike's name was the one that floored them; they all wondered how he made the team.

Amy asked Davey the same question as soon as she saw him. She was wearing the wisdom scarf, so he didn't stretch the truth. "Spike has changed. I just gave him a little reward."

Amy sighed with exasperation. "You made a wish, didn't you?"

Davey tried to look innocent. "I didn't wish for him to make the team. I just wished for him to do his best."

Amy glared at him. "Jimmy won't like it. You're too nice for your own good."

"If it doesn't work out, I'll fix it somehow," Davey replied, hoping he wouldn't have to keep his promise.

❧❦❧❦❧❦❧

That night, something truly incredible happened. Under the ghostly light of a quarter-moon, wolves gathered outside of Houseman's Castle. They came in packs of three or more – over one hundred surrounded the castle by midnight. If Yona had witnessed the event, a legend would have started right then and there. Wolves were territorial animals and never congregated in this manner.

The wolves stood under the nearby trees and began to howl. At first, only a few raised their voices to the sky. Then they all joined in, shattering the calm of the night with an ear-splitting chorus of howls.

Wally, Sineous, Spike, and Wally's wife, Nell, who stayed shut up in the castle most of the time, jumped out of bed and ran to the windows.

"Get out of here!" Wally screamed from his open window. A furious round of howls answered his yell. Wally hurried down to the first floor where he kept two fierce pit bulls, Jaws and Snapper, penned up on a porch. "Go out there and run those wolves off," he ordered, shoving the dogs out the rear door.

Jaws and Snapper ran around to the front of the castle, growling and snarling with fury. Even so, when they saw the huge gathering of wolves under the trees, the dogs took off in the opposite direction. They didn't stop running until they were miles away and didn't return home for a week.

For the rest of the night, Wally and Sineous stood at the windows of his study, firing shotguns at the howling wolves. They cursed, yelled, and shook their fists, yet the determined wolves continued their howling. The shotgun blasts had no effect, apparently missing their targets in the darkness of the night.

When the morning sun finally crept over the horizon, Wally and Sineous were exhausted. The wolves, having voiced their opinion of them all night long, faded back into the forests. Much to Wally's dismay, the wolves returned and repeated their performance on the next night. Wally and Sineous felt like walking zombies when Wednesday finally arrived. Their minds were in a sleep-deprived haze, and the town meeting was that evening.

§ଔ§ଔ§ଔ

On Tuesday, Amy approached Davey with a big frown on her face. "Well, it finally happened. My dad got into an argument with Wally and quit his job."

Davey was shocked. "I didn't know your dad worked for him."

Amy nodded sadly. "Dad hates him, so I never mention it. He was one of the managers at the furniture factory. We've lived in Great

§ 371 ଔ

Oak forever and now we'll probably have to move."

"Why did he quit?"

"Wally made some snide remarks about my Halloween costume and you and I being friends. Dad blew his top and told Wally off."

"Maybe Spike can do something. What if he told his father that he really likes you and is worried about you leaving Great Oak?"

Amy looked as if Davey had lost his mind. "Ha, ha, very funny."

"What harm can it do?"

"None, I guess. A lot of people at the factory depend on my dad. Without him, they'll be lost."

"Don't worry, something will work out. I'll make a wish if necessary."

Amy shook her head. "We can't run to the tree every time there's a problem. That's not the way life should be."

Davey nodded as though agreeing with her. Still, he was going to ask the tree for help whether she liked it or not. The thought of not seeing Amy again was too disturbing.

After school, the Scholar's Team gathered in an empty classroom for their first meeting. The windows of the room overlooked the rack where Amy had parked her new bike, and she was frowning about something when Davey arrived.

Naturally, Davey was curious. "Hey, what's with the frown?"

"Torpedo and Monkey are standing near my bike."

Davey grinned. "They're just guarding it."

"Why would they do that?"

"Spike told them to. He said if anything happens to your bike, he'd rip their heads off. It's his way of making up to you. By the way, I talked to him about your dad."

"What did he say?"

Davey shrugged. "He'll tell his dad about what good friends you've become since being on the Scholar's Team. Maybe it will make a difference."

"Dad won't work for Wally again unless he agrees to make some changes. That probably won't happen, but it's nice of Spike anyway.

Should I thank him?"

Davey shook his head. "Just act friendly; it's all the thanks he needs."

At that moment, Jimmy walked into the room. "G'day mates," he said cheerfully.

Davey waved him over. "Spike told me something interesting today. Apparently, hundreds of wolves stood around his house last night and howled until dawn. He said it was the weirdest thing he's ever seen."

Jimmy was instantly intrigued. "Blimey, it must mean something. I'll tell my dad about it. Maybe he should ask Yona."

"Yeah, I was thinking the same thing," Davey replied.

𝕤𝕺ℭ𝕽𝕤𝕺ℭ𝕽𝕤𝕺ℭ𝕽

On Wednesday evening, a large crowd gathered outside City Hall. Like most buildings in Great Oak, it was almost a hundred years old. Of course, the town was a more prosperous and bustling community when it was built.

City Hall was a classic parthenon-style structure made of limestone. The six Doric columns along the entrance created an impression of grandeur, despite their worn surfaces. At the back of the building, a small auditorium served as the municipal courtroom. It was also where City Council meetings and other public functions occurred. Tonight, the six council members sat behind a long table on an elevated platform, waiting for the doors to open.

City employees had removed the courtroom tables in front of the platform, which left a large open area containing a speaker's podium. A wooden railing separated this area from where the spectators sat. Ten rows of wooden benches provided seating for one hundred people behind the railing. Another twenty could stand in a narrow space behind the benches if they crammed together. Everyone knew the room would be packed for this session, so they were anxious to get inside and find a seat.

𝕤𝕺 373 ℭ𝕽

The meetings normally began at eight o'clock in the evening. At least, that's what the public notices said. Regardless, the meetings rarely started on time because one or more council members were often late. This particular meeting was an exception. It was too important, the risk too great, for any politician to be tardy.

When the front doors opened, the council members sat up and appeared alert. They were dressed in their Sunday best in an effort to look respectable. The future of Great Oak was at stake; a big turnout was expected. What better opportunity could a politician find to impress the voters?

Immediately, a steady stream of people entered the room. There was the usual jostling for the best seats along with the telling of jokes and the saying of hellos. The Three of We found seats with their parents along a row near the front. Before eight o'clock, the room was packed. One of those standing at the very back was Androf Protsky, who had come seeking opportunity.

While the spectators filed in, Wally set up his architectural drawings on easels. His big moment was at hand; he had been practicing his presentation for months and knew it by heart. Despite his preparation, Wally was lethargic and distracted on this night. His hair lacked its usual waviness and his eyes were red and swollen from lack of sleep. Moreover, his mind was so befuddled that he could hardly think straight.

At precisely eight o'clock, Mayor Higgins pounded his gavel on the council table. A few minutes passed before everyone grew quiet, during which he kept tirelessly pounding. Finally, silence filled the room, and he announced the first order of business. Wally Houseman would present his *Progress for Tomorrow Plan.*

Wally stepped forward, looking like a man who had been in a train wreck. He was dressed in his finest suit, yet sweat poured down his splotchy face and a clumsy stagger replaced his usual swagger.

"Hey Wally, are you drunk?" someone yelled from the crowd.

A round of laughter greeted the remark, during which the mayor pounded with his gavel again. The meeting was off to a rowdy start.

When things finally quieted down, Wally began his speech. He stammered and sputtered, but managed to state why Great Oak had fallen on hard times – at least in his opinion. It was all because of cheap labor in places like China. The town's textile and furniture mills could no longer compete. Wisely, he left out the part about his poor management of the factories.

Then Wally described his glorious vision for Great Oak. Tourists and old folks were the answer, according to him. Retired people and those seeking fresh air and outdoor sports were flocking towards the mountains. They needed places to live and things to do.

Wally proclaimed Great Oak had a wonderful opportunity. By combining land from the schools, the park, and his factories, he would create a single tract of a thousand acres. The land would border the river on one side and Main Street on the other. It would offer the scenic views and activities, which the wealthy wanted.

He painted a glowing picture despite his weariness. The world's finest housing and recreational facilities would rise up on this tract. Underground parking for a thousand cars would exist where the park was now. High-rise condominiums, hotels, movie theaters, stores, restaurants, and a golf course would stand above it. The huge complex would stretch all the way to the river, and the town's crisis would end. Jobs would be plentiful and millions of new tax dollars would flow into the city's coffers, but it all hinged on his project.

Wally concluded by stating the sale of the park to him was the only remaining obstacle. Everything else was already in place. The City Council should take advantage of his offer without delay. Oh, what a favor he was doing Great Oak.

The room fell silent when Wally sat down. The council members appeared to be thinking it over. In reality, they had accepted bribes from Wally and were ready to approve his proposal. They studied the audience, looking for signs of their reaction. The response began with a few timid boos; then a chorus of shouts, catcalls, and profane oaths filled the room. Nobody liked what they had heard.

Mayor Higgins, an ethical man who refused to be bought, wasn't willing to let the matter pass easily. He had agreed to hear arguments against Wally's plan and banged his gavel on the table. "We have a long list of speakers on this subject and we'll be here all night if this rowdiness keeps up," he shouted.

That's when Aunt Sally rose to her feet. "Mayor, we can all go home early if you'll let me be first."

The mayor smiled as though Sally was one of his children. "It's okay with me as long as no one objects." After a moment of silence, he nodded at her. "You go right ahead, Sally." For years thereafter, the mayor would laugh whenever he told the story about Aunt Sally's subsequent speech. "Don't ever debate with her," he would chuckle. "She seems nice until she opens her mouth. Then she chews you up and spits you out."

Aunt Sally stepped towards the podium and adjusted the microphone. Her petite and demure figure contrasted vividly with Wally's image. At first, she seemed ill at ease, but the entire room was spellbound as soon as she began speaking; she lambasted Wally right from the beginning. "Let me start by telling everyone a secret. Wally pretends to stand behind this project, but that's a lie. He's actually fronting for the Galaboni family. You may have heard of them – the Las Vegas mafia. If we sell Wally the park, he will quickly sell it to the Galabonis and walk away. He'll make millions in the process, and we'll be stuck with the Galabonis. Is this what you want?"

Once again, cries of outrage erupted. The council members opened their mouths in astonishment. Their bribes seemed paltry when compared to what Wally was making. As for Wally, he was at a loss for words. Nobody knew about his deal with the Galabonis, not even Sineous. Wally was too confounded to offer any denials. *How did she find out?* he wondered. Once more, the mayor's gavel began to pound.

Aunt Sally silenced the room by simply raising her hands and smiling. Everyone gave her their full attention; they wanted to hear what she would say next.

This time, she delivered the fatal blow. She pulled out a document and handed it to the mayor. Then she turned towards the audience. "I have just given the mayor a copy of the deed, which created the park. Gregory Harrison, our founding father, signed it back in 1824. Lawyers call this type of deed a conditional transfer. Apparently Wally didn't do his homework by checking the deed records, so I'm going to read a few important parts of it now."

All eyes turned towards Wally, but he was oblivious to what was happening. His weary mind was still wondering how Aunt Sally had found out about the Galabonis.

Aunt Sally paused and then began to read. "This transfer is subject to the land remaining in a natural state and used as a public park. Should the town stop using the land as such, it shall revert to my then living heirs. Moreover, should there be less than one hundred, fifty-foot tall, oak trees standing on the land at any time, it shall also revert to my heirs. If I have no such heirs, the land shall revert to the Harrison Foundation."

A stunned silence filled the room. Finally, Mayor Higgins burst out laughing and peered over the council table at Aunt Sally. "Why don't you tell us what this means? Make it simple, so even someone like Wally can get it."

Aunt Sally beamed at Wally in triumph. "The deed is perfectly clear. The town cannot legally sell the land to Wally or anyone else. Plus, the town must assure that at least one hundred mature oak trees always grow there in order to use it as a park. If not, it goes back to the Harrisons."

"As a matter of curiosity, how many oak trees are in the park now?" the mayor asked.

Aunt Sally grinned. "To be precise, there are two-hundred and twenty-six."

The mayor winked at Sally. "I sort of figured you'd know. Guess you counted them, huh?"

"Yes sir, just in case someone asked."

The mayor had one more question. "Do you know why he put in the requirement about the trees?"

Aunt Sally had anticipated this question as well. "I was curious myself, so I read all of his old papers. He was a prolific writer, you know. Anyway, back when he created the park, he wrote that he wanted to make sure the town would look after the trees. Since he was very fond of oak trees, he used them as the standard of care."

Mayor Higgins smiled brightly at the spectators. "Well, there you have it, folks. Looks like the town can't sell the park, not even to good old Wally."

A loud chorus of cheers came from the crowd. Some rose and danced in the aisles; others just sat in their seats and laughed. The mayor tried pounding his gavel for a while and then tossed it into the air with a grin.

The celebration went on for at least five minutes. When the room finally calmed down, Aunt Sally finished her speech. "Mayor, our town has other worthy options. My committee has some ideas, which we'll present at your next meeting. In the meantime, I suggest Wally's proposal be voted down."

"I so move," the mayor quickly said. "All in favor, say aye."

The council members were ready to give up at this point. Regardless of Wally's bribes, they had no choice. "Aye," they said in low voices, one after the other.

"Motion passed," the mayor loudly proclaimed. Then he looked sheepishly around for his gavel. When he had tossed it into the air earlier, it had fallen in front of the Council table.

Aunt Sally handed it to him; as she did, he gave her a nod of approval.

"Motion passed," he said again, banging his gavel on the table.

Aunt Sally started towards her seat behind the railing.

"Just a moment, Sally," the mayor said. "Since you're the only one who seems to know anything around here, who are the living heirs of Gregory Harrison?"

"There is only one heir, and he's right here in this room."

Joe Harrison rose from where he was sitting. "That would be me. In case you're wondering, I wouldn't sell the park to Wally or the

Galabonis if they were the last persons on earth."

Everyone stared at Wally for his reaction. He said nothing, but his face turned a dark purple as he hastily pushed his way through the crowd. Jeers and taunts followed his every step, and the doors slammed behind him when he left the room.

Androf had watched everything with veiled emotions. Inwardly, Wally's stupidity and bad luck had excited him. Ubeck had been right; opportunity was at hand. He hurried after Wally, a plan forming in his mind.

∝ Chapter 36 ∞

---

*Fail not to see when the forces of nature
are amiss. Forsooth, evil be afoot, and
thou must make haste and thenceforth
foil the dark plan.*

— Translated from Storia Di Incanto; circa 1885

Dangerous Minds & Devious Plans

ANDROF WALKED a distance behind Wally Houseman as he left
City Hall. He stayed discretely back, wondering where Wally would
go. A man waiting for Wally greeted him as soon as he stepped from
the building. The man was dressed in a long black coat and had a very
ominous look about him.

"Do we own the park now?" the man asked in a low, raspy voice.

Wally angrily swatted him with his cane, yet the man seemed
unaffected by the blows. Then Wally's fury abated and he motioned
with his hand. "Sineous, I need a drink and we have things to
discuss."

Androf stayed in the shadows and followed the two men. He
smiled when they entered The Oak Tavern, an old fashioned bar
down the street. It was the perfect place to tell Wally about his plan.

Ubeck was the one who had urged him to do this. When Aunt
Sally had read the conditions of the deed during the council meeting,
Ubeck had spoken from inside Androf's mind. *Do you remember the
man in Serbia who would not pay tribute? Remember how we killed his*

trees. It was the requirement of one hundred trees, which had jarred Androf's memory.

The Oak Tavern was in a large, gloomy room with an ornately carved bar along one side. The air smelled of stale smoke, spilt-beer, and age. Androf glanced around and then approached a stout man behind the bar.

"I'm looking for Wally Houseman," he said gruffly.

The bartender nodded at a corner table where two men were sitting. "Better leave him alone; he's in a bad mood."

Androf glanced at them. "What are they drinking?"

"Brandy," the bartender replied.

"Give me the bottle and another glass," Androf growled.

The bartender sighed. "Listen, whoever you are. I don't want any trouble."

Androf laid fifty dollars on the bar and glared at him, his face a mask of stone. "There will only be trouble if you don't do as I say."

The bartender squinted at Androf for a second, sizing him up. Finally, he snatched up the money and put a bottle and glass on the bar. Androf took them to where Wally and Sineous were sitting, straddled a chair, and poured himself a drink. Then he offered Wally and Sineous the bottle.

Wally frowned at him suspiciously. "Who are *you?*"

Androf didn't state his real name – after all, this was Ubeck's idea. "I am Ubeck; a man who will help you make millions."

Wally reached for his cane, but as he took in Androf's rough face and bulging muscles, he just grumbled. "Leave me alone!"

Androf was unperturbed by Wally's reaction. "I was at the meeting and heard what was said. You look like a man who is determined to get his way."

"So what," Wally replied.

"So…you took the wrong approach. Now, it's time for something different."

"What's that supposed to mean?"

Androf smiled; he had gotten Wally's attention. "It means that the only one who can actually sell the park is Harrison or the Harrison Foundation."

"They can't sell it as long as the town uses it for a park."

Androf shook his head. "You weren't listening to everything the woman said. Using the land as a park was not the deed's only condition. The land also reverts to the Harrisons if there aren't at least a hundred oak trees standing on it."

Wally glowered at him. "You're speaking in riddles."

Androf locked eyes with Wally, his face stern and hard. "I will tell you a story. If you don't feel like talking after I'm finished, I'll leave."

"The sooner the better!"

Despite his words, Androf could tell Wally was curious, so he began. "Some years ago, a civil war broke out in my country. I led a small army and needed money for food and weapons, so I asked the landowners for contributions. One man, who owned a vast orchard of olive trees, refused. The next night, my men poisoned some of his trees; they died within a few days. After that, the man begged me to take his money."

Suddenly, Wally became interested. "How many trees did you kill?"

"About fifty."

"What kind of poison did you use?"

Androf chuckled at the memory. "We made our own — it was a primitive effort. We used whatever was handy, a mix of alcohol, gasoline, and battery acid. You probably have more *lethal* chemicals at your factory."

"You're saying it's possible to kill trees in a matter of days?"

Androf grinned; Wally was hooked. "The secret lies in getting the chemicals into the tree's roots. We used a long pipe to punch holes under the trees and then poured the chemicals down the pipe. When we were done, we filled the holes with dirt again. The method is undetectable. Some kind of blight appears to be killing the trees."

For the first time in three days, Wally smiled. "I like this idea." Even so, he frowned a few seconds later as he considered it. "What good will it do? If the trees in the park die, the land reverts to Joe Harrison. He'll never sell it to me."

"Harrison is an old man. If he were dead, the Harrison Foundation would own the land. What about them?"

Wally thought it over. There were four trustees of the foundation, Joe Harrison and three others. By coincidence, the others were members of the City Council, men who he had bribed many times. If Harrison were dead, he could surely make a deal with them. There was only one problem – he was running out of time. The Galabonis would not wait forever. "Joe Harrison may be an old man, but he isn't likely to die soon."

"He might have a fatal accident. I have caused such accidents before."

Wally stared at Androf. "This is serious talk. What's in it for you?"

"All I want is money."

"How much money?"

Androf grinned. "Well, let's see. Five thousand dollars should buy enough equipment and chemicals. An additional five thousand will buy you twenty-five dead trees. Of course, I'll have to kill more than the oak trees to make it look like a disease. Taking care of Harrison will cost an extra twenty-five…I can do the entire job for a hundred thousand. You will pay as I produce results." Androf didn't mention his intention to double the price when he was halfway through.

Wally raised his eyebrows. "That's a lot of money."

Androf replied without emotion. "No, the millions you will make is a lot of money. This is just a necessary expense."

Wally began to laugh. "You're a cold-blooded devil, aren't you?"

Androf poured himself another drink. "I've heard that." He pushed the bottle towards Wally and Sineous, and they joined him this time.

Wally turned towards Sineous. "What do you think of this man's plan?"

Sineous licked his lips. His tongue had recently grown longer and now had a blackish tinge. He giggled, as if the question was hilarious.

"I like his scheme – it could be just what we need."

Wally downed his drink and then poured another. "Let's go to my factory. If you find chemicals that will work, kill the first trees tonight. Pick two of the pine trees on the school grounds to avoid suspicion. If the trees die, the job will be yours."

"You want me to do Harrison as well?"

Wally laughed heartily, his black mood lifting. "Yes, everything! When you are done, I may have more work for you. There's a certain woman who should pay for the trouble she's caused."

Androf smiled. "Ah…the woman who spoke at the meeting."

ഇൟരഇൟരഇൟര

Sometime during the next week, Androf's personality went into hibernation. It retreated into a dark corner of his mind, and Ubeck took over. This happened after Androf had killed the first two trees, and Wally had given him one of the black disks to wear. As soon as Androf put on the disk, his personality collapsed. His ego still lingered somewhere in his brain and memories of his past deeds were intact. However, for all intents and purposes, he had become Ubeck.

Androf's twisted brain took comfort in this fact. He had too many enemies – enemies that threatened his every move. The black disk had quickly fueled his paranoia, leaving him paralyzed by fear. Ubeck stepped forward to save the day, confident and decisive. Ubeck wasn't afraid of anything.

After his meeting with Wally, Androf had killed the two pine trees on the school grounds. Within three days, their leaves had turned brown. When Wally saw the dead trees, he gave Androf enough money for his own equipment and chemicals, not wanting him to have anything from his factory in case he was caught.

On Saturday, Androf drove the white van to Greensboro and purchased a motorized pump used for washing windows. Its little engine ran as quiet as a sewing machine and long nozzle was perfect for getting into the roots of the trees. He also purchased drums of

ഇ 384 രു

acid, paint thinner, and chlorine, along with gloves, masks, and other protective clothing.

That same night, he used his new equipment. He selected three trees, one on the school grounds and two at the edge of the park. In this way, it would appear as if the blight had started elsewhere and was spreading towards the park. As a precaution against ravens or wolves, he wore Davey's magic hat. The image that his huge shape created as he stalked through the park was frightening indeed. Still, nobody was there to notice him.

After five days, thirty trees were dead or dying. Nine stood outside the park and twenty-one were within the park grounds. Joe Harrison was beside himself with concern, yet he didn't know why the trees were dying.

Wally paid Androf more money and urged him to kill the trees faster. It had taken Androf a few days to refine his technique, but he was now able to kill fifteen trees each night. He also planned on killing trees along Elm Street, making it seem as if the blight had swept through the entire town. He promised to finish in two weeks.

Wally made only one request. He wanted to be there when Androf poured the chemicals into the roots of the Great Oak. "My family has always hated the tree. I want to see it die."

"Get ready, it will happen in a few days," Androf replied.

೫ଓ೫ଓ೫ଓ

The Three of We immediately noticed the dying trees. They went to the park and searched for Joe Harrison, finding him shaking his head in distress as he looked up at a tall evergreen oak. The tree's leaves had turned brown.

Amy spoke up first. "Mr. Harrison, what's happening to the trees?"

He scratched his head, obviously perplexed. "Amy, I've never seen anything like it. We've had Dutch Elm Disease, Chestnut Blight, Bark Beetles, Root Borers, and every other disease upon occasion, but nothing like this."

"Can't anything stop it?"

"A couple of experts are coming here next week. I tried to get them sooner, but they are busy elsewhere. At the rate this is spreading, we may not have any trees left by then. I've never known of a disease, which could kill trees so quickly. Something just isn't right."

Later that afternoon, Sequoyah met with Yona at the Cherokee village. They sat outside of Yona's log cabin, drinking herb tea. Sequoyah told him about the wolves outside of Houseman's Castle and the trees dying in the park.

Yona listened silently, his lips furrowed into a frown. "Nature is being drawn into the struggle between the spirits," he finally said. "This is a dangerous sign; it may mean the spirits will soon confront each other. Many people could die if such a thing happened. We must destroy the spirit in the cave without delay."

"We have not finished our preparations yet," Sequoyah replied.

Yona cast him a questioning glance. "Elogi Ugithisa and the Ani-Wodi have woven armor from the branches of the tree, and you have made spears and more arrows. What haven't we done?"

"Amy is still translating the old Sabatini books, and Davey is perfecting his magic skill."

Yona turned towards Sequoyah, his eyes keen. "Sometimes we must act before we are ready because the price of waiting is too great. Tell them to hurry. Let them spend another week preparing. Then they must go forward!"

ഇൻഐഇൻഐഇൻഐ

The insistent ringing of his cell phone startled Androf. Irritated, he climbed out of bed and answered it. He had stayed up all night killing trees and didn't like being disturbed.

Yong Chow Lee screamed in his ear. "I've been trying to reach you for a week. Why aren't you answering your phone?"

Using Androf's voice, Ubeck replied. "What do you want, Chinese man?"

"What do I want? I sent you the money, didn't I? Now, you will do your part. The situation has become critical in China. You must kidnap the boy immediately. Call me after you have him."

Ubeck didn't like his arrogance; he wanted to set things straight. "Not so fast; you didn't say how dangerous this boy is. More money is required."

Yong Chow Lee was nearly speechless. "Dangerous? He's only thirteen years old."

Ubeck's words grew harsh. "You are no longer speaking with Androf, the fool. I am Ubeck and I'm telling you the boy is a demon. He has a powerful magic, which protects him. I do not know what game you play, but I will do nothing unless you send more money."

"You are Androf...I recognize your voice."

Ubeck laughed derisively. "Not any more."

Yong Chow Lee began to shout. "What is this talk about demons and magic? Have you gone crazy?"

"Crazy like a fox, Chinese man."

Yong Chow Lee was not a man of long conversations, particularly with an underling like Androf. "Will you kidnap the boy or not?"

"Send the money and we'll see. I want another twenty-five thousand."

Yong Chow Lee's voice grew sinister. "I warned you not to disappoint me, Androf. If you don't follow my orders, you're a dead man."

"As I said before, you are speaking with Ubeck, not Androf. I am not afraid of you or anyone else." Then Androf threw the cell phone against the wall, shattering it into pieces.

Yong Chow Lee stared at the silent phone in disbelief. Androf had placed him in a precarious position. His associates did not tolerate failure, and Androf was now a liability; he knew too much. Frowning with disgust, Yong Chow Lee realized what he must do. He would have to silence Androf and kidnap the boy himself. After thinking for a moment, he dialed another number. Wang Yen answered quickly.

"Wang, I have an urgent job. Pick two of your most able assassins, one an experienced driver, and give them pistols with silencers. Send them with a car tomorrow. The license plates must be untraceable. We are going on a trip and will be gone for three days."

"They will be very expensive," Wang replied.

"Will they follow my orders without hesitation?"

"Most certainly; results are guaranteed."

"They will be worth it," Yong Chow Lee said, his face a mask of anger.

℠ℕ℠ℕ℠ℕ℠ℕ

Spike seemed troubled when Davey saw him on the following Monday. He stared at the floor for a long minute and then looked Davey in the eyes. "Can I tell you a secret? The thing is, I don't want Jimmy or Amy to know. They already don't think much of me."

Davey didn't like keeping anything from Jimmy and Amy, but Spike was a special case. "I won't say anything as long as it doesn't involve them."

Spike sighed. "I'm worried about my dad. I think he's loosing his mind."

Suddenly, Davey's senses were tingling. "What's he done now?"

Spike pulled Davey down the hall until they were alone. "He's the one who has been killing the trees," he whispered.

Davey was shocked. "How do you know?"

"A man has been showing up at our house after dark for the last week. I don't know who he is, but he doesn't work at the factory. Dad doesn't let him come inside; he just talks with him on the front porch, real mysterious like."

"Did you hear what they were saying?"

"Not at first. I saw Dad give him money several times, but I didn't know why until last night. As soon as the man came, I snuck into the bushes and overheard them talking about killing the trees."

"Maybe you should tell your mother?"

"It won't do any good…she gave up on Dad a long time ago. She doesn't approve of the things he does and hardly speaks to him anymore."

"Gee…I'm sorry."

Spike shrugged, and then continued. "Ever since the City Council meeting, Dad has been acting crazy – crazier than usual, I should say. Last night, I heard this man say he was killing the Great Oak on Monday at midnight. Dad said he would meet him there and laughed like some kind of a maniac."

"That's tonight!" Davey exclaimed.

Spike nodded. "I've been thinking about telling the police, but, if I do, they'll put him in jail. I can't be a part of that, no matter how much he deserves it. He would never forgive me."

Davey thought it over. "Maybe I can stop them."

"What can you do? You're just a kid and they're grown men."

"I'll go to the park and catch them. Then I'll say if any more trees die, I'll tell the police. You won't be involved."

Spike shook his head. "It could be dangerous. The man that's killing the trees seems awfully big and mean. For some reason, he's wearing your hat."

"My hat?"

"Yeah, you know – the one from your magician's costume."

Davey thought about this for a moment, completely astonished. *The man who has my hat intends to kill the Great Oak. What does it mean?* "Well, don't worry. I can defend myself," he finally said.

"I remember, but if it comes to that, will you go easy on my dad?"

ℰᏥℰᏥℰᏥ

Davey went to bed at ten o'clock that night – at least, that's what he pretended to do. When he was sure Uncle Bill and Aunt Sally were asleep, he got up and put on his clothes. The house was so quiet he could hear Uncle Bill snoring from down the hall. Bristol was also sleeping peacefully in the hallway.

Davey had decided earlier to wear his magic jewelry to the park; he wanted to be prepared if there was trouble. At the last moment, he also put on Antonio's black cape and the rest of his magician's costume. He caught a glimpse of himself in the mirror and thought about his great grandfather. *Through me, his magic will return tonight.*

Now, all he had to do was find a way out of the house. He considered tiptoeing past Bristol, going down the stairs, and easing out the back door. However, the wooden staircase creaked at every step, and the hinges on the door screeched like someone had stepped on a cat's tail. If Bristol woke up and started barking, he would be in trouble. Still, there wasn't any other way.

Just as he was about to step into the hallway, he heard a tapping on his window. He glanced over and saw the squirrel with its face pressed against the glass. Davey opened the window, and the squirrel immediately indicated he should follow it.

"I'm not sure how to get out," Davey whispered.

The squirrel leaped onto a limb of the tree beside the window and motioned. Davey looked out the window and studied the tree. The squirrel was right; the tree stood close enough for him to grab onto one of its branches. Before long, he had scooted down the tree and was standing on the ground. Then he hurried towards the garage where he kept his bike.

Very quietly, he rolled his bike to the street and climbed onto the seat. The squirrel scampered up Davey's body and took a position on his shoulder. Davey quickly pushed off – they were on their way.

The silvery light of a full moon cast a ghostly glow over the houses along Elm Street. As Davey pedaled furiously towards the park, a sense of excitement filled him. He had an uncanny feeling that it would be a night to remember.

ℭ Chapter 37 ℘

---

*Heed this, oh magician. Magick powere
cometh from within thy mind. As the
river needs water to flow, so doest thou
need rest to restore thy powere.*

— Translated from Storia Di Incanto; circa 1889

The Great Sabatini Returns

THIRTY MINUTES LATER, Yong Chow Lee and his two hired
assassins drove along Elm Street. He sat at the rear of a black Lincoln,
issuing blunt orders to the men in front. To him, the quiet town
seemed defenseless – especially against his little army of killers.

Had Yong Chow Lee arrived half-an-hour earlier, he would have
seen Davey pedaling furiously towards the park, his magician's cape
billowing behind him and a very unusual squirrel perched on his
shoulder. Regardless, the Chinese man thought his timing was
perfect. He wanted to perform his foul deeds while the town slept,
completely unaware of his deadly intentions.

Yong Chow Lee thought over the tasks before him as he scanned
the street for Androf's address. In his mind, his night's work would be
easy, so incredibly easy. His hired men would sneak into Androf's
apartment, knock him out with an anesthetic, and drag his limp body
to the car. Then they would go to Davey Boehm's house and kidnap
the boy in the same way. If someone woke up or resisted – well, that's
why his assassins were along. He wasn't leaving anyone alive to

identify him later.

As soon as his men captured Davey Boehm, they would take off for New York. The boy would be confined in the trunk, all trussed up in a neat little package. Androf's unconscious body would remain in the front seat where it was easily available to his men. Somewhere along the way, they would dispose of the idiot. Throwing him from a high bridge had its appeal.

During his long trip, Yong Chow Lee had studied the two men who accompanied him. He thought they were an odd, but effective team. The man driving the car was Li Ssu, a three-hundred pound man with muscles like coils of steel. He rarely spoke; when he did, he mostly grunted. The other man was Shen Ti Chi, a tall, thin man who moved with the agility of a cat. He could effortlessly kill a man with a single shot from a silenced pistol, an ability earning him the curious nickname of Spit.

At last, Yong Chow Lee saw the address of the house where Androf's garage apartment was located. He ordered Li Ssu to shut off the engine and let the car roll silently up the driveway. The lights in the apartment were out, but there was no sign of Androf's white van. *I hope the idiot is here*, thought Yong Chow Lee.

He quickly gave instructions to Li Ssu and Spit, and they were inside the apartment in a matter of minutes. They returned just as quickly and reported the bad news – the apartment was empty. Yong Chow Lee fumed silently. So far, his simple plan was not working.

Li Ssu and Spit also revealed another interesting fact. They had found twenty-five thousand dollars inside the apartment. *I didn't send him that much, so where did it all come from?* Yong Chow Lee wondered.

Finally, he barked new orders to Li Ssu. "Drive down the street, turn around, and come back. Find a dark spot where we can watch the house without attracting attention. We will wait for Androf to return."

As Li Ssu followed his instructions, Yong Chow Lee ordered him to stop. From his vantage point, he had seen a white van parked at the bottom of the hill. "That looks like Androf's van," he snarled.

℘ℭ℘ℭ℘ℭ

A short time earlier, Wally, Sineous, and Ubeck had met at the north entrance of the park. Wally held his dragon-headed cane and stood watch as Sineous helped Ubeck unload the white van – everything that they needed to kill the Great Oak was there.

As far as Wally knew, the van belonged to Ubeck. Moreover, he thought Ubeck was the name of the man whom he watched. He knew nothing about Androf or the fact that Ubeck's personality had taken control of Androf's body.

Wally raised his eyebrows when he saw Ubeck take a shotgun and baseball bat from the van. "What are those for," he asked with a frown.

Ubeck shrugged. "If someone comes along, we may need them."

Wally gulped and made no reply. Despite his bravado, he was little more than a coward. For a brief moment, he even thought of returning to his castle, but he had dreamed about killing the Great Oak for years. He had to see it – to relish its death by being there. The thought pushed aside his fears and filled him with excitement.

Finally, when Ubeck put on his protective clothing and black top hat, Wally knew they were ready. Then the three men entered the park and headed towards the Great Oak. As the woods closed around them, the lower branches of the trees tore at their bodies. Wally managed a small smile, imagining that the trees were foolishly trying to forestall their dark plan.

Sineous led the way, effortlessly lugging two heavy containers of pre-mixed chemicals. Ubeck came second, pulling his pump on a metal cart. Wally brought up the rear, peering about as though enemies lurked at every bend. When Wally noticed the heavy load Sineous was carrying, he was momentarily startled. *How did Sineous become so strong?* he wondered.

The trees along the path arched above the men, their intertwined

℘ 393 ℭ

branches blocking the moonlight. Every time the wheels on Ubeck's cart squeaked, Wally cringed. He glared at Ubeck, irritated by his confidence and the ridiculous top hat on his head. "Why are you wearing that stupid hat?" he finally asked.

Ubeck offered a sly smile. "Just an extra precaution."

Wally didn't like what he implied. "Precaution against what?"

"Never mind," Ubeck replied curtly, irritating Wally even further.

Before long, they reached the clearing where the Great Oak stood, and Ubeck quickly pulled his cart to the fence around the tree. Sineous giggled fiendishly as he placed his containers beside it and returned to the van for the rest of their supplies. Meanwhile, Wally stared up at the Great Oak, feeling somewhat unsettled. Immediately, Ubeck took out his tools and began to pick the gate's lock.

The moon threw eerie shadows along the limbs of the massive oak. No breeze blew through the clearing, yet the tree's branches swayed of their own accord. An icy shiver crept through Wally as he watched the tree. To him, the scene had a surreal quality; he felt as if the tree were glaring contemptuously at him. "Hurry up. Let's get this done," he snapped as the lock clattered open and the gate swung inward.

"Won't be long now," Ubeck replied, pulling his cart inside the fence. He grabbed a narrow pipe and immediately began using a rubber mallet to hammer it into the tree's roots. A dull thump, thump, thump sounded throughout the clearing while he worked. Soon, he had created a channel for the injection of the chemicals.

Ubeck pulled the pipe out, set his hat on the pump, and put a protective mask over his face. Then he poured the contents of a container into the pump and started its engine. When it was purring smoothly, he picked up the long nozzle at the end of the pump's hose, glanced over at Wally, and signaled his readiness to begin.

Wally felt a triumphant surge of evil. "Do it," he urged, unaware of a man emerging from the shadows behind his back. The man held a double-barreled shotgun, which he shoved against Wally's spine.

"Hold it right there, Houseman," he shouted. "And you inside the fence – turn that machine off."

Wally spun around and found himself looking into the wrinkled face of the park warden. Briefly stunned, he finally stammered out an explanation. "Thank heavens it's you, Joe. I was taking a walk and caught this man. He's doing something to the tree."

Ubeck scowled and then turned off the pump. His movement briefly hid his hand, and he discretely grabbed the baseball bat, concealing it along his side.

Joe motioned with his shotgun. "Cut the bull, Wally; I've caught you red-handed. I suspected a disease wasn't killing these trees and those chemicals are proof of what is. Stand over here in front of me, both of you; I'm taking you to the police station."

Wally frantically pointed his cane at Ubeck. "I haven't done anything. He's the man you should arrest."

Joe turned sideways, distracted by Wally's cane. "Raise your hands and turn around," he ordered, still unaware of the bat in Ubeck's hand.

Wally followed Joe's instructions, whimpering like a naughty child. However, as Ubeck raised his own hands, he threw the bat at Joe. A distance of six feet separated them, and Joe's reflexes were those of a man slowed by age. The bat slammed against his head, staggering him.

Ubeck was upon him in an instant, ripping the shotgun away and punching him several times. As Joe crumpled to the ground, Wally stood with his back turned, hearing the commotion, but afraid to look.

"Put your hands down and get over here," Ubeck growled.

Wally turned and saw Joe's inert figure. "Let's get out of here."

"Don't be stupid – he saw what we were doing. Isn't he that Harrison fellow?"

"Yes…the man you're supposed to kill."

Ubeck laughed heartily. "What a coincidence. Tonight, we'll take care of him as well. I'll tie him up until we finish with the tree. Then his turn will come."

Wally's nerves were shattered. "I've had enough. Do what I'm paying you to do; I'm going home."

Ubeck yanked him forward. "No, you're not! You're standing guard while I do your dirty work." Then he thrust Joe's shotgun towards him. "Keep him covered while I get some rope from the van."

Wally pushed the shotgun away. "I don't want to."

At that moment, Sineous reappeared with two more containers of chemicals. He was unaware of the little drama, which had just unfolded, but his black tongue flickered across his lips as he stared at the unconscious figure of the warden. "Well…well, if it isn't Joe Harrison," he exclaimed, giggling crazily.

Ubeck thrust the shotgun at Sineous this time. "Take it and keep an eye on things. If either of you leave, you'll wind up like this man on the ground. I'll be right back." Then he picked up the baseball bat and stalked out of the clearing.

ഇൻയൻയൻയ

Meanwhile, Davey had left his bike at the east entrance of the park and approached the Great Oak from a different direction. When he reached the clearing, he crouched in the shadows with the squirrel by his side. His eyes went wide when he saw a man pointing a shotgun at the inert figure of the park warden. Wally stood nearby, watching intently. The two men were directly in front of the fence around the Great Oak, fifty-feet away from Davey and the squirrel.

Davey shook his head, realizing his mistake. "I should have told the warden instead of coming here," he whispered to the squirrel. He assumed the man with the shotgun was the one Spike had warned him about – the man killing the trees. He felt like the warden's predicament was his fault and wondered what to do.

Glancing around, he noticed a machine sitting beside the Great Oak. *That must be how they are killing the trees,* he thought. Then a familiar object caught his attention; his magic hat sat on top of the machine. He was startled to see it there, but it also gave him an idea.

Davey looked at the squirrel. "The gate is open. Can you shut it and keep anyone from opening it again? That way, their machine will be locked inside the fence."

The squirrel nodded as if this was not at all difficult.

"Okay, I'm going to distract them by summoning my hat to me. Sneak over to the tree and shut the gate when you see the hat moving. We'll see how a little magic affects them."

The squirrel took off, its black fur blending into the shadows as it scampered through the woods. After a few minutes, Davey focused his mind, picturing the hat floating towards him; it slowly rose into the air and began drifting in his direction. Seconds later, the gate started to close. Its hinges squeaked as it gathered momentum and then clanged shut.

Of course, Wally was unaware of Davey's presence in the clearing. As soon as he saw the hat moving, he turned towards it with a surprised gasp. Immediately, he spun around again when he heard the gate slam shut behind him. "What...who's there?" he exclaimed.

Sineous reacted in a different manner. He noticed a blur of movement inside the fence as the squirrel's dark shape scurried behind the tree and instinctively raised the shotgun and fired. The explosion shattered the silence of the night with an ominous roar. Wally added his own cry of alarm as the noise startled him further.

Behind the backs of the two men, Davey ran forward, plucked his hat from the air, and returned to the shadows. He shoved the hat onto his head and sent a frantic query to the squirrel. *Are you okay?* He heard an answering *yes* inside his head, the hat now allowing him to hear the squirrel's thoughts.

Davey breathed a sigh of relief. He realized the man holding the shotgun was a danger – someone might get hurt if he fired again. He focused his mind and called forth his magic power. As his body pulsed with energy, he sent a stream of lightning into the man's back. He put the entire force of his magic into it, not really knowing how strong it would be.

Sineous didn't stand a chance. Davey watched with amazement as the lightning caught the ill-fated man by surprise, its force jerking him into a spasmodic series of hops and convulsions. The man's fingers involuntarily pulled the other trigger of the shotgun, sending its last load of buckshot harmlessly into the air.

His erratic dance continued for three minutes, during which he emitting a series of howls. When he finally regained control of his body, he glanced around uncertainly, dropped the shotgun, and ran from the clearing. He didn't stop until he reached Houseman's Castle; then he hid in the darkest part of the cellar. Hours passed before he could remember his name.

Wally was alone in the clearing now and terrified. He had watched helplessly as Sineous ran away. "What's happening," he shouted, totally confused. His moment of triumph had disappeared.

Davey felt like it was the perfect time to step from the shadows. He recalled that the Great Sabatini had emerged from an amber cloud during his magic show and willed for a similar cloud to surround him. His hat rested low on his forehead, and the cape hid the rest of his body as he spoke in a ghostly voice, the cloud billowing around him. "The Great Sabatini has returned; leave before it's too late."

Wally turned towards the voice, his mind reeling. He could barely see the figure in the amber cloud, yet it was a frightening sight. He believed the Great Sabatini had indeed come back and reacted as he typically did when facing adversity; he flew into a violent rage. Waving his cane, he rushed at Davey.

The abrupt attack took Davey by surprise. Even so, when he saw Wally waving the dragon-headed cane, another idea formed in his mind. The magic coursing through his blood allowed him to react incredibly fast, and he willed for the amber cloud to billow around Wally as he stepped into the shadows and headed for the Great Oak.

The gate opened when Davey arrived, and he immediately coated the pump with ice. Hours would pass before anyone could start it again. Then he sent a message to the squirrel. *Leave the gate open.*

Very clever, the squirrel replied, as if knowing Davey's plan.

In the meantime, Wally was flailing with the cane at the amber cloud. He cursed and grunted with the effort, but he hit nothing. When the cloud finally drifted away, he seemed bewildered; no one was there. His breath came in labored gasps as he searched for his enemy.

Davey's haunting voice called out again, this time from inside the fence. "Your grandfather was a fool. Think about what happened to him and leave." Davey hoped Wally would take his advice. If not, he wanted to lure him inside the fence.

Wally was too angry to think rationally; he grew even more berserk at the mention of his grandfather. No longer in control of his emotions, he charged again at the figure taunting him.

Davey stood next to the tree and focused his mind as Wally came through the gate. When he was ten feet away, Davey willed for the ground beneath his feet to liquify. Immediately, a swampy hole appeared, and Wally sank to his knees in muck. At that moment, Davey established contact with the dragon-headed cane. The cane's amber eyes suddenly came alive and its head looked at Davey expectantly. *Command me, master.*

Wally struggled against the muck, but it held him fast. Realizing his folly, he glared at Davey, now only a few feet away. Slowly, he recognized the boy that he hated. "You should have died in Los Angeles," he shouted angrily.

Davey saw the menace in Wally's eyes and knew that he posed a threat as long as he was free. With grim determination, he issued an order to the cane. *Restrain him.* The cane responded without hesitation. A wicked flame burst forth from its mouth and it roared in acknowledgement as its wooden shaft expanded into a mass of coils, which began to wrap around Wally's body.

Ever since childhood, Wally had been afraid of snakes. His worst nightmare unfolded, as the cane became a large, slithering serpent. In turn, Wally reached for the black disk around his neck, hoping the talisman of evil would protect him. But when he grasped it, the cane gave him a fierce squeeze and his fingers closed with a reflex so intense that the disk shattered into pieces. The shards of the stone cut into his hand, and he screamed as its evil force streamed into his body. Then a series of wails escaped from his lips, and his mind went blank.

With Wally immobilized, Davey ran to Joe's unmoving figure; the gate closed behind him as he left the enclosure. He put his ear against Joe's chest, listened for a heartbeat, and then smiled with relief. Though unconscious, the warden was still alive. Immediately, Davey attempted to revive him.

Ubeck had been at the van when Sineous fired the shotgun. He grabbed the rope and crept back towards the tree, still carrying his baseball bat. When he neared the clearing, Wally's pathetic wails reached his ears. The sounds were enough to frighten a normal person, but Ubeck ignored them; he peered through the bushes at the edge of the clearing as he cautiously moved forward.

He saw no sign of Sineous, who was supposed to be guarding the warden. Instead, he saw a dark figure bending over his body. The figure had his back turned, but Ubeck knew it wasn't Sineous or Wally. Ever so quietly, he readied his bat and came forward. When he reached the figure, he began a downward swing.

☙ Chapter 38 ❧

---

*Yea, magick be a thing of wondrous
beauty, yet to thine enemies, it shalt oft
seem too fearsome to behold.*

— Translated from Storia Di Incanto; circa 1892

Creatures Of Magic

YONG CHOW LEE'S luck was not improving. After seeing a white van parked at the bottom of the hill, he ordered Li Ssu to drive down Elm Street and pull up beside it. With a quick inspection, he determined it was Androf's van, but there was no sign of Androf. Moreover, he found another ten-thousand dollars inside the glove compartment of the van.

Yong Chow Lee scowled as he studied the thick woods beside the van. "Where are we?" he wondered aloud.

Li Ssu uttered a pig-like grunt and pointed at a sign over the park's entrance. He could not read English, so Spit translated the words on the sign: "Welcome to Harrison Park, home of the Great Oak."

Frowning, Yong Chow Lee asked an obvious question. "Why would Androf be in a park at midnight?"

Li Ssu and Spit both shrugged; they weren't paid to think.

Yong Chow Lee assumed Androf was in the middle of committing some type of crime. *After all, what else did Androf do?* Had he arrived at the van a few minutes earlier, he would have seen Sineous returning for more supplies. That might have told him something. On the other hand, had he remained there a little longer, he would have caught Androf coming for the rope. But impatience was one of Yong Chow Lee's many faults. Another failing was his intense greed.

He instructed Li Ssu to drive around the park while he thought about how to profit from the situation. Before long, he made up his mind. More money was surely involved in whatever Androf was doing. Not only would they sneak up on him; they would also steal *all* of the money. *A little bonus,* he thought.

Yong Chow Lee noted the park had four entrances as they drove around its exterior. Androf had parked his van on the north side, so he decided to approach from a different way. *Which direction will offer the best opportunity?* he wondered. While pondering this question, he heard Sineous fire the shotgun. Seconds later, another shotgun blast occurred. The sounds spurred Yong Chow Lee into action as they reached the west entrance of the park. "Stop here, take your weapons, and be ready to shoot. We're going after Androf," he ordered.

Li Ssu immediately slammed on the brakes, and the three men climbed out of the car. With their pistols raised, they cautiously entered the west side of the park. Since they didn't know where Androf might be, Yong Chow Lee pointed north – the direction of the shotgun blasts. He believed they would find Androf along the way.

℠ℜ℠ℜ℠ℜ

Davey was bending over the warden's unconscious body when an urgent vibration of his necklace alerted him to danger. Seconds later, he saw the moonlit shadow of a figure creeping up behind him. He quickly jumped to his left, just as the figure swung the bat.

Davey's sudden reaction caused the swing to miss his head, yet the tip of the bat caught his shoulder, knocking him sideways. Davey cried out as a searing pain ran down his arm. Scrambling to his feet, he caught a glimpse of a huge, fierce-looking man coming after him. Davey didn't know he was looking at Androf Protsky, a man sent to

Great Oak for the purpose of kidnapping him, but he saw a rope and baseball bat in the man's hands and knew he was in great danger.

Davey tried to run, but the pain in his shoulder slowed him down. The man tossed the bat away, jumped on Davey's back, and bore him to the ground. Davey twisted and turned, yet the man's size and strength gave him the advantage. Soon, he had the rope wrapped around Davey's arms, pinning them against his sides. During the struggle, Davey's hat fell off and the man saw his face. To Davey's surprise, the man reared back as if shocked.

Androf's brief distraction allowed Davey to muster an attack. He worked his hands free of the rope's coils and grabbed onto the man's legs. With all the urgent force of his magic, he sent a stream of intense heat into the man's body. Davey's desperation had magnified his power, delivering an agonizing surprise.

The massive charge propelled Androf into the air, howling like a wild dog. He landed ten feet away, feeling like his insides were on fire. Rolling about on the ground, he slapped furiously at his body, trying to extinguish the searing heat consuming him. Finally, he staggered up, coughing out puffs of smoke as steam rose from his hair.

Androf swayed, glaring at Davey warily. He shook his head in a series of odd twitches as if clearing cobwebs from his mind. Suddenly, he realized Ubeck's personality was no longer controlling his body. He had become Androf again and was facing the demon that he feared. He reached for the black disk around his neck in an effort to bring back Ubeck, but the force of Davey's magic had reduced it to ashes. Androf screamed in a tormented voice. "Ubeck, where are you? Ubeck…come back. I don't want to be Androf."

Davey lay on the ground, too tired to rise. The struggle had drained his strength and his magic power was exhausted. A painful throbbing in his shoulder further sapped his ability to concentrate. He watched the big man who was screaming incoherently. *I'm done for if he comes at me again,* he thought.

As if sensing Davey's weakness, Androf reached for his bat. His sudden anger at Ubeck's desertion overrode his fear of the boy, and he stepped towards him. However, the residual effect of Davey's magic lingered in his legs, making him fall clumsily. Rising again, he took another step. This time, he went three feet before his legs gave out. Determined, he struggled to his feet and came forward once more.

Davey saw the man coming and tried to crawl away. From the corner of his eye, he noticed his hat lying nearby and pulled it onto his head. He did this without conscious thought, but it was a fated blessing. Immediately, a message appeared in his mind.

Unbeknownst to Davey, two dozen ravens had followed him from his house. The birds were floating in the sky above him, their dark feathers shining in the moonlight. They had been waiting for Davey to summon them, but as soon as Davey put the hat on again, they offered to intervene. *You are the one! May we help?*

Davey managed a weak reply. *Yes...please.*

The birds responded with a fierce chorus of caws. They formed an angry triangle as they descended towards Androf, their beaks and claws ready. He heard their harsh cries and terror consumed him. Looking like a rubber-legged clown, he dropped the bat and ran on his feeble legs. He managed to go five feet before he tumbled head-over-heels as the ravens attacked. His sudden fall saved him from certain disaster — only a few of the birds hit their prey. Even so, they left long gashes on his face and hands. Screeching furiously, the ravens swooped upward, readying for another attack.

At that moment, Yong Chow Lee and his men entered the clearing. He ordered his men to spread out and smiled when he saw Androf on his hands and knees. "Androf," he called. "I have come for you."

Androf struggled to his feet, shocked at seeing the three men. He immediately recognized Yong Chow Lee and believed his life was about to end. In desperation, he pointed at Davey. "That is Davey Boehm. I've captured him for you!"

Yong Chow Lee extended a long finger at Androf. "You have caused me a lot of trouble." Then he looked over at the boy who was slowly crawling towards the woods. *What a fortunate coincidence,* he thought; *both Androf and the boy are here.* Without hesitation, he shouted to his men. "Subdue Androf and grab the boy!"

When Davey saw the three men, his mind reeled in confusion. They and their long-barreled pistols seemed even more deadly than the big man attacking him. For some reason, they all appeared to know who he was. He couldn't imagine what they wanted with him. *Is there no end to this?* he wondered, racking his brain for some means of escape.

The ravens immediately realized the threat of the new arrivals. They halted their attack on Androf and dove at the Chinese men instead. At first, the birds caught them by surprise, inflicting pain and making them retreat. Even so, Yong Chow Lee and his men were more dangerous than a severely weakened Androf. They had pistols and were trained marksmen. Soon, the spitting of their silenced weapons filled the air. Five ravens fell to the ground.

Davey's heart sank as he saw the ravens falling from the sky. They were no match for the pistols of the men and he sent them a desperate message. *Leave...you cannot help me now.*

The ravens soared high into the sky, anxiously circling the clearing. They were ready to give their life for the boy and loath to obey.

As Yong Chow Lee watched the ravens, he recalled Androf's story about the birds attacking him. He had thought it was nonsense at the time, but now he wondered. *Perhaps I have misjudged Androf. If he was right about the birds, is he also right about the boy being dangerous?* It seemed ridiculous, yet he motioned to his men. "Surround the boy! When I give the signal, rush him."

Davey watched the Chinese men circling him and tried to summon his magic power. When he felt no answering surge, he knew it was hopeless. Whatever these men wanted, he was powerless to resist. Then he heard the squirrel's voice inside his head. *Ask the Great Sabatini for help.*

Until this moment, the idea had not occurred to him, but he had the hat now, and Yona had said to try using it to speak with his great grandfather's spirit. He looked up at the tree and pictured Antonio's face. *Men came here to harm the tree...now these others are killing the birds. Will you help me stop them?*

At once, the tree's massive limbs began an agitated movement. The loud creeks and groans of the straining wood attracted everyone's attention; they froze briefly, staring in awe at the branches thrashing above their heads. While this sight was somewhat frightening, what happened next was truly dumbfounding. An amber glow spread outward from the massive trunk; it flowed like liquid until it reached the tips of the smallest twigs. Soon, the glow had completely engulfed the tree and its branches ceased their movement.

Yong Chow Lee sensed some sort of unimaginable trouble was coming and shouted new orders at his men. "Shoot Androf, grab the boy, and let's get out of here!"

Androf held up his hands in reckless despair. "Wait – his touch is deadly – let me do it; I know his devious tricks."

At this point, Yong Chow Lee was very alarmed over the strange events unfolding before his eyes. He could not afford to rid himself of any ally, so he decided to give Androf one last chance. "Be quick about it. If you are successful, I will let you live."

Androf picked up the bat and started towards Davey. His legs felt like jelly, but they supported his weight. Li Ssu and Spit backed away from the boy, watching in amusement.

Abruptly, a swirling wind began to blow, picking up leaves and flinging them at the men. As the wind swept through the clearing, an ear-splitting crash came from above their heads. It was the sound of a tremendous force ripping wood apart. The men attacking Davey cowered in disbelief as two enormous limbs tore away from the tree.

Each limb was as big as a normal tree and easily weighed thousands of pounds. The limbs should have plummeted down, yet they rose with grandeur into the air. Yong Chow Lee glanced at Davey and noticed a smile upon his face. *The boy is making this happen*, he thought.

Events happened at lightening speed after that. The two severed limbs circled above the tree, transforming themselves into creatures with raptor-like heads and leafy tail feathers. Four gigantic, bark-covered wings unfolded from their backs and feet with razor-sharp talons emerged from their wooden undersides. As this was happening, a ghostly voice rang out in the clearing. When Davey heard it, he instantly knew the Great Sabatini had indeed returned.

Evil lures you foolish men,
To come here and harm the tree,
Greedy, worthless men of sin,
Oh, how your efforts anger me!

Steal you not my heir away,
Hear my words; begin to cower,
Evil shall not have its day,
Feel instead my magic power!

My heir remains, pure of heart,
Able to confront the beast,
Free he be, his quest to start,
Evil shall not have its feast!

As for you, oh wicked men,
Ye who came for evil's gain,
My mercy, you shall not win,
You will pay the price with pain!

As the voice trailed away, the huge creatures began a slow dive towards the clearing. Their hideous mouths emitted deafening roars and their wings battered the air with sounds like the beating of massive drums. Creaking and groaning as their wooden surfaces strained, their legs reached out.

When Yong Chow Lee saw the creatures coming, he screamed at his men. "Run for the car!" Filled with panic, they streaked towards the west entrance of the park.

Androf turned and headed up the north path, loping clumsily along on his feeble legs. *If I can just reach the van, I can escape,* he thought.

This left Davey and two others in the clearing. The boy had watched the creatures swoop over his head, yet he was not afraid. He had heard the voice of his great grandfather; he was now under his protection. After the creatures zoomed away, a peaceful stillness surrounded the tree. Pulling his cape about his body, Davey closed his eyes for a moment's rest.

Wally was not afraid of the creatures either, but for a decidedly different reason. He lay face up in the pool of muck, his body encased in the coils of the cane. His eyes were open, but his mind wandered in darkness.

The park warden was still unconscious from the effects of Androf's punches. Occasionally he moaned, yet he did not wake up.

ЄꙘЄꙘЄꙘ

Androf almost reached the safety of his van. He burst from the park's entrance just as one of the creatures appeared above his head. When he saw the monster's fierce eyes and snapping jaws, he screamed in terror. Moments later, the creature plucked his body from the ground and carried him high into the air.

As the creature clutched him in its claws, Androf pleaded for mercy. "Don't take me. Ubeck is the one you want…not me…not me." His voice trailed off in the distance as the creature bore him away.

The creature flew over the New River and then released the terrified man. Androf fell ninety feet before he hit the cold waters of the river. The fall broke his legs, but he found a floating log, which kept him from drowning. After clinging to the log for hours, he finally pulled his pain-racked body onto the river's bank. When the police found him the next morning, he was lying there like a beached whale.

ЄꙘЄꙘЄꙘ

Ꙙ 408 ꙅ

Yong Chow Lee and his men ran like terrified rats until they reached their car. The three men huddled inside its interior, unable to comprehend what had happened. Li Ssu sat behind the steering wheel, making no effort to start the engine.

"Idiot! Get us out of here!" Yong Chow Lee finally bellowed.

Li Ssu cranked the engine and pressed the accelerator to the floor. The car leapt away from the curb and roared down the street. Spit stuck his head out a window and looked up at the sky behind them. "One of those creatures is following us," he cried.

As Yong Chow Lee stared out the rear window, the blood drained from his face. The creature was bearing down on them, its amber eyes glowing fiercely. "Faster, it's gaining on us."

Even with its powerful engine, the Lincoln could not outrun the creature. Sabatini magic had created the beast and nothing could thwart its purpose. The huge form landed on the roof of the car and sank its sharp talons into the steel. Then the relentless drumming of its wings lifted the car into the air.

"Shoot it! Shoot it!" Yong Chow Lee yelled.

All three men fired their pistols through the ceiling until they were out of bullets, but they had no effect on the creature's wooden hide. Slowly, it lifted the car high into the sky. Yong Chow Lee opened the rear windows and looked out. He was thinking about jumping until he saw they were two-hundred feet above the ground. The creature turned and headed towards Brown Mountain, the car swinging precariously in the grip of its claws. Occasionally, it let out a thunderous roar; the men screamed at the deafening sound.

Yong Chow Lee thought the creature was going to drop them on the mountain, but when they were over it, the creature slowed. Then it went into a looping dive above a narrow road, which curled along the top of the mountain. "Be ready, the creature is tiring," he said. "If it drops us, hold the wheel firmly and keep it pointed straight. Perhaps, we may survive."

The creature released the car directly above the road at a speed of seventy miles per hour. Li Ssu held the wheel straight as Yong Chow Lee instructed, knowing that even the slightest turn would send the car spinning out of control. It fell a distance of ten feet before the wheels touched the graveled surface. Li Ssu gently tapped the brakes, felt the wheels grab, and grunted with satisfaction.

Yong Chow Lee yelled in triumph as he watched the creature fly away. "We have escaped," he exclaimed, looking at Li Ssu. The joy on his face turned into terror as he glanced through the front windshield. He had seen the road curving sharply thirty yards ahead.

Li Ssu slammed on the brakes, but it was a wasted effort. The car was traveling much too fast to make the curve. When their speed had slowed to forty miles per hour, Yong Chow Lee opened his door and jumped. He rolled like a bowling ball, bouncing off trees and rocks. After his body finally stopped, it lay in a gully alongside the road. He was battered, broken, and unconscious, but still alive.

Li Ssu and Spit were not as fortunate. They stayed in the car and sailed off the mountain like astronauts heading for the moon. Even so, the weight of the engine quickly tuned the car's nose down, and it plunged towards the earth. Four hundred feet below, it hit the side of the mountain and crumpled into a twisted mass of metal. Li Ssu and Spit had only a moment to reflect upon their miserable lives.

സൗൻസൗൻസൗൻ

An hour later, Davey opened his eyes. The moon overhead cast down a peaceful glow on the quiet clearing. He looked up at the tree, surprised to find all of its limbs in place – its majesty fully restored. *Sabatini magic,* he thought with a smile.

Wally still lay in the muck inside the fence, the coils of the dragon-headed cane wrapped around his body. He gave no sign of being aware of anything around him.

Davey walked over to the fence and sent a message to the cane. *Release him and come to me.*

Immediately, the cane resumed its normal shape and flew into his hand. Then Davey willed the earth under Wally's body to assume its natural state, which it quickly did. Wally lay motionless, seemingly unaffected.

Davey was glad his magic power had returned and hurried over to where Joe Harrison lay on the ground. He sent a few soft blasts of icy air across Joe's face and willed for him to wake up. After a few seconds, Joe opened his eyes.

"Are you okay, Mr. Harrison?" he asked with concern.

Joe rubbed his chin and slowly sat up. "Had one heck of a bad dream, but otherwise I feel all right. Where are Wally and the other man?"

Davey pointed to where Wally lay on the ground. "Mr. Houseman is over there. I think he's sick or something. As for the other man, he ran away."

Joe suddenly realized a lot had happened while he was unconscious. He gave Davey a puzzled look. "What are you doing here at this time of night?"

Davey shrugged. "Uh…I came looking for my hat."

Joe stared silently at Davey for a few seconds, his eyes twinkling. "That's your story, huh?"

"Mr. Harrison, it's really complicated. I'm not sure you would believe it."

Joe began to chuckle. "Listen son, I've been around this tree for forty years. I know something magical goes on between it and your family, so I'm not asking more questions. You go on home, and I'll get some help for Wally. He's in a heap of trouble for what he did tonight, that's for sure. When I talk to the police though, I'm not saying a word about you being here."

Davey smiled. "Thank you."

Joe nodded knowingly. "I'm probably the one who should be thanking you. Best as I can tell, you saved my life. You probably saved the Great Oak too, which puts me in your debt. Will you tell me what really happened one of these days?"

Davey grinned. "That's a promise."

❧ Chapter 39 ❧

The Evolution Of Sineous Crop

SINEOUS THRASHED out violently as he slept in the dank cellar of Houseman's Castle. A stabbing pain jolted him every few minutes, yet he slept on. His mind was exploring a dream world filled with shadowy creatures and images of demons. The dream was so alluring that even the pain in his body could not jar him awake.

Three hours before dawn, Sineous finally opened his eyes. He immediately noticed that the changes underway in his body had radically accelerated. The magic energy, which Davey had shot into him, had provided fuel for his final evolution. Steel-like toenails had clawed their way through the leather of his boots, and saw-toothed spines had emerged along his back. In fact, boney spikes and jagged ridges had appeared all along his body, ripping the fabric of his clothes apart.

In fascination, Sineous held his hands before his eyes and marveled at the dagger-like claws protruding from his fingers. His enlarged, pointed ears quivered as he heard every faint sound in the cellar, even the crawling of a beetle ten feet away. With a high-pitched laugh, he studied his new inhuman form. To him, a natural progression was occurring – one that he welcomed.

He pulled off his shredded boots, threw them in a corner, and stood up. A fierce desire consumed him, which he couldn't deny. Leaping silently up the stone steps, he climbed to the fourth floor and entered Wally's study. A dark gloom filled the room; the stuffed animals on the walls seemed to stare at him in shock.

Sineous snarled at their heads as if issuing a challenge. Then he searched through Wally's desk for his stash of black disks. He found six disks in a drawer and placed them around his neck. His long tongue lolled out in pleasure as he felt the icy cold of their evil force rush through his body. Abruptly, another uncontrollable urge came over him. He longed to be free of the confining walls, to be out in the blackness of the night.

With the stealth of a predator, Sineous crept down the stairs and out the front door. The moon had slipped behind dark clouds, but his eyes saw everything with surprising clarity. He ran wildly through the woods and up the hills near the castle. Callused pads of skin protected his feet, and his strange new muscles took him in great leaps across the ground. He lashed out at everything in his way with sweeps of his razor sharp claws.

A small party of deer came wandering through the trees, and Sineous chased them for several miles, howling like a crazed hyena. Three horse-like tails streamed from distinct places on his bald head, one from the center and one above each ear. Their ends beat against his back as he ran, driving him forward. His only emotion was that of brutal savagery. At last, he caught up with the slowest deer and reached out his deadly claws. His arms stretched forward, lengthening of their own accord, and his fingers flexed in anticipation of a kill. However, the deer abruptly zigzagged, and Sineous rammed into a tree instead. Consumed by anger, he forgot the deer and clawed at the tree until its bark was in tatters. Meanwhile, the deer bounded away.

Finally, Sineous grew tired and loped back towards the castle. He looked up at the high walls, hating their confinement. It seemed like a foreign place now. He crept into a thicket of bushes along the front wall and selected a secluded spot. Soon, he curled up like a large animal and fell asleep.

The slamming of a car door woke Sineous several hours later. The sun was rising over the trees, signaling the arrival of morning. He cautiously peered through the bushes and saw two policemen approaching the front door. They rang the doorbell several times and waited patiently until Wally's wife, Nell, opened the door. She greeted the men with a gasp of surprise and then primly pulled her robe around her body.

The older of the two men was Bob Owens, the chief of the town's small police force. He nodded a hello and spoke up immediately. "Sorry for the bad news Nell, but we've got Wally down at the jail. We'd like for you to come with us."

Nell frowned at the men. "What's the old fool done now?"

Bob scratched his head as if embarrassed. "Well, apparently the warden caught him killing the trees in the park last night, but that's only part of it. Wally's had some sort of mental breakdown. We're taking him to the jail in Hickory this afternoon if he doesn't snap out of it; they have a facility for treating people in his condition. We thought you might want to see him first."

Nell hesitated before she replied. "That's just the way Wally is; he acts crazy most of the time," she finally said.

Bob shook his head. "No, this is different – it's like he's in a coma. Doc Holland is examining him as we speak. You might want your own doctor to look at him, and he's going to need an attorney as well."

"Oh, for heavens sake. Just give me a minute to dress," Nell said.

"Wait a second Nell; we'd also like to talk with Sineous. Seeing as how he's Wally's sidekick, we thought he might know something about this."

Nell shouted up the stairs. "Spike, find Sineous and ask him to come down here. And hurry up and get dressed. We're going to the police station. Your *father* is there."

Ten minutes later, both Nell and Spike appeared at the front door, ready to leave. "I looked for Sineous, but he's not around," Spike reported.

Bob nodded. "Come on then. Maybe he'll be back when we return."

Sineous waited until they drove away before he crawled out of the thicket. He had only a vague recollection of what had happened last night. Until the policeman mentioned Wally's name, Sineous hadn't even wondered where he was. Still, Sineous knew one thing for sure. Nobody was putting *him* in jail.

He ran into the house and up the stairs towards his bedroom. While stuffing a few items into a backpack, he glanced at his reflection in a mirror. Although a normal person might have screamed at the hideous image there, Sineous did not. He preened and danced before the mirror, admiring the mottled black and grey surfaces of his skin and the three long tails protruding from his head.

Snarling continuously, he scrambled down to the kitchen and drank a large jug of water. Then he took a raw steak from the refrigerator and gnawed it hungrily. A few minutes later, he left Houseman's Castle, intending never to return. He knew of a place where no one would find him – the cave on Brown Mountain.

ഇൠഇൠഇൠ

Jimmy and Amy were waiting at the bicycle racks when Davey arrived at school. Davey felt terrible; he had a headache, his shoulder hurt, and he had slept for only four hours.

"Bloody heck, you look awful," Jimmy said.

As Amy studied Davey, her intuition came alive. She had seen police in the park on her way to school and had a sneaking suspicion he knew why they were there. "I think you have some explaining to do," she said coolly.

Davey sighed, knowing Jimmy and Amy wouldn't like his story. He started with what Spike had told him about his father killing the

ഇ 415 ൠ

trees and ended with last night's events in the park.

Jimmy frowned after he finished. "Stupid of you to go alone, mate. We're in this together, remember."

"You're lucky you weren't killed," Amy added angrily.

Davey could hardly look at them. "I was just trying to help Spike."

Amy scowled and Davey knew she was furious. "Let's go around the corner where no one can see us," she said, her teeth clenched.

Davey gave Jimmy a questioning glance, but he only nodded towards Amy's departing figure. "Better do as she says; it's the only solution when she's this mad."

Amy was waiting with folded arms when they arrived. "Take off your shirt," she said sharply.

"What?" Davey asked.

Amy stamped her foot impatiently. "Do it! I want to look at your shoulder where the bat hit you. If I say so, you're going to a doctor." Amy had ambitions of being a doctor herself and had a surprising amount of medical knowledge for a thirteen year old.

Jimmy agreed. "Do it, mate."

Davey peeled off his shirt and stood motionless as Amy prodded her fingers at the purplish bruise on his right shoulder. After that, she made him move his arm up and down and watched when he winced at the pain. Finally, she squeezed his shoulder with her hands.

"Go easy will you!" Davey exclaimed. Then he smiled sheepishly, realizing his mistake. "Actually, it doesn't hurt much," he added.

Amy glared into his eyes and shook her finger in his face. "Don't lie to me, Davey Boehm. If you do something stupid like this again, I'm through with you. In the meantime, put on your shirt. You're probably okay, but if your shoulder is not better by tomorrow, you *will* see a doctor. Have I made myself clear?"

"Yes sir," Davey said, managing a feeble smile.

Jimmy had watched their exchange with a glint of amusement in his eyes. When he sensed Amy had calmed down, he cleared his throat. "All right, what should we do now?"

"Let's go see Sequoyah after school and tell him Davey's story,"

Amy said. "Maybe he can look at Davey's shoulder as well."

Jimmy nodded his approval. "Blimey, you've just had two good ideas in a row. My dad also knows a lot about injuries."

Amy glanced at Davey, smiling shyly. "Come on, I'm not letting you out of my sight until then."

Jimmy whispered in Davey's ear as they followed Amy into the school. "You're a lucky bloke, mate. I'd like to have a girlfriend who cares about me that much."

ℰᎧᏒℰᎧᏒℰᎧᏒ

Later that afternoon, the Three of We sat around Sequoyah at the back of the bicycle shop. Davey had just finished a more detailed version of what had happened in the park last night. Earlier, Sequoyah had examined Davey's shoulder and agreed with Amy's opinion – he was probably okay.

"I'm out on a limb here. Your aunt and uncle are my friends and you really should tell them what happened," Sequoyah muttered.

Davey shook his head. "I can't tell them without explaining everything. If I do, they'll think I'm crazy. Who could believe such a story?"

"They might send you away, which is what the evil spirit wants," Jimmy added.

Sequoyah smiled grimly. "The tree sending out flying creatures...I can hardly believe it myself."

"I know, but I saw it happen," Davey replied.

Amy, having thought more about Davey's story, was full of questions. "Who was the big man who attacked you?"

Davey shook his head. "I don't know, but Spike warned me about him. Spike said the man had my hat and was helping Wally kill the trees. He ran away when the flying creatures came."

Amy's questions continued. "Well, who were the men who killed the birds and why did they want to capture you?"

Of course, no one knew the answers, but Sequoyah stated his

Ꮢ 417 Ꭷ

opinion. "It must be as Yona suspected. The evil spirit has summoned others to aid it. Since you thwarted them, at least for the time being, we must hurry before they try again. I will speak with Yona, but we should plan on attacking the spirit this weekend."

Davey sighed. "I'm too tired to think anymore. I'm going home."

Sequoyah looked at Amy and Jimmy after he left. "Davey has a good heart and tries to help everyone. This is a virtue, but it may be clouding his judgment. Yona and I think the evil spirit has targeted him. You must be diligent and watch over him like a hawk."

ഐറെ ഐറെ ഐറെ

That night, Davey went to bed early. He was very tired, yet he thought about the tree and asked it to send him another dream message. Several hours later, he woke up bathed in sweat. The vivid images of a dream lingered in his mind.

His dream was similar to the previous one, but different because Amy, Jimmy, and Spike were also in it. They were flying in the wagon and shouting at each other as the cloud of black spots descended upon them. Once again, he felt the cloud swarming around him like a hive of angry bees.

A relentless buzzing accompanied the cloud, so violently loud and angry it seemed inside Davey's head. Suddenly, the force of the cloud pushed the wagon down. Davey heard Spike yell, "it's the hat…it's the hat," and Amy screamed as the ground rushed towards them. Then the buzzing was gone and the wagon swooped up, leaving the cloud behind. When Davey thought about the dream the next day, he felt as if Spike had saved them.

ഐറെ ഐറെ ഐറെ

Meanwhile, Bob Owens and his small police force were busier than they had been in fifteen years. They had found Androf on the banks of the New River and placed him under arrest after Joe Harrison said

ഐ 418 രെ

that he was the man helping Wally kill the trees. When questioned, Androf said nothing, not even his name. The police took him to the hospital, where surgeons operated on his broken legs. According to them, he wouldn't be walking for a long time, if ever again.

Then Bob and his fellow officers began investigating the car, which had driven off Brown Mountain during the night. They had previously discovered Yong Chow Lee's body alongside the road and taken him to the hospital as well. He was badly injured and babbling incoherently about a hideous creature, which led them to conclude he had taken some kind of mind-altering drug. They also removed the bodies of Li Ssu and Spit from the car and sent them to the morgue. As they probed through the wreckage, they learned several confounding things; a hundred bullet holes were in the roof and spent shell casings littered the inside of the car.

Bob scratched his head when he saw the car's roof looking like a piece of Swiss cheese. "What the heck were they shooting at?" he wondered aloud.

Bob was not a believer in coincidence. He felt like everything would eventually tie together in some way, so he placed a guard outside of Yong Chow Lee's hospital room to prevent his escape. Of course, this wasn't likely since the Chinese man was nearly dead. He also issued a warrant for the arrest of Sineous Crop, who had mysteriously disappeared. Then Bob did something, which helped unravel the mystery. He took pictures of Androf and Yong Chow Lee and circulated them around town. The next day, he received some surprising answers.

Alice Silversmith came forward and identified Androf as Andy Tennison, a nice man who lived in her garage apartment. Bob and his officers searched the apartment and found an odd collection of items. Many were on a list of things recently stolen from a house in Hickory. This prompted Bob's officers to take their pictures of Androf around to Alice's neighbors. Ed Nolen astonished everyone by identifying him as a war criminal from Serbia.

Bob was shocked and confused; he contacted the FBI and asked for help. They came swooping into Great Oak, providing many sordid details about Androf. In the meantime, Bob had run the fingerprints of the three men from the wrecked car through the national database of known felons. He was even more alarmed when the report came back; they were part of an international network of criminals. Somehow, his peaceful little town had become a hotbed of crime.

Bob gladly let the FBI take over at this point. He even told them about Wally's involvement with the notorious Galabonis, just in case they were part of whatever was going on. Then he and his fellow officers went back to patrolling the streets and handing out parking tickets. Nevertheless, Bob stayed alert. One never knew when another crime spree would begin.

₧)(₧₧)(₧₧)(₧

The Three of We met with Sequoyah at the bicycle shop two days later. Sequoyah had talked with Yona, and as expected, he had expressed concern over what had happened. They were in unanimous agreement. The attack on the spirit should proceed without delay.

Davey reported his shoulder was healing, but neither Amy nor Sequoyah was satisfied until they examined him. Finally, they both nodded – his shoulder was definitely okay. Then Davey told them about his latest dream.

"What do you think it means?" Amy asked.

"I've given it a lot of thought; I think the tree is telling us to bring Spike along when we attack the spirit," Davey replied.

"I ain't crazy about the idea," Jimmy grumbled.

"He hasn't been at school since his father was arrested," Amy added.

"Yeah, I know, so I think Amy and I should go see him. She can wear the wisdom scarf and we can ask him questions about the cave. If he answers them truthfully, then I think we should ask him to join us. It will give him a way to make up for the bad things his father has done."

Sequoyah frowned, not liking the idea either. "Wally has been put in a mental ward over in Hickory. They say he's in bad shape; Spike could have his hands full just dealing with that."

Amy saw the worried look on Sequoyah's face. *Protecting Davey from himself isn't easy,* she thought. Even so, she didn't want to disappoint Davey. "The tree hasn't let us down yet, so I think we should try Davey's suggestion," she finally said.

One hour later, Davey and Amy knocked on the door of Houseman's Castle. While they waited, Davey stared at the mildewed walls of the decrepit old structure. "What a gloomy place to live," he muttered, just as Nell Houseman opened the door.

"Amy Pigeon...what a surprise," Nell said pleasantly. "I was just talking to your father earlier. I've asked him to help me run the furniture factory for a while. Actually, it was Spike's idea."

Amy gave Davey a meaningful glance and smiled. "Uh...we came to see Spike, if that's okay. We're on the Scholar's Team together and he hasn't been at school. We're worried about him."

"He'll be glad you came. We're sorting through things, you know, figuring out what to do with the big mess on our hands. He's on the back porch."

Amy motioned towards Davey. "By the way, this is Davey Boehm."

Nell seemed startled for a moment. "Come in Davey, Spike has mentioned you."

Spike was sitting in a chair when they arrived, but he looked away when he saw their faces. They sat down beside him and said nothing for a few seconds.

"Are you okay?" Amy finally asked.

Spike nodded, yet remained silent.

"I'm sorry about your dad. It didn't turn out like I hoped," Davey said.

Spike rose from his chair, walked to the railing, and stared out at the hills behind the castle. Then he turned and looked at Davey. "I knew it was a lost cause. I'm not blaming you for anything, but will you tell me what happened?"

Davey glanced over at Amy and she nodded slightly. Spike was telling the truth – so far. Davey looked him in the eyes. "Can I ask you something first? Will you tell us about the spirit in the cave?"

He seemed stunned by the question. "You know about the spirit?"

"We know a lot, but we need to learn more. It's important; that's why I'm asking."

Spike replied without hesitation. "I have never seen the spirit or been inside the cave, but my father has. He was always talking about it. The spirit is some sort of an evil force. It doesn't like heat and only comes near the mouth of the cave in winter. Its power lies in the way it can affect a person's mind. It has influenced my family for almost a century, making us stupid with meanness and greed. I'd destroy it if I knew how."

Once again, Davey saw Amy nod, so he continued. "If I tell you why we are asking, will you keep it between us?"

Spike didn't conceal his curiosity, but he agreed. "Sure, why not?"

"Amy, Jimmy, and I are going to attack it this weekend. We want you to join us," Davey said quietly.

Spike's response was immediate. "The spirit is dangerous and very powerful. It can twist your mind and make you become its slaves. Look at what it has done to the Housemans."

Amy rose from her chair. "It is a quest, which we are fated to undertake. Our strength lies in our just purpose, and we have the magic of the Sabatinis on our side."

A wistful smile flashed across Spike's face. "Are you serious?"

"You could say…we're deadly serious," Davey replied.

Spike suddenly laughed. "In that case, count me in."

Amy laughed as well. "Let's get comfortable. Davey has a lot to tell you, and it's a very long story."

☙ Chapter 40 ❧

Heed my words, oh fierce magician.
Thou shalt have no finer purpose than
the banishment of evil.

— Translated from Storia Di Incanto; circa 1904

The Battle Begins

DAVEY STOOD at the precipice on Greyhead Mountain, frowning at the gloomy sky. An ominous layer of clouds lingered overhead; a cold wind blew against his face. Amy came up behind him and silently took his hand. He was almost a head taller than she was now, and he solemnly looked down into her eyes.

"Can you fly the wagon in this weather?" she whispered, not wanting Jimmy or Spike to overhear.

Davey gave her hand a squeeze. "Yes, we will do it together."

"Something is troubling you – what is it?"

Davey looked away, his eyes focusing on the vast open space between them and Brown Mountain. "Aunt Sally talked with my mom yesterday; my parents are returning from China. They'll be here next week, and then we'll go back to New York. I didn't want to come here in the first place. Now, I don't want to live anywhere else."

Amy was only thirteen, but she had spent a lot of time thinking about her relationship with Davey. She reached up and touched his face, forcing him to look at her. "Remember what you said when my father quit his job? You told me that something would work out, and it did. So…let me tell you what I believe. You and I were destined to meet; our lives became intertwined from that moment on, and they will stay that way forever."

Davey smiled, taking comfort in her words. "Yes, and we are fated to kill the evil spirit, so let's go do it."

Jimmy and Spike stood twenty yards away, admiring the magic wagon. It no longer was just a carnival wagon; it had become a flying fortress. Yona and the villagers had fastened pointed spikes on the top and sides of the wagon, giving it the appearance of a bristling porcupine. They had made the spikes from branches of the Great Oak to increase the wagon's protective aura.

Davey had used his magic to make some changes in the wagon too. He had created three windows on each side and opened a foot-wide slot across the wall behind the driver's bench. The windows enabled those inside the wagon to look out and throw spears. The slot allowed for the passage of weapons to those on the driver's bench. He had done this without knowing where the ultimate battle would occur. However, if his dreams were right, it might be in the sky.

Yona pounded his staff on the rocky surface of the precipice and motioned for the wagon's four passengers to gather around him. He studied them for a minute and then gave a satisfied nod to Sequoyah, who was standing nearby. At his signal, Sequoyah pulled Spike in front of the chief.

Spike was in awe of the old chief and glanced timidly at him. Yona smiled in return. "I have not performed the naming ceremony for you. We will do it upon your return, but you should know your Cherokee name in the meantime. You are as big as a mountain and you have willingly become a brother warrior. I name you Unvdatlvi Udo!"

Sequoyah translated the words. "It means *Mountain Brother*."

Spike smiled broadly and returned to his place alongside Jimmy. Then Yona called out the Cherokee names of the four warriors and lauded their courage for undertaking a legendary quest. He stepped before each individual, Davey *Little Wolf* Boehm, Jimmy *Strong*

Arrow Surefoot, Amy *Owl With Panther's Eyes* Pigeon, and Spike *Mountain Brother* Houseman. His keen eyes looked into their faces as he whispered words of encouragement. He concluded by engulfing each in a tight embrace and asking the Great Spirit to watch over them.

After Yona finished, Sequoyah instructed the four warriors to line up facing the wagon. Then the Ani-Wodi priests opened several large baskets and took out the armor, which they had woven from the branches and bark of the Great Oak. Their singing voices rose above the wind as they prayed over the pieces and then placed them gravely on the warriors.

When they had completed their tasks, each warrior wore protective plates on their feet, legs, arms, chests, and backs. All but one wore a woven bark helmet with ear flaps and a leather chinstrap. The exception was Davey, who tucked his helmet under his arm, but kept on his magic hat.

Then Elogi Ugithisa stepped forward and painted red war paint on their faces. As she did, her priests sang the battle song and marched around them. Yona and Sequoyah joined in, doing the traditional stomp dance and adding their own animal-like growls. At last, one of the priests handed Elogi Ugithisa a braided leather rope. Attached to one end of the coiled-up rope was a long and intricately carved arrow.

Elogi Ugithisa offered the rope and arrow to Jimmy with an explanation. "Last week, the spirits sent me a dream. In my dream, many braves were fighting a huge wild boar. They were losing until one brave shot an arrow attached to a rope. The arrow pierced the boar's hide, and the rope became entangled in the animal's legs, allowing the braves to kill it. After Yona heard about my dream, he carved this arrow from a branch of the tree, and I boiled the rope for three days in a broth of the tree's leaves. They have the power of the tree's sap in them now."

Jimmy bowed respectfully as he took the weapon. "We thank you for your gifts and blessings."

Sequoyah cleared his throat, fighting to keep tears from forming in his eyes. He hoped Jimmy and his friends weren't undertaking an impossible task. "We put the newly made spears and arrows into the back of the wagon," he said stiffly.

As Davey surveyed his team, he thought they looked magnificent. Only one final task remained. Amy had finished her translation of the magic books, and she and Davey had selected four spells for their armor. Davey had no experience in casting spells, but he followed the book's instructions and cast them anyway.

The books prescribed a specific image for a spell, which the caster formed in his mind and transferred to his target by touch. Davey chose the concentration spell for his armor, the fortitude spell for Amy's armor, the agility spell for Jimmy's armor, and the insight spell for Spike's armor. Each time, he felt a slight tingling in his fingertips, making him think that he had been successful.

"All right, let's get into the wagon," he finally said. "I want Jimmy beside me, and Amy and Spike inside."

Amy felt a slight disappointment. She wanted to sit with Davey, but she knew he was right. Jimmy needed to be up front so Davey could direct the path of his arrows. "Let's go over the plan again," she said.

Davey nodded in agreement. "First, we'll inspect the cave from the air. Next, I'll send the dragon-headed cane in and let its eyes show me what's there. If it's safe, we'll land the wagon and enter the cave. Then I'll shoot fireballs in front of us, driving the spirit into the cave's furthest recess. After we have it cornered, we'll destroy it with a hail of arrows, spears, and fire."

"There's a ledge in front of the cave where the wagon can land," Spike added.

"Okay, let's get aboard," Davey exclaimed, adjusting his hat so that it fit tightly on his head.

Sequoyah had installed seat belts for those sitting on the driver's bench; Davey and Jimmy fastened them around their waists. Amy and Spike were free to roam inside the wagon; they stood at the windows, brandishing their spears. Jimmy put his quiver of arrows across his shoulder and held his bow tightly. Davey focused his mind, and the wagon rose from the precipice. Then it soared into the sky alongside the mountain.

Immediately, a strong gust of wind caught the wagon and bore it upward. Davey concentrated on keeping the wagon level and let the wind carry it along, not fighting the strong currents.

Jimmy looked down and saw Greyhead Mountain rapidly growing smaller beneath them. "Not too high, mate. This ain't no airplane," he cautioned.

"Just getting the feel of it," Davey replied, slowly bringing the nose of the wagon down and angling it towards Brown Mountain. The force of the wind decreased as they went lower, and Davey found that controlling the wagon was easy. While the new spiked branches had made the wagon heavier, the magic in their sap added lifting power.

Before long, Davey could clearly see the jagged cliffs of Brown Mountain. Spike and Amy peered out the windows, and then Spike pointed towards a black spot two thirds of the way up the mountain. "There it is," he shouted. "That's the cave!"

Davey veered left, and the black opening of the cave slowly grew larger as they approached. Jimmy reached over his shoulder, pulled an arrow from his quiver, and notched it into his bowstring. When they were twenty feet above the cave, Davey let the wagon float alongside the mountain. As they peered down at their destination, a sense of dread filled their minds.

The cave was located in the side of a narrow cliff, which jutted out from the mass of the mountain. The cliff rose above the cave for fifty feet and then abruptly sheered off. A narrow trail led from above the cliff to a fifteen-foot wide ledge, which protruded in front of the cave. The mouth of the cave wasn't large, just big enough to permit a normal-sized person to enter. Its dark opening was so obscure, their eyes couldn't penetrate a single foot into its gloomy interior.

Two days ago, the Three of We had asked Spike to recall everything his father had said about the cave. Unfortunately, he knew very little, but they had learned the mouth of the cave opened into a small cavern thirty feet across. At the rear of this cavern, a narrow tunnel wound back into another cavern three times as large. The second cavern is where they would most likely find the spirit.

Now, as they looked down at the cave, an ominous sight suddenly appeared. Sineous Crop stalked from the mouth of the cave, dragging the half-eaten carcass of a small deer. His hideous features made him resemble a monster from a nightmare. Taken completely by surprise, Amy let out a terrified gasp.

Sineous didn't notice the wagon floating high above his head until his sensitive ears heard Amy's muffled cry. With a quick craning of his neck, he glared up at her face. His mouth opened in astonishment and his long black tongue snaked out. To him, the wagon looked like a gigantic flying insect – one meaning him harm. He angrily tossed the deer's carcass aside, fixed his eyes on the wagon, and snarled ferociously.

"Bloody heck, what's that thing?" Jimmy exclaimed.

Amy cried out in horror. "It must be the spirit – shoot it!"

Jimmy glanced quickly at Davey and saw his nod of approval. He pulled back the bowstring, leaned over the side of the wagon, and took aim at the creature.

As Spike looked down, a sudden insight flashed into his mind. Something was very familiar about the inhuman form – the shape of its head. "Wait!" he yelled. "Don't shoot...I think it's Sineous."

Spike's words startled Davey so completely his concentration was briefly broken. This made the wagon lurch sideways and abruptly drop down. Davey quickly focused his mind and brought the wagon under control, but now it floated parallel to the ledge where Sineous stood. Fifteen feet of open space separated them from the creature.

Sineous's eyes narrowed to yellow slits, and he flexed his razor-sharp claws in anticipation. He had lived with the spirit for almost a week; its evil had consumed him. Memories of his former life were completely gone – his only desire was to attack and destroy.

"Talk to him. Call out his name," Davey shouted, thinking they were far enough away from the horrible creature to be safe.

Spike stuck his head through one of the wagon's windows. "Sineous…it's Spike. Can you hear me? Give me a sign if it's you."

Sineous's reaction was immediate. He stooped into a low crouch and sprang at the wagon, roaring like a beast. His movements were so incredibly fast and powerful, Davey was unprepared for the suddenness of his attack. He desperately backed the wagon away from the cliff, but Sineous had been too quick. His body was clinging to the front of the wagon before it moved an inch, his claws digging into the skeletal frame of branches at the bow.

Davey quickly pointed the nose of the wagon up, and it shot high into the open sky. The upward acceleration flattened Sineous against the skeletal frame of branches under the wagon, and a spontaneous chemical reaction occurred as his tainted skin encountered their aura. Wherever his body touched them, his flesh burned as if branded by a hot iron.

Sineous howled in pain and scrambled up the front of the wagon like an angry spider. Soon, he appeared in front of Jimmy's shocked face. Jimmy quickly drew back his bow and loosed an arrow, but Sineous moved with tremendous speed. He made a grasshopper-like leap over Jimmy's head, and the arrow passed beneath his body.

Jimmy frantically twisted around, trying for another shot. However, Sineous had measured his leap perfectly. He came down on the back part of the wagon's roof where Jimmy couldn't easily see him. Unfortunately, Sineous hadn't noticed the spiked tree branches, which protruded from the roof's surface. As he landed, one of the long spikes pierced through his left arm, nearly severing it from his body.

Sineous wailed in agony, impaled on the spike for a moment as its magic power burned through him. Angrily, he pulled free and flattened his body against the roof. From a gaping hole in his arm, a gooey black liquid flowed down. When the drops splattered on the roof, they boiled into ashes and blew away in the wind.

Amy heard the sounds of Sineous on the roof and shouted an alarm. She grabbed her spear and stood at the center window, her head craning out; Spike stood opposite her, looking out the other side. They didn't see Sineous sneaking his right hand through a window behind them until it was too late.

The clawed hand grabbed Amy by her ponytail, yanking her backwards. Amy screamed in panic, dropping her spear as Sineous pulled her towards the window. She grabbed onto the window frame and held on desperately, but her body was halfway through in a matter of seconds. As she looked down at the ground a thousand feet below, she screamed again, knowing that she was about to die.

Hearing Amy's screams, Spike immediately turned and stabbed his spear through the arm dragging her out the window. Sineous released her with a howl of pain, and Spike quickly grabbed Amy's feet; she hung in the air for a moment until Spike hauled her back inside. They tumbled down together as Sineous flapped his arm about on the roof, the imbedded spear searing his flesh.

Amy staggered up and looked into Spike's eyes. "You just saved my life," she muttered.

At this point, Sineous was almost helpless. Both of his arms wouldn't function and he was quickly becoming aware of another problem; his feet were burning. Many years ago, The Great Sabatini had painted the wagon with a varnish made from the tree's sap. The magic power of the varnish was undiminished, and its aura was roasting Sineous like a goose over red-hot coals. He hopped about on burning feet as smoke poured from the pores of his skin. The frantic movements caused his razor-sharp toenails to tear deep gashes in the roof of the wagon. Encouraged, he began a rapid pawing on the roof, hoping to create an opening large enough for him to drop inside.

Amy saw the wood ripping apart above her head and cried out. "He's tearing holes in the roof."

"Use your spear on his feet," Spike shouted, jabbing his spear through the long gashes that Sineous was creating. Amy followed suit, nicking Sineous on the foot several times.

In desperation, Sineous backed into a far corner of the roof where the spears couldn't reach him and fixed his eyes on Davey. He instinctively knew Davey controlled the flying insect, which was slowly stinging him to death. Moreover, he was getting hotter by the minute. While he could no longer use his arms, his legs and feet still functioned and his dagger-like toenails worked perfectly. With the cunning of an animal, he decided to jump on Davey with his feet, cutting him to ribbons with his toes and destroying the insect in the process. Sineous timed his leap and soared high into the air.

Suddenly, the hand of fate intervened; a strong gust of wind made the wagon swerve unexpectedly. Davey let the wind take it, exaggerating the swerve by turning the wagon in a circle. Of course, this completely surprised Sineous. When he came down from his leap, the wagon was not where it was supposed to be. He not only missed Davey, he missed the wagon entirely. He snarled angrily as he somersaulted towards the earth, leaving a faint trail of black smoke behind. After hitting the rocks a thousand feet below, he exploded into a fiery cloud.

Davey circled the wagon for a few minutes as he and his band of warriors regained their senses. *Are we crazy to be doing this?* Davey wondered. *What if there are more of those creatures?* The thought made him shudder.

Amy finally broke the silence. "Come on; let's head back towards the cave. That was probably the worst of it."

"Bloody heck, I hope so. That was one mean and ugly dude," Jimmy exclaimed.

Amy looked at Spike. "Do you still think it was Sineous?"

"Yes…I saw my father's black disks hanging from his neck."

"How did he become such a horrible creature?"

Spike sadly shook his head. "I don't know."

Davey slowly turned the wagon towards the cave. "We'll go back, but if we see any more creatures like him, we're leaving."

"If we can fight them on the ground, you won't have to concentrate on flying the wagon. Then you can use your magic against them," Spike said.

Davey nodded silently, hoping he was right.

∾ Chapter 41 ∾

Yea, though darkness surround thee, hold steadfast to thy just purpose. Fate shall favor the pure of heart.

— Translated from Storia Di Incanto; circa 1910

The Cave Of Evil

AFTER THEIR TERRIFYING experience with Sineous, Davey approached the cave more cautiously. He kept the wagon floating sixty feet from the cliff as he and his team studied the cave, searching for signs of additional creatures. Twenty minutes passed, yet nothing appeared on the ledge or at the mouth of the cave. Finally, Davey sent his dragon-headed cane inside the cave. He wanted to know if anything was lurking near the entrance before landing the wagon.

The cane changed into a sleek dragon with four feathery wings and a spiked tail that whipped about as it flew. The three-foot long dragon circled the wagon with flames pouring from its mouth before streaking into the cave, as if enjoying the astonished stares of the four warriors.

Davey had expected the cane to become the serpent-like beast, which had restrained Wally in the clearing. Nevertheless, he was gradually learning that the cane's unique power allowed it to take many different forms.

"Wow," Spike muttered, shaking his head in amazement. "My dad had the cane for years, yet he never knew it was magical."

"How does it know what to do?" Amy asked.

"I send it mental commands and it lets me see through its eyes as it carries them out," he replied. Then he concentrated on the cane, which had now entered the cave.

The magic hat enhanced Davey's inner vision, and images flashed before his eyes as if he was with the dragon. He kept part of his mind focused on making the wagon stay afloat and part on what the dragon was seeing. His magic skill had increased dramatically over the last week, allowing him to perform these concurrent tasks easily.

The mouth of the cave opened onto a dark cavern, thirty feet across and equally as high. Stalactites hung above the opening like the teeth of a huge monster, dripping a black and slimy liquid. Farther along, more stalactites appeared along the domed roof, coated by the same slime. As the dragon flew, its fiery breath reflected around the stone surfaces of the cave. Everything was wet, slimy, and black as night.

Davey directed the cane to shoot fire at the vile coating on one of the tooth-like stalactites. When the fire touched the odd formation, it burst quickly into flames, burned briefly, and then shattered and fell towards the floor. Unaffected, the cane continued on its way until it reached the end of the chamber.

As the cane approached the opening of the tunnel leading towards the second cavern, Davey saw a fluid shadow retreating into its depths. It was a strangely shifting shape, so incredibly black it stood out against the surrounding rock. Numerous yellow eyes glared menacingly from inside the black form, sending a shiver along Davey's spine. *How very odd,* he thought.

Jimmy noticed Davey trembling. "Any sign of the spirit, mate?"

"I think I just saw it," Davey replied, trying not to sound alarmed.

His companions stared at him in anxious silence, waiting for him to continue. When he did not, Amy shouted impatiently. "Well…what was it like?"

Davey shrugged, briefly lost for words. "I barely saw it, but it gave me the creeps. It was a black and shapeless thing with yellow eyes; it went, or rather flowed, into the tunnel towards the rear cavern."

Amy frowned at his description. "What do you mean by flowed?"

"It was sort of like a dense liquid floating in the air."

Spike nodded gravely. "That's how my dad described it, but he never saw it up close. He said it was magnificent, but I think he actually feared it."

"Did you see any more creatures like the one that attacked us?" Jimmy asked.

"No, but I'm still searching," Davey replied, turning his attention to the cane again. He instructed it to circle the cavern and probe every nook and cranny. To his relief, he saw no other creatures and the spirit didn't reappear. Finally, he ordered the cane to keep watch over the tunnel while he landed the wagon. As it settled on the ledge outside the cave, he turned towards his team. "The front cavern is empty. Does anyone have any last minute thoughts before we go in?"

"I'm ready," Jimmy said.

Amy nodded. "I'm ready too."

"Ditto," said Spike.

Davey looked at them with grim determination. "There's some type of slime coating everything. It seems flammable, so I'm going to set it on fire before we enter. Maybe it will burn off."

The four warriors left the wagon and silently carried their weapons towards the cave, each lost in their own thoughts. When they had gathered outside the cave's entrance, Davey extended his arm towards them. They clasped their hands with his in a silent moment of friendship – their quest was beginning.

Davey summoned the cane out of the cave as he and Amy crouched at the opening. Then she projected the beam of a large flashlight into the interior while he shot a steady stream of fireballs inside. Immediately, they heard the sound of flames erupting. Soon, acrid smoke began to billow from the entrance. They moved away from the opening and waited until the smoke dwindled to a wisp. Finally, Davey sent the cane inside for another look.

The fire had done tremendous damage; stalactites had shattered and fallen from the ceiling, littering the floor with chunks of burning rock. In most places, the slimy liquid had burned away, but flames still flared from the pitted ceiling where the stalactites had been. Davey kept the cane circling the cavern, while they waited for it to cool off.

Thirty minutes later, the four warriors cautiously entered the cave. Amy immediately pointed at where a fiery glow appeared deep inside the cracks and crevices of the rock over their heads. "Look…the cliff is burning above us."

"Yeah, and it stinks in here," Jimmy added.

Davey had been the top student in chemistry class last year and realized the noxious smell posed a threat. "We should check the air as we move forward. These rocks are porous; some kind of volatile chemical has seeped into them."

Amy thought about this for a second and then spoke. "Remember what Yona said about the spirits choosing sanctuaries where they could obtain nourishment from the earth. Maybe the chemical is what nourishes this spirit."

Amy's remark gave Davey an idea. "If we keep burning it, the spirit might die."

Spike nodded. "Yes, but fire consumes the air we breathe as well."

Amy scooped up a handful of dust and tossed it into the air. In the beam of her flashlight, it slowly drifted towards the mouth of the cave. "There's a faint breeze, so air must be entering the cave from another opening."

Spike shook his head. "There's no other entrance. My dad and Sineous searched all over the cliff for one."

"It doesn't have to be a big opening. I've been inside caves where air flows in through narrow crevices between the rocks," Jimmy said.

Davey motioned them forward. "We'll be okay as long as there's fresh air, but I won't start any more fires until we're sure."

"Watch the person beside you and sound off if you feel faint," Spike added.

They hurried across the cavern towards the tunnel. When they arrived, Amy flashed her light inside. Davey noticed the black slime had not permeated the rock walls, which was a relief. As a test, he shot flame into the tunnel and was glad when nothing caught fire. This meant he could shoot fire ahead of them, forcing the spirit back into the rear cavern; they wouldn't have to confront it in the tunnel's narrow space.

Davey sent the cane ahead and watched through its eyes as it inched along. He saw no creatures or shadowy forms and motioned them forward. Amy stayed near Davey, the beam of her flashlight lighting the way. Jimmy and Spike came last, holding their weapons ready.

The tunnel was narrow and winding at first, and so spooky their nerves tingled like taut wires. They could only proceed in single file, which increased their growing anxiety. Davey kept the cane in front of them, watching diligently through its eyes. The air became noticeably cooler, yet they didn't feel lightheaded. Moreover, they didn't detect the chemical smell present in the front cavern.

After a few minutes, they reached a straight section and Davey's necklace began an abrupt vibration. He saw nothing through the eyes of the cane, yet another hideous creature suddenly appeared ten-feet ahead. The creature was identical to Sineous, its mouth open in a terrifying snarl and its claws flexing as it barred the way. Immediately, Jimmy shot three arrows at the creature, but they passed through its body without effect.

"It's another Sineous – run for it," Spike yelled.

Davey, Jimmy, and Spike retreated, but Amy held her ground, her wisdom scarf emitting a putrid smell. "It can't be Sineous; we saw him die," she exclaimed, surprisingly calm.

Davey didn't understand why Amy wasn't retreating. "Come on Amy, get back."

"Wait…the scarf says it's a lie. It must be an illusion, one sent by the spirit to frighten us. If we're not afraid, I think it will go away."

Hoping Amy was right, the four warriors put forth a bold front, even though they were trembling inside. Sure enough, the creature faded as it came forward, disappearing completely before it reached them. Davey noticed a faint buzzing in his head and felt a slight disorientation, but the feeling passed quickly.

"Bloody heck, that was scary," Jimmy muttered.

"The way you faced that thing – it was really brave," Spike said.

Davey smiled and squeezed Amy's hand. "Good job."

They bolstered their courage and went forward again. At last, they rounded a bend and noticed the tunnel widening. "I think we're coming to the rear cavern," Davey said. As Amy sent the beam of her flashlight ahead, he suddenly frowned. "Uh oh, we've got company again."

Standing at the mouth of the cavern was a huge monster. It had the posture of a lion crouched on four stout legs. Black fur, streaked with yellow stripes, covered its body, and three thick necks protruded above its powerful shoulders. Perched at the end of each neck was an alligator-like head with four yellow eyes and a snapping jaw. The thick tail of a scorpion arched across its back as it prepared to attack.

Jimmy turned towards Amy. "Please say that's an illusion."

Amy shrieked in dismay. "No, it's the real deal. Shoot it!"

Jimmy immediately fired his arrows at the monster. In response, it let out a tremendous roar and streaked down the tunnel towards them. Meanwhile, Davey urgently gave the cane new orders. *Keep it away from us.*

The cane responded by assuming a completely new form. It shaped its body into a steel-like grate and magically attached itself to the walls of the tunnel in front of them. Foot-long spikes protruded from the grate, emitting an amber glow.

Jimmy hit the vile creature with more than a dozen arrows before it reached the grate. Each arrow weakened it, yet the monster's three heads snarled and snapped at the grate without retreating. Davey tried coating the monster with ice, but it was unaffected.

"If it was made by the spirit, only heat will harm it," Spike shouted.

Davey could hardly hear Spike's voice over the roaring of the monster; a fierce buzzing had also started inside his head, further hindering his concentration. Even so, he followed Spike's advice and shot hot steam at the creature's body. High-pitched screams came from its three mouths and it doubled its attack on the grate. Sparks filled the air, as the spikes tore away small pieces of the monster's flesh.

Although Davey felt like his head was splitting, he continued to shoot steam, gradually boiling the monster alive. Jimmy fired more arrows, and the monster's three heads looked like pincushions as they darted about, seeking a weak spot in the grate. Then Spike threw a spear, which pierced through one of the monster's three brains, and it fell sideways, unable to maintain its equilibrium.

At that point, the battle was all but won. Then a curious thing happened; instead of dying, the remains of the monster became a fluid mass of black spots and fled towards the rear cavern.

"What's going on? My arrows are laying in the tunnel," Jimmy exclaimed.

"I think the spirit created that thing to test us," Amy said.

"I thought you said it *wasn't* an illusion," Jimmy replied.

"It was real all right. When it couldn't hurt us, it retreated."

Spike nodded in agreement. "We should be ready; it will probably try again with something else."

Davey said nothing during this exchange. His teammates were apparently unaffected during the battle, yet he had felt as if his brain was about to explode. "Did any of you feel a buzzing inside your head?" he finally asked.

They shook their heads, staring at him with concern.

"Well, I did," said Davey, thinking that he should be very careful from now on. Then he instructed the cane to resume its dragon-like form. "Come on; let's see if we can reach the cavern before another attack."

"The cane saved our lives," Jimmy said, picking up his arrows.

Ever so slowly, they crept forward until they were crouched together at the entrance of the cavern. They had plenty of room now, so Jimmy and Spike took positions alongside Amy and Davey. At Davey's signal, Amy flashed the beam of her flashlight into the opening, and he sent the cane inside with its mouth spouting flame.

They stared in astonishment at the sight before their eyes. The cavern was a vast chamber, fifty yards across with a vaulted sixty-foot ceiling. But it wasn't the uncluttered space they had expected. Black columns stood everywhere, formed over the centuries by stalactites joining with stalagmites. The columns were so close together and numerous that they formed a jagged maze stretching throughout the cavern. The black liquid covered everything, and its noxious stench wafted into their nostrils again.

"It's like looking at a stone forest," Amy whispered.

Spike nodded. "An icy forest – feel how cold the air is."

"Those columns are everywhere. They're so tightly formed; it could take us hours to get through." Jimmy muttered.

Spike suddenly grabbed Davey's arm. "Look, there are pools of that slime all over the floor. Maybe the spirit lured us here...maybe it plans to attack us when we get separated in the columns or our feet become stuck."

"Blimey, we'll be sitting ducks and the cane will be unable to protect us like it did in the tunnel," Jimmy exclaimed.

The image made Davey shudder. He was reluctant to enter the cavern after what had happened in the tunnel anyway. "Our other choice is to burn it."

Jimmy grinned. "Go for it. Maybe we'll incinerate the spirit too."

Amy agreed. "I can still feel the breeze, so maybe the smoke will escape through the cliff above us."

"We should be ready to retreat if it doesn't," Spike replied.

"Hurry up and do it before another creature attacks," Jimmy urged.

Amy held her arms out and spoke shakily. "I've got goose bumps."

Davey summoned the cane back and then took a deep breath. "Well, here goes," he said, shooting a powerful stream of fire from his fingers. The fire swept through the cavern like a flamethrower. One by one, the columns ignited, spreading the fire to the vaulted ceiling. Beyond the flames, Davey saw a shadowy form flowing towards the rear of the cavern. It moved by expanding and contracting, one minute a huge black cloud, the next a compact and incredibly dense shape. Imbedded in its opaque surface were hundreds of yellow eyes.

"I see the spirit – it's retreating," Jimmy exclaimed.

Amy nodded. "It's heading for the ceiling in the back; it's trying to get away from the flames."

Davey was anxiously watching the ceiling for a different reason. "I think we should get out of here," he said, pointing to where it was glowing like hot coals.

"Wait…I want to see where the spirit goes," Jimmy said.

They watched as the flames spread at an alarming rate. A few seconds later, a series of small explosions along the ceiling blew pieces of burning rock towards the floor. The falling rocks ignited the slimy pools with a roar and they burst into long tongues of flame. As the cavern turned into an inferno, black smoke flooded into the tunnel.

"Bloody smoke is choking me," Jimmy said, coughing.

"I can hardly breathe," Amy shouted.

Davey knew they had to leave immediately. "Quick, hold your breath and run back to the wagon."

They turned and ran for their lives, which of course was a very good idea. Smoke flowed through the tunnel, making it hard to see, and Davey sent his cane ahead to light the way. They reached the front cavern in a matter of minutes, but a horrible sight greeted their eyes. The fire had jumped over the dense rock around the tunnel and the ceiling was completely ablaze. Small particles of burning rock were falling like rain. Spike was in the lead, and he stopped and retreated towards the safety of the tunnel.

"No, keep going, we'll die in here if we stay," Davey yelled.

Chunks of rock fell all around them as they ran like animals in a blazing forest. They were halfway across the cavern, when Amy tripped and fell hard. She lay unmoving on the floor; her eyes closed. Jimmy, who was directly behind her, hardly broke his stride. He scooped her up in his muscular arms and staggered forward. Moments later, a huge slab of stone crashed upon the spot where she had fallen.

Spike turned to help, his face ashen. "It's okay; I've got her," Jimmy hollered, his breathing labored.

Davey caught up to them and extended his cape over Jimmy's back for protection. "Don't stop – keep going!"

They stumbled from the cave, coughing and choking. Black soot covered their faces, but their armor and Davey's cape had miraculously protected them from harm. Jimmy cradled Amy's limp body in his arms, anxiously watching her face for signs of life. She lay still, apparently unconscious.

"Let's make sure she's breathing," Spike sputtered.

"No, put her in the wagon first," Davey yelled, sensing that their lives depended upon how fast they could get off the cliff.

They scrambled into the wagon, gasping for breath. Jimmy gently put Amy in the back and Spike climbed in after him. Davey leaped onto the driver's bench, desperately focusing his mind. Immediately, the wagon rose and they soared into the sky.

When they were a hundred feet away from the cliff, flames exploded from the mouth of the cave with a deafening roar. The concussion from the blast tilted the wagon sideways; it churned about like a boat on a stormy sea. Davey clung precariously to the bench until he straightened the wagon and it continued its course. Shaking his head at his stupidity, he hastily secured his seat belt.

Meanwhile, Jimmy grabbed a canteen, tore a strip of cloth from his shirt, and soaked it with water. Then he carefully wiped Amy's face with the wet cloth. After a few minutes, she opened her eyes and began to cough.

"Hey, Amy's waking up. I think she's okay," Spike shouted.

With Jimmy and Spike's help, Amy struggled to her feet and they each drank thirstily from the canteen. Spike was passing the canteen towards Davey when Amy suddenly wondered what had happened. "How did I get here? All I remember was running through the cave and falling."

"Jimmy picked you up and carried you out," Spike said.

"If he hadn't, a big piece of rock would have hit you," Davey shouted, so relieved to hear Amy's voice he could hardly speak.

Abruptly, Amy gave Spike and Jimmy a hug. "You each saved my life today."

A big grin spread across Spike's face. "No problem," he muttered.

Jimmy bowed nobly. "A pleasure, little miss."

The wagon was floating a hundred yards away from the cliff now, and Davey turned it so they could all see the cave. "Hey guys, look at the cliff," he shouted.

Jimmy, Amy, and Spike stood at the windows and stared in disbelief. A thick cloud of smoke billowed into the air as flames rose from the cave and the vertical cracks in the cliff. Several minutes later, the front of the cave collapsed with a tremendous roar and slid down the mountain. Above the rear cavern, the narrow cliff tottered precariously as the vertical cracks widened. Then the cliff broke into sections and crashed down upon what was left of the cave. Half of the cliff tumbled to the bottom of the limestone quarry in great slabs. The remaining half crumpled into a huge mound of smoldering rock where the cave had been.

"Awesome...we destroyed the cave," Jimmy exclaimed.

Spike grinned triumphantly. "We destroyed the spirit too."

Jimmy laughed loudly. "Nothing could survive that inferno."

Amy stuck her head through the slot behind the driver's seat. "Davey, we've completed our quest!"

Davey didn't answer. An anxious frown had formed on his face as the smoke drifted away from the cliff. It wasn't the smoke that was worrying him; it was the opaque cloud swirling above the smoldering rocks.

⚜ Chapter 42 ⚜

---

*Yea, when the blackness surrounds thee
and all seems lost, forget ye not the sun
cometh. Light shall follow anon.*

— Translated from Storia Di Incanto; circa 1915

The Swirling Death

DAVEY STUDIED the swirling cloud as it rose like a tornado above the ruins of the cliff. *Is that the spirit?* he wondered, his mind filling with dread. He quickly found out when the churning mass headed for the wagon, its black shape full of yellow eyes. "Prepare for battle," he shouted. "The spirit is alive!"

Jimmy hastily squeezed through the window behind the driver's bench and took his position beside Davey. Spike handed his bow and arrows to him; then he and Amy grabbed their spears. For a few long minutes, they all stared anxiously at the swirling cloud, their hearts beating rapidly.

Amy yelled in frustration. "If the fire didn't kill it, what will?"

"Maybe nothing," Jimmy muttered.

Davey needed time to think about how they should fight the spirit in the open sky, so he flew the wagon away from it. As they gathered speed, Jimmy stood on the driver's bench, watching the spirit over the top of the wagon. "Faster mate, it's gaining on us," he shouted.

"Shoot your arrows. Maybe they will slow it down."

Jimmy fired a few arrows, tearing gaping holes in the black shape.

Regardless, the holes closed after a few seconds as if the arrows had no affect. "My arrows aren't hurting it. If I keep shooting, all my arrows will soon be lost," he yelled in exasperation.

Amy shouted a suggestion from inside the wagon. "Davey, try to fly around the spirit in a circle. If you can see it, you can guide Jimmy's arrows and make them return."

"Do it," Jimmy agreed.

"Okay, but I'm not sure if I can stay away from it."

Amy's plan worked great for about two minutes. When Davey caught sight of the spirit, he sent Jimmy's arrows weaving through it like sewing needles and then brought them back to the wagon. The arrows created numerous holes, but they barely reduced the spirit's speed. Soon, it hovered beside the wagon, buzzing like a vast hive of angry bees. Then it attacked, not as a fluid shape, but as a mass of tiny dots. The dots swarmed in and around the wagon, thick as a black fog. Whenever they touched the surface of the wagon, they exploded with an amber flash.

"The aura of the tree is protecting us," Amy shouted gleefully.

Amy and Spike jabbed their spears at the dots, and Jimmy did the same with an arrow in each hand. The dots disintegrated by the hundreds, creating showers of sparks. Davey concentrated on making the wagon go faster, still trying to outrun the spirit.

"We're killing it," Jimmy shouted as he thrust at the dots.

"Die spirit, die," Spike screamed with each lunge of his spear.

They fought valiantly, not knowing their efforts were having little effect on the spirit. They also didn't realize it was merely distracting them with a portion of its mass. The spirit's main target was Davey. It had found a weakness during the battle in the tunnel – one it was about to exploit. While Jimmy, Amy, and Spike were fighting the dots, the spirit surrounded Davey with a denser mass. Suddenly, it descended upon him.

The mass was so incredibly thick, Davey thought someone had put a hood over his face. Instantly, a fierce buzzing began inside his head. It was the same buzzing that he had felt in the tunnel when they fought the three-headed monster, only ten times stronger and accompanied by a stabbing pain. Sharp needles seemed to be thrusting at his brain, shattering his concentration; he couldn't see or hear, let alone fly the wagon. Slowly his eyes closed as his mind went numb.

Immediately, the wagon began to lose altitude. Its descent wasn't noticeable at first, but then it began to roll from side to side. Jimmy, who was standing up at the time and jabbing at the black dots with his arrows, lost his balance. He briefly flailed at the air and then tumbled off the driver's bench with a cry. Luckily, one of the spiked branches along the front of the wagon snagged his shirt. It held for only a second before ripping through, yet it was long enough for him to get both hands around the branch and cling there precariously.

Hearing Jimmy's cry, Spike stuck his head out one of the windows; he saw Jimmy hanging from the branch, his legs dangling below the wagon. "Hold on, I'm coming," he shouted, climbing through the window. While his feet inched along the branches around the lower part of the wagon, the black dots swarmed against him, exploding whenever they touched his armor. Then he felt the wagon's nose turn down as it went into a dive.

Wondering why the wagon was falling, he clawed his way forward and glanced over at Davey. A shocking sight greeted his eyes. Davey lay on the driver's bench, his body convulsing as the black mass surrounded his head. Spike clung desperately to the side of the wagon, but the angle of its decent was such that he couldn't reach Davey without falling out himself. All he could do was hold on.

Spike yelled urgently at Amy. "Something has happened to Davey. He's not flying the wagon." Then he had a sudden insight. "It's the magic hat – it's allowing the spirit to attack him. Try to replace it with his helmet!"

During the wagon's rapid decline, Amy had fallen against the wall behind the driver's bench. When she heard Spike's yell, she frantically reached through the front window and jerked the magic hat from Davey's head. The black dots flew at her face as she searched for his helmet inside the wagon, making her scream in frustration. Finally, she found the helmet, slammed it onto his head, pulled the flaps over his ears, and fastened the chinstrap. Sparks flew as the black mass angrily hammered against the helmet on Davey's head. He stopped shaking, but didn't open his eyes.

Looking through the window, Amy saw the earth rushing towards them. They were less than five-hundred feet from the ground and falling fast. She pulled Davey into an upright position on the driver's bench and rubbed her hands along his face and neck. "Please…oh please…wake up and fly the wagon," she begged, but he didn't respond. She tried to think of what to do, knowing that they would hit the ground soon.

After a few seconds, a startling idea came to her; the image of the spell for wakefulness from the Sabatini books appeared in her mind. Trying to cast the spell seemed like a ridiculous notion, but she didn't hesitate. With every ounce of concentration that she could muster, she focused on the image and caressed Davey's face. "Wake up…wake up, or we'll all die," she whispered into his ear. Her fingers tingled as she caressed his face.

Amy's voice sounded inside Davey's head like the ringing of a melodic bell. He trusted the voice and wanted to please it above all others. Suddenly, his eyes flashed open. He blinked several times as his confused brain came back to life. Then he realized the wagon was about to crash. Startled into action, he quickly focused his mind and brought the nose of the wagon up. It skimmed along the treetops like a wounded bird as he gradually regained control.

Jimmy felt his feet scraping the tops of the trees and he jerked his legs up. Spike, who was crouched along the front of the wagon, caught Jimmy's legs and held on tight. "It's okay, I've got you," he shouted. As the wagon slowly rose, he helped Jimmy climb back onto the driver's bench.

Jimmy hugged Spike tightly. "Thanks, I thought I was a goner."

Meanwhile, Amy was sitting on the floor of the wagon, almost sobbing. A few minutes passed before she was calm enough to think about what had happened. She looked at her fingers as though amazed. *Did I cast a spell?* she wondered.

The wagon, once more under control, zoomed towards the sky with such speed that it pulled away from the spirit. During the brief respite, Spike climbed back inside and Jimmy secured his seatbelt. Fortunately, his bow and arrows had not fallen out during the wagon's descent. They assumed their battle positions, each wondering how much more they could take.

At last, Davey pointed the wagon towards the spirit. Jimmy began shooting his arrows; this time they had more effect. The holes closed slower than before and the spirit wasn't moving as fast. Davey kept the wagon a comfortable distance away as he circled the black mass. "I think it's getting tired," he said, his confidence growing.

Amy stuck her head through the window. "What about you?"

"I'm okay – at least I think I am."

"The spirit doesn't act like it wants to fight anymore," Spike said.

"Yona said it would die if it didn't find another sanctuary quickly," Amy remarked.

Jimmy managed a smile. "That's what I'm hoping."

Davey felt the air getting warmer; the grey sky of the morning was clearing. A few minutes later, several rays of sunlight poked through the clouds. The spirit responded to the sun by contracting into a denser shape and streaking away from the wagon, spiraling downward.

"Bloody heck, it's running away," Jimmy exclaimed.

"Go after it. The sunlight is making it weaker," Spike shouted.

Davey accelerated the wagon and caught up with the spirit, keeping a distance of fifty feet between them. As the clouds parted, he had a clear view of the countryside below. "Look, it's heading towards Great Oak," he said, pointing at the town some distance away.

"Maybe there's another sanctuary there," Jimmy said.

Immediately, Amy realized what the spirit was doing. "No…Great Oak is where the tree is. Remember what Yona said; when two opposite spirits confront each other, a great calamity results. That's what the spirit wants now."

Davey quickly understood. "Thousands of people could be killed, including our families."

"But how can we stop it?" Jimmy shouted.

Davey thought for a second; then a plan formed in his mind. "Spike, pass up the arrow and rope that Elogi Ugithisa and Yona made. Jimmy, tie the free end of the rope onto the front of the wagon and get ready to shoot the arrow."

When Jimmy had tied the rope to a large iron ring beneath the driver's bench, he nodded. "Okay, I'm ready, but how are we going to stop the spirit with this?"

"I'm going to weave it into a net. If I'm right, the spirit won't be able to break through it because of the aura in the rope."

Davey sped up until the wagon was directly behind the spirit. It swirled twenty yards ahead, unaware of their plan. Davey flew the wagon closer until they were fifteen – then ten yards away. "Shoot," he cried at last, and Jimmy launched the arrow. As it streaked forward, Davey mentally directed the arrow around the spirit in a series of interwoven loops. When he was finished, the rope had formed a crude net encircling its black mass.

In the meantime, they had reached the sky above Great Oak. Davey slowed the wagon, and the rope grew taut. The spirit, unable to escape the net, slowed as well.

"It's working; you're a genius," Jimmy exclaimed.

For the next thirty minutes, a furious tug-of-war ensued. The spirit fought against the net, its yellow eyes glaring at Davey as it tried to drag the wagon down. In turn, Davey increased his concentration and steered the wagon higher. They spun around in a frantic struggle, repeating the process numerous times, but neither gaining an advantage. The spirit seemed to grow increasingly berserk, bucking against the net like a huge wild stallion that resisted capture. It zigzagged and reeled in frenzied loops, changing directions in sharp turns that violently whipped the wagon from side to side.

Jimmy fired arrows repeatedly, and Davey directed them into the spirit; small pieces of the spirit's mass tore away, dissolving in the sunlight as they fell towards the earth. However, the harsh rocking of the wagon was taking a toll on its frame. The wood creaked and groaned in protest; then the eighty-year old lashings that held the underlying skeleton of tree branches in place began to split apart. One after another, the branches began to pop loose, some dropping to the earth below and others trailing beneath the wagon, still attached by a flimsy strip of leather.

Each lost branch represented a diminishment of flying power, making Davey struggle more and more to keep the wagon airborne. Finally, he restrained Jimmy with his hand. "No more arrows. I need to use all of my mental skills to fly the wagon."

He pulled the spirit high into the sky one last time and tried to hold it in the rays of the sun, but the spirit was still too strong. Gradually, they began to descend. This time, Davey couldn't prevent it. "I can't restrain it any longer," he gasped.

At that moment, the spirit executed another series of sharp turns. As it did, a horrendous groan filled the air and the wagon began to shake violently. Immediately, Amy cried out in dismay. "The wagon is coming apart."

Davey turned and saw that the left front panel of the wagon was beginning to separate from its adjoining side. A foot-wide gap had appeared – a gap that was growing wider by the minute. This caused a shocking realization. If the spirit continued to make sharp turns and pull against the net, the front of the wagon was going to tear away.

Unable to hide his concern, Davey shouted to Jimmy. "Quick, untie the rope and fasten it to something *inside* the wagon."

Aware of the pending disaster, Jimmy hastened to obey. He climbed down to where the rope was attached to the iron ring below the driver's bench and tried to untie the knot. After a few seconds, he called up to Davey. "It's too tight; I can't undo it while the spirit is pulling against it."

"Try cutting it with a knife," Davey said, his voice strained.

Jimmy drew his hunting knife from his belt and began sawing at the rope. Unfortunately, his efforts were futile; the sap that Elogi Ugithisa had boiled into the rope had made it as tough as steel. "Bloody heck – I can't even scratch it," Jimmy yelled.

Spike grabbed the window frame behind the driver's bench with his beefy hands in an effort to hold the front of the wagon together. Another sharp turn by the spirit, followed by a loud screech and a further widening of the gap, indicated his lack of success. "It's still separating; I can't stop it," he grunted as the wagon began to tilt at an odd angle.

Amy screamed in frustration. "Davey, do something. The spirit will get away, and we'll crash if the front comes off."

Davey racked his brain for a solution, but he couldn't think of one. Moreover, his concentration was getting weaker by the minute. "Jimmy, climb into the back. I'll join you in a second. Maybe I can make what's left of the wagon float to the ground when it breaks up."

"Can't you think of anything else?" Amy cried, her voice barely audible above the creaking and groaning of the wagon.

Davey shook his head. "No – I'm fresh out of ideas."

"Pray for a miracle," Jimmy yelled as he began to climb into the wagon.

"That's it," Spike shouted. "Davey can wish for a miracle."

"I'll try," Davey said, immediately focusing his mind. Regretfully, the mental exertion of keeping the wagon afloat had weakened his ability to concentrate on more than one thing at a time. He didn't feel the connection with the tree that usually accompanied a wish.

"Oh no…look!" Amy suddenly cried, pointing towards Great Oak.

Jimmy stared at where Amy was pointing; what he saw horrified him. Three black clouds were rising towards them from below. "Blimey – what are those?"

Amy shook her head in dismay. "Somehow, the spirit has summoned help."

"We're done for now," Spike exclaimed.

Davey studied the new shapes anxiously. They were wavering dark masses, not at all like the spirit, yet they were heading directly at them. Abruptly, Davey pulled his helmet off and shouted at Amy. "Quick, give me my hat."

"Are you crazy? Remember what happened before," Jimmy yelled.

Amy handed him the hat. "I hope you know what you're doing."

Davey pulled the hat on and pointed at the rapidly approaching shapes. "Look at the center. Do you see the triangle?" Then he laughed as a thousand thoughts filled his head. *You are the one,* they cried in unison.

The three wavering masses converged as they drew near. When Amy, Jimmy, and Spike realized their composition, they stared in astonishment. Birds of every size, shape, and kind were flying in formation, thousands of them. A hundred ravens were leading the way.

Davey smiled – he knew just what to do now. He briefly took his mind off the wagon and pictured the Great Oak instead. He was creating a protective spell – not one from the magic books – a spell of his own making. When he was ready, he cast the spell as a thought message to the birds by using his hat. *Fill your minds with this image and hear no other thoughts but mine. Then attack the evil spirit. The tree will protect you and together, we will kill it.*

The tree protects us, the birds cried as they descended upon the spirit with a relentless barrage of jabbing beaks and ripping claws. The spirit writhed inside the net, trying to escape the furious onslaught; the wagon rose, no longer dragged down by the spirit's pull. Spike's hold on the front of the wagon intensified as he strained to keep it in place. Without the spirit's constant tug, the gap between the walls grew no wider.

Davey rallied his concentration and towed the spirit into the fierce rays of the sun once again. The huge cloud of birds surrounded it, darting in and out as they continued their attack. Shredded pieces of the spirit tried to escape, only to wither away in the sunlight. The battle lasted for almost an hour, during which the spirit's shape dwindled to a small, black ball inside the net. Then Jimmy shot an arrow into its evil core; it burst into flames, burned for a minute, and the ashes blew away on the wind.

The four warriors burst into cheers – the evil spirit was dead at last. The birds had turned a near disaster into a great victory.

As Jimmy reeled in the rope, the birds landed on the wagon, so numerous that they covered every inch of its surface. They excitedly cawed and chirped as Davey kept the wagon floating calmly in the sky. Amy, Jimmy, and Spike watched in disbelief. They had seen many incredible things on this day, but this was the most intriguing. Davey let the birds have their fun for a while and then raised his hand. The birds grew silent at once.

He thought back to his first morning in Great Oak, to when the birds had filled the tree outside his window. *Did they know this day was coming?* he wondered. Just as he had imagined then, he knew the birds wanted to hear a speech now, so he began a flowery oration. He lauded them endlessly for their bravery and thanked them for saving the day. When he was finished, they broke into a rowdy chorus, reminding him of their initial welcome. Then, with a glorious fluttering of wings, they rose en masse and flew away.

Jimmy watched them go, shaking his head. "Unbelievable...I can't wait to tell Yona.

Amy began to crawl through the front window. "May I sit beside Davey now?"

A grin spread across Jimmy's face. "As long as you fasten your seat belt; I'll ride in back with my pal, Mountain Brother."

Thirty minutes later, Davey brought the wagon in for a landing at the Cherokee village. As it floated over the village, they waved at the crowd gathered below. A huge celebration was beginning; every villager was there, beating drums, blowing flutes, shaking rattles, and shouting joyfully.

For the next three hours, they told the villagers about their battle with the spirit. Each time they finished, someone asked them to tell it again. Both children and adults gathered around them, and the feasting and dancing seemed like it would never end. Finally, when they were ready to leave, they had a private moment. They stood at the wagon and inspected its battle-scarred exterior. Many of the branches had splintered or fallen off, burn marks covered its surface from the incineration of the black dots, the roof was in tatters, and the front sat askew because of the separated side.

Davey felt a sudden sadness. "It took quite a beating."

Amy fondly touched its side. "Yona said the villagers will repair it and hang our armor and weapons on the walls of the Council House."

"Now, I know how a rock star feels," Jimmy said with a smile.

Spike grinned. "This has been the best day of my life."

"Thanks to you, we all survived," Amy said.

Davey looked at Spike, having already obtained Amy and Jimmy's agreement to what he was going to say next. "A month ago, Amy, Jimmy, and I formed a team. We called ourselves the Three of We. Then you joined us, and we did something extraordinary together. As a result, we are changing our name. The Three of We have become the Four of Us. Whenever one is in need, the others will help. That's our promise to each other."

Spike nodded. "You can count on me. I don't know where my mom and I will be, but I won't forget."

Jimmy suddenly frowned. "Are you leaving Great Oak?"

"Mom thinks we'll have to sell the furniture factory because of my dad's debts. Then we'll probably move away out of shame."

Davey listened without saying a word. Amy squeezed his hand; she was sure he was thinking about his own departure from Great Oak. Had she looked into his face, she would have seen the twinkle in his eyes.

As for Davey, new ideas were flooding into his mind — ones that he couldn't wait to share with the tree.

✧ Chapter 43 ✦

---

*And so, believe you now in magic? The
answer is up to you. Only the magician
knows; what is illusion and what is true!*

— Written by The Great Sabatini; circa 1925

A New Beginning

THE RESIDENTS OF GREAT OAK greeted the new day with a
surprising feeling of optimism. They were unaware of the battle above
their little town yesterday, yet they sensed their lives were different.
Was it just their imagination, or had the sky become clearer, the air
fresher, and the song of the birds sweeter?

It was Sunday, and the churches in Great Oak were suddenly full
of people. Their pastors glanced happily at the faces lining the pews of
their respective houses. The attendance was astonishing, and they
rallied to the occasion by delivering their best ever sermons on hope
and charity.

Of course, the Four of Us knew the reason for these feelings of
elation. The evil spirit was dead; the Great Oak was radiating its
benevolence without interference. They celebrated by riding their
bikes around the park in the afternoon, stopping every so often to
admire the healthy glow around the tree – good fortune was surely
coming.

Three days later, Davey, Aunt Sally, and Uncle Bill picked up Davey's parents at the airport. Janie and Walter stared in bewilderment at Davey when they saw his smiling face. The tall, tanned, and muscular boy wasn't at all like the son they had left behind.

"My, how you have grown," Janie cried as she hugged Davey fiercely.

"Look at these muscles," Walter exclaimed, pounding Davey on the back.

Davey grinned, imagining what they would say if he told him about the battle with the spirit. "You were right, Dad. Living in a small town is good for me."

Walter was amazed; his son didn't often say he was right about anything. "I knew you'd like Great Oak, but are you excited about returning to New York?"

Davey shook his head. "Not exactly...I like it here." *And I hope you will like it too,* he thought.

"Well, I'm glad it worked out," Walter replied. "You can come for a visit next summer if your aunt and uncle are willing."

"Of course, he can come anytime," Aunt Sally said, looking a bit teary-eyed.

Davey wanted to keep his parents in Great Oak for a while so the tree could work its magic upon them. After a lot of thought, he had figured out how to do it. "Hey Dad, I'm the captain of the Scholar's Team at school...our first match is next week. Would it be okay if we stayed until then?" he asked innocently.

Walter looked at Janie and saw her excited nod. Naturally, she loved the idea of having a longer visit with her sister. "Captain of the Scholar's Team, huh? Well, I like the sound of that! We can stay if it's okay with your aunt and uncle."

Uncle Bill laughed. "Walter, my vote doesn't count. Ever since our wives became millionaires, I don't have much say anymore."

Walter stared at him blankly. "Millionaires?"

Uncle Bill's eyes twinkled merrily. "There's a little matter of five million in gold coins, which was left behind by the Sabatinis. I'll tell you about it on the ride home."

The Scholar's Team had their competition on the following Tuesday. They were up against Hickory, which had won the regional contest for the last five years. Eunice Bluestone had nearly gone berserk when she learned Hickory would be Great Oak's first opponent. She paced along the aisle of the school bus as the team headed towards the match, generally making a nuisance of herself.

Linda finally pulled Eunice into the seat alongside her. "Sit down...you are getting on everyone's nerves. They're a smart group of kids; they'll do fine."

"You didn't see the way Hickory made fools of us last year. It was disgraceful," Eunice snapped, thinking Linda was much too relaxed.

Even so, Linda turned out to be right; her team performed admirably. When the judges declared them the winner, Eunice could hardly believe her ears. Her greatest triumph came when Hickory's principal, Delia Smoot, congratulated her.

"We'll be a force to reckon with from now on," Eunice replied confidently.

Delia smiled. "You do have some smart kids, but they'll move on to high school in a few years. Besides, I'm sure Linda Peabody would rather work in a real school – Hickory for example."

Eunice's face showed her shock. "Delia Smoot, you wouldn't dare!"

Delia cackled as she walked away. "You know me, Eunice. I'm very daring."

After that remark, Linda heard an endless amount of praise from Eunice on their return trip. Moreover, she gave Linda a twenty percent raise. *Will wonders never cease?* Linda thought with a bemused smile.

That evening, Ed took Linda to dinner in celebration of the

victory. They ate at Mama Lilly's, a cozy restaurant known for its small band of musicians. Linda thought her day couldn't get any better as the musicians gathered around their table and played her favorite song, but she was in for a surprise. When the song ended, Ed knelt down and the entire dining room fell silent. "Linda Peabody, will you marry me?" he asked, holding out a beautiful engagement ring.

Linda smiled radiantly, even though tears were streaming down her face. "Well of course, but what took you so long to ask?"

Everyone in the dining room cheered when they heard her answer, and the musicians played Linda's favorite song all over again. At that moment, Aunt Gilda came walking out from a little alcove where she had been watching. Ed chuckled at Linda's surprised face as he seated Aunt Gilda at their table. "I knew you'd want your aunt here to help us celebrate."

Linda was so thrilled she could hardly speak. "How long have you two been cooking this up?" she finally asked.

Aunt Gilda giggled merrily. "We've been discussing it for weeks. Ed was afraid you might say no, but Charles told me otherwise."

Linda nodded knowingly. "Charles is a very wise man."

"Spirit dear, Charles is a very wise spirit. That reminds me, Charles wants you and Ed to live with us in Charlesville after you're married. There's lots of room, and I will leave the house to you when I join him in the hereafter."

Linda turned to Ed, clearly excited. "What do you think?"

Ed considered it for a moment and then smiled. "Well, I've almost finished my remodeling, so I guess we can sell my house. Since Gilda and I are already pals, and Charles seems mighty handy to have around, I think it's a great idea."

Aunt Gilda hugged Ed tightly. "You are such a kind man; welcome to the family. You can remodel Charlesville all you like."

They stayed at the restaurant until it closed. Many of the guests came by their table, offering congratulations and telling them about their own engagements. Aunt Gilda paid close attention, and Linda smiled with amusement, knowing she was gathering material for new stories – some great entrées, no doubt.

On the next day, the rumor mill was abuzz over Linda's forthcoming marriage. Naturally, Amy heard the news first and repeated it to Davey with great fanfare. He didn't seem the least bit surprised, which aroused her suspicions. "What have you been up to?" she asked with raised eyebrows.

"I think we'll be hearing more good news before long."

Amy stamped her foot impatiently. "Davey, tell me right this minute."

"You'll have to wait and see."

Amy was clearly exasperated. "What about your parents? They *were* going back to New York after the Scholar's Team match, but they're still here."

"Yes, and they're no longer in a hurry to leave."

Amy thought for a moment. "Dad has been meeting with your father and Nell Houseman, but he won't tell me why. I think they're discussing a business transaction."

Davey grinned happily. "There you go. You know as much as I do."

ဆၣဆၣဆၣ

While the town's outlook improved, the futures of Androf Protsky, Yong Chow Lee, and Wally Houseman grew bleaker. Of the three, Wally's fate was the worst. He remained in a facility for the criminally insane, his doctors unable to say if a recovery was possible. Androf's plight was almost as desperate. Criminal charges were now pending against him in Great Oak as well as Europe. But despite Yong Chow Lee's serious injuries, his fate was less certain. There was no proof of his involvement in any crimes.

When the FBI informed Androf of their decision to turn him over to the European police, he suddenly became talkative. Knowing the Europeans would be merciless, he made a deal with the FBI and revealed the details of Yong Chow Lee's kidnapping scheme. In return, they allowed Androf to plead guilty to a lesser sentence in the United States. Eventually, both Androf and Yong Chow Lee received twenty-year prison terms.

ΣᴑᏟᏒᏕᴑᏟᏒᏕᴑᏟᏒ

Three weeks after the death of the evil spirit, the town held a party in the park. No one knew what they were celebrating, but it didn't matter. The people were in a festive mood and winter was pleasingly late – enough reason for a party in their minds.

On the day of the celebration, the entire town shut down at two o'clock. People crowded into the park, filling the clearing in front of the pavilion by mid-afternoon. Their faces were all smiles when they saw the picnic tables covering the grounds and the booths giving out free hot dogs, hamburgers, and cups of punch. Overhead, flags flew gaily in a breeze warmed by a bright sun. It was nearly December, yet the temperature was a balmy seventy degrees. Even the weather was cooperating.

As the crowd ate, the music of the Great Oak Windings floated in the air, creating a jovial atmosphere. Thirty minutes passed, and then Mayor Higgins led a small group of people onto the pavilion. They sat down in chairs facing the clearing while the mayor tapped on a microphone to test the sound.

"Mayor, we can hear you fine," someone shouted from the back of the clearing.

The crowd hushed quickly, sensing some important announcements were forthcoming. They recognized most of the small group on the pavilion, but it was an odd mix of folks. Moreover, three of the faces were completely unfamiliar. "Who are the strangers? Why are two of them wearing Cherokee robes?" they whispered among themselves.

The mayor cleared his throat and began to speak. "One hundred and sixty years ago, our founding fathers stood on this spot and

ᎰᏅ 459 ᏕᏅ

named our town. At first, we grew and prospered, but then we lost our way. Today, I'm declaring a new beginning. These folks up here will tell you about it."

The mayor motioned one of the strangers forward and introduced her. "This elegant lady is Elogi Ugithisa, the high priestess of the Cherokee village on Greyhead Mountain. I have asked her to begin these proceedings with a prayer, so give her a Great Oak welcome."

A gentle clapping of hands came from the crowd as they glanced at each other in surprise. They couldn't recall a Cherokee villager ever attending a Great Oak party, not to mention a high priestess. The mayor was acting very strangely in their opinion.

Elogi Ugithisa's resonant voice rang out in the clearing. "Oh Great Spirit, we greet you with our thanks for this day. We see the sun shine and the trees grow. We hear the birds sing and the animals call. We feel the love of our families and friends. Oh Great Spirit, you honor us with your blessings…for this we give our thanks."

The clearing was silent after she finished; then a thunderous round of applause broke out. Her simple words had touched their hearts and they clapped for a long minute as she sat down.

The mayor resumed after a brief pause. "Now, let's welcome a man whom many of you have heard about, but never seen. He is Yona, Chief of the Cherokee village."

Yona walked towards the microphone, his keen eyes surveying the audience. When he had everyone's attention, he began. "The Cherokee have lived beside the people of Great Oak for many moons, yet we have not been friends. Recently, we came to know four young people from your village. We gave them Cherokee names and took them into our hearts. I wish for Little Wolf, Strong Arrow, Owl with Panther's Eyes, and Mountain Brother to stand."

Davey, Jimmy, Amy, and Spike rose, and then Yona continued. "These four braves have performed a great service; we will speak of their valor for many generations. They also taught me something important. You see, I learned we share common goals with the people of Great Oak. We each seek peace, prosperity, and a place to live in harmony with nature…so this is our pledge to you. The Cherokee are your friends; we will help the people of Great Oak prosper."

The magnitude of Yona's words stunned the crowd. They had rarely heard such an offer of friendship and certainly hadn't expected it from the fierce old chief. Almost as one, they stood up and cheered. Then they stared at the Four of Us, wondering why the chief was so impressed with them. Weren't they just ordinary kids?

The mayor rushed to the microphone again. "You haven't heard everything, folks. Stay in your seats and give a welcome to our very own Nell Houseman."

No applause came from the crowd. While Nell was a Great Oak native, they couldn't overcome their dislike for her husband. For the most part, they pitied her for being married to him. On the other hand, they were suspicious of what she was going to say.

The poor response didn't surprise Nell; she hurriedly began her speech. "The Housemans have been part of Great Oak since its beginning and shared in its early success. Unfortunately, we weren't good managers or even good citizens. After my husband's most recent folly, I was ready to move away. My son, Spike, has convinced me otherwise. Therefore, I'm here to tell you what I have done to make amends."

Nell turned towards four others who were sitting behind her. Everyone waited in anticipation as Uncle Bill, Walter Boehm, Sequoyah, and Tom Pigeon stepped forward. Something big was happening; they could sense it.

Nell smiled for the first time as she faced them. "Three days ago, I sold the Houseman's furniture and textile factories to these individuals. They are an experienced team and can make our factories profitable. Moreover, they have promised that no more jobs will be lost. Better yet, they hope to create new ones in the future."

Each of the new owners stepped forward and spoke briefly after that. They talked about new furniture designs, improved equipment, and increased efficiencies; ideas that Wally had refused to consider. When they were finished, Nell concluded with a few more remarks.

"Spike and I are also trying to make the Houseman's other properties productive for Great Oak. In the near future, we will reopen the quarry on Brown Mountain and hire a hundred people. There's new demand for the limestone there; if we do it right, we will all prosper."

The crowd rose to their feet, giving Nell and the new factory owners a hearty round of cheers. What a great party this was; they hadn't been so excited in years. Everyone knew Nell was a good person, despite her idiot of a husband. In addition, they liked what the new factory owners had to say.

Mayor Higgins beamed at the crowd. "All right folks, there you have it – a new beginning. Now, let's not get complacent like we did in the past. Pay attention to who is running things in this town. Two City Council seats are up for election next year, and I have asked Sally Winston and Sequoyah Surefoot to apply for the jobs. Please let them know if you like the idea."

The crowd cheered loud and long, nodding in agreement. As far as they were concerned, there was no point in even holding an election. Sally and Sequoyah were hands down winners. The mayor smiled happily and pointed at the bandstand. Immediately, the Great Oak Windings started playing again. "Stick around and enjoy the music. There's popcorn, cotton candy, and cherry pie at the booths," he exclaimed.

Later, as the sun sank slowly in the western sky, the Four of Us sat together. Every few minutes, someone came by and asked what they had done to impress the Cherokee. They gave vague answers to the many questions, knowing no one would believe the truth.

"What's this about the Harrison Foundation?" Spike asked Davey when they had a moment to themselves.

Davey grinned. "Joe Harrison fired the old trustees. He's asked Aunt Sally, Sequoyah, and me to take their places."

"I've never heard of a kid being a trustee of a foundation," Spike replied.

"He wants a member of the younger generation on the board, but I also think he did it because I saved him from that Protsky guy."

"And nearly got killed in the process," Amy added.

"Hey, we were *all* almost killed by the evil spirit," Davey said.

"Have you told your parents about our quest?" Jimmy asked.

"No, but I did tell them about my inherited magic skill. Mom had heard the old rumors about her grandparents being witches, and she was worried. Chief Yona helped by telling her the truth about Antonio and Alicia."

"I hope you didn't tell them about the tree granting your wishes," Amy said.

Davey shook his head. "They may never be ready for *that*."

"Have your parents bought a house yet?" Jimmy asked.

"Oh yeah, I forgot to tell you. Ed Nolen is selling the old Sabatini house to us. It'll be great living near my aunt and uncle."

Amy looked thoughtful. "I wonder if there's more secrets there."

"I think so. When we were at the house today, my necklace was vibrating like crazy."

"I'm so happy. Everything is working out," Amy said.

Davey chuckled. "Get this...Aunt Sally just found out she's having a baby."

"Wow, it could be another magician," Jimmy muttered.

Amy smiled at Davey. "All of this is your doing, isn't it?"

"I just had a long talk with the tree. I didn't make any wishes."

"Who cares, I think it's all great," Spike said.

"I still feel bad about your dad," Davey replied.

"I hate to say it, but my mom and I are a lot happier with him somewhere else. Maybe we'll have a normal life now."

At that moment, Amy saw Yona and Elogi Ugithisa leaving the clearing. "I'll be right back," she said, and then ran towards them.

Yona saw her coming and smiled warmly. "We were just leaving."

Amy hugged each of them affectionately. "I'm so glad I caught you. I've wanted to ask you about something."

Yona stared into her face as if expecting her question. "Ask freely, Owl with Panther's Eyes."

Amy hoped she wasn't being foolish. "I've been wondering; I cast a spell when the wagon was falling and can use the wisdom scarf. How can I do these things without any magic skill?"

Yona's eyes twinkled. "Perhaps the answer lies in something I recently learned. I was mistaken about your ancestor, Morning Dove. She was not from the bird clan; she was an Ani-Wodi priestess."

His words stunned her. "What are you saying?"

Elogi Ugithisa gently put her arm around Amy. "The Ani-Wodi have special abilities; you may have inherited some unique talents from your ancestor."

"You mean…like Davey's magic skill?" Amy asked, her eyes filling with excitement.

Elogi Ugithisa smiled. "Something like that. Come to the village when you can. We'll find out."

Davey noticed that Amy seemed distracted when she returned and studied her briefly. "Are you okay?" he finally asked.

She replied by changing the subject. "Can we visit the tree before the sun sets?"

"Good idea," Davey said, rising from his chair.

Spike started to get up too, but Jimmy placed a discrete hand on his arm. "Let them go alone," he whispered. "She's got something on her mind."

Davey glanced at Jimmy and Spike. "Are you guys coming?"

"Nah, you go ahead. Spike and I will bask in our glory here," Jimmy said.

Amy took Davey's hand as soon as they left the clearing, and they walked through the park without speaking. Amy wanted to tell him about her conversation with Yona and Elogi Ugithisa, but she wasn't sure how he would react. When they reached the tree, the gate opened and the squirrel popped in front of them, clearly thrilled by their visit.

"The squirrel appears just like you said," Amy exclaimed with delight.

The squirrel performed its usual welcoming flurry of somersaults and then scrambled up the trunk, signaling for Davey to follow. "Go ahead, I'll wait for you," Amy said. Then the squirrel did something unexpected; it pointed at Amy and motioned again.

Davey grinned. "The squirrel wants you to climb the tree too."

"But how?" Amy asked, glancing at the limbs above her head.

"Just follow me," Davey said, leading the way. Before long, they were both sitting on the lowest branch of the tree.

Amy looked down in amazement. "I've got goose bumps all over."

The squirrel barked at them from a branch above their heads and then ran halfway up the tree. "We are being invited to go higher," Davey explained.

They reached the little platform near the top of the tree in fifteen minutes and sat down. The rays of the setting sun shimmered over the horizon in shades of red, orange, blue, and yellow, painting a glorious picture. Then Amy let out a gasp of surprise as the tree began to gently sway, apparently pleased by their presence.

A sense of contentment came over Amy and she felt happier than she could ever remember being. "It's so beautiful and peaceful...I don't want to leave," she said softly.

Davey stared at her in astonishment; he had suddenly realized the importance of what had happened. "Amy, you have climbed the tree," he exclaimed.

She laughed softly. "Well of course, that's how I got here."

"No...listen. It's the tree's way of saying it favors you."

Davey's remark reminded Amy of what she had wanted to tell him. "Elogi Ugithisa thinks I have some kind of magic skill," she blurted out.

At that moment, the squirrel interrupted them by leaping joyously along the branches above their heads. It finally hopped into Davey's lap, a leather pouch in its hands. Davey took the pouch and opened it slowly. Inside, he found an ornately painted deck of cards. "Are these what my great grandfather used to predict the future?"

The squirrel nodded its head vigorously, gently took the cards from Davey, and placed them into Amy's hands. There was no mistaking its intent. Amy was the one who would use the cards.

Davey and Amy looked at each other in surprise. Soon, they both began to laugh. They stayed in the tree until the sun set, happily imagining all sorts of future adventures. Then they bid the tree goodbye and Davey walked Amy home. *I wonder what tomorrow will bring,* he thought while they strolled along.

ℬℭℬℭℬℭ

That night, as the residents of Great Oak dreamed blissfully of their new beginning, Wally Houseman opened his eyes for the first time in a month. He woke up in a locked room of the Waldorf Asylum for the Criminally Insane, one hundred and fifty miles away.

The room was completely dark, but Wally wasn't troubled. His yellow eyes penetrated the gloom as if it was daylight. He held his hand in front of his face – the hand where the shards of the black disk had cut into his palm. Not even a scar was visible.

With a fiendish giggle, Wally crept from his bed and twirled in a circle. He laughed uproariously as a spray of black spots fell away from his body; they rejoined his whirling figure seconds later.

A single window was set in the far wall. Unbreakable glass and steel bars covered the opening, although it was too small for a person to pass through. Wally swirled over to the window, held his face inches from the glass, and blew against it. His breath was so cold it could make a stone crack. Before long, two inches of ice covered both sides of the glass. Then he hit the window with his fist, shattering it into a hundred pieces.

Wally stepped back to the center of the room and began a crazy, whirling dance. Faster and faster he turned, his shrill laughter echoing along the halls. The other inmates held their ears and screamed in terror at the sound. Finally, whirling so fast that he was nothing more than a fluid mass of dots, his body poured through the window and out into the night.

Wally had only one conscious thought as he spun away. *This time, it will be different.*

So ends *The Sabatini Prophecy...*

The story continues in *The Terces Dimension.*
(Scheduled for Release in 2007)

ʚ Acknowledgments ɞ

I was fortunate to have the help and support of many during the writing of *The Sabatini Prophecy*. In particular, I would like to thank my publisher, Axiom House, for the wonderful guidance, editorial assistance, and helpful suggestions during the three-year creative process. I would also like to thank my wife, Kathy, daughter, Jennifer, and sister-in-law, Helen, for their contributions, including a lot of tireless reading of the many versions of different chapters.

In addition, I would like to thank the many test readers of the novel for their insightful comments, suggestions, and words of encouragement. Listed in alphabetical order, they are: David Blair, Tim Blair, Chap Chappell, Jordan Deuink, Eliza Geary, Steven Giesler, Chris Hellwig, Morgan Hellwig, Colleen Heptig, Anna Hicks, Sylvia Hicks, Patrick Jones, Lauren Krohn, Michael Krohn, Gillie Logan, Jim Offutt, Lauren Salomon, Margaret Sharpe, and Kelly Troncoso.

Finally, I would like to thank Michael Hayes for the creation of the original cover art. He brought the flying wagon to life and captured the battle with Sineous Crop as if reading my mind. Look for the *free* computer wallpaper featuring this artwork on the Axiom House website, www.axiomhouse.com.

I would also like to comment on a few aspects of the book. While it is a work of fiction, I tried to stay true to the history, folklore, and customs of the Cherokee whenever possible. In addition and to my knowledge, there is no town named Great Oak in the Blue Ridge Mountains. Any resemblance to towns in the area is unintended. However, the *Brown Mountain Lights* are a real phenomenon, which has been formally studied by the scientific community. Although theories abound, a complete understanding of these lights may require further investigation.